*ix years. Not so long in the lifespan of a drow. And yet—in counting the months, the weeks, the days, the hours—it seemed to me as if I had been away from Mithril Hall a hundred times that number. The place was another lifetime, another way of life, a mere stepping stone to . . .*

*To what? To where?*

*I ride the waves along the Sword Coast now, the wind and spray in my face. My ceiling is the rush of clouds and the canopy of stars; my floor, the creaking boards of a swift, well-weathered ship. Beyond that lies the azure blanket, flat and still, heaving and falling, hissing in the rain and exploding under the fall of a breaching whale.*

*Is this, then, my home?*

# Novels by R.A. Salvatore

FORGOTTEN REALMS

# PASSAGE to DAWN

## R.A. Salvatore

Wizards
OF THE COAST

# PASSAGE TO DAWN

First Printing: August 1996.
First Paperback Edition: August 1997.
Printed in the United States of America.
Library of Congress Catalog Card Number: 96-60820
Excerpt from *The Summoning* ©2000 Wizards of the Coast, Inc.
All rights reserved.

9 8 7 6 5 4

620-T8571P

ISBN: 0-7869-0750-9

U.S., CANADA,
ASIA, PACIFIC, & LATIN AMERICA
Wizards of the Coast, Inc.
P.O. Box 707
Renton, WA 98057-0707
+1-800-324-6496

EUROPEAN HEADQUARTERS
Wizards of the Coast, Belgium
P.B. 2031
2600 Berchem
Belgium
+32-70-23-32-77

Visit our web site at **www.wizards.com/forgottenrealms**

# PROLOGUE

he was beautiful, shapely, and pale-skinned with thick, lustrous hair cascading halfway down her naked back. Her charms were offered openly, brazenly, conveyed to him at the end of a gentle touch. So gentle. Little brushing fingers of energy tickled his chin, his jawbone, his neck.

Every muscle of his body tensed and he fought for control, battled the seductress with every bit of willpower remaining in him after so many years.

He didn't even know why he resisted anymore, didn't consciously remember what offerings of the other world, the real world, might be fueling his stubbornness. What were "right" and "wrong" in this place? What might be the price of pleasure?

What more did he have to give?

The gentle touch continued, soothing his trembling muscles, raising goose bumps across his skin wherever those fingers brushed. Calling to him. Bidding him to surrender.

Surrender.

He felt his willpower draining away, argued against his stubbornness. There was no reason to resist. He could have soft sheets and a comfortable mattress; the smell—the awful reek so terrible that even years had not allowed him to get used to it—could be taken away. She could do that with her magic. She had promised him.

Falling fast, he half-closed his eyes and felt the touch continuing, felt it more keenly than before.

He heard her snarl, a feral, bestial sound.

Now he looked past her. They were on the lip of a ridge, one of countless ridges across the broken, heaving ground that trembled as if it were a living thing, breathing, laughing at him, mocking him. They were up high. He knew that. The ravine beyond the ridge was wide, and yet he could not see more than a couple of feet beyond the edge. The landscape was lost in the perpetual swirling grayness, the smoky pall.

The Abyss.

Now it was his turn to growl, a sound that was not feral, not primal, but one of rationale, of morality, of that tiny spark that remained in him of who he had been. He grabbed her hand and forced it away, turning it, twisting it. Her strength in resisting confirmed his memories, for it was supernatural, far beyond what her frame should have allowed.

Still, he was the stronger and he forced the hand away, turned it about, then set his stare upon her.

Her thick hair had shifted a bit, and one of her tiny white horns had poked through.

"Do not, my lover," she purred. The weight of her plea nearly broke him. Like her physical strength, her voice carried more than was natural. Her voice was a conduit of charms, of deceit, of the ultimate lie that was all this place.

A scream erupted from his lips and he heaved her backward with all his strength, hurled her from the ridge.

Huge batlike wings unfolded behind her and the succubus hovered, laughing at him, her open mouth revealing horrid fangs that would have punctured his neck. She laughed and he knew that although he had resisted, he had not won, could never win. She had almost broken him this time, came closer to it than the last, and would be closer still the next. And so she laughed at him, mocked him. Always mocking him!

He realized that it had been a test, always a test. He knew who had arranged it and was not surprised when the whip tore into his back, laying him low. He tried to take cover, felt the intense heat building all around him, but knew that there was no escape.

A second snapping had him crawling for the ledge. Then

came a third lash, and he grabbed on to the lip of the ridge, screamed, and pulled himself over, wanting to pitch into the ravine, to splatter his corporeal form against the rocks. Desperate to die.

Errtu, the great balor, twelve feet of smoking deep red scales and corded muscles, casually walked to the edge and peered over. With eyes that had seen through the mists of the Abyss since the dawn of time, Errtu sought out the falling form, then reached out to him.

He was falling slower. Then he was not falling at all. He was rising, caught in a telekinetic web, reeled in by the master. The whip was waiting and the next lash sent him spiraling, mercifully, into unconsciousness.

Errtu did not retract the whip's cords. The balor used the same telekinetic energy to wrap them about the victim, binding him fast. Errtu looked back to the hysterical succubus and nodded. She had done well this day.

Drool slipped over her bottom lip at the sight of the unconscious form. She wanted to feast. In her eyes, the table was set and waiting. A flap of her wings brought her back to the ledge and she approached cautiously, seeking some way through the balor's defenses.

Errtu let her get close, so close, then gave a slight tug on the whip. His victim flopped away weirdly, jumping past the balor's perpetual flames. Errtu shifted a step to the side, putting his bulk between the victim and the succubus.

"I must," she whined, daring to move a bit closer, half-walking and half-flying. Her deceivingly delicate hands reached out and grasped at the smoky air. She trembled and panted.

Errtu stepped aside. She inched closer.

The balor was teasing her, she knew, but she could not turn away, not with the sight of this helpless one. She whined, knowing she was going to be punished, but she could not stop.

Taking a slightly roundabout route, she walked past the balor. She whined again, her feet digging a firm hold that she might rush to the prone victim and taste of him at least once before Errtu denied her.

Out shot Errtu's arm, holding a sword that was wrought

3

of lightning. He lifted it high and uttered a command and the ground jolted with the strength of a thunderstroke.

The succubus waited and leaped away, running for the ledge and then flying off of it, shrieking all the while. Errtu's lightning hit her in the back and sent her spinning, and she was far below the edge of the ridge before she regained control.

Back on the ledge, Errtu gave her not another thought. The balor was thinking of his prisoner, always of his prisoner. He enjoyed tormenting the wretch, but had to continually sublimate his bestial urges. He could not destroy this one, could not break him too far, else the victim would hold no value for the balor. This was but one being, and measured against the promise of freedom to walk again on the Prime Material Plane, that did not seem so much.

Only Drizzt Do'Urden, the renegade dark elf, the one who had banished Errtu to a hundred years in the Abyss, could grant that freedom. The drow would do that, Errtu believed, in exchange for the wretch.

Errtu turned his horned, apelike head to look over one massive shoulder. The fires that surrounded the balor burned low now, simmering as was Errtu's rage. Patience, the balor reminded himself. The wretch was valuable and had to be preserved.

The time was coming, Errtu knew. He would speak with Drizzt Do'Urden before another year had passed on the Material Plane. Errtu had made contact with the witch, and she would deliver his message.

Then the balor, one of the true tanar'ri, among the greatest denizens of the lower planes, would be free. Then Errtu could destroy the wretch, could destroy Drizzt Do'Urden, and could destroy every being that loved the renegade drow.

Patience.

# Part 1

## WIND AND SPRAY

ix years. Not so long in the life span of a drow, and yet, in counting the months, the weeks, the days, the hours, it seemed to me as if I had been away from Mithril Hall a hundred times that number. The place was removed, another lifetime, another way of life, a mere stepping stone to . . .

To what? To where?

My most vivid memory of Mithril Hall is of riding away from the place with Catti-brie at my side, is the view in looking back over the plumes of smoke rising from Settlestone to the mountain called Fourthpeak. Mithril Hall was Bruenor's kingdom, Bruenor's home, and Bruenor was among the most dear of friends to me. But it was not my home, had never been so.

I couldn't explain it then, and still cannot. All should have been well there after the defeat of the invading drow army. Mithril Hall shared prosperity and friendship with all of the neighboring communities, was part of an assortment of kingdoms with the power to protect their borders and feed their poor.

All of that, but still Mithril Hall was not home. Not for me, and not for Catti-brie. Thus had we taken to *the road, riding west to the coast, to Waterdeep.*

*I never argued with Catti-brie—though she had certainly expected me to—concerning her decision to leave Mithril Hall. We were of like minds. We had never really set down our hearts in the place; we had been too busy, in defeating the enemies who ruled there, in reopening the dwarven mines, in traveling to Menzoberranzan and in battling the dark elves who had come to Mithril Hall. All that completed, it seemed time to settle, to rest, to tell and to lengthen tales of our adventures. If Mithril Hall had been our home before the battles, we would have remained. After the battles, after the losses . . . for both Catti-brie and Drizzt Do'Urden, it was too late. Mithril Hall was Bruenor's place, not ours. It was the war-scarred place where I had to again face the legacy of my dark heritage. It was the beginning of the road that had led me back to Menzoberranzan.*

*It was the place where Wulfgar had died.*

*Catti-brie and I vowed that we would return there one day, and so we would, for Bruenor was there, and Regis. But Catti-brie had seen the truth. You can never get the smell of blood out of the stones. If you were there when that blood was spilled, the continuing aroma evokes images too painful to live beside.*

*Six years, and I have missed Bruenor and Regis, Stumpet Rakingclaw, and even Berkthgar the Bold, who rules Settlestone. I have missed my journeys to wondrous Silverymoon, and watching the dawn from one of Fourthpeak's many rocky perches. I ride the waves along the Sword Coast now, the wind and spray in my face. My ceiling is the rush of clouds and the canopy of stars; my floor is the creaking boards of a swift, well-weathered ship, and beyond that, the azure blanket, flat and still, heaving and rolling, hissing in the rain and exploding under the fall of a breaching whale.*

*Is this my home? I know not. Another stepping stone, I would guess, but whether there really is a road that would lead me to a place called home, I do not know.*

*Nor do I think about it often, because I've come to realize that I do not care. If this road, this series of stepping stones, leads nowhere, then so be it. I walk the road with friends, and so I have my home.*

—Drizzt Do'Urden

# Chapter 1
## THE SEA SPRITE

rizzt Do'Urden stood on the very edge of the beam, as far forward as he could go, one hand grasping tight the guide rope of the flying jib. This ship was a smooth runner, perfect in balance and ballast and with the best of crews, but the sea was rough this day and the *Sea Sprite* cut and bounced through the rolls at full sail, throwing a heavy spray.

Drizzt didn't mind. He loved the feel of the spray and the wind, the smell of the brine. This was freedom, flying, skimming the water, skipping the waves. Drizzt's thick white hair flipped in the breeze, billowing like his green cape behind him, drying almost as fast as the water wetted it. Splotches of white caked salt could not lessen the luster of his ebony skin, which glistened with wetness. His violet eyes sparkled with joy as he squinted at the horizon and caught a fleeting glimpse of the sails of the ship they pursued.

Pursued and would catch, Drizzt knew, for there was no ship north of Baldur's Gate that could outrun Captain Deudermont's *Sea Sprite*. She was a three-masted schooner, new in design, light and sleek and full of sail. The square-rigged caravel they were chasing could put up a fair run in a straight line, but anytime the bulkier vessel altered its course even the slightest bit, the *Sea Sprite* could angle inside it, gaining ground. Always gaining ground.

That was what she was meant to do. Built by the finest engineers and wizards of Waterdeep, funded by the lords of that city, the schooner was a pirate chaser. How thrilled Drizzt had been to discover the good fortunes of his old friend, Deudermont, with whom he had sailed all the way from Waterdeep to Calimshan in pursuit of Artemis Entreri when the assassin had captured Regis the halfling. That journey, particularly the fight in Asavir's Channel when Captain Deudermont had won—with no small help from Drizzt and his companions—against three pirate ships, including the flagship of the notorious Pinochet, had caught the attention of sailors and merchants all along the Sword Coast. When the Lords of Waterdeep had completed this schooner, they had offered it to Deudermont. He loved his little two-master, the original *Sea Sprite,* but no seaman could resist this new beauty. Deudermont had accepted a commission in their service and, they had granted him the right to name the vessel and allowed him to handpick his crew.

Drizzt and Catti-brie had arrived in Waterdeep sometime after that. When the *Sea Sprite* next put in to the grand harbor of the seaport, and Deudermont found his old friends, he promptly made room for them among his crew of forty. That was six years and twenty-seven voyages ago. Among those who monitored the shipping lanes of the Sword Coast, particularly among the pirates themselves, the schooner had become a scourge. Thirty-seven victories, and still she sailed.

Now number thirty-eight was in sight.

The caravel had noticed them, from too far away to see the flag of Waterdeep. That hardly mattered, for no other ship in the region carried the distinctive design of the *Sea Sprite,* the three masts of billowing triangular, lateen sails. Up came the caravel's square rigs, and so the chase was on in full.

Drizzt was at the point, one foot on the lion-headed ram, loving every second. He felt the sheer power of the sea bucking beneath him, felt the spray and the wind. He heard the music, loud and strong, for several of the *Sea Sprite*'s crewmen were minstrels and whenever the chase was on, they took up their instruments and played rousing songs.

"Two thousand!" Catti-brie yelled down from the crow's nest. It was a measure of the distance yet to gain. When her estimate got down to five hundred, the crew would move to their battle posts, three going to the large ballista mounted on a pivot atop the flying deck in the *Sea Sprite*'s stern, two going to the smaller, swiveling crossbows mounted to the forward corners of the bridge. Drizzt would join Deudermont at the helm, coordinating the close combat. The drow's free hand slipped to the hilt of one of his scimitars at the thought. The *Sea Sprite* was a vicious foe from a distance. It had crack archers, a skilled ballista team, a particularly nasty wizard, an evoker full of fireballs and lightning bolts, and of course, Catti-brie with her deadly bow, Taulmaril the Heartseeker. But it was in close, when Drizzt and his panther companion—Guenhwyvar—and the other skilled warriors could get across, that the *Sea Sprite* was truly deadly.

"Eighteen hundred!" came Catti-brie's next call. Drizzt nodded at the confirmation of their speed, though the gain was truly startling. The *Sea Sprite* was running faster than ever. Drizzt had to wonder if her keel was even getting wet!

The drow dropped a hand into his pouch, feeling for the magical figurine that he used to summon the panther from the Astral Plane, wondering if he should even call to Guenhwyvar this time. The panther had been aboard for much of the last week, hunting the hundreds of rats that threatened the ship's food stores, and was likely exhausted.

"Only if I need you, my friend," Drizzt whispered. The *Sea Sprite* cut hard to starboard and Drizzt had to take up the guide rope in both hands. He steadied himself and remained silent, his gaze to the horizon, to the square-rigged ship growing larger by the minute. Drizzt felt deep within himself, mentally preparing for the coming battle. He immersed himself in the hiss and splash of the water below him, in the rousing music cutting the wind, and in Catti-brie's calls.

Fifteen hundred, a thousand.

"Black cutlass, lined in red!" the young woman shouted down when, thanks to her spyglass, she was able to discern the design on the snapping flag of the caravel.

Drizzt didn't know the insignia, didn't care about it. The caravel was a pirate ship, one of the many who had overstepped their bounds near Waterdeep's harbors. As in any waters with trading routes, there had always been pirates on the Sword Coast. Until the last few years, though, the pirates had been somewhat civil, following specific codes of conduct. When Deudermont had defeated Pinochet in Asavir's Channel, he had subsequently let the pirate go free. That was the way, the unspoken agreement.

No longer was that the case. The pirates of the north had become bolder and more vicious. Ships were no longer simply looted, but the crews, particularly if any females were aboard, were tortured and murdered. Many ruined hulks had been found adrift in the waters near Waterdeep. The pirates had crossed the line.

Drizzt, Deudermont, and all the *Sea Sprite*'s crew, were being paid handsomely for their work, but down to every last man and woman (with the possible exception of the wizard, Robillard) they weren't chasing pirates for the gold.

They were fighting for the victims.

"Five hundred!" Catti-brie called down.

Drizzt shook himself from his trance and looked to the caravel. He could see the men on her decks now, scrambling, preparing for the fight, an army of ants. The *Sea Sprite*'s crew was outnumbered, possibly two to one, Drizzt realized, and the caravel was heavily armed. She carried a fair-sized catapult on her stern deck, and probably a ballista beneath that, ready to shoot out from the open windows.

The drow nodded and turned back to the deck. The crossbows fixed on the bridge and the ballista were manned; many of the crew lined the rail, testing the pull of their longbows. The minstrels played on as they would right up until the boarding began. High above the deck, Drizzt spotted Catti-brie, Taulmaril in one hand, her spyglass in the other. He whistled to her and she gave a quick wave in response, her excitement obvious.

How could it be otherwise? The chase, the wind, the music, and the knowledge that they were doing good work here. Smiling widely, the drow skittered back along the beam and then the rail, joining Deudermont at the wheel. He noticed Robillard the wizard, looking bored as usual, sitting on the edge of the poop deck. Every so often he waved one hand in the direction of the mainmast. Robillard wore a huge ring on that hand, a silver band set with a diamond, and its sparkle now came from more than a reflection of the light. With every gesture from the wizard, the ring loosed its magic, sending a strong gust of wind into the already straining sails. Drizzt heard the creak of protest from the mainmast and understood their uncanny speed.

"Carrackus," Captain Deudermont remarked as soon as the drow was beside him. "Black cutlass outlined in red."

Drizzt looked at him curiously, not knowing the name.

"Used to sail with Pinochet," Deudermont explained. "First mate on the pirate's flagship. He was among those we battled in Asavir's Channel."

"Captured?" Drizzt asked.

Deudermont shook his head. "Carrackus is a scrag, a sea troll."

"I do not remember him."

"He has a penchant for staying out of the way," Deudermont replied. "Likely he dove overboard, taking to the depths as soon as Wulfgar turned us about to ram his ship."

Drizzt remembered the incident, the incredible pull of his strong friend that nearly turned the original *Sea Sprite* on its stern, right into the faces of so many surprised pirates.

"Carrackus was there, though," Deudermont continued. "By all reports, it was he who rescued Pinochet's wounded ship when I set him adrift outside of Memnon."

"And is the scrag allied with Pinochet still?" Drizzt asked.

Deudermont nodded grimly. The implications were obvious. Pinochet couldn't come after the troublesome *Sea Sprite* personally because in return for his freedom he had sworn off vengeance against Deudermont. The pirate had other ways of repaying enemies. He had many allies like Carrackus who were not bound by his personal oath.

Drizzt knew at that moment that Guenhwyvar would be needed and he took the intricate figurine from his pouch. He studied Deudermont carefully. The man stood tall and straight, slender but well-muscled, his gray hair and beard neatly trimmed. He was a refined captain, his dress impeccable, as at home in a grand ball as on the open sea. Now his eyes, so light in hue that they seemed to reflect the colors about them rather than to possess any color of their own, revealed his tension. Rumors had followed the *Sea Sprite* for many months that the pirates were organizing against the vessel. With confirmation that this caravel was allied with Pinochet, Deudermont believed that this might be more than a chance crossing.

Drizzt glanced back at Robillard, who was up on one knee now, arms outstretched and eyes closed, deep in meditation. Now the drow understood the reason Deudermont had put them at such a reckless speed.

A moment later, a wall of mist rose around the *Sea Sprite,* dimming the view of the caravel, which was now barely a hundred yards away. A loud splash to the side told them that the catapult had begun firing. A moment later, a burst of fire erupted in the air before them, dissipating into a cloud of hissing steam as they and their defensive mist wall streamed through it.

"They've a wizard," Drizzt remarked.

"Not surprising," Deudermont was quick to reply. He looked back to Robillard. "Keep your measures defensive," he ordered. "We can take them with ballista and bow!"

"All the fun for you," Robillard called back dryly.

Deudermont managed a smile, despite his obvious tension.

"Bolt!" came a cry, several cries, from forward. Deudermont instinctively spun the wheel. The *Sea Sprite* leaned into the leeward turn so deeply that Drizzt feared they would capsize.

At the same moment, Drizzt heard a rush of wind to his right as a huge ballista bolt ripped past, snapping a line, skipping off the edge of the poop deck right beside a surprised Robillard and rebounding to tear a small hole in the crossjack—the sail on the mizzenmast.

"Secure that line," Deudermont instructed coolly.

Drizzt was already going that way, his feet moving impossibly fast. He got the snapping line in hand and quickly tied it off, then got to the rail as the *Sea Sprite* straightened. He looked to the caravel, now barely fifty yards ahead and to starboard. The water between the two ships rolled wildly. Whitecaps spit water that was blown into mist, caught in a tremendous wind.

The crew of the caravel didn't understand, and so they put their bows in line and began firing, but even the heaviest of their crossbow quarrels was turned harmlessly aside as it tried to cut through the wall of wind that Robillard had put between the ships.

The archers of the *Sea Sprite,* accustomed to such tactics, held their shots. Catti-brie was above the wind wall as was the archer poised in the crow's nest of the other ship—an ugly seven-foot-tall gnoll with a face that seemed more canine than human.

The monstrous creature loosed its heavy arrow first, a fine shot that sank the bolt deep into the mainmast, inches below Catti-brie's perch. The gnoll ducked below the wooden wall of its own crow's nest, readying another arrow.

No doubt the dumb creature thought itself safe, for it didn't understand Taulmaril.

Catti-brie took her time, steadied her hand as the *Sea Sprite* closed.

Thirty yards.

Her arrow went off like a streak of lightning, trailing silver sparks and blasting through the feeble protection of the caravel's crow's nest as though it were no stronger than a sheet of old parchment. Splinters and the unfortunate lookout were thrown high into the air. The doomed gnoll gave a shriek, bounced off the crossbeam of the caravel's mainmast, and spun head over heels to splash into the sea, quickly left behind by the speeding ships.

Catti-brie fired again, angling down, concentrating on the catapult crew. She hit one man, a half-orcish brute by the looks of him, but the catapult launched its load of burning pitch.

The caravel's gunners hadn't properly compensated for the sheer speed of the *Sea Sprite* and the schooner crossed under the pitch and was long gone by the time it hit the water, hissing in protest.

Deudermont brought the schooner alongside the caravel, barely twenty yards of water between them. Suddenly the water in that narrow channel stopped its wind-whipped turmoil and the archers of the *Sea Sprite* let fly many of their arrows that sported small gobs of flaming pitch.

Catti-brie let fly for the catapult itself this time, her enchanted arrow blasting a deep crack along the machine's throwing beam. *Sea Sprite*'s deadly ballista drove a heavy bolt right into the caravel's hull at sea level.

Deudermont spun the wheel to port, angling away, satisfied with the pass. More missiles, many flaming, soared between the ships before Robillard created a wall of blocking mist behind the *Sea Sprite*'s stern.

The caravel's wizard put a lightning bolt right into the mist. Though the energy was dispersed somewhat, it crackled all about the edges of the *Sea Sprite*, knocking several men to the deck.

Drizzt, leaning far over the rail and straining to watch the caravel's deck with his hair flying wildly from the energy of the lightning bolt, spotted the wizard, amidships, near the mainmast. Before the *Sea Sprite*, now running perpendicular to the pirate ship, was too far away, the drow called upon his innate powers, summoned a globe of impenetrable darkness and dropped it over the man.

He clenched his fist when he saw the globe moving along the caravel's deck, for he had hit the mark and the globe's magic had caught the wizard. It would follow and blind him, until he found some way to counter the magic. Even more than that, the ten-foot ball of blackness marked the dangerous wizard clearly.

"Catti-brie!" Drizzt cried.

"I have him!" she replied, and Taulmaril sang out, once and then again, sending two streaks into that ball of blackness.

Still it continued its run. Catti-brie hadn't dropped the wizard, but surely she and Drizzt had given the man something to think about!

A second ballista bolt soared out from the *Sea Sprite*, cutting across the bow of the caravel, and then a fireball from Robillard exploded high in the air before the rushing ship. The caravel, not agile and no longer equipped with an able wizard, rushed right into the explosions. As the fireball disappeared, both masts of the square-rigger were tipped in flames, giant candles on the open sea.

The caravel tried to respond with its catapult, but

Catti-brie's arrows had done their work and the throwing beam split apart as soon as the crew cranked too much tension on it.

Drizzt rushed back to the wheel. "One more pass?" he asked Deudermont.

The Captain shook his head. "Time for only one," he explained. "And no time to stop and board."

"Two thousand yards! Two ships!" Catti-brie called out.

Drizzt looked at Deudermont with sincere admiration. "More of Pinochet's allies?" he asked, already knowing the answer.

"That caravel alone could not defeat us," the seasoned captain coolly added. "Carrackus knows that and so would Pinochet. She was to lead us in."

"But we were too fast for that tactic," Drizzt reasoned.

"Are you ready for a fight?" Deudermont asked slyly.

Before the drow could even answer, Deudermont pulled hard and the *Sea Sprite* leaned into a starboard turn until it came about to face the slowed caravel. The square-sailed ship's topmasts were burning and half her was crew busy trying to repair the rigging, to at least keep her under half-sail. Deudermont angled his ship to intercept, to cut across the prow, in what the archers called a "bow rake."

And the wounded caravel couldn't maneuver out of harm's way. Her wizard, though blinded, had kept the presence of mind to put up a wall of thick mist, the standard and effective defensive seaboard tactic.

Deudermont measured his angle carefully, wanting to turn the *Sea Sprite* right against the edge of that mist and the whipping water, to get as close to the caravel as he could. This was their last pass, and it had to be devastating or else the caravel would be able to limp into the fight with its sister ships, which were closing fast.

There came a flash on the square-rigged ship's deck, a spark of light that countered Drizzt's darkness spell.

From her high perch above the defensive magic, Catti-brie saw it. She was already training on the darkness when the wizard emerged. The robed man went immediately into a chant, meaning to hurl a devastating spell in the path of the *Sea Sprite* before she could cross the caravel's bow, but only a couple of words had escaped his lips when he felt a tremendous thump against his chest and heard the planks of the ship's deck splinter behind him. He looked down at the blood beginning to pour onto the decking and realized that he was sitting, then lying, and all the world grew dark.

The wall of mist the wizard had put up fell away.

Robillard saw it, recognized it, and clapped his hands and sent twin bolts of lightning slashing across the caravel's deck, slamming the masts and killing many pirates. The *Sea Sprite* crossed in front of the caravel, and the archers let fly. So, too, did the ballista crew, but they did not hurl a long spear this time. They used a shortened and unbalanced bolt, trailing a chain lined with many-pronged grapnels. The contraption twirled as it flew, entangling many lines, fouling up the caravel's rigging.

Another missile, a living missile, six hundred pounds of sleek and muscled panther, soared from the *Sea Sprite* as she crossed by and caught the caravel's beam.

"Are you ready, drow?" Robillard called, seeming excited for the first time this fight.

Drizzt nodded and motioned to his fighting companions, the score of veterans who comprised the *Sea Sprite*'s crack boarding crew. They scrambled toward the wizard from all sections of the ship, dropping their bows and drawing out weapons for close melee. By the time Drizzt, leading the rush, got near to Robillard, the wizard already had a shimmering field—a magical door—on the deck beside him. Drizzt didn't hesitate, charging right through, scimitars in hand. One of them, Twinkle, glowed a fierce blue.

Out the other end of Robillard's magical tunnel he came, arriving in the midst of many surprised pirates aboard the caravel. Drizzt slashed left and right, clearing a hole in their ranks, and he darted through, his feet a blur. He turned sharply, fell to the side and rolled as one archer shot harmlessly above him. He came back to his feet, darted straight for the bowman and cut him down.

More of the *Sea Sprite*'s warriors poured through the gate and the middle of the caravel erupted in wild battle.

The confusion on the caravel's bow was no less as Guenhwyvar, all teeth and claws she seemed, slashed and tore through the mass of men who wanted nothing more than to be away from this mighty beast. Many were pulled down under those powerful claws, and several others simply turned to the side and leaped overboard, ready to take their chances with the sharks.

Again the *Sea Sprite* bent low in the water, Deudermont pulling her hard to port, angling away from the caravel and turning to meet the charge of the coming duo head-on. The tall captain smiled as he heard the fighting on the ship behind him, confident in his boarding party, though they were still likely outnumbered two to one.

The dark elf and his panther tended to even such odds.

From her high perch, Catti-brie picked several more shots, each one taking down a strategically-placed pirate archer, and one driving through a man to kill the pirate goblin sitting next to him!

Then the young woman turned her attention away from the caravel, looking forward in order to direct the *Sea Sprite*'s movements.

Drizzt ran and rolled, leaped in confusing spins and always came down with his scimitars angled for an enemy's most vital areas. Under his boots, he wore bands of gleaming mithril rings secured around black material, enchanted for speed. Drizzt had taken these from Dantrag Baenre, a famed drow weaponmaster. Dantrag had used them as bracers to speed his hands, but Drizzt understood the truth of the items. On his ankles, they allowed the drow to run and dart like a wild hare.

He used them now, along with his amazing agility, to confuse the pirates, to keep them unsure of where he was, or where they could next expect him to be. Whenever one of them guessed wrong and was caught off guard, Drizzt seized the opportunity and came in hard, scimitars slashing away. He made his way generally forward, seeking to join up with Guenhwyvar, the fighting companion who knew him best and complimented his every move.

He didn't quite get there. The rout on the caravel was nearly complete, many pirates dead, others throwing down their weapons, or throwing themselves overboard in sheer desperation. One of the crew, the most seasoned and most fearsome, a personal friend of Pinochet, wasn't so quick to surrender.

He emerged from his cabin under the forward bridge, his body bent over because the low construction of the ship would not accommodate his ten-foot height. He wore only a sleeveless red vest and short breeches, which barely covered his scaly green skin. Limp hair the color of seaweed hung below his broad shoulders. He carried no weapon fashioned on a smithy's anvil but, his dirty claws and abundant teeth seemed deadly enough.

"So the rumors were true, dark elf," he said in a wet, bubbly voice. "You have returned to the sea."

"I do not know you," Drizzt said, skidding to a stop a cautious distance from the scrag. He guessed the pirate to be Carrackus, the sea troll Deudermont had spoken of, but could not be sure.

"I know you!" the scrag growled. He charged, his clawed hands slashing for Drizzt's head.

Three quick steps brought Drizzt out of the monster's path. The drow dropped to one knee and spun about, both scimitars slashing across, blades barely an inch apart.

More agile than Drizzt expected, the opponent turned the opposite way and twirled, pulling in his trailing leg. The drow's scimitars barely nicked the monster as they passed.

The scrag charged, meaning to bury Drizzt where he knelt, but again the drow was too quick for such a straightforward tactic. He came up to his feet and started left, then, as the scrag took the bait and began to turn, Drizzt came back fast to the right, underneath the monster's swinging arm.

Twinkle stabbed a hip and Drizzt's other blade followed with a deep cut along the scrag's side.

Drizzt accepted the backhand his opponent launched his way, knowing that the off-balance scrag couldn't put much of its formidable strength and weight behind it. The long and skinny arm thudded off the drow's shoulder and then off his parrying blades as he spun to face the lurching brute.

Now it was Drizzt's turn to charge, lightning fast and straight ahead. He slid Twinkle under the elbow of the outstretched scrag arm, drawing a deep gash and then hooked

21

the fine-edged and curving blade underneath the hanging flap of skin. His other scimitar poked for the scrag's chest, slipped past the frantic block of the other arm.

There was only one way for the off-balance monster to move. Drizzt knew that, anticipated the scrag's retreat perfectly. The drow secured his grip on Twinkle, even braced his shoulder against the weapon's hilt to hold it firm. The scrag roared in agony and dove back and to the side, directly opposite the angle of Twinkle's nasty bite. The sickly flesh peeled from the scrag's arm, all the way from its biceps to its wrist. The torn lump fell to the deck with a sickening thud.

His black eyes filled with outrage and hatred. The scrag looked down to the exposed bone, to the writhing lump of troll flesh on the deck. And finally, to Drizzt, who stood casually, scimitars crossed down low in front of him.

"Damn you, Drizzt," the monstrous pirate growled.

"Strike your colors," Drizzt ordered.

"You think you have won?"

In response, Drizzt looked down to the slab of meat.

"It will heal, foolish dark elf!" the pirate insisted.

Drizzt knew that the scrag spoke truly. Scrags were close relatives of trolls, horrid creatures renowned for their regenerative powers. A dead dismembered troll could come back together.

Unless . . .

Drizzt called upon his innate abilities once more, that small part of magic inherent in the dark elf race. A moment later, purplish flames climbed the towering scrag's form, licking at green scales. This was only faerie fire, harmless light the dark elves could use to outline their opponents. It had no power to burn, nor could it prevent the regenerative process of a troll.

Drizzt knew that; he was betting that the monster did not.

The scrag's gruesome features twisted in an expression of sheer horror. He flailed his good arm, beat it against his leg and hip. The stubborn purple flames would not relent.

"Strike your colors and I will release you of the flames that your wounds might heal," Drizzt offered.

The scrag snapped a look of pure hatred at the drow. He took a step forward, but up came Drizzt's scimitars. He decided he didn't want to feel their bite again, especially if the flames prevented him from healing!

"We will meet again!" the scrag promised. The creature wheeled about to see dozens of faces—Deudermont's crew and captured pirates—staring at him in disbelief. He howled and charged across the deck, scattering those in the way of the furious rush. The pirate leaped from the rail, back to the sea, back to his true home where he might heal.

So quick was Drizzt that he got across the deck and managed yet another hit on him before the scrag got off the rail. The drow had to stop there, unable to pursue and fully aware that the sea troll would indeed regenerate to complete health.

He hadn't even gotten a curse of frustration out of his mouth when he saw a fast movement to his side, a rush of black. Guenhwyvar leaped past Drizzt, flew out from the rail, and splashed into the sea right behind the troll.

The panther disappeared under the azure blanket and the rough and choppy waves quickly covered any indication that the scrag and the cat had gone in.

Several of the *Sea Sprite*'s boarding party peered intently over the rail, worried for the panther who had become such a friend to them.

"Guenhwyvar is in no danger," Drizzt reminded them, producing the figurine and holding it high so that all could see. The worse the scrag could do was send the panther back to the Astral Plane, where the cat would heal any wounds and be ready to return to Drizzt's next call. Still, the drow's expression was not bright as he considered the spot where Guenhwyvar had gone in, as he considered that the panther might be in pain.

The deck of the captured caravel went perfectly quiet, save the creaking of the old vessel's timbers.

An explosion to the south turned all heads, all eyes strained to perceive tiny sails, still far away. One of the pirate ships had turned away; the other caravel was burning while the *Sea Sprite* literally sailed circles about her. Flash after flash of silver streaking arrows came from the

*Sea Sprite's* crow's nest, battering the hull and masts of the damaged, seemingly helpless ship.

Even from this great distance, the people on the captured caravel could see the pirate flag go down the mainmast, colors struck in surrender.

That brought a cheer from the *Sea Sprite's* boarding party, a rousing yell that was halted abruptly by churning waters just off the side of the caravel. They saw green scales and black fur tumbling in the turmoil. A scrag arm floated out from the mass, and Drizzt was able to sort the confusing scene out enough to realize that Guenhwyvar had gotten onto the scrag's back. Her forelegs were tight about the monster's shoulders, her back legs were kicking, raking wildly, and the panther's powerful jaws were clamped tight onto the back of the scrag's neck.

Dark blood stained the sea, mixing with torn pieces of the pirate's flesh and bone. Soon enough, Guenhwyvar sat still, teeth and claws securely in place on the back of the dead, floating scrag.

"Better fish the thing out," one of the *Sea Sprite's* boarding party remarked, "or we'll be growing a whole crew o' stinking trolls!"

Men arrived at the rail with long gaff hooks and began the gruesome task of hauling in the carcass. Guenhwyvar got back to the caravel easily enough, clambering over the rail and then giving a good shake, spraying water on all those nearby.

"Scrags don't heal if they're out o' the sea," a man remarked to Drizzt. "We'll haul this one up the yardarm to dry, then burn the damned thing."

Drizzt nodded. The boarding party knew their duty well enough. They would organize and supervise the captured pirates, freeing the rigging and getting the caravel as seaworthy as possible for the trip back to Waterdeep.

Drizzt looked to the southern horizon and saw the *Sea Sprite* returning. The damaged pirate ship limped alongside.

"Thirty-eight and thirty-nine," the drow muttered.

Guenhwyvar gave a low growl in reply and shook vigorously again, soaking her dark elf companion.

# Chapter 2
## THE FIRST MESSENGER

aptain Deudermont seemed out of place indeed as he strolled down Dock Street, the infamous, rough and tumble avenue that lined Waterdeep Harbor. His clothes were fine and perfectly tailored to his tall and thin frame, his posture was perfect, and his hair and goatee meticulously groomed. All about him, the scurvy sea dogs who had put in for their weeks ashore staggered out of taverns, reeking of ale, or fell down unconscious in the dust. The only thing protecting them from the many robbers lurking in the area was the fact that they had no money or valuables to steal.

Deudermont ignored the sights, and didn't fancy himself any better than those sea dogs. In fact, there was an aspect of their way of life that intrigued the gentlemanly captain, an honesty that mocked the pretentious courts of nobles.

Deudermont pulled his layered cloak tighter about his neck, warding off the chill night breeze that blew in off the harbor. Normally one would not walk alone down Dock Street, not even in the light of noonday, but Deudermont felt secure. He carried his decorated cutlass at his side, and knew how to use it well. Even more than that, the word had been passed through every tavern and every pier in Waterdeep that the *Sea Sprite*'s captain had been afforded the personal protection of the Lords of Waterdeep, including some very powerful wizards who would seek out and destroy anyone bothering the captain or his crew while they were in port. Waterdeep was the *Sea Sprite*'s haven, and so Deudermont thought nothing of walking alone down Dock Street. He was more curious than fearful when a wrinkled old man, bone skinny and barely five feet tall, called to him from the edge of an alleyway.

Deudermont stopped and looked about. Dock Street was quiet, except for the overspill of sound from the many taverns and the groan of old wood against the incessant sea breeze.

"Ye's is Doo-dor-mont-ee, asin't yer?" the old seabones called softly, a whistle accompanying each syllable. He smiled widely, almost lewdly, showing but a couple of crooked teeth set in black gums.

Deudermont stopped and eyed the man patiently, silently. He felt no compulsion to answer the question.

"If ye be," the man wheezed, "then oi've got a bit o' news for yer. A warnin' from a man yer's is rightly fearin'."

The captain stood tall and impassive. His face showed none of the questions that raced about in his mind. Who would he be afraid of? Was the old dog talking of Pinochet? That seemed likely, especially considering the two caravels the *Sea Sprite* had escorted into Waterdeep Harbor earlier that week. But few in Waterdeep had any contact with the pirate, whose domain was much farther to the south, south of Baldur's Gate even, in the straights near the Moonshae Isles.

But who else might the man be talking about?

Smiling still, the sea dog motioned for Deudermont to come to the alley. The captain didn't move as the old man turned and took a step in.

"Well, be yer fearin' old Scaramundi?" the sea dog whistled.

Deudermont realized it could be a disguise. Many of the greatest assassins in the Realms could look as helpless as this one, only to put a poisoned dagger into their victim's chest.

The sea dog came back to the entrance to the alley, then walked right out into the middle of the street toward Deudermont.

No disguise, the captain told himself, for it was too complete, too perfect. Besides, he recollected that he had seen this same old man before, usually sitting right near to this very same alleyway, which probably served as his home.

What then? Might there be an ambush set down that alley?

"Have it yer own way then," the old man wheezed as he

threw up one hand. He leaned heavily on his walking stick and started back to the alley, grumbling. "Just a messenger, I be, and not fer carin' if yer hears the news or not!"

Deudermont cautiously looked all around again. Seeing nobody nearby, and no likely hiding spots for an ambush party, he moved to the mouth of the alleyway. The old sea dog was ten short paces in, at the edge of the slanting shadows cast by the building to the right, and barely visible in the dimness. He laughed and coughed and moved in yet another step.

One hand on the hilt of his cutlass, Deudermont cautiously approached, scanning carefully before each step. The alleyway seemed empty enough.

"Far enough!" Deudermont said suddenly, stopping the sea dog in his tracks. "If you have news for me, then speak it, and speak it now."

"Some things shouldn't be said too loudly," the old man replied.

"Now," Deudermont insisted.

The salty sea dog smiled widely and coughed, perhaps laughing. He ambled back a few steps, stopping barely three feet from Deudermont.

The smell of the man nearly overwhelmed the captain, who was accustomed to powerful body odors. There wasn't much opportunity to bathe on a ship at sea and the *Sea Sprite* was often out for weeks, even months, at a time. Still, the combination of cheap wine and old sweat gave this one a particularly nasty flavor that made Deudermont scrunch up his face, even put a hand over his nose to try to intercept some of the fumes.

The sea dog, of course, laughed hysterically at that.

"Now!" the captain insisted.

Even as the word left Deudermont's lips, the sea dog reached out and caught him by the wrist. Deudermont, not afraid, turned his arm, but the old man held on stubbornly.

"I want you to tell me of the dark one," the sea dog said, and it took Deudermont a moment to realize that the man's dockside accent was gone.

"Who are you?" Deudermont insisted, and he tugged fiercely, to no avail. Only then did Deudermont realize the truth of the superhuman grip; he might as well have been pulling against one of the great fog giants that lived on the reef surrounding Delmarin Island, far to the south.

"The dark one," the old man repeated. With hardly any effort, he yanked Deudermont deeper into the alleyway.

The captain went for his cutlass, and though the old man held Deudermont's right hand fast, he could fight fairly well with his left. It was somewhat awkward extracting the curving blade from its sheath with that hand, and before the cutlass came fully free, the old man's free hand shot forward, open-palmed, to slam Deudermont in the face. He flew backward, crashing against the wall. Keeping his wits about him, he drew out the blade, transferred it to his now-free right hand, and slashed hard at the ribs of the approaching sea dog.

The fine cutlass gashed deep into the sea dog's side, but he didn't even flinch. Deudermont tried to block the next slap, and the next after that, but his defenses simply were not strong enough. He tried to get his cutlass in line to parry, but the old man slapped it away, sent it spinning from his hand, then resumed the battering. Open palms came in with the speed of a striking snake, heavy blows that knocked Deudermont's head tilting, and he would have fallen, except that the old man grabbed him by the shoulder and held him fast.

Through bleary eyes, Deudermont peered at his foe. Confusion crossed his stern features as his enemy's face began to melt away and then to reform.

"The dark one?" he, *it*, asked again, and Deudermont hardly heard the voice, his voice, so dumbfounded was he at the spectacle of his own face leering back at him.

\* \* \* \* \*

"He should be here by now," Catti-brie remarked, leaning on the bar.

She was growing impatient, Drizzt realized, and not because Deudermont was late—the captain was often detained at one function or another in Waterdeep—but because the sailor on the other side of her, a short and stocky man with a thick beard and curly hair, both the color of a raven's wing, kept bumping into her. He apologized each time, looking over his shoulder to regard the beautiful woman, often winking and always smiling.

Drizzt turned so that his back was against the waist-high bar. The Mermaid's Arms was nearly empty this night. The weather had been fine and most of the fishing and merchant fleets were out. Still, the place was loud and rowdy, full of sailors relieving months of boredom with drink, companionship, much bluster and even fisticuffs.

"Robillard," Drizzt whispered, and Catti-brie turned and followed the drow's gaze to see the wizard slipping through the crowd, moving to join them at the bar.

"Good evening," the wizard said without much enthusiasm. He didn't look at the companions as he spoke, and didn't wait for the bartender to come near, merely waggled his fingers and a bottle and a glass magically came to his place. The bartender started to protest, but a pile of copper pieces appeared in his hand. The bartender shook his head with disdain, never caring much for the *Sea Sprite*'s wizard and his arrogant antics, and moved away.

"Where is Deudermont?" Robillard asked. "Squandering my pay, no doubt."

Drizzt and Catti-brie exchanged smiles wrought of continued disbelief. Robillard was among the most distant and caustic men either of them had ever known, more grumpy even than General Dagna, the surly dwarf who served as Bruenor's garrison commander at Mithril Hall.

"No doubt," Drizzt replied.

Robillard turned to regard him with an accusing, angry glare.

"Of course, Deudermont's one to steal from us all the time," Catti-brie added. "Takes a fancy to the finest o' ladies and the finest o' wine, and is free with what's not his to be free with."

A growl escaped Robillard's thin lips and he pushed off the bar and walked away.

"I'd like to know that one's tale," Catti-brie remarked.

Drizzt nodded his accord, his eyes never leaving the departing wizard's back. Indeed, Robillard was a strange one, and the drow figured that something terrible must have happened to him somewhere in his past. Perhaps he had unintentionally killed someone, or had been rejected by a true love. Perhaps he had seen too much of wizardry, had looked into places where a man's eyes were not meant to go.

Catti-brie's simple spoken thought had sparked a sudden interest within Drizzt Do'Urden. Who was this Robillard, and what precipitated his perpetual boredom and anger?

"Where is Deudermont?" came a question from the side, breaking Drizzt's trance. He turned to see Waillan Micanty, a lad of barely twenty winters, with sandy-colored hair, cinnamon eyes and huge dimples that always showed because Waillan never seemed to stop smiling. He was the youngest of the *Sea Sprite*'s crew, younger even than Catti-brie, but with an uncanny eye on the ballista. Waillan's shots were fast becoming legend, and if the young man lived long enough, he would no doubt assemble quite a reputation along the Sword Coast. Waillan Micanty had put one ballista bolt through the window of a pirate captain's quarters at four hundred yards and had skewered the pirate captain as the man was buckling on his cutlass. The momentum of the heavy spear had hurled the pirate right through his closed cabin door and out onto the deck. The pirate ship struck her colors immediately, the capture ended before the fighting had really even begun.

"We are expecting the man," Drizzt answered, his mood brightening simply at the sight of the beaming young man. Drizzt couldn't help but notice the contrast between this youngster and Robillard, who was probably the oldest of the crew, except for Drizzt.

Waillan nodded. "Should be here by now," he remarked under his breath, but the drow's keen ears caught every word.

"You are expecting him?" Drizzt was quick to ask.

"I need to speak with him," Waillan admitted, "about a possible advance on earnings." The young man blushed deep red and moved close to Drizzt so that Catti-brie could not hear. "A lady friend," he explained.

Drizzt found his smile widening even more. "The captain is overdue," he said. "I'm sure he will not be much longer."

"He was less than a dozen doors down when I last saw him," Waillan said. "Near to the Foggy Haven and heading this way. I thought he'd beat me here."

For the first time, Drizzt grew a bit concerned. "How long ago was that?"

Waillan shrugged. "I been here since the fight before," he said.

Drizzt turned and leaned back against the bar. He and Catti-brie exchanged concerned looks this time, for many minutes had passed since the previous two fights. There wasn't much to interest the captain between the Mermaid's Arms and the place Waillan spoke of, certainly nothing that should have detained Deudermont for this long.

Drizzt sighed and took a long swallow of the water he was drinking. He looked to Robillard, now sitting by himself, though a table not far from the man held open chairs beside the four that were occupied by members of the *Sea Sprite*'s crew. Drizzt wasn't too concerned. Perhaps Deudermont had forgotten some business, or had simply changed his mind about coming to the Mermaid's Arms this night. But still, Dock Street in Waterdeep was a dangerous place, and the drow ranger's sixth sense, that warrior instinct, told him to be wary.

\* \* \* \* \*

Deudermont, practically senseless, did not know how long the beating went on. He was lying on the cold ground now, that much he knew. The thing, whatever it was, having assumed his exact form, clothing, even weapons, was sitting on his back. The physical torture was not so great anymore, but even worse than the beating, the captain felt the creature within his mind, probing his thoughts, gaining knowledge that it could no doubt use against his friends.

*You will taste fine,* Deudermont heard in his thoughts. *Better than the old Scaramundi.*

Despite the unreality of it all, the lack of true sensation, the captain felt his stomach churning. He believed he knew, in that distant corner of consciousness, what monster had come to him. Dopplegangers were not common in the Realms, but the few who had made themselves known had certainly caused enough havoc to secure the wretched reputation of the alien race.

Deudermont felt himself being lifted from the ground. So strong was the grasp of the creature that the captain felt as if he were weightless, simply floating to his feet. He was spun around to face the thing, to face himself, and he expected then to be devoured.

"Not yet," the creature replied to his unspoken fears. "I need your thoughts, good Captain Deudermont. I need to know enough about you and your ship to sail it out of Waterdeep Harbor, far to the west and far to the south, to an island that few know, but many speak of."

The thing's smile was tantalizing and Deudermont had just focused fully on it when the creature's head shot forward, its forehead slamming him in the face, knocking him senseless. Some time later—he did not know how many seconds might have passed—Deudermont felt the cold ground against his cheek once more. His hands were tightly bound behind his back, his ankles likewise strapped, and a tight gag was about his mouth. He managed to turn his head enough to see the creature, wearing his form still, bending over a heavy iron grate.

Deudermont could hardly believe the strength of the thing as it lifted that sewer covering, a mass of metal that had to weigh near to five hundred pounds. The creature casually leaned it against the wall of a building, then turned and grabbed Deudermont, dragging him to the opening and unceremoniously dropping him in.

The stench was awful, worse than the captain would have expected even from a sewer, and when he managed to shift about and get his face out of the muck, he understood the source.

Scaramundi, it had to be Scaramundi, lay beside him, caked in blood, more than half of his torso torn away, eaten by the creature. Deudermont jumped as the sewer grate clanked back into place, and then he lay still, horrified and helpless, knowing that he would soon share the same grisly fate.

# Chapter 3

# THE MESSAGE, SUBTLY TOLD

ome time later, Drizzt was beginning to worry. Robillard had already left the Mermaid's Arms, disgusted that his captain, as he had put it, "couldn't be counted on." Waillan Micanty was still at the bar beside Drizzt, though the young man had taken up a conversation with another sailor on the other side of him.

Drizzt, his back to the bar, continued to survey the crowd, perfectly at ease among the sailors. It hadn't always been so. Drizzt had come through Waterdeep only twice before he and Catti-brie had left Mithril Hall, first on his way to Calimport chasing Entreri, and on the return trip, when he and his friends were making their way back to reclaim Mithril Hall. Drizzt had made that first passage through the city in disguise, using a magical mask to appear as a surface elf. The second journey through, made without the mask, had been a trickier proposition. The *Sea Sprite* had put into Waterdeep Harbor in early morning but, at Deudermont's request, Drizzt and his friends had waited until after dark to leave the city for the road to the east.

Upon his return to Waterdeep with Catti-brie six years ago, Drizzt had dared to walk openly as a drow. It had been an uncomfortable experience, eyes were upon him every step, and more than one ruffian had challenged him. Drizzt had avoided those challenges, but knew that sooner or later, he would have to fight, or even worse, he would be slain from afar, likely by a hidden bowman, for no better reason than the color of the skin.

Then the *Sea Sprite* had put in and Drizzt had found Deudermont, his old friend and a man of considerable reputation among the docks of the great city. Soon after, Drizzt had become widely accepted in Waterdeep, particularly all along Dock Street, because of his personal reputation, spread in no small way by Captain Deudermont. Wherever the *Sea Sprite* docked, it was made clear that Drizzt Do'Urden, this most unusual of dark elves, was a member of her heroic crew. Drizzt's road had been easier, had even become comfortable.

And through it all, Catti-brie and Guenhwyvar had been beside him. He looked to them now, the young woman sitting at a table with two of the *Sea Sprite*'s crew, the great panther curled up on the floor about her legs. Guenhwyvar had become a mascot to the patrons of the Mermaid's Arms, and Drizzt was glad that he could sometimes call in the cat, not for battle, but simply for companionship. Drizzt wondered which reason would hold this day. Catti-brie had requested the panther, saying her feet were cold, and Drizzt had agreed, but in the back of the drow's mind was the realization that Deudermont might be in trouble. Guenhwyvar might be needed for more than companionship.

The drow surely relaxed a moment later, blew out a deep sigh of relief as Captain Deudermont walked into the Mermaid's Arms, glanced around, then focused on Drizzt and sidled up to the bar.

"Calimshan wine," the doppleganger said to the bartender, for it had scoured Deudermont's mind and knew that to be the man's customary drink. In the short time they had spent together, the doppleganger had learned much of Captain Deudermont and of the *Sea Sprite*.

Drizzt turned about and leaned over the bar. "You are late," he remarked, trying to feel the captain out, trying to discern if there had been any trouble.

"A minor problem," the impostor assured him.

"What is it, Guen?" Catti-brie asked softly as the panther's head came up, the cat looking in the direction of Drizzt and Deudermont, her ears flattened against her head and a low growl resonating from her strong body. "What do ye see?"

Guenhwyvar continued to watch the pair closely, but Catti-brie dismissed the cat's temperament, figuring there must be a rat or the like in the far corner beyond Drizzt and the captain.

"Caerwich," the impostor announced to Drizzt.

The ranger regarded the man curiously. "Caerwich?" he echoed. Drizzt knew the name; every sailor along the Sword Coast knew the name of the tiny island, which was too small and remote to appear on the vast majority of nautical charts.

"We must put out at once for Caerwich," the impostor explained, looking Drizzt directly in the eye. So perfect was the disguise of the doppleganger that Drizzt hadn't the slightest idea that anything was amiss.

Still, the request sounded strange to Drizzt. Caerwich was a shipboard story, a tale of a haunted island that played home to a blind witch. Many doubted its existence, though some sailors claimed to have visited the place. Certainly Drizzt and Deudermont had never spoken of it. For the captain to announce that they must go there caught the drow completely by surprise.

Again Drizzt studied Deudermont, this time noting the man's stiff mannerisms, noting how uncomfortable Deudermont seemed in this place, which had always been his favorite among the taverns of Dock Street. Drizzt believed something had unnerved Deudermont. Whatever had delayed his arrival at the Mermaid's Arms—Drizzt figured it to be a visit by one of Waterdeep's secretive lords, perhaps even mysterious Khelben—had upset Deudermont greatly. Perhaps Deudermont's announcement wasn't so out of place. Many times in the last six years, the *Sea Sprite,* the tool of Waterdeep's Lords, had been assigned private, unusual missions, and so the drow accepted the information without question.

What both Drizzt and the doppleganger hadn't counted on was Guenhwyvar, who crouched so low that her belly brushed against the floor as she inched for Deudermont's back, her ears flat.

"Guenhwyvar!" Drizzt scolded.

The doppleganger spun about, putting its back to the wooden bar just as Guenhwyvar charged in, coming up high and pinning the creature to the bar. Had the doppleganger kept its wits and played the innocent victim, it might have talked its way out of the predicament. But the creature recognized Guenhwyvar, or at least the fact that this panther was not of the Prime Material Plane. And if the doppleganger instinctively recognized that about the panther, it figured the panther would recognize the same.

Purely on instinct, the creature batted Guenhwyvar with its forearm, the weight of the blow launching the six-hundred pound cat halfway across the wide room.

No human could do that, and when the impostor looked again at Drizzt, it found that the drow had his scimitars in hand.

"Who are you?" Drizzt demanded.

The creature hissed and grabbed at the blades, catching one. Drizzt struck, tentatively and with the flat of his free blade, for he feared that this might be Deudermont under some type of enchantment. He smacked the impostor on the side of the neck.

The creature caught the blade in its open hand, and it rushed forward and bowled Drizzt aside.

The rest of those in the tavern were up then, most thinking it one of the typical fights. But the crew of the *Sea Sprite,* particularly Catti-brie, realized the absolute strangeness of the scene.

The doppleganger made for the door, slapping aside the one confused sailor, one of the *Sea Sprite*'s crewmen, who stood in its way.

Catti-brie had her bow ready, and she put an arrow, trailing silvery sparks, into the wall right beside the creature's head. The doppleganger spun to face her, hissed loudly, and was subsequently buried by six hundred pounds of flying panther. This time Guenhwyvar recognized the strength of her foe and by the time the two had sorted out their tumble, the great cat was sitting on the doppleganger's back, her powerful jaws clamped tight on the nape

37

of the thing's neck. Drizzt was there in an instant, followed closely by Catti-brie, Waillan Micanty and the rest of the crew, and more than a few curious onlookers, including the proprietor of the Mermaid's Arms, who wanted to get a look at the damage from that enchanted arrow.

"What are you?" Drizzt demanded, grabbing the impostor by the hair and turning its head so that he could look into its face. Drizzt rubbed his free hand across the thing's cheek, looking for makeup, but found none. He barely got his fingers away before the doppleganger bit at them.

Guenhwyvar growled and tightened her jaws, forcing the creature's face to slam hard back into the floor.

"Go and check out Dock Street!" Drizzt called to Waillan. "Near to where you last saw the captain!"

"But . . ." Waillan protested, pointing to the prone form.

"This is not Captain Deudermont," Drizzt assured him. "This is not even human!"

Waillan motioned to several of the *Sea Sprite*'s crew and headed out, followed by many other sailors who called themselves friends of the apparently missing captain.

"And call for the Watch!" Drizzt yelled after them, referring to the famed Waterdeep patrols. "Be ready with your bow," Drizzt said to Catti-brie and she nodded and fitted another arrow to the bowstring.

Working with Guenhwyvar, the drow managed to get the doppleganger fully subdued and standing against a wall. The bartender offered some heavy rope, and they tightly bound the doppleganger's hands behind its back.

"I ask you one more time," Drizzt began threateningly. The creature merely spat in his face and began laughing, a diabolical sound indeed.

The drow did not respond with force, just stared hard at this impostor. Truly Drizzt's heart was low then, for the way the impostor looked at him, laughed at him, only at him, sent a shiver along his spine. He wasn't afraid for his own safety, never that, but he feared that his past had caught up with him once again, that the evil powers of Menzoberranzan had found him here in Waterdeep, and that the good Captain Deudermont had fallen because of him.

If true, it was more than Drizzt Do'Urden could bear.

"I offer your life in exchange for Captain Deudermont," the drow said.

"It's not your place to be bargaining with the . . . whatever it might be," remarked one sailor whom Drizzt did not know. The drow, scowling fiercely, turned to face the man, who went silent and backed away, having no desire to invoke the wrath of a dark elf, especially one of Drizzt's fighting reputation.

"Your life for Deudermont," Drizzt said again to the doppleganger. Again came that diabolical laughter and the creature spat in Drizzt's face.

Left, right, left came Drizzt's open palms in rapid succession, battering the creature's face. The last punch bent the thing's nose, but it reformed, right before Drizzt's eyes, to perfectly resemble the unmarred nose of Captain Deudermont.

That image, combined with the continuing laughter, sent ripples of rage through the drow and he slugged the impostor with all his strength.

Catti-brie wrapped her arms about Drizzt and pulled him away, though the mere sight of her reminded Drizzt of who he was and shamed him for his rash, out-of-control actions.

"Where is he?" Drizzt demanded, and when the creature continued to taunt him, Guenhwyvar came up on her hind legs, resting one forepaw on each shoulder, and putting her snarling visage barely an inch from the doppleganger's face. That quieted the creature, for it knew that Guenhwyvar recognized the truth of its existence, and knew that the angry panther could utterly destroy it.

"Get a wizard," one sailor offered suddenly.

"Robillard!" exclaimed another, the last of the *Sea Sprite*'s crew, besides Drizzt and Catti-brie, in the tavern. "He'll know how to get the information out of this thing."

"Go," Catti-brie agreed, and the man rushed out.

"A priest," offered another man. "A priest will better deal with . . ." The man paused, not knowing what to make of this impostor.

Through it all, the doppleganger remained passive, matching Guenhwyvar's stare but making no threatening moves.

The crewman had barely exited the tavern when he was passed by another of the *Sea Sprite*'s hands, heading back in with the news that Deudermont had been found.

Out they went, Drizzt shoving the doppleganger along, Guenhwyvar on the other side of the creature and Catti-brie behind it, her bow up and ready, an arrow tip nearly touching the back of the thing's head. They came into the alley even as the sewer grate was being pried open, one sailor promptly dropping into the smelly hole to help his captain out.

Deudermont eyed the doppleganger, eyed the perfect image of himself, with open contempt. "You may as well assume your natural form," he said to the thing. Drawing himself up straight, he brushed off some of the muck, regaining his dignity in an instant. "They know who I am, and know what you are."

The doppleganger did nothing. Drizzt kept Twinkle tight against the side of its neck, Guenhwyvar remained alert on the other side, and Catti-brie went over to Deudermont, supporting the injured man.

"Might I lean on your bow?" the captain asked, and Catti-brie, with hardly a thought, quickly handed it over.

"Must be a wizard," Deudermont said to Drizzt, though the captain suspected differently. The injured Deudermont took the offered bow and leaned on it heavily. "If he utters a single, uncalled for syllable, slash his throat," he instructed.

Drizzt nodded and pressed Twinkle a bit closer. Catti-brie moved to take Deudermont's arm, but he waved her ahead, then followed closely.

\* \* \* \* \*

Far away, on a smoky layer of the Abyss, Errtu watched the unfolding scene with pure delight. The trap had been set, not as the great tanar'ri had expected when he had sent the doppleganger to Waterdeep, but set anyway, and perhaps more deliciously, more unexpectedly, more chaotically.

Errtu understood Drizzt Do'Urden well enough to know that the mention of Caerwich was all the bait that was needed. Something awful had happened to them that night and they would not let it pass, would go willingly to the mentioned island and discover the source.

The mighty fiend was having more fun than he had known in years. Errtu could have delivered the message to Drizzt more easily, but this intrigue—the doppleganger, the blind witch who waited at Caerwich—was the fun of it all.

The only thing that would be more fun for Errtu was tearing Drizzt Do'Urden apart, little piece by little piece, devouring his flesh before his very eyes.

The balor howled at that thought, figuring that it would soon enough come to pass.

* * * * *

Deudermont straightened as much as possible and continued to wave away any offered help. The captain put on a good face, and stayed close behind Catti-brie as she moved slowly toward the alley exit, toward Drizzt and Guenhwyvar and the captured doppleganger.

Deudermont watched that strange creature most carefully of all. He understood the evil of the thing, had felt it up close. Deudermont hated the thing for the beating it had given him, but in assuming the captain's form, the thing had violated him in a way that he could not tolerate. Looking at the creature now, as it wore the features of the *Sea Sprite*'s Captain, Deudermont could barely keep his anger in check. He kept very close to Catti-brie, watching, anticipating.

Near to Dock Street, Drizzt stood quietly beside the bound impostor. The drow and the many crewmen nearby were focused on the injured captain, and none of them noticed as the creature began to shift its malleable form once more, reshaping its arms so that they slipped and twisted free of the bonds.

Drizzt just got his second scimitar out after the creature suddenly shoved him aside. The doppleganger bolted for the alley's exit with Guenhwyvar close behind. Wings sprouted from the doppleganger's back and it leaped high, meaning to fly off into the night.

41

Guenhwyvar charged and sprang mightily in pursuit while Captain Deudermont slipped an arrow from the quiver on Catti-brie's hip. The woman, sensing the theft, spun about as the bow came up. She cried out, fell to the side and Deudermont let fly.

The doppleganger was more than twenty feet off the ground by the time Guenhwyvar began her leap, but still the great panther caught up to the flying monster, her jaws catching a firm hold on the creature's ankle. That limb shifted and reformed immediately, making the panther's grasp tentative. Then came the silver-streaking arrow, slamming the doppleganger square in the back, right between the wings.

Down came Guenhwyvar, landing lightly on padded paws, and down came the doppleganger, dead before it ever hit the ground.

Drizzt was there in an instant, the others rushing to catch up with him.

The creature began to shift its form again. Its newest features melted away, to be replaced by a humanoid appearance the likes of which none of the gathering had ever seen. Its skin was perfectly smooth, the fingers of its slender hand showing no distinguishable grooves. It was completely hairless, and everything about it seemed perfectly unremarkable. It was a lump of humanoid-shaped clay and nothing more.

"Doppleganger," Deudermont remarked. "It would seem that Pinochet is not pleased by our latest exploits."

Drizzt nodded, allowing himself to agree with the captain's reasoning. This incident wasn't about him, wasn't about who he was and where he came from.

He had to believe that.

\* \* \* \* \*

Errtu thoroughly enjoyed the spectacle, and was glad that he would not have to pay off his hired master of disguise. It bothered the fiend for a moment that his guide for the *Sea Sprite*'s voyage to the virtually unchartered island had just gone away, but the balor held his faith. The seeds had been sown; the doppleganger had teased Deudermont about the destination, and Drizzt had heard the exact name of the island and would pass it on to the captain. The balor knew neither were cowards, both were resourceful and curious.

Errtu knew Drizzt and Deudermont would find their way to Caerwich and the blind seer who held the fiend's message. Soon enough.

# Chapter 4

# UNASKED FOR "ASSISTANCE"

he *Sea Sprite* put back out two weeks later, her course south. Captain Deudermont explained that they had business pending in Baldur's Gate, one of the largest ports on the Sword Coast, about halfway between Waterdeep and Calimshan. No one questioned Deudermont openly, but many felt that he seemed on edge, almost indecisive, a mannerism they had never experienced with the confident captain before.

That demeanor changed four days out of Waterdeep Harbor, when the *Sea Sprite*'s lookout caught sight of a square-rigger sporting a deck covered with sailors. Caravels were ordinarily crewed by forty to fifty men. A pirate ship, wanting to attack swiftly with overwhelming odds, and then bring the booty quickly to shore, might carry three times that number. Pirate ships didn't carry cargo; they carried warriors.

If Deudermont had seemed indecisive before, not so now. Up came the *Sea Sprite*'s sails to full. Catti-brie hooked Taulmaril over her shoulder and began the climb to the crow's nest, and Robillard was ordered to take his place on the poop deck and to use his magic to further fill the sails. But the natural wind was already strong from the northwest, from astern it already filled the sails of both the *Sea Sprite* and the running pirate ship, and the chase would be a long one.

At center deck, the ship's musicians took up a rousing

tune, and Drizzt came back from the forward beam earlier than usual to stand beside Deudermont at the wheel.

"Where will we tow her once captured?" the drow asked, a usual question on the high seas. They were still closer to Waterdeep than to Baldur's Gate, but the wind was from the north generally, favoring a southern course.

"Orlumbor," Deudermont answered without hesitation.

Drizzt was surprised by that. Orlumbor was a rocky, windswept island halfway between Waterdeep and Baldur's Gate, an independent city-state, lightly populated and hardly equipped to hold a caravel full of pirates.

"Will the shipwrights even take her?" the drow asked doubtfully.

Deudermont nodded, his face stern. "Orlumbor owes much to Waterdeep," he explained. "They will hold her until another ship of Waterdeep arrives to tow her away. I will instruct Robillard to use his powers to contact the Lords of Waterdeep."

Drizzt nodded. It seemed perfectly logical, yet perfectly out of place. The drow understood now that this was no ordinary run for the normally patient *Sea Sprite*. Never before had Deudermont left off a captured ship and crew for another to pick up in his wake. Time had never seemed an issue out here, amidst the steady and eternal roll of the sea. The *Sea Sprite* would normally run until she found a pirate ship, snag her or sink her, then return to one of the friendly ports and hand her over, however long that might take.

"Our business in Baldur's Gate must be urgent," the drow remarked, cocking a suspicious eye the captain's way.

Deudermont turned to look at him directly, to stare long and hard at Drizzt for the first time this voyage. "We are not going to Baldur's Gate," he admitted.

"Then where?" Drizzt's tone showed that he was not surprised by that revelation.

The captain shook his head and turned his stare forward, adjusting the wheel slightly to keep them in line with the running caravel.

Drizzt accepted that. He knew that Deudermont had graced him by even admitting that they would not sail for Baldur's Gate. He also knew that the captain would confide in him as Deudermont needed. Their business now at hand was the pirate ship, still far ahead, her square sails barely visible on the blue line of the horizon.

"More wind, wizard!" Deudermont casually called back to Robillard, who grunted and waved his hand at the captain. "We'll not catch her before dusk unless we have more wind."

Drizzt offered a smile to Deudermont, then made his way forward, back to the beam, to the smell and the spray, to the hissing sound of the *Sea Sprite*'s run, to the solitude he needed to think and to prepare.

They ran for three hours before the caravel was close enough for Catti-brie, in the crow's nest with her spyglass, to even confirm that it was indeed a pirate ship. The day was long then, the sun halfway from peak to the western horizon, and the chasers knew they would be cutting this one close. If they couldn't catch the pirate ship before sunset, she would sail off into the darkness. Robillard had some spells to try to keep track of her movements, but the pirate ship no doubt had a wizard of her own, or a cleric, at least. Though neither would likely be very powerful, certainly not as accomplished as Robillard, such tracking spells were easily defeated. Also, pirates never ventured too far from their secret ports, and the *Sea Sprite* certainly couldn't chase this one all the way home, where her friends might be waiting.

Deudermont didn't seem overly concerned. They had lost pirates to the night before, and would again. There would always be another outlaw to chase. But Drizzt, keeping a covert eye on the captain, never remembered seeing him quite this casual. Obviously, it had something, or everything, to do with the incident in Waterdeep and the mysterious destination that Deudermont would not discuss.

The drow tightened his hold on the line of the flying jib and sighed. Deudermont would tell him in his own time.

The wind lessened and the *Sea Sprite* made up some ground. It seemed as though this pirate ship might not get away after all. The band of minstrels, which had broken up during the long and tedious middle hours of the chase, came back together again and took up the tune. Drizzt knew that soon the pirates would hear the music, it would reach to them across the waves, a harbinger of their doom.

Now things seemed back to normal, more relaxed despite the fact that a battle seemed imminent. Drizzt tried to convince himself that Deudermont was calm because he had known they would catch the pirate ship. Everything was back to normal.

"Spray astern!" came a cry, turning all hands about.

"What is that?" more than one voice cried. Drizzt looked to Catti-brie, who had her spyglass aimed behind the *Sea Sprite*, and was shaking her head curiously.

The drow skittered along the rail, pulling up to a halt amidships, and leaning out to catch his first glimpse of the unknown pursuer. He saw a high wedge of spray, the spray the giant dorsal fin of a killer whale might make if any whale in all the world could move so quickly. But this was no natural animal, Drizzt knew instinctively, and so did everyone else aboard the *Sea Sprite*.

"She's going to ram!" warned Waillan Micanty, near to the ballista mounted on the ship's stern. Even as he spoke, the strange rushing pursuer veered to starboard and cut by the *Sea Sprite* as though she was standing still.

No whale, Drizzt realized as the creature, or whatever it was, plowed past, twenty yards from the *Sea Sprite*, but close enough to lift a wall of water against the side of the schooner. The drow thought he saw a form inside that spray, a human form.

"It's a man!" Catti-brie called from above, confirming Drizzt's suspicions.

All the crew watched in disbelief as the speeding creature rushed away from the *Sea Sprite*, closing the ground to the caravel.

"A wizard?" Deudermont asked Robillard.

Robillard shrugged, as did all of the others nearby, none of them having any explanation whatsoever. "The more important question," the wizard finally said, "would be to inquire as to the loyalty of this newcomer. Friend, or foe?"

Apparently, those on the caravel didn't know the answer to that either, for some stared silently from the rail, while others picked up crossbows. The pirate ship's catapult crew even launched a ball of flaming pitch at the newcomer, but he was moving too fast for them to gauge the distance and the missile hissed harmlessly into the surf. Then the rushing man moved up alongside the caravel, easily outpacing her. The wake diminished and then disappeared in an instant, to reveal a robed man wearing a heavy pack and standing atop the waves, waving his arms frantically and calling out. He was too far from the *Sea Sprite* now for any of the crew to make out exactly what he was saying.

"Suren he's to casting a spell!" Catti-brie yelled down from the crow's nest. "He's—" She stopped abruptly, drawing a concerned look from Drizzt, and though the drow couldn't make her out clearly from his angle so far below, he could tell that she was confused and could see that she was shaking her head, as if in denial of something.

Those on the deck of the *Sea Sprite* struggled to figure out exactly what was going on. They saw a flurry of activity near the rail facing the man as he stood upon the water. They heard shouts and the clicking sound of crossbows firing, but if any bolts struck the man, he did not show it.

Suddenly, there came a tremendous flash of fire that dissipated immediately into a huge cloud of thick fog, a ball of white where the caravel had been. And it was growing! Soon the cloud covered the water-walking spellcaster as well, and spread out thick and wide. Deudermont kept his course straight and fast, but when he finally neared the location, he had to slow to a drifting crawl, not daring to enter the unexplained bank. Frustrated, cursing under his breath, Deudermont turned the *Sea Sprite* broadside to the misty veil.

All hands stood ready along the rail. The heavy mounted crossbows were armed and ready, as was the ballista on the *Sea Sprite*'s stern deck.

Finally, the fog began to lift, to roll back under the press of the stiff breeze. A ghostly figure appeared just within the veil, standing on the water, chin in palm, looking disconcertingly at the spot where the caravel had been.

"Ye're not to believe this," Catti-brie called down to Drizzt, a groan accompanying her words.

Indeed, Drizzt did not, for he also came to recognize the unexpected arrival. He noted the carmine robe, decorated with wizardly runes and outrageous images. These were stick figures, actually, depicting wizards in the throes of spellcasting, something an aspiring wizard the ripe age of five might draw in a play spellbook. Drizzt also recognized the hairless, almost childish face of the man—all dimples and huge blue eyes—and the brown hair, long and straight, pulled back tight behind the man's ears so that they stood out from his head at almost right angles.

"What is it?" Deudermont asked the drow.

"Not what," Drizzt corrected. "But who." The drow gave a short laugh and shook his head in disbelief.

"Who then?" Deudermont demanded, trying to sound stern though Drizzt's chuckles were both comforting and infectious.

"A friend," Drizzt replied, and he paused and looked up at Catti-brie. "Harkle Harpell of Longsaddle."

"Oh, no," Robillard groaned from behind them. Like every wizard in all the Realms, Robillard had heard the tales of Longsaddle and the eccentric Harpell family, the most unintentionally dangerous group of wizards ever to grace the multiverse.

As the moments passed and the fog cloud continued to dissipate, Deudermont and his crew relaxed. They had no idea of what had happened to the caravel until the cloud was nearly gone, for then they spotted the pirate ship, running fast, far, far away. Deudermont almost called for full sails, meaning to give chase once more, but he looked to the lowering sun, gauged the distance between his ship and his adversary, and decided that this one had gotten away.

The wizard, Harkle Harpell, was in clear sight now, just a dozen yards or so beyond the *Sea Sprite*'s starboard bow. Deudermont gave the wheel over to a crewman and walked with Drizzt and Robillard to the closest point. Catti-brie came down the mainmast to join them.

Harkle stood impassively, chin in hand, staring at the spot where the caravel had been. He rolled with the swells, up high and down low, and continually tapped his foot upon the sea. It was a strange sight, for the water moved away from him, his water-walking enchantment preventing his foot from actually making any contact with the salty liquid.

Finally, Harkle looked back at the *Sea Sprite,* at Drizzt and the others. "Never thought of that," he admitted, shaking his head. "Aimed the fireball too low, I suppose."

"Wonderful," Robillard muttered.

"Are you coming aboard?" Deudermont asked the man, and the question, or the sudden realization that he was not aboard any ship, seemed to break Harkle from his trance.

"Ah, yes!" he said. "Actually a good idea. Glad I am that I found you." He pointed down at his feet. "I do not know how much longer my spell—"

As he spoke the words, the spell apparently expired, for under he went, plop, into the sea.

"Big surprise," remarked Catti-brie, moving to the rail to join the others.

Deudermont called for poles to fish the wizard out, then looked to his friends in disbelief. "He came out on the high seas with such a tentative enchantment?" the captain asked incredulously. "He might never have found us, or any other friendly ship, and then . . ."

"He is a Harpell," Robillard answered as though that should explain everything.

"Harkle Harpell," Catti-brie added, her sarcastic tone accentuating the wizard's point.

Deudermont just shook his head, taking some comfort in the fact that Drizzt, standing beside him, was obviously enjoying all of this.

# Chapter 5
## A PASSING THOUGHT

rapped in a blanket, his robes hanging on the mast high above him to dry in the wind, the waterlogged wizard sneezed repeatedly, spraying those around him. He simply couldn't contain himself and got Deudermont right in the face when the captain came up for an introduction.

"I give to you one Harkle Harpell of Longsaddle," Drizzt said to Deudermont. Harkle extended his hand, and the blanket fell away from him. The skinny wizard scrambled to retrieve it, but was too late.

"Get this one a meal," Catti-brie snickered from behind. "Suren he could use a bit o'meat on that bum."

Harkle blushed a deep red. Robillard, who had already met the Harpell, just walked away, shaking his head and suspecting that exciting times were yet to come.

"What brings you here," Deudermont asked, "so far from shore, on the open seas?"

Harkle looked to Drizzt. "I came on invitation," he said at length, seeming somewhat perturbed when the drow made no move to answer for him.

Drizzt eyed him curiously.

"I did!" protested the wizard. "On your word." He spun about to regard Catti-brie. "And yours!"

Catti-brie looked to Drizzt, who shrugged and held his hands out to the sides, having no idea of what Harkle might be talking about.

"Oh, well, well, well, a fine 'hello,' I suppose," the exasperated wizard stammered. "But then, I expected it, though I hoped a drow elf would have a longer memory. What do you say to someone you meet again after a century?

51

Couldn't remember his name, could you? Oh, no, no. That would be too much trouble."

"What are you talking about?" Drizzt had to ask. "I remember your name."

"And a good thing, too!" Harkle roared. "Or I would really be mad!" He snapped his fingers indignantly in the air, and the sound sobered him. He stood for a long moment, seeming thoroughly confused, as though he had forgotten what in the world he was talking about.

"Oh, yes," Harkle said at length and looked straight at Drizzt. The wizard's stern expression soon softened to one of curiosity.

"What are you talking about?" Drizzt asked again, trying to prompt Harkle.

"I do not know," the wizard admitted.

"You were telling me what brought you out here," Deudermont put in.

Harkle snapped his fingers again. "The spell, of course!" he said happily.

Deudermont sighed. "Obviously, it was a spell," the captain began slowly, trying to find a path that would garner some useful information from the rambling mage.

"Not 'a' spell," Harkle retorted. "*The* spell. My new spell, the fog of fate."

"The fog of fate?" Deudermont echoed.

"Oh, very good spell," Harkle began excitedly. "Expedites things, you know. Get on with your life and all that. Shows you where to go. Puts you there even, I think. But it doesn't tell you why." The wizard moved one hand up to tap at his chin, and his blanket slipped down again, but he didn't seem to notice. "I should work on that part. Yes, yes, then I would know why I was here."

"Ye're not even knowin'?" Catti-brie asked, and she faced the rail, even leaned over it somewhat, so she wouldn't have to look at Harkle's bony buttocks.

"Answering an invitation, I suppose," Harkle replied.

Catti-brie's expression was purely doubtful, as was Drizzt's.

"It's true!" Harkle protested vehemently. "Oh, so convenient of you to forget. Shouldn't say things you don't mean,

I say! When you, both of you"—he looked from one to the other, waggling his finger—"passed through Longsaddle six years ago, you mentioned that you hoped our paths might cross once more. 'If ever you find yourself near to us.' That is exactly what you said!"

"I do not—" Drizzt began, but Harkle waved him silent, then rushed to the oversized pack he had carried with him, which was drying on the deck. His blanket slipped down farther, but the wizard was too consumed by his task to notice. Catti-brie didn't bother to look away, she just snickered and shook her head.

Harkle pulled a small flask from his pack, retrieved his blanket for modesty's sake, and bounced back over to stand before Drizzt. Snapping his fingers defiantly in the air before the drow, the wizard popped off the cork.

From the flask came a voice, Catti-brie's own voice. "If you ever find yerself near to us," she said, "do look in."

"So there," Harkle said in superior tones as he plopped the cork back into place. He stood for a long moment, hands on hips, until Drizzt's smile became inviting. "And just where are we?" the wizard asked, turning to Deudermont.

The captain looked to the drow ranger, and Drizzt could offer only a shrug in reply. "Come, and I will show you," Deudermont said, leading the wizard toward his cabin. "And I will get you some proper clothes to wear until your robes have dried."

When the two were gone, Catti-brie, walked back over to her friend. Robillard stood not so far away, glaring at them both.

"Pray we find no more pirates to fight until we can be rid of our cargo," the wizard said.

"Harkle will try to help," Catti-brie replied.

"Pray hard," Robillard muttered and walked away.

"You should be more careful of what you say," Drizzt remarked to Catti-brie.

"Could have been yer own voice just as well as me own," the young woman shot back. "And besides, Harkle did try to help in the fight."

"It could as easily have been us he engulfed, in stream or in fire," Drizzt promptly reminded her.

Catti-brie sighed and had no words to reply. They turned to the door of Deudermont's cabin, where the captain stood with Harkle, about to enter.

"So that was the fog of fate you cast at our pirate friends, eh?" Deudermont asked, trying to sound impressed.

"Huh?" Harkle answered. "That? Oh, no, no, that was a fireball. I am good at casting those!" The Harpell paused and lowered his eyes, following Deudermont inside. "Except that I aimed too low," Harkle admitted quietly.

Catti-brie and Drizzt looked to each other, then to Robillard. "Pray," all three whispered in unison.

\* \* \* \* \*

Drizzt and Catti-brie dined privately with Deudermont that night, the captain seeming more animated than he had since they had put out from Waterdeep. The two friends tried to apologize for Harkle's arrival several times, but Deudermont brushed such thoughts away, even hinted that he was not so upset about the Harpell's arrival.

Finally Deudermont sat back in his chair, wiped his neatly-groomed goatee with a satin napkin and stared hard at the two friends, who fell silent, understanding that the captain had something important to tell them.

"We are not in this area by chance," Deudermont admitted bluntly.

"And not going to Baldur's Gate," reasoned Drizzt, who had suspected all along. The *Sea Sprite* was supposedly running to Baldur's Gate, but Deudermont hadn't been careful about staying close to the coast, the more direct route, the safer route, and the route most likely to allow them to find and capture pirates.

Again there ensued a long pause, as though the captain had to settle things in his own mind before admitting them openly. "We're turning west for Mintarn," Deudermont said.

Catti-brie's jaw dropped open.

"A free port," Drizzt reminded, and warned. The island of Mintarn had a well-earned reputation as a haven for pirates and other fugitives, a rough and tumble place. How might the *Sea Sprite,* the hunter of justice, be received in such a port?

"A free port," Deudermont agreed. "Free for pirates and free for the *Sea Sprite,* in need of information."

Drizzt didn't openly question the captain, but his doubting expression spoke volumes.

"The Lords of Waterdeep have given the *Sea Sprite* over to me completely," Deudermont said, somewhat harshly. "She's my ship, under my word alone. I can take her to Mintarn, to the Moonshaes, all the way to Ruathym, if I so please, and let no one question me!"

Drizzt sat back in his seat, stung by the harsh words and surprised that Deudermont, who had professed to be his friend, had so treated him as a subordinate.

The captain winced openly at the sight of the drow's disappointment. "My pardon," he said quietly.

Drizzt came forward in his seat, leaning his elbows on the table to bring himself closer to Deudermont. "Caerwich?" he asked.

Deudermont eyed him directly. "The doppleganger spoke of Caerwich, and so to Caerwich I must go."

"And do ye not think ye'll be sailing right into a trap?" Catti-brie put in. "Going right where they're wanting ye to go?"

"Who?" Deudermont asked.

"Whoever sent the doppleganger," Catti-brie reasoned.

"Who?" Deudermont asked again.

Catti-brie shrugged. "Pinochet?" she queried. "Or mighten it be some other pirate that's had his fill o' the *Sea Sprite*?"

Deudermont leaned back in his seat again, as did Drizzt, all three sitting in silence for several long moments. "I cannot, nor do I believe that you can, continue to sail up and down the Sword Coast as though nothing at all has happened," the captain explained. Drizzt closed his lavender eyes, expecting this answer and agreeing with the logic. "Someone powerful, for doppleganger hirelings are neither common nor cheap, desires my demise and the end of the *Sea Sprite,* and I intend to find out who it might be. I've never run from a fight, nor has my crew, and any who are not prepared to go to Caerwich may disembark in Mintarn and catch a sail back to Waterdeep, paid by my own coffers."

"Not a one will go," Catti-brie admitted.

"Yet we do not even know if Caerwich truly exists," Drizzt remarked. "Many claim to have been there, but these are the tales of seagoing men, tales too often exaggerated by drink or by bluster."

"So we must find out," Deudermont said with a tone of finality. Neither Drizzt nor Catti-brie, both willing to face trouble head-on, offered a word of disagreement. "Perhaps it is not such a bad thing that your wizard friend arrived," the captain went on. "Another wizard knowledgeable in the mystical arts might help us to sort through this mystery."

Catti-brie and Drizzt exchanged doubtful looks; Captain Deudermont obviously didn't know Harkle Harpell! They said no more about it, though, and finished the meal discussing more pertinent matters of the everyday handling of the ship and crew. Deudermont wanted to go to Mintarn, so Drizzt and Catti-brie would follow.

After the meal, the two friends strolled out onto the nearly-deserted deck of the schooner, walking under a canopy of brilliant stars.

"Ye were relieved at the captain's tale," Catti-brie remarked.

After a moment of surprise, Drizzt nodded.

"Ye thought the attack in Waterdeep had to do with yerself, and not with Deudermont or the *Sea Sprite*," Catti-brie went on.

The drow simply stood and listened, for, as usual, the perceptive young woman had hit his feelings exactly, had read him like an open book.

"Ye'll always be fearing that every danger comes from yer home," Catti-brie said, moving to the rail and looking over at the reflection of the stars in the rolling waters.

"I have made many enemies," Drizzt replied as he joined her.

"Ye've left them buried in yer tracks," Catti-brie said with a laugh.

Drizzt shared in that chuckle, and had to admit that she was right. This time, he believed, it wasn't about him. For several years now, he had been a player in the larger drama of the world. The personal element of the danger that had followed him every step since his initial departure from Menzoberranzan seemed a thing of the past. Now, under the stars and with Catti-brie beside him, thousands of miles and many years from Menzoberranzan, Drizzt Do'Urden felt truly free, and carefree. He did not fear the trip to Mintarn, or to any mysterious island beyond that, whatever the rumors of haunts might be. Never did Drizzt Do'Urden fear danger. He lived on the edge willingly, and if Deudermont was in trouble, then Drizzt was more than ready to take up his scimitars.

As was Catti-brie, with her bow, Taulmaril, and the magnificent sword, Khazid'hea, always ready at her hip. As was Guenhwyvar, ever-faithful companion. Drizzt did not fear danger; only guilt could bend his stoic shoulders. This time, it seemed, he carried no guilt, no responsibility for the attack and for the *Sea Sprite*'s chosen course. He was a player in Deudermont's drama, a willing player.

He and Catti-brie basked in the wind and the spray, watched the stars silently for hours.

# Chapter 6
## THE NOMADS

ierstaad, son of Revjak, knelt on the soft turf, his knee pocking the ground. He was not tall by the standards of the Icewind Dale nomads, barely topping six feet, and was not as muscular as most. His hair was long and blond, his eyes the color of the sky on the brightest of days, and his smile, on those rare occasions that he displayed it, beamed from a warm soul.

Across the flat tundra Kierstaad could see the snow-capped top of Kelvin's Cairn. It was the lone mountain in the thousand square miles of the land called Icewind Dale, the windswept strip of tundra between the Sea of Moving Ice and the northwestern spur of the Spine of the World mountains. If he were to move but a few miles toward the mountain, Kierstaad knew that he would see the tips of the masts of the fishing ships sailing Lac Dinneshere, second largest of the three lakes in the region.

A few miles to a different world, Kierstaad realized. He was just a boy, really, having seen only seventeen winters. But in that time, Kierstaad had witnessed more of the Realms and of life than most in the world would ever know. He had traveled with many warriors to the call of Wulfgar, from Icewind Dale to a place called Settlestone, far, far away. He'd celebrated his ninth birthday on the road, removed from his family. At the age of eleven, the young barbarian lad had battled goblins, kobolds, and drow elves, fighting beside Berkthgar the Bold, leader of Settlestone. It was Berkthgar who had decided that the time had come for the barbarian peoples to return to Icewind Dale—their ancestral home—and the ways of their forebears.

Kierstaad had seen so much, had lived two different lives, it seemed, in two different worlds. Now he was a nomad, a hunter out on the open tundra, approaching his eighteenth birthday and his first solitary hunt. Looking at Kelvin's Cairn, though, and knowing of the fishing ships on Lac Dinneshere, on Maer Dualdon to the west, and on Red-waters to the south, Kierstaad realized how narrow his existence had truly become, and how much wider was the world—a world just a few short miles from where he now knelt. He could picture the markets in Bryn Shander, the largest of the ten towns surrounding the lakes. He could imagine the multicolored garments, the jewels, the excitement, as the merchant caravans rolled in with the spring, the southerners bartering for the fine scrimshaw carved from the head bone of the three lakes' abundant knuckle-head trout.

Kierstaad's own garments were brown, like the tundra, like the reindeer he and his people hunted, like the tents they lived in.

Still, the young man's sigh was not a lament for what was lost to him, but rather a resignation that this was now his way, the way of his ancestors. There was a simple beauty to it, Kierstaad had to admit, a toughness, too, that hardened the body and the soul. Kierstaad was a young man, but he was wise beyond his years. A family trait, so it was said, for Kierstaad's father, Revjak, had led the unified tribes after Wulfgar's departure. Calm and always in control, Revjak hadn't left Icewind Dale to go to war in Mithril Hall, explaining that he was too old and set in his ways. Revjak had stayed on with the majority of the barbarian people, solidifying the alliance between the nomadic tribes, and also strengthening the ties with the folk of Ten-Towns.

Revjak hadn't been surprised, but was pleased at the return of Berkthgar, of Kierstaad—his youngest child—and of all the others. Still, with that return came many questions concerning the future of the nomadic tribes and the leadership of the barbarian people.

"More blood?" came a question, drawing the young man from his contemplations. Kierstaad turned to see the other hunters, Berkthgar among them, moving up behind him.

Kierstaad nodded and pointed to the red splotch on the brown ground. Berkthgar had speared a reindeer, a fine throw from a great distance, but only had wounded the beast, and it had taken flight. Always efficient, particularly when dealing with this animal that gave to them so very much, the hunters had rushed in pursuit. They would not wound an animal to let it die unclaimed. That was not their way. It was, according to Berkthgar, "the wasting way of the men who lived in Ten-Towns, or who lived south of the Spine of the World."

Berkthgar walked up beside the kneeling young man, the tall leader locking his own stare on distant Kelvin's Cairn. "We must catch up to the beast soon," Berkthgar stated. "If it gets too close to the valley, the dwarves will steal it."

There were a few nods of agreement and the hunting party started off at a swift pace. Kierstaad lagged behind this time, his steps weighed by his leader's words. Ever since they had left Settlestone, Berkthgar had spoken ill of the dwarves, the folk who had been their friends and allies, Bruenor's folk, who had fought in a war of good cause beside the barbarians. What had happened to the cheers of victory? His most vivid memory of the short couple of years in Settlestone was not of the drow war, but of the celebration that had followed, a time of great fellowship between the dwarves, the curious svirfneblin, and the warriors who had joined in the cause from several of the surrounding villages.

How had that all changed so dramatically? Barely a week on the road out of Settlestone, the story of the barbarian existence there had begun to change. The good times were no longer spoken of, replaced by tales of tragedy and hardship, of the barbarians lowering their spirits to menial tasks not fit for the Tribe of the Elk, or the Tribe of the Bear, or any of the ancestral tribes. Such talk had continued all the way around the Spine of the World, all the way back to Icewind Dale, and then, gradually, it had died away.

Now, with rumors that the several score of the dwarves had returned to Icewind Dale, Berkthgar's critical remarks had begun anew. Kierstaad understood the source. The rumors said that Bruenor Battlehammer himself, the Eighth King of Mithril Hall, had returned. Shortly after the drow war, Bruenor had given the throne back over to his ancestor, Gandalug, Patron of Clan Battlehammer, who had returned from centuries of magical imprisonment at the hands of the drow elves. Even at the height of their alliance, relations between Berkthgar and Bruenor had been strained, for Bruenor had been the adoptive father of Wulfgar, the man who stood tallest in the barbarians' legends. Bruenor had forged mighty Aegis-fang, the warhammer which, in the hands of Wulfgar, had become the most honored weapon of all the tribes.

But then, with Wulfgar gone, Bruenor would not give Aegis-fang over to Berkthgar.

Even after his heroic exploits in the battle of Keeper's Dale against the drow, Berkthgar had remained in Wulfgar's shadow. It seemed to perceptive Kierstaad, that the leader had embarked on a campaign to discredit Wulfgar, to convince his proud people that Wulfgar was wrong, that Wulfgar was not a strong leader, that he was even a traitor to his people and their gods. Their old life, so said Berkthgar, one of roaming the tundra and living free of any bonds, was the better way.

Kierstaad liked his life on the tundra, and wasn't certain that he disagreed with Berkthgar's observations concerning which was the more honorable lifestyle. But the young man had grown up admiring Wulfgar, and Berkthgar's words about the dead leader did not sit well with him.

Kierstaad looked to Kelvin's Cairn as he ran along the soft, spongy ground, and wondered if the rumors were true. Had the dwarves returned, and if so, was King Bruenor with them?

And if he was, could it be possible that he brought with him Aegis-fang, that most powerful of warhammers?

Kierstaad felt a tingle at that thought, but it was lost a moment later when Berkthgar spotted the wounded reindeer and the hunt was on in full.

\* \* \* \* \*

"Rope!" Bruenor bellowed, hurling to the floor the twine the shopkeeper had offered him. "Thick as me arm, ye durned orc-brain! Ye thinking that I'm to hold up a tunnel with that?"

The flustered shopkeeper scooped up the twine and rambled away, grumbling with every step.

Standing at Bruenor's left, Regis gave the dwarf a scowl.

"What?" demanded the red-bearded dwarf, leaping to face the portly halfling directly. There weren't many people that the four-and-a-half foot dwarf could look down on, but Regis was one of them.

Regis ran both his plump hands through his curly brown hair and chuckled. "It is good that your coffers run deep," the halfling said, not afraid of blustery Bruenor in the least. "Otherwise Maboyo would throw you out into the street."

"Bah!" the dwarf snorted, straightening his lopsided, one-horned helmet as he turned away. "He's needing the business. I got mines to reopen, and that's meaning gold for Maboyo."

"Good thing," Regis muttered.

"Keep flapping yer lips," Bruenor warned.

Regis looked up curiously, his expression one of blank amazement.

"What?" Bruenor insisted, turning to face him.

"You *saw* me," Regis breathed. "And you just saw me again."

Bruenor started to reply, but the words got caught in his throat. Regis was standing on Bruenor's left, and Bruenor had lost his left eye in a fight in Mithril Hall. After the war between Mithril Hall and Menzoberranzan, one of the most powerful priests of Silverymoon had cast healing spells over Bruenor's face, which was scarred from forehead, down diagonally across the eye, to the left side of his jaw. The wound was an old one by that point, and the cleric had predicted that his work would do little more than cosmetic repair. Indeed, it took several months for a new eye to appear, deep within the folds of the scar, and some time after that for the orb to grow to full size.

Regis pulled Bruenor closer. Unexpectedly, the halfling covered Bruenor's right eye with one hand, pointed a finger of his other hand, and jabbed it at the dwarf's left eye.

Bruenor jumped and caught the poking hand.

"You can see!" the halfling exclaimed.

Bruenor grabbed Regis in a tight hug, even swung him completely about. It was true, the dwarf's sight had returned in his left eye!

Several other patrons in the store watched the emotional outburst, and as soon as Bruenor became aware of their stares, and even worse, their smiles, he dropped Regis roughly back to the floor.

Maboyo arrived then, his arms full with a coil of heavy rope. "Will this meet your desires?" he asked.

"It's a start," Bruenor roared at him, the dwarf turning suddenly sour again. "I need another thousand feet."

Maboyo stared at him.

"Now!" Bruenor roared. "Ye get me the rope or I'm out for Luskan with enough wagons to keep me and me kin supplied for a hunnerd years!"

Maboyo stared a moment longer, then gave up and headed for his storeroom. He had known the dwarf meant to clean him out of many items as soon as Bruenor had entered his store with a heavy purse. Maboyo liked to dole out supplies slowly, over time, making each purchase seem precious and extracting as much gold from the customer as possible. Bruenor, the toughest bargainer this side of the mountains, didn't play that game.

"Getting back your vision didn't do much to improve your mood," Regis remarked as soon as Maboyo was out of sight.

Bruenor winked at him. "Play the game, Rumblebelly," the dwarf said slyly. "Suren this one's glad we're back. Doubles his business."

True enough, Regis understood. With Bruenor and two hundred of Clan Battlehammer back in Icewind Dale, Maboyo's store—the largest and best-stocked in all of Bryn Shander, in all of Ten-Towns—stood to do well.

Of course, that meant Maboyo would have to put up with the surliest of customers. Regis chuckled privately at the thought of the battles the shopkeeper and Bruenor would fight, just as it had been nearly a decade before, when the rocky valley just south of Kelvin's Cairn chimed with the ringing of dwarven hammers.

Regis spent a long while staring at Bruenor. It was good to be home.

# Part 2
## THE FOG OF FATE

e are the center. In each of our minds—some may call it arrogance, or selfishness—we are the center, and all the world moves about us, and for us, and because of us. This is the paradox of community, the one and the whole, the desires of the one often in direct conflict with the needs of the whole. Who among us has not wondered if all the world is no more than a personal dream?

I do not believe that such thoughts are arrogant or selfish. It is simply a matter of perception; we can empathize with someone else, but we cannot truly see the world as another person sees it, or judge events as they affect the mind and the heart of another, even a friend.

But we must try. For the sake of all the world, we must try. This is the test of altruism, the most basic and undeniable ingredient for society. Therein lies the paradox, for ultimately, logically, we each must care more about ourselves than about others, and yet, if, as rational beings we follow that logical course, we place our needs and desires above the needs of our society, and then there is no community.

*I come from Menzoberranzan, city of drow, city of self. I have seen that way of selfishness. I have seen it fail miserably. When self-indulgence rules, then all the community loses, and in the end, those striving for personal gains are left with nothing of any real value.*

*Because everything of value that we will know in this life comes from our relationships with those around us. Because there is nothing material that measures against the intangibles of love and friendship.*

*Thus, we must overcome that selfishness and we must try; we must care. I saw this truth plainly following the attack on Captain Deudermont in Waterdeep. My first inclination was to believe that my past had precipitated the trouble, that my life course had again brought pain to a friend. I could not bear this thought. I felt old and I felt tired. Subsequently learning that the trouble was possibly brought on by Deudermont's old enemies, not my own, gave me more heart for the fight.*

*Why is that? The danger to me was no less, nor was the danger to Deudermont, or to Catti-brie or any of the others about us.*

*Yet my emotions were real, very real, and I recognized and understood them, if not their source. Now, in reflection, I recognize that source, and take pride in it. I have seen the failure of self-indulgence; I have run from such a world. I would rather die because of Deudermont's past than have him die because of my own. I would suffer the physical pains, even the end of my life. Better that than watch one I love suffer and die because of me. I would rather have my physical heart torn from my chest, than have my heart of hearts, the essence of love, the empathy and the need to belong to something bigger than my corporeal form, destroyed.*

*They are a curious thing, these emotions. How they fly in the face of logic, how they overrule the most basic instincts. Because, in the measure of time, in the measure of humanity, we sense those self-indulgent instincts to be a weakness, we sense that the needs of the community must outweigh the desires of the one. Only when we admit to our failures and recognize our weaknesses can we rise above them.*

*Together.*

—Drizzt Do'Urden

# Chapter 7
## MINTARN

t took some effort for Drizzt to spot the panther. The island of Mintarn, four hundred miles southwest of Waterdeep, was cloaked in thick trees, and Guenhwyvar was perfectly blended, reclining on a branch twenty feet from the ground, camouflaged so well that a deer might walk right under the cat, never realizing its doom.

Guenhwyvar was not hunting deer this day. The *Sea Sprite* had put into port barely two hours before, flying no flag, no colors at all, and with her name covered by tarps. The three-masted schooner was likely recognizable, though, for she was unique along the Sword Coast, and many of the rogues now visiting the free port had run from her in the past. So it was that Drizzt, Catti-brie and Deudermont had been approached soon after they had entered the Freemantle, a tavern just off the docks.

Now they waited for their contact, half expecting an ambush in the thick woods barely a hundred yards from the town common.

There and then, Deudermont could truly appreciate the value of such loyal and powerful friends. With Drizzt and Catti-brie, and ever-alert Guenhwyvar keeping watch, the captain feared no ambush, not if all the pirates of the Sword Coast rose against him! Without these three around him, Deudermont would have been terribly vulnerable. Even Robillard, undeniably powerful but equally unpredictable, could not have afforded the captain such comfort. More than their skill, Deudermont trusted in these three for their loyalty. They'd not desert him, not one of them, no matter the risk.

70

Guenhwyvar's ears flattened and the panther gave a low growl, a sound the other three felt in their bellies rather than heard with their ears.

Drizzt went into a low crouch and scanned the region, he pointed east and north, then slipped into the shadows, silent as death. Catti-brie moved behind a tree and fixed an arrow to Taulmaril's bowstring. She tried to follow Drizzt's movements, using them to discern the approach of their contact, but the drow was gone. It seemed he had simply vanished soon after he had entered the thick growth. As it turned out, she didn't need Drizzt's movements as a guide, for their visitors were not so adept at traveling silently and invisibly through the woods.

Deudermont stood calmly in the open, his hands folded behind his back. Every now and then he brought out one hand to adjust the pipe that hung in his mouth. He, too, sensed the proximity of other men, several men, taking up positions in the woods about him.

"You do not belong here," came an expected voice from the shadows. The speaker, a tiny man with small dark eyes and huge ears poking out from under his bowl-cut brown hair, had no idea that he had been spotted twenty steps from his current position, which was still more than a dozen yards from the captain. He did not know that his seven companions, too, were known to Drizzt and Catti-brie, and especially to Guenhwyvar. The panther was a moving shadow among the branches, positioning herself close enough to get to four of the men with a single leap.

Off to the speaker's left side, one of his companions spotted Catti-brie and brought his own bow up, putting an arrow in line with the woman. He heard a rustle, but before he could react, a dark form rushed past him. He gave a short yelp, fell back, and saw the forest green of a cape swish past. Then the form was gone, leaving the man stunned and unharmed.

"Brer'Cannon?" the man addressing Deudermont asked, and there came rustling from several positions.

"I'm okay," a shaken Brer'Cannon replied quickly, straightening himself and trying to understand what that pass had been about. He figured it out when he at last looked back to his bow and saw that the bowstring had been cut. "Damnation," Brer'Cannon muttered, scanning the brush frantically.

"I am not accustomed to speaking with shadows," Deudermont called out clearly, his voice unshaken.

"You are not alone," the speaker replied.

"Nor are you," Deudermont said without hesitation. "So do come out and let us be done with this business—whatever business you might have with me."

More rustling came from the shadows, and more than one whispering voice told the speaker, a man named Dunkin, to go talk to the *Sea Sprite*'s captain.

At last, Dunkin mustered the courage to stand up and come forward, taking one step and looking all around, then another step and looking all around. He walked right under Guenhwyvar and didn't know it, which brought a smile to Deudermont's lips. He walked within three feet of Drizzt and didn't know it, but he did spot Catti-brie, for the woman was making no real effort to conceal herself behind the tree just to the side of the small clearing where Deudermont stood.

Dunkin fought hard to regain his composure and his dignity. He walked to within a few paces of the tall captain and straightened himself. "You do not belong here," he said in a voice that cracked only once.

"It was my understanding that Mintarn was a free port," Deudermont replied. "Free for scalawags only?"

Dunkin pointed a finger and started to reply, but the words apparently did not suffice and he stopped after uttering only a meaningless grunt.

"I have never known of any restrictions placed on vessels desiring to dock," Deudermont went on. "Surely my ship is not the only one in Mintarn Harbor flying no colors and with her name covered." The last statement was true enough. Fully two-thirds of all the vessels that put into the free port did so without any open identification.

"You are Deudermont and your ship is the *Sea Sprite*, out of Waterdeep," Dunkin said, his tone accusing. He tugged at his ear as he spoke, a nervous tick, the captain reasoned.

Deudermont shrugged and nodded.

"A law ship," Dunkin went on, finding some courage at

last. He let go of his ear. "Pirate hunter, and here, no doubt, to—"

"Do not presume to know my intentions," Deudermont interrupted sharply.

"The *Sea Sprite*'s intentions are always known," Dunkin retorted, his voice equally firm. "She's a pirate hunter, and yes, there are indeed pirates docked in Mintarn, including one you chased this very week."

Deudermont's expression grew stern. He understood that this man was an official of Mintarn, an emissary from his tyrancy, Tarnheel Embuirhan, himself. Tarnheel had made his intentions of keeping Mintarn in line with its reputation as a free port quite clear to all the lords along the Sword Coast. Mintarn was not a place to settle vendettas, or to chase fugitives.

"If we came in search of pirates," Deudermont said bluntly, "the *Sea Sprite* would have come in under the flag of Waterdeep, openly and without fear."

"Then you admit your identity," accused Dunkin.

"We hid it only to prevent trouble for your port," Deudermont replied easily. "If any of the pirates now in Mintarn Harbor sought retribution, we would have had to sink them, and I am certain that your overlord would not approve of so many wrecks under the waves of his harbor. Is that not exactly why he sent you to find me in the Freemantle, and why he bade you to come out here with your bluster?"

Dunkin again seemed to not be able to find the words to reply.

"And you are?" Deudermont asked, prompting the nervous man.

Dunkin straightened once more, as if remembering his station. "Dunkin Tallmast," he said clearly, "emissary of His Tyrancy, Lord Tarnheel Embuirhan of the free port of Mintarn."

Deudermont considered the obviously phoney name. This one had probably crawled onto Mintarn's docks years ago, running from another scalawag, or from the law, and over time had found his way into Tarnheel's island guard. Dunkin was not a great choice as an emissary, Deudermont realized. Not practiced in diplomacy and not long on courage. But the captain refused to underestimate Tarnheel, reputably a proficient warrior who had kept the relative peace on Mintarn for many years. Dunkin was no imposing diplomat, but Tarnheel had probably decided that he would be the one to meet with Deudermont for a reason, possibly to make the *Sea Sprite*'s captain understand that he and his ship were not considered very important to his tyrancy.

Diplomacy was a curious game.

"The *Sea Sprite* has not sailed in to engage with any pirates," Deudermont assured the man. "Nor in search of any man who might be in hiding on Mintarn. We have come to take on provisions, and in search of information."

"About a pirate," Dunkin reasoned, seeming not pleased.

"About an island," Deudermont replied.

"A pirate island?" Dunkin retorted, and again his tone made the question seem more of an accusation.

Deudermont pulled the pipe from his mouth and stared hard at Dunkin, answering the question without uttering a word.

"It is said that nowhere in all the Realms can a greater concentration of the most seasoned sea dogs be found than on Mintarn," Deudermont began at length. "I seek an island that is as much legend as truth, an island known to many through tales, but to only a few by experience."

Dunkin didn't reply, and didn't seem to have any idea of what Deudermont might be talking about.

"I will make you a deal," the captain offered.

"What have you to bargain with?" Dunkin replied quickly.

"I, and all of my crew, will remain on the *Sea Sprite*, quietly, and far out in the harbor. Thus will the peace of Mintarn remain secure. We have no intention of hunting any on your island, even known outlaws, but many might seek us out, foolishly thinking the *Sea Sprite* vulnerable while in port."

Dunkin couldn't help but nod. Back in the Freemantle, he had already heard whispers hinting that several of the ships now in port were not pleased to see the *Sea Sprite*, and might join together against her.

"We will remain out of the immediate dock area," Deudermont said again, "and you, Dunkin Tallmast, will find for me the information I desire." Before Dunkin could respond, Deudermont tossed him a pouch full of gold coins. "Caerwich," the captain explained. "I want a map to Caerwich."

"Caerwich?" Dunkin echoed skeptically.

"West and south, by tales I've heard," Deudermont replied.

Dunkin gave a sour look and moved to toss the coins back, but Deudermont raised a hand to stop him. "The Lords of Waterdeep will not be pleased to learn that Mintarn's hospitality was not extended to one of their ships," the captain was quick to point out. "If you are not a free port for the legal ships of Waterdeep, then you proclaim yourself an open haven only to outlaws. Your Lord Tarnheel will not be pleased at the results of such a proclamation."

It was as close to a threat as Deudermont wanted to get, and he was much relieved when Dunkin clutched the bag of coins tightly once more.

"I will speak with his tyrancy," the short man asserted. "If he agrees . . ." Dunkin let it go at that, waving his hand.

Deudermont popped the pipe back into his mouth and nodded to Catti-brie, who came out of hiding, her bow relaxed, all arrows replaced in her quiver. She never blinked as she walked past Dunkin, and he matched her stare.

His resolve melted a moment later, though, when Drizzt slipped out of the brush to the side. And if the sight of a drow elf wasn't enough to fully unnerve the man, surely the sudden presence of a six-hundred pound black panther dropping to the ground barely five feet to Dunkin's side, was.

\* \* \* \* \*

Dunkin rowed out to the *Sea Sprite* the very next day. Despite the fact that Deudermont welcomed him warmly, he came aboard tentatively, as though he was in awe of this vessel that was so fast becoming a legend along the Sword Coast.

They greeted Dunkin on the open deck, in full view of the crew. Guenhwyvar was at rest in her astral home, but Robillard and Harkle joined the others this time, standing together, and Drizzt thought that a good thing. Perhaps Robillard, an adept wizard, could keep Harkle's powers under control, the drow reasoned. And perhaps Harkle's perpetual smile would rub off on the grumpy Robillard!

"You have my information?" Deudermont asked, coming right to the point. The *Sea Sprite* had sat calm and undisturbed thus far, but Deudermont held no illusions about their safety in Mintarn Harbor. The captain knew that no less than a dozen ships now in port desired their demise, and the sooner the schooner was out of Mintarn, the better.

Dunkin motioned to the door to the captain's private quarters.

"Out here," Deudermont insisted. "Give it over and be gone. I've not the time for any delays, and I need no privacy from my crew."

Dunkin looked around and nodded, having no desire to debate the point.

"The information?" Deudermont asked.

Dunkin started, as if surprised. "Ah, yes," he stuttered. "We have a map, but it's not too detailed. And we cannot be sure, of course, for the island you seek might be no more than legend, and then, of course, there would be no correct map."

His humor was not appreciated, he soon realized, and so he calmed himself and cleared his throat.

"You have my gold," Deudermont said after yet another long pause.

"His tyrancy wishes a different payment," Dunkin replied. "More than the gold."

Deudermont's eyes narrowed dangerously. He put his pipe in his mouth deliberately and took a long, long draw.

"Nothing so difficult," Dunking was quick to assure. "And my lord offers more than a simple map. You'll need a wizard or a priest to create a hold large enough to carry ample supplies."

"That would be us," Harkle put in, draping an arm over Robillard's shoulders as he spoke, then quickly withdrawing it upon seeing the grumpy wizard's threatening scowl.

"Ah, yes, but no need, no need," Dunkin blurted. "For his tyrancy has a most wonderful chest, a magical hold, it is, and he will give it to you on loan, along with the map, for the pouch of gold, which was not so much, and one other little favor."

"Speak it," demanded Deudermont, growing weary of the cryptic game.

"Him," said Dunkin, pointing to Drizzt.

Only Drizzt's quick reaction, lifting a blocking arm, kept Catti-brie from leaping forward and punching the man.

"Him?" Deudermont asked incredulously.

"Just to meet with the drow," Dunkin quickly explained, realizing that he was treading on dangerous ground here. The water was cold about Mintarn and the man had no desire for a long swim back to shore.

"A curiosity piece?" Catti-brie snapped, pushing against Drizzt's blocking arm. "I'll give ye something for yer stupid tyrant!"

"No, no," Dunkin tried to explain. He never would have gotten the words out of his mouth, would have been tossed overboard for simply making the seemingly absurd request, had not Drizzt intervened, a calming voice that revealed no offense taken.

"Explain your lord's desire," the drow said quietly.

"Your reputation is considerable, good drow," Dunkin stammered. "Many pirates limping into Mintarn speak of your exploits. Why, the main reason that the *Sea Sprite* has not been . . ." He stopped and glanced nervously at Deudermont.

"Has not been attacked in Mintarn Harbor," Deudermont finished for him.

"They wouldn't dare come out and face you," Dunkin dared to finish, looking back to Drizzt. "My lord, too, is a warrior of no small reputation."

"Damn," Catti-brie muttered, guessing what was to come, and Drizzt, too, could see where this speech was leading.

"Just a contest," Dunkin finished. "A private fight."

"For no better reason than to prove who is the better," Drizzt replied distastefully.

"For the map," Dunkin reminded him. "And the chest, no small reward." After a moment's thought, he added, "You will have those whether you win or lose."

Drizzt looked at Catti-brie, then to Deudermont, then to all the crew, who were making no effort anymore to disguise the fact that they were listening intently to every word.

"Let us be done with it," the drow said.

Catti-brie grabbed him by the arm, and when he turned to face her, he realized that she did not approve.

"I cannot ask you to do such a thing," Deudermont said.

Drizzt looked at him directly, and with a smile. "Perhaps my own curiosity over who is the better fighter is no less than Tarnheel's," he said, looking back to Catti-brie, who knew him and knew his motivations better than that.

"Is it any different than your own fight with Berkthgar over Aegis-fang before the dark elves came to Mithril Hall?" Drizzt asked simply.

True enough, Catti-brie had to admit. Before the drow war, Berkthgar had threatened to break the alliance with Bruenor unless the dwarf turned Aegis-fang over to him, something Bruenor would never do. Catti-brie had gone to Settlestone and had ended the debate by defeating Berkthgar in the challenge of single combat. In light of that memory, and the drow's duty now, she let go of Drizzt's arm.

"I will return presently," Drizzt promised, following Dunkin to the rail, and then into the small boat.

Deudermont, Catti-brie, and most of the other crewmen, watched them row away, and Catti-brie noticed the sour expression on the captain's face, as though Deudermont was somewhat disappointed, something the perceptive young woman understood completely.

"He's not wanting to fight," she assured the captain.

"He is driven by curiosity?" Deudermont asked.

"By loyalty," Catti-brie answered. "And nothing more. Drizzt is bound by friendship to ye and to the crew, and if a simple contest against the man will make for an easier sail, then he's up to the fight. But there's no curiosity in Drizzt. No stupid pride. He's not for caring who's the better at sword-play."

Deudermont nodded and his expression brightened. The young woman's words confirmed his belief in his friend.

The minutes turned into an hour, then into two, and the conversation on the *Sea Sprite* gradually shifted away from Drizzt's confrontation to their own situation. Two ships, square-riggers both, had sailed out of Mintarn. Neither had gone out into the open sea, but rather, had turned into the wind just beyond the harbor, tacking and turning so that they remained relatively still.

"Why don't they just drop their anchors?" Waillan asked a crewman who was standing near him on the poop deck, just behind the *Sea Sprite*'s deadly ballista.

Catti-brie and Deudermont, near the center of the ship, overheard the remark and looked to each other. Both knew why.

A third ship put up her lower sails and began to drift out in the general direction of the *Sea Sprite*.

"I'm not liking this," Catti-brie remarked.

"We may have been set up," Deudermont replied. "Perhaps Dunkin informed our sailor friends here that the *Sea Sprite* would be without a certain dark elf crewman for a while."

"I'm for the nest," Catti-brie said. She slung Taulmaril over her shoulder and started up the mainmast.

Robillard and Harkle came back on deck then, apparently aware of the potentially dangerous situation. They nodded to Deudermont and moved astern, beside Waillan and his ballista crew.

Then they waited, all of them. Deudermont watched the creeping movements of the three ships carefully, and then a fourth pushed off from Mintarn's long docks. Possibly they were being encircled, the captain knew, but also he knew that the *Sea Sprite* could put up anchor and be out to sea in mere minutes, especially with Robillard's magic aiding the run. And all the while, between the ballista and the archers, particularly Catti-brie and that devastating bow of hers, the *Sea Sprite* could more than match any barrage they offered.

Deudermont's primary concern at that moment was not for his ship, but for Drizzt. What fate might befall the drow if they had to leave him behind?

That notion disappeared, but a new fear materialized when Catti-brie, spyglass in hand, yelled down that Drizzt was on his way back. Deudermont and many others followed the woman's point and could just make out the tiny rowboat in front and to starboard of the third ship drifting out of the harbor.

"Robillard!" Deudermont yelled.

The wizard nodded and peered intently to spot the craft.

He began casting a spell immediately, but even as the first words left his mouth, a catapult on the third pirate ship let fly, dropping a bail of pitch into the water right beside the rowboat, nearly capsizing her.

"Up sails!" Deudermont cried. "Weigh anchor!"

Catti-brie's bow hummed, streaking arrow after arrow back toward the drifting caravel, though the ship was still more than three hundred yards away.

All the harbor seemed to come to life immediately. The two ships farther out put up full sails and began their turn to catch the wind, the third ship launched another volley at the rowboat, and the sails of the fourth ship, indeed a part of the conspiracy, unfurled.

Before Robillard's spell began its effect, a third ball of pitch hit just behind the rowboat, taking part of her stern with her. Still, the enchantment caught the tiny craft, a directed wave of water grabbing at her and speeding her suddenly in the direction of the *Sea Sprite*. Drizzt put up the now-useless oars while Dunkin bailed frantically, but even though they made great progress toward the schooner, the damaged rowboat could not stay afloat long enough to get to the *Sea Sprite*'s side.

Robillard recognized that fact and as the craft floundered, the wizard dispelled his magic, else Drizzt and Dunkin would have been drowned beneath the enchanted wave.

Deudermont's mind worked furiously, trying to measure the distance and the time before the pirates would catch them. He figured that as soon as the sails were up, he would have to turn the *Sea Sprite* in toward the harbor, for he would not leave Drizzt behind, no matter the risk.

His calculations quickly shifted when he saw that Drizzt, Dunkin in tow, was swimming furiously toward the ship.

Dunkin was even more surprised by this turn of events than was Deudermont. When the rowboat went under, the man's first instinct told him to get away from the drow. Drizzt's carried twin scimitars and wore a suit of chain mail. Dunkin wore no encumbering equipment and figured that the drow would cling to him and likely drown them both. To Dunkin's surprise, though, Drizzt could not only stay above the water, but could swim impossibly fast.

The chain mail was supple, cunningly forged of the finest materials and to drowlike design by Buster Bracer of Clan Battlehammer, one of the finest smithies in all the Realms. And Drizzt wore enchanted anklets, allowing him to kick his feet incredibly fast. He caught up to Dunkin and dragged the man out in the direction of the *Sea Sprite* almost immediately, closing nearly a quarter of the distance before the startled man even gained his wits enough about him to begin swimming on his own.

"They are coming fast!" Waillan cried happily, thinking his friend would make it.

"But they lost the chest!" Robillard observed, pointing to the floundering rowboat. Right behind the wreckage and coming faster still was the third pirate ship, her sails now full of wind.

"I will get it!" cried Harkle Harpell, wanting desperately to be of some use. The wizard snapped his fingers and began an enchantment, as did Robillard, realizing that they had to somehow slow the pursuing caravel if Drizzt was to have any chance of making it to the *Sea Sprite*.

Robillard stopped his casting almost immediately, though, and looked to Harkle curiously.

Robillard's eyes widened considerably as he considered a fish that appeared suddenly on the deck at Harkle's feet. "No!" he cried, reaching for the Harpell, figuring out what type of spell Harkle had enacted. "You cannot cast an extra dimension on an item enchanted with an extra dimension!"

Robillard had guessed correctly; Harkle was trying to pull in the sinking magical chest by creating an extra-dimensional gate in the region where the rowboat and the chest went down. It was a good idea, or would have been, except that the chest Tarnheel had promised to the *Sea Sprite* was a chest of holding—a contained extra-dimensional space that could hold much more volume than would be indicated by the item's size and weight. The problem was that extra-dimensional spells and items did not usually mesh correctly. Throwing a bag of holding into a chest of holding, for example, could tear a rift in the multiverse, spewing everything nearby into the Astral Plane, or even worse, into the unknown space between the planes of existence.

81

"Oops," Harkle apologized, realizing his error and trying to let go of his enchantment.

Too late. A huge wave erupted right in the area where the rowboat had gone down, rocking the approaching caravel and rolling into Drizzt and Dunkin, hurling them toward the *Sea Sprite*. The water churned and danced, then began to roll, forming a giant whirlpool.

"Sail on!" Deudermont cried as ropes were thrown out to Drizzt and Dunkin. "Sail on, for all our lives!"

The sails fell open, and crewmen immediately pulled to put them against the wind. At once the *Sea Sprite* lurched and rolled away, gliding swiftly out of the harbor.

Things were not as easy for the pursuing caravel. The pirate ship tried to tack and turn, but was too close to the mounting whirlpool. She crested the lip and was pulled sideways violently, many of her crew being tossed overboard into the turmoil. Around she went, once and then twice. Those aboard the *Sea Sprite* watched her sails diminish as she sank lower and lower into the spin.

But other than horrified Harkle, the eyes of those on the *Sea Sprite* had to go outward, to the two vessels lying in wait. Robillard called up a mist, understanding that Deudermont's intent was not to engage, but to slip by, out into the open waters. Waillan's crew fired at will, as did the archers, while several crewmen, Deudermont among them, hauled Drizzt and a very shaken Dunkin Tallmast aboard.

"Sealed," Drizzt said to Deudermont with a wry smile, producing a capped scroll tube that obviously contained the map to Caerwich.

Deudermont clapped him on the shoulder and turned to go to the wheel. Both surveyed the situation, and both figured that the *Sea Sprite* would have little trouble slipping through this trap.

The situation looked bright, to those looking forward. But hanging over the stern rail, Harkle Harpell could only watch in dismay. Rationally, he knew that his unintentional catastrophe had probably saved Drizzt and the other man in the rowboat, and probably would make the *Sea Sprite*'s run all the easier, but the gentle Harkle could not suffer the sights of the turmoil within the whirlpool and the screams of the drowning men. He muttered, "oh, no," over and over, searched his mind for some spell that might help the poor men of the caravel.

But then, almost as suddenly as it had appeared, the whirlpool dissipated, the water flattening to perfect, glassy calm. The caravel remained, hanging so low to the side that her sails nearly touched the water.

Harkle breathed a deep sigh of relief and thanked whatever gods might be listening. The water was full of sailors, but they all seemed close enough to get to the swamped hull.

Harkle clapped his hands happily and ran down from the poop deck, joining Deudermont and Drizzt by the wheel. The engagement was on in full by then, with the two square-riggers trading shots with the *Sea Sprite,* though none of the three were close enough to inflict any real damage.

Deudermont eyed Harkle curiously.

"What?" asked the flustered mage.

"Have you any more fireballs in you?" Deudermont asked.

Harkle paled. So soon after the horror of the whirlpool, he really didn't have the heart to burn up another vessel. But that wasn't what sly Deudermont had in mind.

"Put one in the water between our enemies," the captain explained, then looked to Drizzt. "I'll run for the mist and swing to port, then we'll have time to contend with only one of the pirate ships up close."

Drizzt nodded. Harkle brightened, and was more than happy to comply. He waited for Deudermont's signal, then skipped a fireball just under the waves. There came a flash and then a thick cloud of steam.

Deudermont headed straight for it, and the square-riggers predictably turned to cut off such an escape. Soon before plunging into the mist, Deudermont cut hard to port, skimming the cloud and angling outside the pirate ship farthest to the left.

They would pass close, but that didn't bother Deudermont much, not with the *Sea Sprite*'s speed and Robillard's magical defenses.

An explosion soon changed Deudermont's mind, a heavy ball of iron shearing through Robillard's defensive shields and snipping through a fair amount of rigging as well.

"They've got a smokepowder gun!" Harkle roared.

"A what?" Drizzt and Deudermont asked at the same time.

"Arquebus," Harkle whimpered, and his hands began spinning large circles in the air. "Big arquebus."

"A what?" the two asked again.

Harkle couldn't begin to explain, but his horrified expression spoke volumes. Smokepowder was a rare and dangerous thing, a fiendish concoction of Gondish priests that used sheer explosive energy to launch missiles from metal barrels, and oftentimes, to inadvertently blow apart the barrels. "One in ten," was the saying among those who knew smokepowder best, meaning that one in ten attempts to fire would likely blow up in your face. Harkle figured these pirates must truly despise the *Sea Sprite* to risk such a dangerous attack.

But still, even if the one in ten rule held true, nine in ten could take the *Sea Sprite* out of the water!

Harkle knew that he had to act as the seconds passed, as the others, even Robillard, looked on helplessly, not understanding what they were suddenly up against. Smokepowder was more common in the far eastern reaches of the Realms, and had even been used in Cormyr, so it was said. Of course, there were rumors that it had surfaced just a bit on the Sword Coast, mostly aboard ships. Harkle considered his options, considered the volume of smokepowder and its volatility, considered the weapons he had at his disposal.

"A metal cylinder!" Catti-brie called down from the crow's nest, spotting the targeting gun through the steam.

"With bags near to it?" Harkle cried back.

"I cannot see!" Catti-brie called, for the cloud continued to drift and to obscure her vision of the pirate ship's deck.

Harkle knew that time was running out. The smokepowder cannon wasn't very accurate, but it didn't have to be, for one of its shots could take down a mast, and even a glancing hit on the hull would likely blow a hole large enough to sink the schooner.

"Aim for it!" Harkle cried out. "For the cylinder and the decking near to it!"

Catti-brie was never one to trust in Harkle Harpell, but his reasoning then seemed unusually sound. She put up

Taulmaril and sent off an arrow, then another, thinking to disable the crew near to the cylinder, if not take out the weapon itself. Through the fog, she saw the sparks as one enchanted arrow skipped off the cylinder, then heard a cry of pain as she nailed one of the gunners.

The *Sea Sprite* ran on, nearing the pirate ship. Harkle bit at his fingernails. Dunkin, who also knew of smoke-powder guns, tugged at his large ears.

"Oh, turn away the ship," Harkle bade Deudermont. "Too close, too close. They'll fire it off again right into our faces, and knock us under the waves."

Deudermont didn't know how to respond. He had already learned that Robillard's magic couldn't stop the smoke-powder weapon. Indeed, when the captain glanced back to Robillard, he found the wizard frantically creating gusts of wind to speed their passage, apparently with no intent of even trying to stop a second shot. Still, if the captain tried to turn to port, he would likely be in range of that weapon for some time, and if he tried to veer to starboard, he might not be able to even get past the pirate ship and into the cloud, might ram the ship head-on. Even if they could then defeat the crew of this ship, her two remaining friends would have little trouble in overcoming the *Sea Sprite*.

"Get the wizard and get to them," Deudermont said to Drizzt. "And get the cat. We need you now, my friend!"

Drizzt started to move, but Harkle, spotting the light of a torch near to where Catti-brie had pointed out the cylinder, shouted out "no time!" and dove flat to the deck.

From on high, Catti-brie saw the torch, and with its light, she also saw the large sacks that Harkle had inquired about. She instinctively aimed for the torchbearer, thinking to slow the smokepowder crew, but then took a chance and agreed with Harkle, shifting her aim slightly and letting fly, straight for the pile of sacks on the pirate's decking.

Her arrow streaked in the instant before the man put the torch to the cannon, as the *Sea Sprite* was running practically parallel to the pirate ship. It was just an instant, but in that time, the torchbearer was foiled, was blown into the air as the streaking arrow sliced into the sacks of volatile smokepowder.

The pirate ship nearly stood straight up on end. The fireball was beyond anything Harkle, or even Robillard, had ever seen, and the sheer concussion and flying debris nearly cleaned the *Sea Sprite*'s deck of standing crewmen, and tore many holes in the schooner's lateen sails.

The *Sea Sprite* lurched wildly, left and right, before Deudermont could regain his senses and steady the wheel. But she plowed on, leaving the trap behind.

"By the gods," Catti-brie muttered, truly horrified, for where the pirate square-rigger had been, there was now only flotsam and jetsam, splinters, charred wood, and floating bodies.

Drizzt, too, was stunned. Looking on the carnage, he thought he was previewing the end of the world. He had never seen such devastation, such complete carnage, not even from a powerful wizard. Enough smokepowder could flatten a mountain, or a city. Enough smokepowder could flatten all the world.

"Smokepowder?" he said to Harkle.

"From Gondish priests," the wizard replied.

"Damn them all," muttered Drizzt, and he walked away.

Later that day, as the crew worked to repair the tears in the sails, Drizzt and Catti-brie took a break and leaned on the rail of the schooner's bow, looking down at the empty water and considering the great distance they had yet to travel.

Finally Catti-brie couldn't stand the suspense any longer. "Did ye beat him?" she asked.

Drizzt looked at her curiously, as though he didn't understand.

"His tyrancy," Catti-brie explained.

"I brought the map," Drizzt replied, "and the chest, though it was lost."

"Ah, but Dunkin promised it whether ye won or lost," the young woman said slyly.

Drizzt looked at her. "The contest was never important," he said. "Not to me."

"Did ye win or lose?" Catti-brie pressed, not willing to let the drow slip out of this one.

"Sometimes it is better to allow so important a leader

and valuable an ally to retain his pride and his reputation," Drizzt replied, looking back to the sea, then to the mizzenmast, where a crewman was calling for some assistance.

"Ye let him beat ye?" Catti-brie asked, not seeming pleased by that prospect.

"I never said that," Drizzt replied.

"So he beat ye on his own," the young woman reasoned.

Drizzt shrugged as he walked away toward the mizzenmast to help out the crewman. He passed by Harkle and Robillard, who were coming forward, apparently meaning to join Drizzt and Catti-brie at the rail.

Catti-brie continued to stare at the drow as the wizards walked up. The woman did not know what to make of Drizzt's cryptic answers. Drizzt had let Tarnheel win, she figured, or at least had allowed the man to fight him to a draw. For some reason the young woman did not understand, she didn't want to think that Tarnheel had actually beaten Drizzt; she didn't want to think that anyone could beat Drizzt.

Both Robillard and Harkle were smiling widely as they considered the young woman's expression.

"Drizzt beat him," Robillard said at last.

Startled, Catti-brie turned to the wizard.

"That is what you were wondering about," Robillard reasoned.

"We watched it all," Harkle said. "Oh, of course we did. A good match." Harkle went into a fighting crouch, his best imitation of Drizzt in combat, which of course seemed a mockery to Catti-brie. "He started left," Harkle began, making the move, "then ran to the right so quickly and smoothly that Tarnheel never realized it."

"Until he got hit," Robillard interjected. "His tyrancy was still swinging forward, attacking a ghost, I suppose."

That made sense to Catti-brie; the move they had just described was called "the ghost step."

"He learned better, he did!" howled Harkle.

"Suffice it to say that his tyrancy will not be sitting down anytime soon," Robillard finished, and the two wizards exploded into laughter, as animated as Catti-brie had ever seen Robillard.

The young woman went back to the rail as the two walked away, howling still. Catti-brie was smiling too. She now knew the truth of Drizzt's claims that the fight wasn't important to him. She'd make certain that she teased the drow about it in the days to come. She also was smiling because Drizzt had won.

For some reason, that was very important to Catti-brie.

# Chapter 8
## SEA TALK

epairs continued on the *Sea Sprite* for two days, preventing her from putting up her sails in full. Even so, with the strong breeze rushing down from the north, the swift schooner made fine speed southward, her sails full of wind. In just over three days, she ran the four hundred miles from Mintarn to the southeasternmost point of the great Moonshae Isles, and Deudermont turned her to the west, due west, for the open sea, running just off the southern coast of the Moonshaes.

"We'll run for two days with the Moonshaes in sight," Deudermont informed the crew.

"Are you not making for Corwell?" Dunkin Tallmast, who always seemed to be asking questions, was quick to interrupt. "I think I should like to be let off at Corwell. A beautiful city, by all accounts." The little man's cavalier attitude was diminished considerably when he began tugging at his ear, that nervous tick that revealed his trepidation.

Deudermont ignored the pesty man. "If the wind holds, tomorrow, mid-morning, we'll pass a point called Dragon Head," he explained. "Then we'll cross a wide harbor and put in at a village, Wyngate, for our last provisions. Then it's the open sea, twenty days out, I figure, twice that without the wind."

The seasoned crew understood it would be a difficult journey, but they bobbed their heads in accord, not a word of protest from the lot of them—with one exception.

"Wyngate?" Dunkin protested. "Why, I'll be a month in just getting out of the place!"

"Whoever said that you were leaving?" Deudermont

asked him. "We shall put you off where we choose . . . after we return."

That shut the man up, or at least changed his train of thought, for before Deudermont could get three steps away, Dunkin shouted at him. "*If* you return, you mean!" he called. "You have lived along the Sword Coast all your stinking life. You know the rumors, Deudermont."

The captain turned slowly, ominously, to face the man. Both were quite conscious of the murmurs Dunkin's words had caused, a ripple of whispers all across the schooner's deck.

Dunkin did not look at Deudermont directly, but scanned the deck, his wry smile widening as he considered the suddenly nervous crew. "Ah," he moaned suspiciously. "You haven't told them."

Deudermont didn't blink.

"You wouldn't be leading them to an island of legend without telling them all of the legend?" Dunkin asked in sly tones.

"The man enjoys intrigue," Catti-brie whispered to Drizzt.

"He enjoys trouble," Drizzt whispered back.

Deudermont spent a long moment studying Dunkin, the captain's stern gaze gradually stealing the little man's stupid grin. Then Deudermont looked to Drizzt—he always looked to Drizzt when he needed support—and to Catti-brie, and neither seemed to care much for Dunkin's ominous words. Bolstered by their confidence, the captain turned to Harkle, who seemed distracted, as usual, as though he hadn't even heard the conversation. The rest of the crew, at least those near to the wheel, had heard, and Deudermont noted more than one nervous movement among them.

"Tell us what?" Robillard asked bluntly. "What is the great mystery of Caerwich?"

"Ah, Captain Deudermont," Dunkin said with a disappointed sigh.

"Caerwich," Deudermont began calmly, "may be no more than a legend. Few claim to have been there, for it is far, far away from any civilized lands."

"That much, we already know," Robillard remarked. "But if it is just a legend and we sail empty waters until we are forced to return, then that bodes no ill for the *Sea Sprite*. What is it that this insignificant worm hints at?"

Deudermont looked hard at Dunkin, wanting at that moment to throttle the man. "Some of those who have been there," the captain began, choosing his words carefully, "claim that they witnessed unusual visions."

"Haunted!" Dunkin interrupted dramatically. "Caerwich is a haunted island," he proclaimed, dancing around to cast a wild-eyed stare at each of the crewmen near to him. "Ghost ships and witches!"

"Enough," Drizzt said to the man.

"Shut yer mouth," Catti-brie added.

Dunkin did shut up, but he returned the young woman's stare with a superior look, thinking he had won the day.

"They are rumors," Deudermont said loudly. "Rumors I would have told you when we reached Wyngate, but not before." The captain paused and looked around once more, this time his expression begging friendship and loyalty from the men who had been with him so very long. "I would have told you," he insisted, and everyone aboard, except perhaps for Dunkin, believed him.

"This sail is not for Waterdeep, nor against any pirates," Deudermont went on. "It is for me, something I must do because of the incident on Dock Street. Perhaps the *Sea Sprite* sails into trouble, perhaps to answers, but I must go, whatever the outcome. I would not force any of you to go along. You signed on to chase pirates, and in that regard, you have been the finest crew any captain could wish for."

Again came a pause, a long one, with the captain alternately meeting the gaze of each man, and of Catti-brie and Drizzt, last of all.

"Any who do not wish to sail to Caerwich may disembark at Wyngate," Deudermont offered. It was an extraordinary offer that widened the eyes of every crewman. "You will be paid for your time aboard the *Sea Sprite,* plus a bonus from my personal coffers. When we return . . ."

"If you return," Dunkin put in, but Deudermont simply ignored the troublemaker.

"When we return," Deudermont said again, more firmly, "we will pick you up at Wyngate. There will be no questions of loyalty asked, and no retribution by any who voyaged to Caerwich."

Robillard snorted. "Is not every island haunted?" he asked with a laugh. "If a sailor were to believe every whispered rumor, he'd not dare sail the Sword Coast at all. Sea monsters off of Waterdeep! Coiled serpents of Ruathym! Pirates of the Nelanther!"

"That last one's true enough!" one sailor piped in, and everyone gave a hearty laugh.

"So it is!" Robillard replied. "Seems some of the rumors might be true."

"And if Caerwich is haunted?" another sailor asked.

"Then we'll dock in the morning," Waillan answered, hanging over the rail of the poop deck, "and put out in the afternoon."

"And leave the night for the ghosts!" yet another man finished, again to hearty laughter.

Deudermont was truly appreciative, especially to Robillard, from whom the captain had never expected such support. When the roll was subsequently called, not a single one of the *Sea Sprite*'s crew meant to get off at Wyngate.

Dunkin listened to it all in sheer astonishment. He kept trying to put in some nasty flavoring to the rumors of haunted Caerwich, tales of decapitation and the like, but he was shouted or laughed down every time.

Neither Drizzt nor Catti-brie was surprised by the unanimous support for Deudermont. The *Sea Sprite*'s crew, they both knew, had been together long enough to become true friends. These two companions had enough experience with friendship to understand loyalty.

"Well, I mean to get off at Wyngate," a flustered Dunkin said at last. "I'll not follow any man to haunted Caerwich."

"Who ever offered you such a choice?" Drizzt asked him.

"Captain Deudermont just said . . ." Dunkin started, turning to Deudermont and pointing an accusing finger the captain's way. The words stuck in his throat, though, for Deudermont's sour expression explained that the offer wasn't meant for him.

"You cannot keep me here!" Dunkin protested. "I am the emissary of his tyrancy. I should have been released in Mintarn."

"You would have been killed in Mintarn Harbor," Drizzt reminded him.

"You will be released in Mintarn," Deudermont promised. Dunkin knew what that meant.

"When we might have a proper inquiry as to your part in the attempted ambush of the *Sea Sprite*," Deudermont went on.

"I did nothing!" Dunkin cried, tugging his ear.

"It is convenient that so soon after you informed me that Drizzt's presence aboard the *Sea Sprite* was preventing any pirate attacks, you arranged to take Drizzt from our decks," Deudermont said.

"I was almost killed by that very ambush!" Dunkin roared in protest. "If I had known that the scalawags were after you, I never would have rowed out into the harbor."

Deudermont looked to Drizzt.

"True enough," the drow admitted.

Deudermont paused a moment, then nodded. "I find you innocent," he said to Dunkin, "and agree to return you to Mintarn after our journey to Caerwich."

"You will pick me back up at Wyngate, then," Dunkin reasoned, but Deudermont shook his head.

"Too far," the captain replied. "None of my crew will disembark at Wyngate. And now that I must return to Mintarn, I will return from Caerwich by a northerly route, passing north of the Moonshaes."

"Then let me off at Wyngate and I'll find a way to meet you in a northern town of the Moonshaes," Dunkin offered.

"Which northern town?" Deudermont asked him.

Dunkin had no answers.

"If you wish to leave, you may get off at Wyngate," Deudermont offered. "But I cannot guarantee your passage back to Mintarn from there." With that, Deudermont turned and walked to his cabin. He entered without looking back, leaving a frustrated Dunkin standing droop-shouldered by the wheel.

"With your knowledge of Caerwich, you will be a great

asset to us," Drizzt said to the man, patting him on the shoulder. "Your presence would be appreciated."

"Ah, come along then," Catti-brie added. "Ye'll find a bit o' adventure and a bit o' friendship. What more could ye be asking for?"

Drizzt and Catti-brie walked away, exchanging hopeful smiles.

"I am new to this, too," Harkle Harpell offered to Dunkin. "But I am sure that it will be fun." Smiling, bobbing his head stupidly, the dimpled wizard bounded away.

Dunkin moved to the rail, shaking his head. He did like the *Sea Sprite*, he had to admit. Orphaned at a young age, Dunkin had taken to sea as a boy and had subsequently spent the bulk of his next twenty years as a hand on pirate vessels, working among the most ruthless scalawags on the Sword Coast. Never had he seen a ship so full of comradery, and their escape from the pirate ambush in Mintarn had been positively thrilling.

He had been nothing but a complaining fool over the last few days, and Deudermont had to know of his past, or at least to suspect that Dunkin had done some pirating in his day. Yet the captain was not treating him as a prisoner, and, by the words of the dark elf, they actually wanted him to go along to Caerwich.

Dunkin leaned over the rail, took note of a school of bottle-nosed dolphins dancing in the prow waves and lost himself in thought.

\* \* \* \* \*

"You're thinking about them again," came a voice behind the sullen dwarf. It was the voice of Regis, the voice of a friend.

Bruenor didn't answer. He stood on a high spot along the rim of the dwarven valley, four miles south of Kelvin's Cairn, a place known as Bruenor's Climb. This was the dwarf king's place of reflection. Though this column of piled stones was not high above the flat tundra, barely fifty feet up, every time he climbed the steep and narrow trail it seemed to Bruenor as though he was ascending to the very stars.

Regis huffed and puffed as he clambered up the last twenty feet to stand beside his bearded friend. "I do love it up here at night," the halfling remarked. "But there will not be much night in another month!" he continued happily, trying to bring a smile to Bruenor's face. His observation was true enough. Far, far in the north, Icewind Dale's summer days were long indeed, but only a few hours of sun graced the winter sky.

"Not a lot o' time up here," Bruenor agreed. "Time I'm wantin' to spend alone." He turned to Regis as he spoke, and even in the darkness, the halfling could make out the scowling visage.

Regis knew the truth of that expression. Bruenor was more bark than bite.

"You would not be happy up here alone," the halfling countered. "You would think of Drizzt and Catti-brie, and miss them as much as I miss them, and then you would be a veritable growling yeti in the morning. I cannot have that, of course," the halfling said, waggling a finger in the air. "In fact, a dozen dwarves begged me to come out here and keep up your cheer."

Bruenor huffed, but had no reasonable response. He turned away from Regis, mostly because he did not want the halfling to see the hint of a smile turning up the corners of his mouth. In the six years since Drizzt and Catti-brie had gone away, Regis had become Bruenor's closest friend, though a certain dwarven priestess named Stumpet Rakingclaw had been almost continually by Bruenor's side, particularly of late. Giggled whispers spoke of a closer bond growing between the dwarf king and the female.

But it was Regis who knew Bruenor best, Regis who had come out here when, Bruenor had to admit, he truly needed the company. Since the return to Icewind Dale, Drizzt and Catti-brie had been on the old dwarf's mind almost continually. The only things that had saved Bruenor from falling into a deep depression had been the sheer volume of work in trying to reopen the dwarven mines, and Regis, always there, always smiling, always assuring Bruenor that Drizzt and Catti-brie would return to him.

"Where do you think they are?" Regis asked after a long moment of silence.

Bruenor smiled and shrugged, looking to the south and west, and not at the halfling. "Out there," was all that he replied.

"Out there," Regis echoed. "Drizzt and Catti-brie. And you miss them, as do I." The halfling moved closer, put a hand on Bruenor's muscled shoulder. "And I know that you miss the cat," Regis said, once again drawing the dwarf from dark thoughts.

Bruenor looked at him and couldn't help but grin. The mention of Guenhwyvar reminded Bruenor not only of all the conflict between himself and the panther, but also that Drizzt and Catti-brie, his two dear friends, were not alone and were more than able to take care of themselves.

The dwarf and halfling stood for a long time that night, in silence, listening to the endless wind that gave the dale its name and feeling as though they were among the stars.

\* \* \* \* \*

The gathering of supplies went well at Wyngate and the *Sea Sprite*, fully provisioned and fully repaired, put out and soon left the Moonshaes far behind.

The winds diminished greatly, though, just a day off the western coast of the Moonshaes. They were out in the open ocean with no land in sight.

The schooner could not be completely calmed, not with Robillard aboard. But still, the wizard's powers were limited; he could not keep the sails full of wind for very long, and settled for a continual fluttering that moved the ship along slowly.

Thus the days passed, uneventful and hot, the *Sea Sprite* rolling in the ocean swells, creaking and swaying. Deudermont ordered strict rationing three days out of Wyngate, as much to slow the rising incidents of seasickness as to preserve the food stores. At least the crew wasn't worried about pirates. Few other ships came out this far, certainly no cargo or merchant vessels, nothing lucrative enough to keep a pirate happy.

The only enemies were the seasickness, the sunburn, and the boredom of days and days of nothing but the flat water.

They found some excitement on the fifth day out. Drizzt, on the forward beam, spotted a tail fin, the dorsal fin of a huge shark, running parallel to the schooner. The drow yelled up to Waillan, who was in the crow's nest at the time.

"Twenty footer!" the young man called back down, for from his high vantage point, he could make out the shadow of the great fish.

All of the crew came on deck, yelling excitedly, taking up harpoons. Any thoughts they might have had of spearing the fish dissolved into understandable fear, though, as Waillan continued to call down numbers, as they all came to realize that the shark was not alone. The counts varied—many of the dorsal fins were hard to spot amidst the suddenly churning water—but Waillan's estimate, undoubtedly the most accurate, put the school at several hundred.

Several hundred! And many of them were nearly as large as the one Drizzt had spotted. Words of excitement were fast replaced by prayers.

The shark school stayed with the *Sea Sprite* throughout the day and night. Deudermont figured that the sharks did not know what to make of the vessel, and though no one spoke the words, all were thinking along the same lines, hoping that the voracious fish didn't mistake the *Sea Sprite* for a running whale.

The next morning, the sharks were gone, as suddenly and inexplicably as they had come. Drizzt spent the better part of the morning walking the rails of the ship, even climbing up the mainmast to the crow's nest a few times. The sharks were gone, just gone.

"They're not answering to us," Catti-brie remarked late that morning, meeting Drizzt as he came down the mast from one of his skyward jaunts. "Never that. Suren they're moving in ways they know, but we cannot."

It struck Drizzt as a simple truth, a plain reminder of how unknown the world about him really was, even to those, like Deudermont, who had spent the bulk of their lives on the sea. This watery world, and the great creatures that inhabited it, moved to rhythms that he could never truly understand. That realization, along with the fact that the horizon from every angle was nothing but flat water, reminded Drizzt of how small they really were, of how overwhelming nature could be.

For all his training, for all his fine weapons, for all his warrior heart, the ranger was a tiny thing, a mere speck on a blue-green tapestry.

Drizzt found that notion unsettling and comforting all at once. He was a small thing, an insignificant thing, a single swallow to the fish that had easily paced the *Sea Sprite*. And yet, he was a part of something much bigger, a single tile on a mosaic much huger than his imagination could even comprehend.

He draped an arm comfortably across Catti-brie's shoulder, connected himself to the tile that complimented his own, and she leaned against him.

\* \* \* \* \*

The winds picked up the next day, and the schooner rushed on, to the applause of every crewman. Robillard's mirth disappeared soon after, though. The wizard had spells to tell of impending weather, and he informed Deudermont that the new winds were the forerunners of a substantial storm.

What could they do? There were no ports nearby, no land at all, and so Deudermont ordered everything battened down as much as was possible.

What followed was among the worst nights of Catti-brie's life. It was as bad as any storm anyone aboard the schooner had ever suffered. Deudermont and the forty crewmen huddled belowdecks as the *Sea Sprite* rode out the storm, the long and slender ship tossing about wildly, nearly going over more than once.

Robillard and Harkle worked frantically. Robillard was on the deck for most of the storm, sometimes having to take cover below and view the deck through a magical, disembodied eye. All the while, he enacted spells to try and counter the fierce winds. Harkle, with Guenhwyvar and a handful of crewmen beside him, scrambled about on all fours in the lowest hold, dodging rats and shifting crates of foodstuff as they inspected the hull. The Harpell had a spell to keep the area well lit, and others that could enlarge wood to seal cracks. The crewmen carried tarred lengths of rope that they hammered in between any leaking boards.

Catti-brie was too sick to move—so were many others. The tossing got so bad at one point that many of the crew had to tie themselves down to stop from bouncing off the walls or crushing each other. Poor Dunkin got the worst of it. In one particularly bad roll, the small man, reaching at the time for an offered length of rope, went flying head over heels and slammed into a beam so violently that he dislocated a shoulder and broke his wrist.

There was no sleep that night aboard the *Sea Sprite*.

The ship was listing badly to port the next morning, but she was still afloat and the storm had passed without a single loss of life. The crew, those who were able, worked through the morning, trying to get up a single sail.

About midday, Catti-brie called down from the crow's nest, reporting that the air was alive with birds to the north and west. Deudermont breathed a deep sigh of relief. He had feared that the storm had blown them off course and that they would not be able to recover in time to put in at the Gull Rocks, the last charted islands on the way to Caerwich. As it was, they were well to the south of their intended course, and had to work frantically, particularly poor Robillard and Harkle. Both of the wizards had bluish bags under their eyes that showed their exhaustion from both the physical and magical strain.

Somehow, the *Sea Sprite* managed to veer enough to get to the rocks. The place was aptly named. The Gull Rocks were no more than a series of barren stones, most smaller than the *Sea Sprite*, many large enough for only two or three men to stand upon. A couple of the rocks were substantial, one nearly a mile across, but even these large ones were more white than gray, thick with guano. As the

*Sea Sprite* neared the cluster, thousands and thousands of seagulls, a veritable cloud of them, fluttered in the air all about her, squawking angrily at the intrusion to this, their private domain.

Deudermont found a little inlet where the water was more calm, where repairs could be done in peace, and where each of the crew could take turns off of the ship, to calm their churning stomachs, if nothing else.

Later on that day, at the highest point on the Gull Rocks, perhaps fifty feet above sea level, Deudermont stood with Drizzt and Catti-brie. The Captain was looking south using the spyglass, though he obviously expected to find nothing but flat water.

It had taken them nearly two weeks to cover the five hundred miles from the westernmost spur of the Moonshaes to the Gull Rocks, nearly double the time Deudermont had expected. Still, the captain remained confident that the provisions would hold and they would find their way to Caerwich. Nothing much had been said about the island since the *Sea Sprite* had put out of Wyngate. Nothing openly, at least, for Drizzt had overheard the nervous whispers of many of the crew, talk of ghosts and the like.

"Five hundred behind us and five hundred to go," Deudermont said, the spyglass to his eye and his gaze to the south and west. "There is an island not far south of here where we might gain more provisions."

"Do we need them?" Drizzt asked.

"Not if make good speed to Caerwich, and good speed on the return," Deudermont replied.

"What're ye thinking then?" Catti-brie asked.

"I grow weary of delays, and weary of the journey," Deudermont replied.

"That's because yer fearin' what's at its end," Catti-brie reasoned bluntly. "Who's for knowin' what we'll find in Caerwich, if even there is a Caerwich?"

"She's out there," the captain insisted.

"We can always stop at this other island on our return," Drizzt offered. "Certainly we've enough provisions to get to Caerwich."

Deudermont nodded. They would make straight for

Caerwich then, the last leg of their journey out. The captain knew the stars—that was all he would have available to take him from the Gull Rocks to Caerwich. He hoped that the map Tarnheel had provided was accurate.

He hoped that Caerwich truly existed.

And still, a part of him hoped that it did not.

# Chapter 9
## CAERWICH

ow small is this island of Caerwich?" Catti-brie asked Deudermont. Another week of sailing had slipped past, this one uneventfully. Another week of emptiness, of solitude, though the schooner was fully crewed and there were few places where someone could be out of sight of everyone else. That was the thing about the open ocean, you were never physically alone, yet all the world seemed removed. Catti-brie and Drizzt had spent hours together, just standing and watching, each lost, drifting on the rolls of the azure blanket, together and yet so alone.

"A few square miles," the captain answered absently, as though the response was an automatic reflex.

"And ye're thinkin' to find it?" An unmistakable edge showed in the woman's voice, drawing a lazy stare from Drizzt, as well as from Deudermont.

"We found the Gull Rocks," Drizzt reminded Catti-brie, trying to brighten her mood though he, too, was getting that unmistakable edge of irritation to his voice. "They are not much larger."

"Bah, they're known to all," Catti-brie retorted. "A straight run west."

"We know where we are, and where we must go," Deudermont insisted. "There is the matter of the map; we're not sailing blindly."

Catti-brie glanced over her shoulder and cast a scowl at Dunkin, the provider of the map, who was hard at work scrubbing the poop deck. The woman's sour expression alone answered Deudermont's claim, told the captain how reliable she believed that map might be.

"And the wizards have new eyes that see far," Deudermont said. True enough, Catti-brie realized, though she wondered how reliable the "eyes" in question might be. Harkle and Robillard had taken some birds from the Gull Rocks, and claimed that they could communicate with them through use of their magic. The gulls would help, the two wizards declared, and each day, they set them flying freely, ordering them to report back with their findings. Catti-brie hadn't thought much about the wizards and in truth, all but two of the ten birds they had taken had not returned to the *Sea Sprite*. Catti-brie figured the birds had more likely flown all the way back to the Gull Rocks, probably laughing at the bumbling wizards all the way.

"The map is all we have had since we left Mintarn," Drizzt said softly, trying to erase the young woman's fears and the anger that was plain upon her fair, sunburned features. He sympathized with Catti-brie, because he was sharing those negative thoughts. They had all known the odds, and thus far, the journey had not been so bad—certainly not as bad as it might have been. They had been out for several weeks, most of that time on the open ocean, yet they had not lost a single crewman and their stores, though low, remained sufficient. Thank Guenhwyvar and Harkle for that, Drizzt thought with a smile, for the panther and the wizard had cleared the ship of the bulk of her pesky rats soon after they had departed from Wyngate.

But still, despite the logical understanding that the journey was on course and going well, Drizzt could not help the swells of anger that rose up in him. It was something about the ocean, he realized, the boredom and the solitude. Truly the drow loved sailing, loved running the waves, but too long in the open ocean, too long in looking at emptiness as profound as could be found in all the world, grated on his nerves.

Catti-brie walked away, muttering. Drizzt looked to Deudermont, and the experienced captain's smile relieved the drow of a good measure of his worry.

"I have seen it before," Deudermont said quietly to him. "She will relax as soon as we sight Mintarn, or as soon as we make the decision to turn back to the east."

"You would do that?" Drizzt asked. "You would forsake the words of the doppleganger?"

Deudermont thought long and hard on that one. "I have come here because I believe it to be my fate," he answered. "Whatever the danger that is now pursuing me, I wish to meet it head-on and with my eyes wide open. But I'll not risk my crew more than is necessary. If our food stores become too diminished to safely continue, we will turn back."

"And what of the doppleganger?" Drizzt asked.

"My enemies found me once," Deudermont replied casually, and truly the man was a rock for Drizzt and for all the crew, something solid to hold onto in a sea of emptiness. "They will find me again."

"And we will be waiting," Drizzt assured him.

\* \* \* \* \*

As it turned out, the wait, for Caerwich at least, was not a long one. Less than an hour after the conversation, Harkle Harpell bounded out of Deudermont's private quarters, clapping his hands excitedly.

Deudermont was the first to him, followed closely by a dozen anxious crewmen. Drizzt, at his customary spot on the forward beam, came to the rail of the flying bridge to survey the gathering. He realized what was going on immediately, and he glanced upward, to Catti-brie, who was peering down intently from the crow's nest.

"Oh, what a fine bird, my Reggie is!" Harkle beamed.

"Reggie?" Deudermont, and several others nearby, asked.

"Namesake of Regweld, so fine a wizard! He bred a frog with a horse—no easy feat that! Puddlejumper, he called her. Or was it Riverjumper? Or maybe . . ."

"Harkle," Deudermont said dryly, his tone bringing the wizard from the rambling confusion.

"Oh, of course," babbled Harkle. "Yes, yes, where was I? Oh, yes, I was telling you about Regweld. What a fine man. Fine man. He fought valiantly in Keeper's Dale, so say the tales. There was one time . . ."

"Harkle!" Now there was no subtle coercion in Deudermont's tone, just open hostility.

"What?" the wizard asked innocently.

"The damned seagull," Deudermont growled. "What have you found?"

"Oh, yes!" Harkle replied, clapping his hands. "The bird, the bird. Reggie. Yes, yes, fine bird. Fastest flyer of the lot."

"Harkle!" a score of voices roared in unison.

"We have found an island," came a reply from behind the flustered Harpell. Robillard stepped onto the deck and appeared somewhat bored. "The bird returned this day chattering about an island. Ahead and to port, and not so far away."

"How large?" Deudermont asked.

Robillard shrugged and chuckled. "All islands are large when seen through the eyes of a seagull," he answered. "It could be a rock, or it could be a continent."

"Or even a whale," Harkle piped in.

It didn't matter. If the bird had indeed spotted an island out here, out where the map indicated that Caerwich should be, then Caerwich, it must be!

"You and Dunkin," Deudermont said to Robillard, and he motioned to the wheel. "Get us there."

"And Reggie," Harkle added happily, pointing to the seagull, which had perched on the very tip of the mainmast, right above Catti-brie's head.

Drizzt saw a potential problem brewing, given the bird's position, the woman's sour mood and the fact that she had her bow with her. Fortunately, though, the bird flew off at Harkle's bidding without leaving any presents behind.

Had it not been for that bird, the *Sea Sprite* would have sailed right past Caerwich, within a half mile of the place without ever sighting it. The island was circular, resembling a low cone, and was just a few hundred yards in diameter. It was perpetually shrouded in a bluish mist that looked like just another swell in the sea from only a short distance away.

As the schooner approached that mist, drifting quietly at half sail, the wind turned colder and the sun seemed somehow less substantial. Deudermont did a complete circle of the island, but found no particularly remarkable place, nor any area that promised an easy docking.

Back in their original spot, Deudermont took the wheel from Dunkin and turned the *Sea Sprite* straight toward Caerwich, slowly slipping her into the mist.

"Ghost wind," Dunkin remarked nervously, shuddering in the sudden chill. "She's a haunted place, I tell you." The small man tugged at his ear ferociously, suddenly wishing that he had gotten off the schooner at Wyngate. Dunkin's other ear got tugged as well, but not by his own hand. He turned about to look eye to eye with Drizzt Do'Urden. They were about the same height, with similar builds, though Drizzt's muscles were much more finely honed. But at that moment, Drizzt seemed much taller to poor Dunkin, and much more imposing.

"Ghost wi—" Dunkin started to say, but Drizzt put a finger to his lips to silence him.

Dunkin leaned heavily on the rail and went silent.

Deudermont ordered the sails lower still and brought the schooner to a creeping drift. The mist grew thick about them and something about the way the ship was handling, something about the flow of the water beneath them, told the captain to be wary. He called up to Catti-brie, but she had no answers for him, more engulfed by blinding mist than he.

Deudermont nodded to Drizzt, who rushed off to the forward beam and crouched low, marking their way. The drow spotted something a moment later, and his eyes widened.

A pole was sticking out of the water, barely fifty yards ahead of them.

Drizzt eyed it curiously for just an instant, then recognized it for what it was: the top of a ship's mast.

"Stop us!" he yelled.

Robillard was into his spellcasting before Deudermont agreed to heed the warning. The wizard sent his energy out directly in front of the *Sea Sprite,* brought up a ridgelike swell of water that halted the ship's drifting momentum. Down came the *Sea Sprite's* sails, and down dropped the anchor with a splash that seemed to echo ominously about the decks for many seconds.

"How deep?" Deudermont asked the crewmen manning the anchor. The chain was marked in intervals, allowing them to gauge the depth when they put the anchor down.

"A hundred feet," one of them called back a moment later.

Drizzt rejoined the captain at the wheel. "A reef, by my guess," the drow said, explaining his call for a stop. "There is a hulk in the water barely two ship-lengths ahead of us. She's fully under, except for the tip of her mast, but standing straight. Something brought her down in a hurry."

"Got her bottom torn right off," Robillard reasoned.

"I figure us to be a few hundred yards from the beach," Deudermont said, peering hard into the mist. He looked to the stern. The *Sea Sprite* carried two small rowboats, one hanging on either side of the poop deck.

"We could circle again," Robillard remarked, seeing where the captain's reasoning was leading. "Perhaps we will find a spot with a good draw."

"I'll not risk my ship," Deudermont replied. "We will go in using the rowboat," he decided. He looked to a group of nearby crewmen. "Drop one," he instructed.

Twenty minutes later, Deudermont, Drizzt, Catti-brie, the two wizards, Waillan Micanty and a very reluctant and very frightened Dunkin glided away from the *Sea Sprite*, filling their rowboat so completely that its rim was barely a hand above the dark water. Deudermont had left specific instructions with those remaining on the *Sea Sprite*. The crew was to put back out of the mist a thousand yards and wait for their return. If they had not returned by nightfall, the *Sea Sprite* was to move out away from the island, making one final run at Caerwich at noon the next day.

After that, if the rowboat had not been spotted, she was to sail home.

The seven moved away from the *Sea Sprite*, Dunkin and Waillan on the oars and Catti-brie peering over the prow, expecting to find a reef at any moment. Farther back, Drizzt knelt beside Deudermont, ready to point out the mast he had spotted.

Drizzt couldn't find it.

"No reef," Catti-brie said from the front. "A good and deep draw, by me own guess." She looked back to Drizzt and especially to Deudermont. "Ye might've bringed her in right up to the damned beach," she said.

Deudermont looked to the drow, who was scanning the mist hard, wondering where that mast had gone to. He was about to restate what he had seen when the rowboat lurched suddenly, her bottom scraping on the rocks of a sharp reef.

They bumped and ground to a halt. They might have gotten hung up there, but a spell from Robillard brought both wizards, Deudermont and Catti-brie floating above the creaking planks of the boat, while Drizzt, Dunkin and Waillan cautiously brought the lightened boat over.

"All the way in?" Drizzt remarked to Catti-brie.

"It wasn't there!" the young woman insisted. Catti-brie had been a lookout for more than five years, and was said to have the best eyes on the Sword Coast. So how, she wondered, had she missed so obvious a reef, especially when she was looking for exactly that?

A few moments later, Harkle, at the very stern of the rowboat, gave a startled cry and the others turned to see the mast of a ship sticking out of the water right beside the seated wizard.

Now the others, especially Drizzt, were having the same doubts as Catti-brie. They had practically run over that mast, so why hadn't they seen it?

Dunkin tugged furiously at his ear.

"A trick of the fog," Deudermont said calmly. "Bring us around that mast." The command caught the others off guard. Dunkin shook his head, but Waillan slapped him on the shoulder.

"Hard on the oar," Waillan ordered. "You heard the captain."

Catti-brie hung low over the side of the rowboat, curious to learn more about the wreck, but the mist reflected in the water, leaving her staring into a gray veil whose secrets she could not penetrate. Finally, Deudermont gave up on gathering any information out here, and commanded Waillan and Dunkin to put straight in for the island.

At first, Dunkin nodded eagerly, happy to get off the water. Then, as he considered their destination, he alternated pulls on the oar with pulls on his ear.

The surf was not strong, but the undertow was and it

pulled back against the rowboat's meager progress. The island was soon in sight, but it seemed to hang out there, just beyond their grasp, for many moments.

"Pull hard!" Deudermont ordered his rowers, though he knew that they were doing exactly that, were as anxious as he to get this over with. Finally, the captain looked plaintively to Robillard, and the wizard, after a resigned sigh, stuck his hand into his deep pockets, seeking the components for a helpful spell.

Still up front, Catti-brie peered hard through the mist, studying the white beach for some sign of inhabitants. It was no good; the island was too far away, given the thick fog. The young woman looked down instead, into the dark water.

She saw candles.

Catti-brie's face twisted in confusion. She looked up and rubbed her eyes, then looked back to the water.

Candles. There could be no mistake about it. Candles . . . *under the water.*

Curious, the woman bent lower and looked more closely, finally making out a form holding the closest light.

Catti-brie fell back, gasping. "The dead," she said, though she couldn't get more than a whisper out of her mouth. Her sharp movements alone had caught the attention of the others, and then she hopped right to her feet, as a bloated and blackened hand grabbed the rim of the rowboat.

Dunkin, looking only at Catti-brie, screamed as she drew out her sword. Drizzt got to his feet and scrambled to get by the two oarsmen.

Catti-brie saw the top of the ghost's head come clear of the water. A horrid, skeletal face rose to the side of the boat.

Khazid'hea came down hard, hitting nothing but the edge of the boat and driving right through the planking until it was at water level.

"What are you doing?" Dunkin cried. Drizzt, at Catti-brie's side, wondered the same thing. There was no sign of any ghost, there was just Catti-brie's sword wedged deeply into the planking of the rowboat.

"Get us in!" Catti-brie yelled back. "Get us in!"

Drizzt looked at her hard, then looked all around. "Candles?" he asked, noticing the strange watery lights.

That simple word sparked fear in Deudermont, Robillard, Waillan and Dunkin, sailors all, who knew the tales of sea ghosts, lying in wait under the waves, their bloated bodies marked by witchlight candles.

"How pretty!" said an oblivious Harkle, looking overboard.

"Get us to the beach!" Deudermont cried, but he needn't have bothered, for Waillan and Dunkin were pulling with all of their strength.

Robillard was deep into spellcasting. He summoned a wave right behind the small craft and the rowboat was lifted up and sent speeding toward shore. The jolt of the sudden wave knocked Catti-brie to the deck and nearly sent Drizzt right over.

Harkle, entranced by the candles, wasn't so fortunate. As the wave crested, coming right over the tide line, he tumbled out.

The rowboat shot ahead, sliding hard onto the beach.

In the surf, ten yards offshore, a drenched Harkle stood up.

A dozen grotesque and bloated forms stood up around him.

"Oh, hello . . ." the friendly Harpell started, and then his eyes bulged and nearly rolled from their sockets.

"Eeyah!" Harkle screamed, plowing through the undertow and toward the shore.

Catti-brie was already up and in position, lifting Taulmaril and fitting an arrow. She took quick aim and let fly.

Harkle screamed again as the arrow streaked right past him. Then he heard the sickening thump and splash as an animated corpse hit the water, and understood that he was not the woman's target.

Another arrow followed closely, taking out the next nearest zombie. Harkle, as he came to more shallow water, tore himself free of grabbing weeds and quickly outdistanced the other monsters. He had just cleared the water, putting a few feet of moist sand behind him, when he heard the roar of flames and glanced back to see a curtain of fire separating him from the water, and from the zombies.

He ran the rest of the way up the beach to join the other

six by the rowboat and expressed his thanks to Robillard, shaking the wizard so hard that he broke the man's concentration.

The curtain of blocking fire fell away. Where there had been ten zombies, there were now a score, and more were rising from the water and the weeds.

"Well done," Robillard said dryly.

Catti-brie fired again, blasting away another zombie.

Robillard waggled the fingers of one hand and a bolt of green energy erupted from each of them, soaring down the beach. Three hit one zombie in rapid succession, dropping it to the water. Two sped past, burning into the next monster in line and likewise sending it down.

"Not very creative," Harkle remarked.

Robillard scowled at him. "You can do better?"

Harkle snapped his fingers indignantly, and so the challenge was on.

Drizzt and the others stood back, weapons ready, but knowing better than to charge down at their foes in the face of wizardly magic. Even Catti-brie, after a couple of more shots, lowered her bow, giving the competing spellcasters center stage.

"A Calimshan snake charmer taught me this one," Harkle proclaimed. He tossed a bit of twine into the air and chanted in a cracking, high-pitched voice. A line of seaweed came alive to his call, rose up like a serpent and immediately wrapped itself about the nearest zombie, yanking the thing down under the surf.

Harkle smiled broadly.

Robillard snorted derisively. "Only one?" he asked, and he launched himself into the throes of another spell, spinning and dancing and tossing flakes of metal into the air. Then he stopped and pivoted powerfully, hurling one hand out toward the shore. Shards of shining, burning metal flew out, gained a momentum all their own, and sent a barrage into the zombies' midst. Several were hit, the ignited metals clinging to them stubbornly, searing through the weeds and the remnants of clothing, through rotted skin and bone alike.

A moment later, a handful of the gruesome zombies tumbled down.

"Oh, simple evocation," Harkle chided and he answered Robillard's spell by pulling out a small metal rod and pointing it toward the water.

Seconds later, a lightning bolt blasted forth. Harkle aimed it at the water and the bolt blasted in, spreading wide in a circular pattern, engulfing many monsters.

How weird, even funny, that sight appeared! Zombie hair popped up straight and the stiff-moving things began a strange, hopping dance, turning complete circles, rolling this way and that before spinning down under the waves.

When it was over, the zombie ranks had been cut in half, though more were rising stubbornly all along the beach.

Harkle smiled widely and snapped his fingers again. "Simple evocation," he remarked.

"Indeed," muttered Robillard.

Catti-brie had eased her bowstring by this point, and was smiling, sincerely amused, as she regarded her companions. Even Dunkin, so terrified a moment before, seemed ready to laugh aloud at the spectacle of the battling wizards. In looking at the pair, Deudermont was glad, for he feared that the sight of such horrid enemies had defeated his team's heart for this search.

It was Robillard's turn and he focused on a single zombie that had cleared the water and was ambling up the beach. He used no material components this time, just chanted softly and waved his arms in specific movements. A line of fire rushed out from his pointing finger, reaching out to the unfortunate target monster and then shrouding it in flames, an impressive display that fully consumed the creature in but a few moments. Robillard, concentrating deeply, then shifted the line of fire, burning away a second monster.

"The scorcher," he said when the spell was done. "A remnant from the works of Agannazar."

Harkle snorted. "Agannazar was a minor trickster!" he declared, and Robillard scowled.

Harkle reached into a pocket, pulling forth several components. "Dart," he explained, lifting the item. "Powdered rhubarb and the stomach of an adder."

"Melf!" Robillard cried happily.

"Melf indeed!" echoed Harpell. "Now there was a wizard!"

"I know Melf," said Robillard.

Harkle stuttered and stopped his casting. "How old are you?" he asked.

"I know Melf's work," Robillard clarified.

"Oh," said Harkle and he went back to casting.

To prove h s point, Robillard reached into his own pocket and producec a handful of beads that smelled of pine tar. Harkle caugł t the aroma, but paid it little heed as he was in the throes of the final runes of his own spell by then.

The dart zipped out from Harkle's hand, rocketing into the belly of the closest zombie. Immediately it began to pump forth acid, boring an ever-widening hole right through the creature. The zombie grasped futilely at the wound, even bent low as if it meant to peer right through itself.

Then it fell over.

"Melf!" Harkle proclaimed, but he quieted when he looked back to Robillard and saw tiny meteors erupting from the wizard's hand, shooting out to blast mini-fireballs among the zombie ranks.

"Better Melf," Harkle admitted.

"Enough of this foolishness," Captain Deudermont put in. "We can simply run up off the beach. I doubt they will pursue." Deudermont's voice trailed away as he realized that neither wizard was paying him much heed.

"We are not on the ship," was all that indignant Robillard would reply. Then to Harkle, he said, "Do you admit defeat?"

"I have not yet begun to boom!" declared the obstinate Harpell.

Both launched themselves into spells, among the most powerful of their considerable repertoires. Robillard pulled out a tiny bucket and shovel, while Harkle produced a snakeskin glove and a long, painted fingernail.

Robillard cast first, his spell causing a sudden and violent excavation right at the feet of the closest zombies. Beach sand flew wildly. The monsters walked right into the pit, falling from sight. Robillard shifted his angle and muttered a single word, and another pit began, not far to the side of the first.

"Dig," he muttered to Harkle, between chants.

"Bigby," Harkle countered. "You know of Bigby?"

Robillard blanched despite his own impressive display. Of course he knew of Bigby! He was one of the most powerful and impressive wizards of all time, on any world.

Harkle's spell began as a gigantic disembodied hand. It was transparent and hovered over the beach, in the area near Robillard's first pit. Robillard looked hard at the hand. Three of the fingers were extended, pointing toward the hole, but the middle finger was curled back and under the thumb.

"I have *improved* on Bigby," Harkle boasted. A zombie ambled between the gigantic hand and the hole.

"Doink!" commanded the Harpell and the hand's middle finger popped out from underneath the thumb, slamming the zombie on the side of the head and launching it sideways into the pit.

Harkle turned a smug smile at Robillard. "Bigby's Snapping Digits," he explained. He focused his thoughts on the hand again, and it moved to his will, gliding all along the beach and "doinking" zombies whenever they came within range.

Robillard didn't know whether to roar in protest or howl in laughter. The Harpell was good, he had to admit, very good. But Robillard wasn't about to lose this one. He took out a diamond, a gem that had cost him more than a thousand gold pieces. "Otiluke," he said defiantly, referring to yet another of the legendary and powerful wizards whose works were the staples of a magician's studies. Now it was Harkle's turn to blanch, for he had little knowledge of the legendary Otiluke.

When Robillard considered that diamond, and the quickly diminishing ranks of their monstrous adversaries, he had to wonder if it was really worth the price. He snapped his fingers with a revelation, popped the diamond back into his pocket and took out a thin sheet of crystal instead.

"Otiluke," he said again, choosing another variation of the same spell. He cast the spell and immediately, all along the beach, the surf simply froze, locking fast in the thick ice those zombies who had not yet come out of the water.

"Oh, well done," Harkle admitted as Robillard slapped his hands together in a superior motion, wiping himself clean of the zombies and of Harkle. The spells had cleared the beach of enemies, and so the fight was apparently over.

But Harkle couldn't let Robillard have the last word, not that way. He looked to the zombies struggling in the ice, and then glowered at Robillard. Deliberately, he reached into his deepest pocket and pulled forth a ceramic flask. "Super hero-ism," he explained. "You have perhaps heard of Tenser?"

Robillard put a finger to pursed lips. "Oh, yes," he said a moment later. "Of course, crazy Tenser." Robillard's eyes went wide as he considered the implications. Tenser's most renowned spell reportedly transformed a wizard into a war-rior for a short duration—a berserk warrior!

"Not the Tenser!" Robillard yelled, tackling Harkle where he stood, pinning the man down before he could pop the cork off the potion flask.

"Help me!" Robillard begged, and the others were there in a moment. The battle, and the contest, was at its end.

They pulled themselves together and Deudermont announced that it was time to get off the beach.

Drizzt motioned to Catti-brie and immediately moved out front, more than ready to be on the move. The woman didn't immediately follow. She was too intent on the continuing, now-friendly, exchange between the wizards. Mostly, she was watching Robillard, who seemed much more animated and happy. She thought perhaps Harkle Harpell was indeed having a positive effect on the man.

"Oh, that digging spell worked so very well with my Bigby variation," she heard Harkle say. "You really must teach it to me. My cousin, Bidderdoo, he is a werewolf, and he has this habit of burying everything about the yard, bones and wands and the like. The dig spell will help me to recover . . ."

Catti-brie shook her head and rushed to catch up with Drizzt. She skidded to an abrupt stop, though, and looked back to the rowboat. More particularly, she looked back to Dunkin Tallmast, who was seated in the beached craft, shaking his head back and forth. Catti-brie motioned to the others and they all went back to the man.

"I wish to go back to the boat," Dunkin said sternly. "One of the wizards can get me there." As he spoke, the man was clutching the rail so tightly that the knuckles on both his hands had whitened for lack of blood.

"Come along," Drizzt said to him.

Dunkin didn't move.

"You have been given a chance to witness what few men have ever seen," the ranger said. As he spoke, Drizzt took out the panther figurine and dropped it on the sand.

"You know more about Caerwich than any other aboard the *Sea Sprite*," Deudermont added. "Your knowledge is needed."

"I know little," Dunkin retorted.

"But still more than any other," Deudermont insisted.

"There is a reward for your assistance," Drizzt went on, and Dunkin's eyes brightened for an instant—until the drow explained what he meant by the word "reward."

"Who knows what adventure we might find here?" Drizzt said excitedly. "Who knows what secrets might be unveiled to us?"

"Adventure?" Dunkin asked incredulously, looking to the carnage along the beach, and to the zombies still frozen in the water. "Reward?" he added with a chuckle. "Punishment, more likely, though I have done nothing to harm you, any of you!"

"We are here to unveil a mystery," Drizzt said, as though that fact should have piqued the man's curiosity. "To learn and to grow. To live as we discover the secrets of the world about us."

"Who wants to know?" Dunkin snapped, deflating the drow and dismissing his grandiose speech. Waillan Micanty, inspired by the drow's words, had heard enough of the whining little man. The young sailor moved to the side of the beached rowboat, tore Dunkin's hands free of the rail and dragged the man onto the sand.

"I could have done that with much more flair," Robillard remarked dryly.

"So could Tenser," said Harkle.

"*Not* the Tenser," Robillard insisted.

"Not the Tenser?"

"Not the Tenser," Robillard reiterated, in even tones of finality. Harkle whimpered a bit, but did not respond.

"Save your magic," Waillan said to both of them. "We may need it yet."

Now it was Dunkin's turn to whine.

"When this is over, you will have a tale to widen the eyes of every sailor who puts in at Mintarn Harbor," Drizzt said to the small man.

That seemed to calm Dunkin somewhat, until Catti-brie added, "If ye live."

Drizzt and Deudermont both scowled at her, but the woman merely grinned innocently and walked away.

"I will tell his tyrancy," Dunkin threatened, but no one was listening to him anymore.

Drizzt called to Guenhwyvar and when the panther came onto the beach, the seven adventurers gathered around Deudermont. The captain drew a rough outline of the island in the sand. He put an X on the area indicating their beach, then another one outside his drawing, to show the location of the *Sea Sprite.*

"Ideas?" he asked, looking particularly at Dunkin.

"I've heard people speak of 'the Witch of the Moaning Cave,'" the small man offered sheepishly.

"There might be caves along the coast," Catti-brie reasoned. "Or up here." She put her finger down onto Deudermont's rough drawing, indicating the one mountain, the low cone that comprised the bulk of Caerwich.

"We should search inland before we put back out into the sea," Deudermont reasoned, and none of them had to follow his gaze to the frozen zombies to be reminded of the dangers along the shore of Caerwich. And so off they trudged, inland, through a surprisingly thick tangle of brush and huge ferns.

Almost as soon as they had left the openness of the beach behind, sounds erupted all about them—the hoots and whistles of exotic birds, and throaty howling calls that none of them had heard before. Drizzt and Guenhwyvar took up the point and flanks, moving off to disappear into the tangle without a sound.

Dunkin groaned at this, not liking the fact that his immediate group had just become smaller. Catti-brie chuckled at him, drawing a scowl. If only Dunkin knew how much safer they were with the drow and his cat moving beside them.

They searched for more than an hour, then took a break in a small clearing halfway up the low conical mountain. Drizzt sent Guenhwyvar off alone, figuring that the cat could cover more ground in the span of their short break than they would search out the rest of the day.

"We will come down the back side of the cone, then move southward, all the way around and back to the boat," Deudermont explained. "Then back up and over the cone, and then to the north."

"We may have walked right past the cave without ever seeing it," Robillard grumbled. It was true enough, they all knew, for the tangle was so very thick and dark, and the mist had not diminished in the least.

"Well, perhaps our two wizards could be of use," Deudermont said sarcastically, "if they hadn't been so absorbed in wasting their spells to prove a point."

"There were enemies to strike down," Harkle protested.

"I could've cut 'em down with me bow," said Catti-brie.

"And wasted arrows!" Harkle retorted, thinking he had her in a logic trap.

Of course, the others all knew, Catti-brie's quiver was powerfully enchanted. "I don't run out of arrows," she remarked, and Harkle sat back down.

Drizzt interrupted then, abruptly, by hopping to his feet and staring hard into the jungle. His hand went to the pouch that held the onyx figurine.

Catti-brie jumped to her feet, taking up Taulmaril, and the others followed suit.

"Guenhwyvar?" the woman asked.

Drizzt nodded. Something had happened to the panther, but he wasn't sure of what that might be. On a hunch, he took out the figurine, placed it on the ground, and called to the panther once more. A moment later, the gray mist appeared, and then took form, Guenhwyvar pacing nervously about the drow.

"There's two of them things?" Dunkin asked.

"Same cat," Catti-brie explained. "Something sent Guen home."

118

Drizzt nodded and looked to Deudermont. "Something that Guenhwyvar could find again," he reasoned.

Off they went, through the tangle, following Guenhwyvar's lead. Soon they came to the northern slopes of the cone, and behind a curtain of thick hanging moss, they found a dark opening. Drizzt motioned to Guenhwyvar, but the panther would not go in.

Drizzt eyed her curiously.

"I'm going back to the boat," Dunkin remarked. He took a step away, but Robillard, tired of the man's foolishness, drew out a wand and pointed it right between Dunkin's eyes. The wizard said not a word, he didn't have to.

Dunkin turned back to the cave.

Drizzt crouched near to the panther. Guenhwyvar would not enter the cave, and the drow had no idea of why that might be. He knew that Guenhwyvar was not afraid. Might there be an enchantment on the area that prevented the panther from entering?

Satisfied with that explanation, Drizzt drew out Twinkle, the fine scimitar glowing its customary blue, and motioned for his friends to wait. He slipped past the mossy curtain, waited a moment so that his eyes could adjust to the deeper gloom, then moved in.

Twinkle's light went away. Drizzt ducked to the side, behind the protection of a boulder. He realized that he was not moving as quickly as expected, his enchanted anklets were not aiding him.

"No magic," he reasoned, and then it seemed perfectly clear to him why Guenhwyvar would not enter. The drow turned to go back out, but found his impatient friends already slipping in behind him. Both Harkle and Robillard wore curious expressions. Catti-brie squinted into the gloom, one hand fiddling with the suddenly useless cat's eye pendant strapped to her forehead.

"I have forgotten all of my spells," Harkle said loudly, his voice echoing off the bare wall of the large cave. Robillard slapped his hand over Harkle's mouth.

"Ssssh!" the calmer wizard hissed. When he thought about what Harkle had said, though, Robillard had his own outburst. "As have I!" he roared, and then he slapped his hand over his own mouth.

"No magic in here," Drizzt told them. "That is why Guenhwyvar could not enter."

"Might be that is what sent the cat home," Catti-brie added.

The discussion ended abruptly, and all heads swung about to regard Waillan as the light of a makeshift torch flared brightly.

"I'll not walk in blindly," the young sailor explained, holding high the burning branches he had strapped together.

None of them could argue. Just the few feet they had gone past the cave's entrance had stolen most of the light, and their senses hinted to them that this was no small place. The cave felt deep, and cool. It seemed as if the sticky humidity of the island air had been left behind outside.

As they moved in a bit farther, the torchlight showed them that their senses were telling the truth. The cave was large and roughly oval in shape, perhaps a hundred feet across at its longest point. It was uneven, with several different levels across its broken floor and gigantic stalactites leering down at them.

Drizzt was about to suggest a systematic exploration, when a voice cut the stillness.

"Who would seek my sight?" came a cackle from the rear of the cave, where there appeared to be a rocky tier a dozen feet above the party's present level. All of the group squinted through the gloom. Catti-brie tightened her grip on Taulmaril, wondering how effective the bow might be without its magic.

Dunkin turned back for the door, and out came Robillard's wand, though the wizard's gaze was firmly set ahead, upon the tier of boulders. The small man hesitated, then realized that Robillard had no power against him, not in here.

"Who would seek my sight?" came the cackling question again.

Dunkin bolted out through the moss.

As one, the group looked back to the exit.

"Let him go," Deudermont said. The captain took the torch from Waillan and moved forward slowly, the other five following in his wake. Drizzt, ever cautious, moved to the shadows offered by the side wall of the cave.

The question came a third time, in rehearsed tones as though the witch was not unaccustomed to visits by sailors. She showed herself to them then, moving out between a tumble of boulders. The hag was old, ancient, wearing a tattered black shift and leaning heavily on a short and polished staff. Her mouth was open—she seemed to be gasping for breath—showing off a single, yellow tooth. Her eyes, appearing dull even from a distance, did not blink.

"Who will bear the burden of knowledge?" she asked. She kept her head turned in the general direction of the five for a short while, then broke into cackling laughter.

Deudermont held his hand up, motioning for the others to halt, then boldly stepped forward. "I will," he announced. "I am Deudermont of the *Sea Sprite,* come to Caerwich . . ."

"Go back!" the hag yelled at him so forcefully that the captain took a step backward before he realized what he was doing. Catti-brie bent her bow a bit more, but kept it low and unthreatening.

"This is not for you, not for any man!" the hag explained. All eyes shifted to regard Catti-brie.

"It is for two, and only two," the hag went on, her croaking voice rhythmic, as though she was reciting a heroic poem. "Not for any man, or any male whose skin browns under the light of the sun."

The obvious reference sent Drizzt's shoulders slumping. He came out of the shadows a moment later, and looked to Catti-brie, who seemed as crestfallen as he in the sudden realization that this was, after all, about Drizzt once more. Deudermont had almost been killed in Waterdeep, and that the *Sea Sprite* and her crew were in peril, a thousand miles from their usual waters, because of his legacy.

Drizzt sheathed his blades and walked over to Catti-brie, and together they moved past the startled captain, and out in front to face the blind witch.

"My greetings, renegade of Daermon N'a'shezbaernon," the blind witch said, referring to Drizzt's ancient family name, a name that few outside of Menzoberranzan would know. "And to you, daughter of a dwarf, who hurled the mightiest of spears!"

That last sentence caught the pair off guard, and confused them for just a moment, until they realized the reference. The witch must be speaking of the stalactite that Catti-brie had dropped, the great "spear" that drove through the dome of House Baenre's chapel! This was about them, about Drizzt's past, and the enemies they thought they had left behind.

The blind hag motioned for them to come closer, and so they did, walking with as much heart as they could muster. They were barely ten feet from the ugly woman when they stopped. They were several feet below her as well, a fact that made her— someone who knew what she should not have known—seem all the more imposing. The crone pulled herself up as high as she could, showing great effort in trying to straighten her bowed shoulders, and aligned her sightless orbs straight with those of Drizzt Do'Urden.

Then she recited, quietly and quickly, the verse Errtu had given her:

No path by chance but by plot,
Further steps along the road of his father's ghost.
The traitor to Lloth is sought
By he who hates him most.

The fall of a house, the fall of a spear,
Puncture the Spider Queen's pride as a dart.
And now a needle for Drizzt Do'Urden to wear
'Neath the folds of his cloak, so deep in his heart.

A challenge, renegade of renegade's seed,
A golden ring thee cannot resist!
Reach, but only when the beast is freed
From festering in the swirl of Abyss.

Given to Lloth and by Lloth given
That thee might seek the darkest of trails.
Presented to one who is most unshriven
And held out to thee, for thee shall fail!

So seek, Drizzt Do'Urden, the one who hates thee most.
A friend, and too, a foe, made in thine home that was
     first.
There thee will find one feared a ghost
Bonded by love and by battle's thirst.

The blind hag stopped abruptly, her sightless eyes lingering, her entire body perfectly still, as though the recital had taken a great deal of her strength. Then she drifted back between the stones, moving out of sight.

Drizzt hardly noticed her, just stood, shoulders suddenly slumped, strength sapped by the impossible possibility. "Given to Lloth," he muttered helplessly, and only one more word could he speak, "Zaknafein."

# Chapter 10
## KIERSTAAD'S HEART

hey came out of the cave to find Guenhwyvar sitting calmly atop a pinned Dunkin. Drizzt waved the cat off the man and they departed.

Drizzt was hardly conscious of the journey back across the island to the rowboat. He said nothing all the way, except to dismiss Guenhwyvar back to her astral home as soon as they realized that they would face no resistance on the beach this time. The ice was gone and so were the zombies. The others, respecting the drow's mood, understanding the unnerving information the hag had given him, remained quiet as well.

Drizzt repeated the blind seer's words over and over in his mind, vainly trying to commit them to memory. Every syllable could be a clue, Drizzt realized, every inflection might offer him some hint as to who might be holding his father prisoner. But the words had come too suddenly, too unexpectedly.

His father! Zaknafein! Drizzt could hardly breathe as he thought of the sudden possibility. He remembered their many sparring matches, the years they had spent in joyful and determined practice. He remembered the time when Zaknafein had tried to kill him, and he loved his father even more for that, because Zaknafein had come after him only in the belief that his beloved Drizzt had gone over to the dark ways of the drow.

Drizzt shook the memories from his mind. He had no time for nostalgia now; he had to focus on the task so suddenly at hand. As great as was his elation at the thought that Zaknafein might be returned to him, so was his trepidation. Some powerful being, either a matron mother, or perhaps even Lloth herself, held the secret, and the hag's words implicated Catti-brie as well as Drizzt. The ranger cast a sidelong glance at Catti-brie, who was lost in apparently similar contemplations. The hag had intimated that all of this, the attack in Waterdeep and the journey to this remote island, had been arranged by a powerful enemy who sought revenge not only upon Drizzt, but upon Catti-brie.

Drizzt slowed and let the others get a few steps ahead as they dragged the rowboat to the surf. He released Catti-brie from his gaze, and, momentarily at least, from his thoughts, going back to privately reciting the hag's verse. The best thing he could do for Catti-brie, and for Zaknafein, was to memorize it, all of it, as exactly as possible. Drizzt understood that consciously, but still, the possibility that Zaknafein might be alive, overwhelmed him, and all the verses seemed fuzzy, a distant dream that the ranger fought hard to recollect. Drizzt was not alert as they splashed back off the beach of Caerwich. His eyes focused only on the swish of the oars under the dark water, and so intent was he that if a horde of zombies had risen up against them from the water, Drizzt would have been the last to draw a weapon.

As it turned out, they got back to the *Sea Sprite* without incident and Deudermont, after a quick check with Drizzt to assure that they were done with their business on the island, wasted no time in putting the ship back out to sea. Deudermont called for full sails the moment they got out of the enveloping fog of Caerwich, and the swift schooner soon put the misty island far, far behind. Only after Caerwich was out of sight did Deudermont call Drizzt, Catti-brie, and the two wizards into his private quarters for a discussion of what had just transpired.

"You knew what the old witch was speaking about?" the captain asked Drizzt.

"Zaknafein," the drow replied without hesitation. He noticed that Catti-brie's expression seemed to cloud over. The woman had been tense all the way back from the cave, almost giddy, but it seemed to Drizzt that she was now merely crestfallen.

"And our course now?" Deudermont asked.

"Home, and only home," Robillard put in. "We have no provisions, and we still have some damage to repair from the storm that battered us before we made the Gull Rocks."

"After that?" the captain wanted to know, looking directly at Drizzt as he asked the question.

Drizzt was warmed by the sentiment, by the fact that Deudermont was deferring to his judgment. When the drow gave no immediate response, the captain went on.

" 'Seek the one who hates you most,' the witch said," Deudermont reasoned. "Who might that be?"

"Entreri," Catti-brie answered. She turned to a surprised Deudermont. "Artemis Entreri, a killer from the southlands."

"The same assassin we once chased all the way to Calimshan?" Deudermont asked.

"Our business with that one never seems to be finished," Catti-brie explained. "He's hating Drizzt more than any—"

"No," Drizzt interrupted, shaking his head, running a hand through his thick white hair. "Not Entreri." The drow understood Artemis Entreri quite well, too well. Indeed Entreri hated him, or had once hated him, but their feud had been more propelled by blind pride, the assassin's need to prove himself the better, than by any tangible reason for enmity. After his stay in Menzoberranzan, Entreri had been cured of that need, at least somewhat. No, this challenge went deeper than the assassin. This had to do with Lloth herself, and involved not only Drizzt, but Catti-brie, and the dropping of the stalactite mount into the Baenre chapel. This pursuit, this proverbial golden ring, was based in pure and utter hatred.

"Who then?" Deudermont asked after a lengthy silence.

Drizzt could not give a definite answer. "A Baenre, most likely," he replied. "I have made many enemies. There are dozens in Menzoberranzan who would go to great lengths to kill me."

"But how do you know it is someone from Menzoberranzan?" Harkle interjected. "Do not take this the wrong way, but you have made many enemies on the surface as well!"

"Entreri," Catti-brie said again.

Drizzt shook his head. "The hag said, 'A foe made in the

home that was first,' " Drizzt explained. "An enemy from Menzoberranzan."

Catti-brie wasn't sure that Drizzt had correctly repeated the witch's exact words, but the evidence seemed irrefutable.

"So where to start?" Deudermont, playing the role of moderator and nothing more, asked them all.

"The witch spoke of otherworldly influence," Robillard reasoned. "She mentioned the Abyss."

"Lloth's home," Drizzt added.

Robillard nodded. "So we must get some answers from the Abyss," the wizard reasoned.

"Are we to sail there?" Deudermont scoffed.

The wizard, more knowledgeable in such matters, merely smiled and shook his head. "We must bring a fiend to our world," he explained, "and extract information from it. Not so difficult or unusual a task for those practiced in the art of sorcery."

"As you are?" Deudermont asked him.

Robillard shook his head and looked to Harkle.

"What?" the distracted Harpell said dumbly as soon as he noticed every gaze upon him. The wizard was deep in thought, also trying to reconstruct the blind witch's verse, though from his vantage point in the cave, he hadn't heard every word.

"As you are," Robillard explained, "practiced in matters of sorcery."

"Me?" he squeaked. "Oh, no. Not allowed at the Ivy Mansion, not for twenty years. Too many problems. Too many fiends walking around eating Harpells!"

"Then who will get us the answers?" Catti-brie asked.

"There are wizards in Luskan who practice sorcery," Robillard offered, "as do some priests in Waterdeep. Neither will come cheaply."

"We have the gold," Deudermont said.

"That is the ship's gold," Drizzt put in. "For all crew of the *Sea Sprite*."

Deudermont waved a hand at him as he spoke, the captain shaking his head with every syllable. "Not until Drizzt Do'Urden and Catti-brie came aboard have we enjoyed such a business and such a profit," he told the drow. "You are a part of the *Sea Sprite,* a member of her crew, and all will donate their share as you would donate yours to help another."

Drizzt could find no argument against that offer, but he did note a bit of grumbling when Robillard added, "Indeed."

"Waterdeep or Luskan, then?" Deudermont asked Robillard. "Do I sail north of the Moonshaes, or south?"

"Waterdeep," Harkle unexpectedly answered. "Oh, I would choose the priest," the wizard explained. "A goodly priest. Better with fiends than a wizard because the wizard might have other duties or questions he wishes to ask of the beast. Not good to get a fiend too involved, I say."

Drizzt, Catti-brie and Deudermont looked at the man curiously, trying to decipher what he was talking about.

"He is right," the *Sea Sprite*'s wizard quickly explained. "A goodly priest will stick to the one task, and we can be sure that such a person will call to a fiend only to better the cause of good, of justice." He looked at Drizzt as he said this, and the drow got the feeling that Robillard was suddenly questioning the wisdom of this search, the wisdom of following the blind witch's words. Questioning the course, and perhaps, Drizzt realized, the motive.

"Freeing Zaknafein from the clutches of Lloth, or of a matron mother would be a just act," Drizzt insisted, a bit of anger seeping into the edges of his voice.

"Then a goodly priest is our best choice," the *Sea Sprite*'s wizard replied casually, no apologies forthcoming.

\* \* \* \* \*

Kierstaad looked into the black, dead eyes of the reindeer lying still, so very still, upon the flat tundra, surrounded by the colorful flowers that rushed to bloom in Icewind Dale's short summer. He had killed the deer cleanly with one throw of his great spear.

Kierstaad was glad of that. He felt little remorse at the sight of the magnificent beast, for the survival of his people depended upon the success of the hunt. Not a bit of this proud animal would be wasted. Still, the young man was glad that the kill, his *first* kill, had been clean. He looked into the eyes of the dead animal and gave thanks to its spirit.

Berkthgar came up behind the young hunter and patted him on the shoulder. Kierstaad, too overwhelmed by the spectacle, by the sudden realization that in the eyes of the tribe he was no more a boy, hardly noticed as the huge man strode past him, a long knife in hand.

Berkthgar crouched beside the animal and shifted its legs out of the way. His cut was clean and perfect, long practiced. Only a moment later, he turned about and stood up, holding his bloody arms out to Kierstaad, holding the animal's heart.

"Eat it and gain the deer's strength and speed," the barbarian leader promised.

Kierstaad took the heart tentatively and brought it near to his lips. This was part of the test, he knew, though he had no idea that this would be expected of him. The gravity in Berkthgar's voice was unmistakable, he could not fail. No more a boy, he told himself. Something savage welled in him at the smell of the blood, at the thought of what he must do.

"The heart holds the spirit of the deer," another man explained. "Eat of that spirit."

Kierstaad hesitated no longer. He brought the blackish-red heart to his lips and bit deeply. He was hardly conscious of his next actions, of devouring the heart, of bathing in the spirit of the slain deer. Chants rose around him, the hunters of Berkthgar's party welcoming him to manhood.

No more a boy.

Nothing more was expected of Kierstaad. He stood impassively to the side while the older hunters cleaned and dressed the reindeer. This was indeed the better way for he and his people, living free of the bonds of wealth and the ties to others. In that, at least, Kierstaad knew that Berkthgar was right. Yet, the young man continued to bear no ill will toward the dwarves or the folk of Ten-Towns, and had no intention of allowing any lies to diminish his respect for Wulfgar, who had done so much good for the tribes of Icewind Dale.

Kierstaad looked to the harvesting of the reindeer, so complete and perfect. No waste and no disrespect for the proud animal. He looked to his own bloody hands and arms, felt a line of blood running down his chin to drip onto the spongy soil. This was his life, his destiny. Yet what did that mean? More war with Ten-Towns, as had happened so many times in the past? And what of relations with the dwarves who had returned to their mines south of Kelvin's Cairn?

Kierstaad had listened to Berkthgar throughout the last few weeks. He had heard Berkthgar arguing with Revjak, Kierstaad's father and the accepted leader of the Tribe of the Elk, at present the one remaining tribe on Icewind Dale's tundra. Berkthgar would break away, Kierstaad thought as he looked at the gigantic man. Berkthgar would take the other young warriors with him and begin anew the Tribe of the Bear, or one of the other ancestral tribes. Then the tribal rivalry that had for so long been a way of life for Icewind Dale's barbarians would begin anew. They would fight for food or for good ground as they wandered the tundra.

It was one possibility only, Kierstaad reasoned, trying to shake the disturbing thoughts away. Berkthgar wanted to be the complete leader, wanted to emulate and then surpass the legend of Wulfgar. He could not do that if he splintered the remaining barbarians, who in truth were not yet numerous enough to support any separate tribes of any real power.

Wulfgar had united the tribes.

There were other possibilities, but as he thought about it, none of them sat well with him.

Berkthgar looked up from the kill, smiling widely, accepting Kierstaad fully and with no ulterior motives. Yet Kierstaad was the son of Revjak, and it seemed to him now that Berkthgar and his father might be walking a troubled course. The leader of a barbarian tribe could be challenged.

That notion only intensified when the successful hunting party neared the deerskin tent encampment of the tribe, only to intercept one Bruenor Battlehammer and another dwarf, the priestess Stumpet Rakingclaw.

"You do not belong here!" Berkthgar immediately growled at the dwarven leader.

"Well met to yerself too," Stumpet, never the one to sit back and let others speak for her, snarled at Berkthgar. "Ye're forgettin' Keeper's Dale, then, as we've heard ye were?"

"I do not speak to females on matters of importance," Berkthgar said evenly.

Bruenor moved quickly, extending an arm to hold the outraged Stumpet back. "And I'm not for talking with yerself," Bruenor replied. "Me and me cleric have come to see Revjak, the leader of the Tribe of the Elk."

Berkthgar's nostrils flared. For a moment, Kierstaad and the others expected him to hurl himself at Bruenor, and the dwarf, bracing himself and slapping his many-notched axe across his open palm, apparently expected it, too.

But Berkthgar, no fool, calmed himself. "I, too, lead the hunters of Icewind Dale," he said. "Speak your business and be gone!"

Bruenor chuckled and walked past the proud barbarian, moving into the settlement. Berkthgar howled and leaped, landing right in Bruenor's path.

"Ye led in Settlestone," the red-bearded dwarf said firmly. "And ye might be leadin' here. Then again, ye might not. Revjak was king when we left the dale and Revjak's king still, by all word I'm hearing." Bruenor's judging gray eyes never left Berkthgar as he walked past the huge man once more.

Stumpet turned up her nose and didn't bother to eye the giant barbarian.

For Kierstaad, who liked Bruenor and his wild clan, it was a painful meeting.

* * * * *

The wind was light, the only sound the creaking timbers of the *Sea Sprite* as it glided quietly eastward on calm waters. The moon was full and pale above them as it crossed a cloudless sky.

Catti-brie sat on the raised platform of the ballista, huddled near to a candle, every so often jotting something down on parchment. Drizzt leaned on the rail, his parchment rolled and in a pocket of his cloak. On Deudermont's wise instructions, all six who had been in the blind witch's cave were to write down the poem as they remembered it. Five of them could write, an extraordinary percentage. Waillan, who was not skilled with letters would dictate his recollection to both Harkle and Robillard, who would separately pen the words, hopefully without any of their own interpretations.

It hadn't taken Drizzt long to write down the verse, at least the parts he remembered most clearly, the parts he considered vital. He understood that every word might provide a necessary clue, but he was simply too excited, too overwhelmed to pay attention to minute details. In the poem's second line, the witch had spoken of Drizzt's father, and had intimated at Zaknafein's survival several times thereafter. That was all that Drizzt could think of, all that he could hope to remember.

Catti-brie was more diligent, her written record of the verse far more complete. But she, too, had been overwhelmed and surprised, and simply couldn't be certain of how accurate her recording might be.

"I would have liked to share a night such as this with him," Drizzt said, his voice shattering the stillness so abruptly that the young woman nearly jabbed her quill through the fragile parchment. She looked up to Drizzt, whose eyes were high, his gaze focused on the moon.

"Just one," the drow went on. "Zaknafein would have loved the surface night."

Catti-brie smiled, not doubting the claim. Drizzt had spoken to her many times about his father. Drizzt's soul was the legacy of his father's, not of his evil mother's. The two were alike, in combat and in heart, with the notable exception that Drizzt had found the courage to walk away from Menzoberranzan, whereas Zaknafein had not. He had remained with the evil dark elves and had eventually come to be sacrificed to the Spider Queen.

"Given to Lloth and by Lloth given."

The true line came suddenly to Catti-brie. She whispered it once aloud, hearing the ring and knowing it to be exact, then went back to her parchment and located the line. She had written, "for" instead of "to," which she quickly corrected.

Every little word could be vital.

"I suspect that the danger I now face is beyond anything we have ever witnessed," Drizzt went on, talking to himself as much as to Catti-brie.

Catti-brie didn't miss his use of the personal pronoun, instead of the collective. She too was involved, a point that she was about to make clear, but another line came to her, jogged by Drizzt's proclamation.

"That thee might seek the darkest of trails."

Catti-brie realized that was the next line and her quill went to work. Drizzt was talking again, but she hardly heard him. She did catch a few words, though, and she stopped writing, her gaze lifting from the parchment to consider the drow. He was speaking again of going off alone!

"The verse was for us two," Catti-brie reminded him.

"The dark trail leads to my father," Drizzt replied, "a drow you have never met."

"Yer point being?" Catti-brie asked.

"The trail is for me to walk . . ."

"With meself," Catti-brie said determinedly. "Don't ye be doing that again!" she scolded. "Ye walked off once on me, and nearly brought ruin upon yerself and us all for yer stupidity!"

Drizzt swung about and eyed her directly. How he loved this woman! He knew that he could not argue the point with her, knew that whatever arguments he might present, she would defeat them, or simply ignore them.

"I'm going with ye, all the way," Catti-brie said, no compromise in her firm tone. "And me thinkin's that Deudermont and Harkle, and maybe a few o' the others're coming along, too. And just ye try to stop us, Drizzt Do'Urden!"

Drizzt began to reply, but changed his mind. Why bother? He would never talk his friends into letting him walk this dark course alone. Never.

He looked back out to the dark sea and to the moon and stars, his thoughts drifting back to Zaknafein and the "golden ring," the witch had held out to him.

"It will take at least two weeks to get back to port," he lamented.

"Three, if the wind doesn't come up strong," Catti-brie put in, her focus never leaving the all-important parchment.

Not so far away, on the main deck just below the rail of the poop deck, Harkle Harpell rubbed his hands eagerly. He shared Drizzt's lament that all of this would take so very long, and had no stomach for another two or three weeks of rolling about on the empty water.

"The fog of fate," he mouthed quietly, thinking of his new, powerful spell, the enchantment that had brought him out to the *Sea Sprite* in the first place. The opportunity seemed perfect for him to energize his new spell once more.

# Chapter 11
## BREWING STORM

evjak's smile widened nearly enough to take in his ears when he saw that the rumors were true, that Bruenor Battlehammer had returned to Icewind Dale. The two had lived side by side for the first forty years of Revjak's life, but during that time the barbarian had little experience with Bruenor, other than as enemies. But then Wulfgar had united the nomadic tribes and cast them into the war as allies of the folk of Ten-Towns and the dwarves of Clan Battlehammer against evil Akar Kessel and his goblinoid minions.

On that occasion, less than a decade before, Revjak had come to appreciate the strength and fortitude of Bruenor and of all the dwarves. In the few weeks that had followed, before Bruenor and Wulfgar had set out to find Mithril Hall, Revjak had spent many days with Bruenor and had forged a fast friendship. Bruenor was going to leave, but the rest of Clan Battlehammer would remain in Icewind Dale until Mithril Hall was found, and Revjak had taken on the responsibility of tightening the friendship between the giant barbarians and the diminutive dwarves. He had done such a fine job that many of his people, Berkthgar included, had opted to go south with Clan Battlehammer to join in the fight to reclaim Mithril Hall, and there they had stayed for several years.

It seemed to wise Revjak that Berkthgar had forgotten all of that, for when the giant warrior entered the tent to join in the meeting with Bruenor and Stumpet, his face was locked in a deep and unrelenting scowl.

"Sit, Berkthgar," Revjak bade the man, motioning to a spot beside him.

Berkthgar held out his hand, indicating that he would remain standing. He was trying to be imposing, Revjak knew, towering over the seated dwarves. If hardy Bruenor was bothered at all, though, he didn't show it. He reclined comfortably on the thick blanket of piled skins so that he did not have to crook his neck to look up at the standing Berkthgar.

"Ye're still looking like yer last meal didn't taste so good," the dwarf remarked to Berkthgar.

"Why has a king come so far from his kingdom?" Berkthgar retorted.

"No more a king," Bruenor corrected. "I gived that back to me great-great-great-great grandfather."

Revjak looked at the dwarf curiously. "Gandalug?" he asked, remembering the improbable story Berkthgar had told him of how Bruenor's ancestor, the original Patron of Clan Battlehammer and the founder of Mithril Hall, had returned from the dead as a prisoner of the drow elves.

"The same," Stumpet answered.

"Yerself can call me prince," Bruenor said to Berkthgar, who huffed and looked away.

"Thus you have returned to Icewind Dale," Revjak intervened, before the discussion could turn ugly. It seemed to the barbarian leader that Bruenor did not appreciate the level of antipathy Berkthgar had cultivated for the dwarves—either that, or Bruenor simply didn't care. "You're here to visit?"

"To stay," Bruenor corrected. "The mines are being opened as we sit here talkin'. Cleaning out the things that've crawled in and fixing the supports. We'll be taking ore in a week and hammering out goods the day after that."

Revjak nodded. "Then this is a visit for purposes of business," he reasoned.

"And for friendship," Bruenor was quick to reply. "Better if the two go together, I say."

"Agreed," Revjak said. He looked up to notice that Berkthgar was chewing hard on his lip. "And I trust that your clan will be fair with its prices for goods that we need."

"We've got the metal, ye've got the skins and the meat," Bruenor answered.

"You have nothing that we need," Berkthgar interjected suddenly and vehemently. Bruenor, smirking, looked up at him. After returning the look for just a moment, Berkthgar looked directly to Revjak. "We need nothing from the dwarves," the warrior stated. "All that we need is provided by the tundra."

"Bah!" Bruenor snorted. "Yer stone speartips bounce off good mail!"

"Reindeer wear no mail," Berkthgar replied dryly. "And if we come to war with Ten-Towns and the allies of Ten-Towns, our strength will put the stone tips through anything a dwarf can forge."

Bruenor sat up straight and both Revjak and Stumpet tensed, fearing that the fiery red-bearded dwarf would pounce upon Berkthgar for such an open threat.

Bruenor was older and wiser than that, though, and he looked instead to Revjak. "Who's speaking for the tribe?" the dwarf asked.

"I am," Revjak stated firmly, looking directly at Berkthgar.

Berkthgar didn't blink. "Where is Aegis-fang?" the giant man asked.

There it was, Bruenor thought, the point of it all, the source of the argument from the very beginning. Aegis-fang, the mighty warhammer forged by Bruenor himself as a gift to Wulfgar, the barbarian lad who had become as his son.

"Did you leave it in Mithril Hall?" Berkthgar pressed, and it seemed to Bruenor that the warrior hoped the answer would be yes. "Is it hanging useless as an ornament on a wall?"

Stumpet understood what was going on here. She and Bruenor had discussed this very point before they had set out on the return to Icewind Dale. Berkthgar would have preferred it if they had left Aegis-fang in Mithril Hall, hundreds and hundreds of miles away from Icewind Dale. So far away, the weapon would not have cast its shadow over him and his own great sword, Bankenfuere, the Northern Fury. Bruenor would hear nothing of such a course, though. Aegis-fang was his greatest accomplishment, the pinnacle of his respectable career as a weaponsmith, and even more importantly, it was his only link to his lost son. Where Bruenor went, Aegis-fang went, and Berkthgar's feelings be damned!

Bruenor hedged for a moment on the question, as if he was trying to figure out the best tactical course. Stumpet was not so ambivalent. "The hammer's in the mines," she said determinedly. "Bringed by Bruenor, who made it."

Berkthgar's scowl deepened and Stumpet promptly attacked.

"Ye just said the dale'll give ye all ye're needin'," the priestess howled. "Why're ye caring for a dwarf-made hammer, then?"

The giant barbarian didn't reply, but it seemed to both Bruenor and Revjak as if Stumpet was gaining the upper hand here.

"Of course that own sword ye wear strapped to yer back was not made in the dale," she remarked. "Ye got it in trade, and it, too, was probably made by dwarves!"

Berkthgar laughed at her, but there was no mirth in Revjak's tent, for his laugh seemed more of threat than of mirth.

"Who are these dwarves who call themselves our friends?" Berkthgar asked. "And yet they will not give over to the tribe a weapon made legendary by one of the tribe."

"Yer talk is getting old," Bruenor warned.

"And you are getting old, dwarf," Berkthgar retorted. "You should not have returned." With that, Berkthgar stormed from the tent.

"Ye should be watchin' that one," Bruenor said to Revjak.

The barbarian leader nodded. "Berkthgar has been caught in a web spun of his own words," he replied. "And so have many others, mostly the young warriors."

"Always full o' fight," Bruenor remarked.

Revjak smiled and did not disagree. Berkthgar was indeed one to be watched, but in truth, there was little Revjak could do. If Berkthgar wanted to split the tribe, enough would agree and follow him so that Revjak could not stop him. And even worse, if Berkthgar demanded the Right of Challenge for the leadership of the united tribe, he would have enough support so that Revjak would find it difficult to refuse.

Revjak was too old to fight Berkthgar. He had thought the ways of the barbarians of Icewind Dale changed when Wulfgar had united the tribes. That is why he had accepted the offered position as leader when Wulfgar had left, though in the past such a title could be earned only by inheritance or by combat, by deed or by blood.

Old ways died hard, Revjak realized, staring at the tent flap through which Berkthgar had departed. Many in the tribe, especially those who had returned from Mithril Hall, and even a growing number of those who had remained with Revjak waxed nostalgic for the freer, wilder days gone by. Revjak often happened upon conversations where older men retold tales of the great wars, the unified attack upon Ten-Towns, wherein Wulfgar was captured by Bruenor.

Their nostalgia was misplaced, Revjak knew. In the unified attack upon Ten-Towns, the warriors had been so completely slaughtered that the tribes had barely survived the ensuing winter. Still, the stories of war were always full of glory and excitement, and never words of tragedy. With the excitement of Berkthgar's return along with the return of Bruenor and the dwarves, many remembered too fondly the days before the alliance.

Revjak would indeed watch Berkthgar, but he feared that to be all he could do.

\* \* \* \* \*

Outside the tent, another listener, young Kierstaad, nodded his agreement with Bruenor's warning. Kierstaad was truly torn, full of admiration for Berkthgar but also for Bruenor. At that moment though, little of that greater struggle entered into the young man's thoughts.

Bruenor had confirmed that Aegis-fang was in the dale!

\* \* \* \* \*

"Might be the same storm that hit us near the Gull Rocks," Robillard remarked, eyeing the black wall that loomed on the eastern horizon before the *Sea Sprite.*

"But stronger," Deudermont added. "Taking power from the water." They were still in the sunshine, six days out from Caerwich, with another eight to the Moonshaes, by Deudermont's figuring.

The first hints of a head wind brushed against the tall captain's face, the first gentle blows of the gales that would soon assault them.

"Hard to starboard!" Deudermont yelled to the sailor at the wheel. "We shall go north around it, north around the Moonshaes," he said quietly, so that only Robillard could hear. "A straighter course to our port."

The wizard nodded. He knew that Deudermont did not want to turn to the north, where the wind was less predictable and the waters choppier and colder, but he understood that they had little choice at this point. If they tried to dodge the storm to the south, they would wind up near the Nelanther, the Pirate Isles, a place the *Sea Sprite,* such a thorn in the side of the pirates, did not want to be.

So, north they would go, around the storm, and around the Moonshaes. That was the hope, anyway. In looking at the wall of blackness, often creased by a shot of lightning, Robillard was not sure they could run fast enough.

"Do go and fill our sails with your magical wind," Deudermont bade him, and the captain's quiet tone showed that he obviously shared the wizard's trepidation.

Robillard moved to the rail of the poop deck and sat down, slipping his legs under the rail so that he was facing the mainmast. He held his left hand up toward the mast and called on the powers of his ring to create a gust of wind. Such a minor enchantment would not tax the powers of the wizard's mighty ring, and so Robillard enacted it again and again, filling the sails, launching the *Sea Sprite* on a swift run.

Not swift enough. The black wall closed in on them, waves rocking the *Sea Sprite* and soon turning her ride into more of a bounce than a run. A grim choice lay before Deudermont. He could either drop the sails and batten everything down in an attempt to ride out the storm, or keep up the run, skirting the edge of the storm in a desperate attempt to slip off to the north of it.

"Luck be with us," the captain decided, and he tried the run, keeping the sails full until, at last, the storm engulfed them.

She was among the finest ships ever built, crewed by a handpicked group of expert sailors that now included two powerful wizards, Drizzt, Catti-brie and Guenhwyvar, and she was captained by one of the most experienced and well-respected seamen anywhere along the Sword Coast. Great indeed were the powers of the *Sea Sprite* when measured by the standards of man, but tiny she seemed now in the face of the sheer weight of nature. They tried to run, but like a skilled hunter, the storm closed in.

Guide ropes snapped apart and the mast itself bent for the strain. Robillard tried desperately to counter, so did Harkle Harpell, but even their combined magic could not save the mainmast. A crack appeared along the main vertical beam, and the only thing that saved it was the snapping of the horizontal guide beam.

Out flapped the sail, knocking one man from the rigging to splash into the churning sea. Drizzt moved immediately, yelling to Guenhwyvar, calling the panther to his side and then sending her over the rail in search of the sailor. Guenhwyvar didn't hesitate—they had done this before. Roaring all the way, the cat splashed into the dark water and disappeared immediately.

Rain and hail pelted them, as did the walls of waves that splashed over the bow. Thunder boomed all about the tossing ship, more than one bolt of lightning slamming into the tall masts.

"I should have stopped the run sooner!" Deudermont cried, and though he screamed with all his strength, Drizzt, standing right beside him, could barely hear him over the roar of the wind and the pounding of the thunder.

The drow shook his head. The ship was nearly battened down, most of the crew had gone below, and still the *Sea Sprite* was being tossed wildly. "We are on the edges because of the run," the drow said firmly. "If you had stopped earlier, we would be in the heart of the storm and surely doomed!"

Deudermont heard only a few of the words, but he understood the gist of what his dark elven friend was trying to communicate. Grateful, he put a hand on Drizzt's shoulder, but suddenly went flying away, slamming hard against the rail and nearly toppling over, as a huge wave nearly lay the *Sea Sprite* down on her side.

Drizzt caught up to him in an instant, the drow's enchanted bracers and sheer agility allowing him to navigate on the rocking deck. He helped the captain to his feet and the two struggled for the hatch.

Deudermont went down first, Drizzt stopping to survey the deck, to make sure that everyone else had gone below. Only Robillard remained, wedged in with his thighs pressing against the rail, cursing the storm and throwing magical gusts into the teeth of the raging wind. The wizard noticed that Drizzt was looking at him, and he waved the drow away, then pointed to his ring, reminding Drizzt that he had enough magical power to save himself.

As soon as he got into the cramped deck below, Drizzt took out the panther figurine. He had to hope that Guenhwyvar had found the sailor and had him in her grasp, for if he waited any longer, the man would surely be drowned anyway. "Go home, Guenhwyvar," he said to the statue.

He wanted to call Guenhwyvar back almost immediately, to find out if the man had been saved, but a wave slammed the ship and the figurine flew off into the darkness. Drizzt scrambled, trying to follow its course, but it was too cramped and too dark.

In the blackness belowdecks, the terrified crew had no way of really knowing if this was the same storm that had battered them before. If it was, then it had indeed intensified, for this time, the *Sea Sprite* was tossed about like a toy. Water washed over them from every crack in the deck above, and only their frantic bailing, coordinated and disciplined despite the darkness and the terror, kept the ship afloat. It went on for more than two hours, two horrible gut-wrenching hours, but Drizzt's estimate of the value of Deudermont's run was accurate. The *Sea Sprite* was on the fringe of the storm, not in its heart; no ship in all the Realms could have survived this storm in full.

Then all went quiet, except for the occasional thunder boom, growing ever more distant. The *Sea Sprite* was listing badly to port, but she was up.

Drizzt was the first on deck, Deudermont right behind him. The damage was extensive, especially to the mainmast.

"Can we repair her?" Drizzt asked.

Deudermont didn't think so. "Not without putting into port," he replied, not bothering to mention the fact that the nearest port might be five hundred miles away.

Catti-brie came up soon after, bearing the onyx figurine. Drizzt wasted no time in calling to the panther, and when the cat came on deck, she was escorted by a very sorry-looking sailor.

"There is a tale for your grandchildren," Deudermont said in a chipper voice to the man, clapping him on the shoulder and trying to keep up the morale of those near him. The stricken sailor nodded sheepishly as two other crewmen helped him away.

"So fine a friend," Deudermont remarked to Drizzt, indicating Guenhwyvar. "The man was surely doomed."

Drizzt nodded and dropped a hand across Guenhwyvar's muscled flank. Never did he take the cat's friendship for granted.

Catti-brie watched the drow's actions intently, understanding that saving the sailor was important to Drizzt for reasons beyond the drow's altruistic demeanor. Had the sailor drowned, that would have been one more weight of guilt laid across the shoulders of Drizzt Do'Urden, one more innocent sacrificed because of the ranger's dark past.

But that had not come to pass, and it seemed for a moment as if the *Sea Sprite* and all of her crew had survived. That happy notion fell away a moment later, though, when Harkle bounded over, asking a simple, but poignant question. "Where is Robillard?"

All eyes turned to regard the forward rail of the poop deck, to see that the rail had split apart in precisely the spot where Drizzt had last seen the wizard.

Drizzt's heart nearly failed him and Catti-brie rushed to the rail and began surveying the empty water.

Deudermont didn't seem so upset. "The wizard has ways to escape the storm," the captain assured the others. "It has happened before."

True enough, Drizzt and Catti-brie realized. On several occasions Robillard had left the *Sea Sprite* by use of his magic in order to attend a meeting of his guild in Waterdeep, even though the ship was sailing waters hundreds of miles removed from that city at the time.

"He cannot drown," Deudermont assured them. "Not while he wears that ring."

Both the friends seemed satisfied with that. Robillard's ring was of the Elemental Plane of Water, a powerfully enchanted device that gave the wizard many advantages on the sea, no matter the strength of a storm. He might have been hit by lightning, or might have been knocked unconscious, but more likely, he had been swept away from the *Sea Sprite* and forced to use his magic to get clear of the storm long before the ship ever did.

Catti-brie continued her scan, and Drizzt joined her.

Deudermont had other business to attend to, he had to figure out how he was going to get the *Sea Sprite* into a safe port. They had weathered the storm and survived, but that might prove to be a temporary reprieve.

Harkle, in watching the captain's movements and in surveying the extensive damage to the schooner, knew it too. He moved quietly to Deudermont's cabin, hiding his eagerness until he was safely locked away. Then he rubbed his hands together briskly, his smile wide, and took out a leather book.

Glancing around to ensure that no one was watching, Harkle opened a magical tome, one of the components he needed for his newest, and perhaps most powerful spell. Most of the pages were blank—all of them had been blank until Harkle had first cast his fog of fate. Now the first few pages read as a journal of Harkle's magical ride to join the *Sea Sprite,* and, he was glad to see, of his continuing experiences with the ship. To his absolute amazement, for he hadn't dared look so extensively at the journal before, even the blind seer's poem was there, word for word.

The fog of fate was working still, Harkle knew, for neither he nor any other man had penned a single word into the journal. The continuing enchantment of the spell was recording the events!

This exceeded Harkle's wildest expectations for the fog of fate. He didn't know how long this might continue, but he understood that he had stumbled onto something very special here. And something that needed a little boost. The *Sea Sprite* was dead in the water, and so was the quest that had apparently befallen Drizzt and Catti-brie, and by association, Harkle. Harkle wasn't one to be patient, not now. He waved his hand over the first of the many blank pages, chanting softly. He reached into a pouch and produced some diamond dust, sprinkling it sparingly onto the first of the still-blank pages.

Nothing happened.

Harkle continued for nearly an hour, but when he emerged from the cabin, the *Sea Sprite* was still listing, still drifting aimlessly.

Harkle rubbed the stubble on his unshaven face. Apparently, the spell needed more work.

* * * * *

Robillard stood on top of the rolling water, tapping his foot impatiently. "Where is that brute?" he asked, referring to the water elemental monster he had summoned to his aid. He had sent the creature in search of the *Sea Sprite,* but that had been many minutes ago.

Finally, the azure blanket before the wizard rolled up and took on a roughly humanoid shape. Robillard gurgled at it, asking the creature in its own watery language if it had found the ship.

It had, and so the wizard bade the elemental to take him to it. The creature held out a huge arm. It appeared watery, but was in truth much more substantial than any normal liquid. When the wizard was comfortably in place, the monster whisked him away with the speed of a breaking wave.

# Chapter 12
## THE FOG OF FATE

he crew worked through the afternoon, but they seemed to be making little progress on the extensive damage the ship had taken. They could hoist one of the sails, the mizzen-sail, but they couldn't control it to catch the wind, or to steer the ship in any desired direction.

Thus was their condition when Catti-brie called out an alert from the crow's nest. Deudermont and Drizzt rushed side by side to see what she was calling about, both fearing that it might be a pirate vessel. If that was the case, damaged as she was and without Robillard, the proud *Sea Sprite* might be forced to surrender without a fight.

No pirate blocked their path, but directly ahead loomed a curtain of thick fog. Deudermont looked up to Catti-brie, and the young woman, having no explanation, only shrugged in reply. This was no usual occurrence. The sky was clear, except for this one fog bank, and the temperature had been fairly constant.

"What would cause such a mist?" Drizzt asked Deudermont.

"Nothing that I know of," the captain insisted. "Man some oars!" he yelled out to the crew. "Try to put up a sail. Let us see if we can navigate around it."

By the time Deudermont turned his attention back to the sea before them, however, he found Drizzt shaking his head doubtfully, for the fog already loomed much nearer. It was not stationary.

"It is approaching us," the captain breathed in disbelief.

"Swiftly," Drizzt added, and then the drow, with his keen ears, heard the chuckle of Harkle Harpell and knew in his heart that this was the wizard's work. He turned in time to

146

see the man disappearing through the hatch belowdecks, and started to follow. Drizzt stopped before he reached the hatch, though, hearing Deudermont's gasp and the nervous cries of many crewmen.

Catti-brie scrambled down the rigging. "What is it?" she asked, near desperation.

Into the gray veil they went. The sound of splashing water went away, as did any sensation of movement. Crewmen huddled together and many drew out their weapons, as if expecting some enemy to climb aboard from the dark mist.

It was Guenhwyvar who gave Drizzt the next clue of what might be going on. The panther came to Drizzt's side, ears flattened, but her expression and demeanor showing more curiosity than fear.

"Dimensional," the drow remarked.

Deudermont looked at him curiously.

"This is Harkle's doing," Drizzt said. "The wizard is using his magic to get us off the open sea."

Deudermont's face brightened at that notion, so did Catti-brie's—at least until both of them took a moment to consider the source of their apparent salvation.

Catti-brie looked out at the thick fog. Suddenly, drifting in a damaged ship across empty waters did not seem like such a bad thing.

\* \* \* \* \*

"What do you mean?" Robillard roared. He slapped his hands together fiercely and translated his question into the watery, gurgling language of the water elemental.

The reply came without hesitation, and Robillard knew enough of such a creature to understand that it had the means to know the truth of the matter. This one had been cooperative, as elemental creatures go, and Robillard did not believe that it was lying to him.

The *Sea Sprite* was gone, vanished from the sea.

Robillard breathed a sigh of relief when he heard the next reply, that the ship had not sunk, had simply drifted out of the waters.

"Harkle Harpell," the wizard reasoned aloud. "He has gotten them into a port. Well done!" Robillard considered his own situation then, alone and so far from land. He commanded the elemental to keep him moving in a generally easterly direction, and explained that he would need the creature until the next dawn. Then he took out his spellbook, a fabulous leatherbound and watertight work, and moved its golden tassel bookmark to the page containing his teleportation spell.

Then the wizard sat back and relaxed. He needed to sleep, to gather his strength and his energy. The elemental would see to his safety for now, and in the morning he would use his spell to put him in his private room in the guild hall in Waterdeep. Yes, the wizard decided, it had been a difficult and boring few weeks, and now was a good time for some restful shore leave.

Deudermont would just have to catch up with him later.

\* \* \* \* \*

The *Sea Sprite* drifted in a surreal stillness, no sound of water or wind, for many minutes. The fog was so thick about them that Drizzt had to hang very low over the rail to even see the water. He didn't dare reach out and touch that gray liquid, not knowing what Harkle's spell, if this was indeed Harkle's spell, might be doing.

At last they heard a splash, the lap of a wave against the prow of the ship. The fog began to thin almost immediately, but though they couldn't see their surroundings, everyone on board sensed that something had changed.

"The smell," Catti-brie remarked, and the heads of all those near her bobbed in agreement. Gone was the salty aroma, so thick that it left a taste in your mouth, replaced by a crisp summer scent, filled with trees, flowers, and the slick feel of an inlet swamp. The sounds, too, had changed, from the empty, endless whistle of the wind and the muted splashes of deep water to the gentle lapping of lesser waves and the trilling of . . .

"Songbirds?" Drizzt asked.

The fog blew away, and all of the crew breathed a sigh

of relief, for they were near to land! To the left loomed a small island, tree-covered, centered by a small castle and dotted with large mansions. A long bridge stretched in front of the *Sea Sprite,* reaching from the island to the shore, to the docks of a fair-sized, walled town. Behind the town, the ground sloped up into tall mountains, a landmark that no sailor could miss, but that Deudermont did not know. Many boats were about, though none much bigger than the rowboats the *Sea Sprite* carried astern. All the crews stood, staring blankly at the magnificent sailing ship.

"Not Waterdeep," Deudermont remarked. "Nor anywhere near to the city that I know of."

Drizzt surveyed the area, studying the coastline that curled back behind them. "Not the open sea," he replied.

"A lake," Catti-brie reasoned.

All three of them looked at each other for a moment, then yelled out, "Harkle!" in unison. The Harpell, expecting the call, scrambled out of the hatch and bounded right up beside them, his expression full of cheer.

"Where are we?" Deudermont demanded.

"Where the fates wanted us to be," the mage said mysteriously, waving his arms, the voluminous sleeves of his robe flying wide.

"I'm thinking ye'll have to do better than that," Catti-brie put in dryly.

Harkle shrugged and lowered his arms. "I do not know for sure, of course," he admitted. "The spell facilitates the move—not a random thing—but wherever that might be, I cannot tell."

"The spell?" Deudermont asked.

"The fog of fate," Drizzt answered before Harkle could. "The same spell that brought you to us."

Harkle nodded through the drow's every word, his smile wide, his expression one of pride and accomplishment.

"You put us in a lake!" Deudermont roared angrily.

Harkle stammered for a reply, but a call from the water cut the private conversation short. "Yo ho, *Sea Sprite!*"

The four went to the rail, Drizzt pulling the hood of his cloak over his head. He didn't know where they were, or what reception they might find, but he felt it likely that the greeting would be less warm if these sailors discovered that the *Sea Sprite* carried a drow elf.

A fair-sized fishing boat had pulled up alongside, its crew of six studying the schooner intently. "You've seen battle," an old graybeard, seeming to be the skipper of the fishing boat, reasoned.

"A storm," Deudermont corrected. "As fierce a blow as I've ever known."

The six fishermen exchanged doubting looks. They had been on the water every day for the last month and had seen no storms.

"Far from here," Deudermont tried to explain, recognizing the doubting expressions.

"How far can you get?" the old graybeard asked, looking about at the ever-present shoreline.

"Ye'd be surprised," Catti-brie answered, casting a sidelong glance at the blushing Harkle.

"Where did you put in?" the graybeard asked.

Deudermont held his hands out wide. "We are the *Sea Sprite,* out of Waterdeep."

The doubting expressions turned into open smirks. "Waterdeep?" the graybeard echoed.

"Are we in another world?" Catti-brie whispered to Drizzt, and the drow found it hard to honestly comfort her, especially with Harkle Harpell behind it all.

"Waterdeep," Deudermont said evenly, seriously, with as much conviction as he could muster.

"You're a long way from home, captain," another of the fishermen remarked. "A thousand miles."

"Fifteen hundred," the graybeard corrected.

"And all of it land," another added, laughing. "Have you wheels on the *Sea Sprite*?" That brought a chuckle from the six and from several other crews of boats moving close to investigate.

"And a team of horses I'd like to see," a man on another boat put in, drawing more laughter.

Even Deudermont managed a smile, relieved that he and his ship were apparently still in the Realms. "Wizard's work," he explained. "We sailed the Sea of Swords, five hundred miles southwest of the Moonshaes, when the storm found us and left us drifting. Our wizard"—Deudermont looked over to Harkle—"cast some enchantment to get us into port."

"He missed," howled a man.

"But he got us off of the open sea," Deudermont said when the laughter died away. "Where we surely would have perished. Pray tell me, good sailors, where are we?"

"This is Impresk Lake," the graybeard replied, then pointed to shore, to the walled town. "Carradoon."

Deudermont didn't recognize the names.

"Those are the Snowflakes," the skipper continued, indicating the mountains.

"South," Catti-brie said suddenly. All eyes turned to her. "We are far south of Waterdeep," she said. "And if we sailed south from the lake, we'd get to the Deepwash, then to Vilhon Reach in the Inner Sea."

"You have the place," the graybeard announced. "But you'd not draw enough water to get that ship to Shalane Lake."

"And unless you've wings with those wheels, you won't be sailing over the Cloven Mountains!" the man beside the graybeard roared. But the laughter was subdued now, all the sailors, on the *Sea Sprite* and on the fishing boats, digesting the gravity of the situation.

Deudermont blew a long sigh and looked to Harkle, who cast his gaze to the deck. "We'll worry about where we are going later," Deudermont said. "For now, the task is to repair the *Sea Sprite.*" He turned to the graybeard. "I fear that your lake hasn't enough draw," he said. "Is there a long wharf, where we might put in for repairs?"

The skipper pointed to Carradoon Island, and one long dock jutting out in the direction of the *Sea Sprite.*

"The draw is deeper on the northern side of the island," the man next to him remarked.

"But the long dock is privately owned," a third fisherman put in.

"We'll get permission to put her in," the graybeard said firmly.

"But the task is not so easy," Deudermont interjected.

151

"We've not the sails, nor the steering to navigate. And I do not know these waters, obviously."

"Put out some lines, Captain . . ."

"Deudermont," the *Sea Sprite*'s captain replied. "Captain Deudermont."

"My name's Terraducket," the graybeard said. "Well met." He signaled to all the other boats as he spoke, and already they were swarming about the *Sea Sprite,* trying to get in position.

"We'll get you in to the docks, and Carradoon has a fair number of shipwrights to help in your repairs," Terraducket went on. "Even on that mast, though we'll have to find a tall tree indeed to replace it! Know that it will cost you a fair number of stories about your sailing adventures on the Sea of Swords, if I know my fellows!"

"We've a fair number to tell!" Deudermont assured him.

The ropes went out and the fishing fleet put in line and began to guide and tow the great schooner.

"The brotherhood of sailors extends to those upon the lakes," Drizzt remarked.

"So it would seem," Deudermont agreed. "If we had crew to replace, I'd know where to begin my search." The captain looked over to Harkle, who was still staring forlornly at the deck. "You did well, Master Harpell," Deudermont said, and the wizard's face brightened as he looked up at the man. "We would have perished in the uncharted waters so far from the Moonshaes, and now we shall live."

"But on a lake," Harkle replied.

Deudermont waved that notion away. "Robillard will find us, and the two of you will find a way to put us back where we belong, I do not doubt. For now, my ship and my crew are safe, and that is all that matters. Well done!"

Harkle verily glowed.

"But why are we here?" Catti-brie had to ask.

"The fog of fate," Drizzt and Harkle said in unison.

"And that means that there is something here that we need," the wizard went on.

"Need for what?" Catti-brie asked.

"For the quest, of course!" Harkle roared. "That is what this is all about, is it not?" He looked around as if that should explain everything, but saw that the stares coming back at him were not looks of comprehension. "Before the storm, we were heading for . . ."

"Waterdeep," Deudermont answered. "Your spell has not put us closer to Waterdeep."

Harkle waved his hands frantically. "No, no," he corrected. "Not for Waterdeep, but for a priest, or perhaps a wizard, in Waterdeep."

"And you think that we're more likely to find a spellcaster of the power we need here than in Waterdeep?" Drizzt asked incredulously. "In this tiny town so far from home?"

"Good Captain Terraducket," Harkle called.

"Here," came the reply from farther away than before, for Terraducket's fishing boat had moved forward to join in the towing line.

"We seek a priest," Harkle said. "A very powerful priest . . ."

"Cadderly," Terraducket interrupted without hesitation. "Cadderly Bonaduce. You'll not find a more powerful priest in all the Realms!" Terraducket boasted, as if this Cadderly was the property of all of Carradoon.

Harkle cast a superior glance at his friends. "Fog of fate," he remarked.

"And where might we find this Cadderly?" Deudermont asked. "In Carradoon?"

"No," came Terraducket's reply. "Two day's march out, into the mountains, in a temple called the Spirit Soaring."

Deudermont looked to Harkle, no more doubting questions coming to surface.

Harkle clapped his hands together. "Fog of fate!" he said again. "Oh, and it all fits so well," he said excitedly, as though another thought had just popped into his head.

"Fits like the *Sea Sprite* in a lake," Catti-brie put in sarcastically, but Harkle just ignored her.

"Don't you see?" the wizard asked them all, excited once more and flapping those winglike arms. "*Sea Sprite* and Spirit Soaring. SS and SS, after all! And fog of fate, ff."

"I'm needin' a long sleep," Catti-brie groaned.

"And HH!" Harkle bellowed. Drizzt looked at him curiously. "Harkle Harpell!" the excited wizard explained, then he poked a finger the drow's way. "And DD for Drizzt Do'Urden! FF for fog of fate, and SS and SS, HH and DD! And you . . ." he pointed at Catti-brie.

"Doesn't work," the young woman assured him.

"Doesn't matter," Drizzt added. Deudermont was biting hard on his lip, trying not to steal Harkle's moment of glory with a burst of laughter.

"Oh, there's something in the letters," Harkle said, speaking to himself more than to the others. "I must explore this!"

"Explore yer mind," Catti-brie said to him, and then she added under her breath, so that only Drizzt and Deudermont could hear, "Better take a big lantern and a dwarf's cave pack."

That brought a snicker.

"But your father!" Harkle yelled suddenly, leaping at Catti-brie. She barely held back from slugging him, so great was her surprise.

"Me father?" she asked.

"BB!" Harkle, Drizzt, and Deudermont all said together, the drow and the captain feigning excitement.

Catti-brie groaned again.

"Yes, yes. Bruenor Battlehammer," Harkle said to himself, and started walking away. "BB. Oh, I must explore the correlation of the letters, yes, I must."

"While ye're thinkin' on it, find the correlation of BF," Catti-brie said to him. The distracted wizard nodded and rambled along, making a straight path to Deudermont's private quarters, which Harkle had practically taken over.

"BF?" the captain asked Catti-brie.

"Babbling fool," she and Drizzt replied together, drawing yet another laugh from those nearby. Still, neither Drizzt nor Catti-brie, Deudermont nor any of the others could dismiss the fact that the "babbling fool" had apparently saved the *Sea Sprite,* and had put them closer to their goal.

# Part 3

THE NATURE OF EVIL

hey are the absolutes, the pantheon of ideals, the goodly gods and the evil fiends, forever locked in the struggle for the souls of the mortals. The concept that is Lloth is purely evil; that of Mielikki, purely good. As opposite as black and white, with no shades of gray in between.

Thus are the concepts, good and evil. Absolute, rigid. There can be no justification for a truly evil act; there is no shade of gray. While an act of good often brings personal gain, the act itself is absolute as its measure is based on intent. This is epitomized by our beliefs in the pantheon, but what of the mortal races, the rational beings—the humans and the races of elvenkind and dwarvenkind, the gnomes and the halflings, the goblinoids and giantkin? Here the question muddles, the absolutes blend.

To many, the equation is simple: I am drow, drow are evil, thus I am evil.

They are wrong. For what is a rational being if not a choice? And there can be no evil, nor any good, without intent. It is true that in the Realms there are races and cultures, particularly the goblinoids, which show

157

*a general weal of evil, and those, such as the surface elves, which lean toward the concept of good. But even in these, which many consider personifications of an absolute, it is the individual's intents and actions that ultimately decide. I have known a goblin who was not evil; I am a drow who has not succumbed to the ways of his culture. Still, few drow and fewer goblins can make such claims, and so the generalities hold.*

*Most curious and most diverse among the races are the humans. Here the equation and the expectations muddle most of all. Here perception reins supreme. Here intent is oft hidden, secret. No race is more adept than humans at weaving a mask of justification. No race is more adept than humans at weaving a mask of excuses, at ultimately claiming good intent. And no race is more adept at believing its own claims. How many wars have been fought, man against man, with both armies espousing that god, a goodly god, was on their side and in their hearts?*

*But good is not a thing of perception. What is "good" in one culture cannot be "evil" in another. This might be true of mores and minor practices, but not of virtue. Virtue is absolute.*

*It must be. Virtue is the celebration of life and of love, the acceptance of others and the desire to grow toward goodness, toward a better place. It is the absence of pride and envy, the willingness to share our joys and to bask in the accomplishments of others. It is above justification because it is what truly lies in each and every heart. If a person does an evil act, then let him weave his mask, but it will not hide the truth, the absolute, from what is naked within his own heart.*

*There is a place within each of us where we cannot hide from the truth, where virtue sits as judge. To admit the truth of our actions is to go before that court, where process is irrelevant. Good and evil are intents, and intent is without excuse.*

*Cadderly Bonaduce went to that place as willingly and completely as any man I have known. I recognize that growth within him, and see the result, the Spirit Soaring, most majestic and yet most humble of human accomplishments.*

*Artemis Entreri will go to that place. Perhaps not until the moment of his death, but he will go, as we all must eventually go, and what agony he will realize when the truth of his evil existence is laid bare before him. I pray that he goes soon, and my hope is not born of vengeance, for vengeance is an empty prayer. May Entreri go of his own volition to that most private place within his heart to see the truth and, thus, to correct his ways. He will find joy in his penance, true harmony that he can never know along his present course.*

*I go to that place within my heart as often as I am able in order to escape the trap of easy justification. It is a painful place, a naked place, but only there might we grow toward goodness; only there, where no mask can justify, might we recognize the truth of our intents, and thus, the truth of our actions. Only there, where virtue sits as judge, are heroes born.*

—Drizzt Do'Urden

# Chapter 13
## THE SPIRIT SOARING

rizzt, Catti-brie, Deudermont, and Harkle
encountered no trouble as they left Carradoon
for their trek into the Snowflake Mountains.
The drow kept the cowl of his cloak pulled low,
and everyone in town was so excited by the
presence of the schooner that none paid too much attention
to the group as they departed.

Once they got past the gate, the foursome found the
going easy and safe. Guided around any potential problems
by the drow ranger, they found nothing remarkable, nothing exciting.

Given what they had all been through over the last few
weeks, that was just the way they wanted it.

They chatted easily, mostly with Drizzt explaining to
them the nature of the wildlife about them—which birds
went with which chatter, and how many deer had made the
beds of flattened needles near to one grove of pines. Occasionally the conversation drifted to the task at hand, to the
blind seer's poem. This put poor Harkle in quite a predicament. He knew that the others were missing obvious
points, possibly critical points in the verse, for with his
journal, he had been able to scrutinize the poem thoroughly. The wizard wasn't sure how much he could intervene, though. Fog of fate had been created as a passive
spell, a method for Harkle to facilitate, and then witness
dramatic unfolding events. If he became an active partici-
pant in those events by letting another of the players in
this drama glance at his enchanted journal, or by using
what the journal had shown to him, he would likely ruin
the spell.

Certainly Harkle could use his other magical abilities if fate led them to battle, and certainly he could use his intuition, as in the discussion on the *Sea Sprite* when they had first agreed that they needed to see a sorcerer or a priest. But direct intervention, using information given by the facilitation of the spell, would alter the future perhaps, and thus defeat the intentions of fate. Harkle's spell had never been created for such a purpose; the magic had its edges. Poor Harkle didn't know how far he could push that boundary. In living his forty years surrounded by wizards at least as outrageous as he, he understood all too well the potentially grave side effects of pushing magic too far.

So Harkle let the other three babble through their discussions of the poem, nodding his head and agreeing with whatever seemed to be the most accepted interpretation of any given line. He avoided any direct questions, though his halfhearted shrugs and mumbled responses brought many curious looks.

The trails climbed higher into the mountains, but the going remained easy, for the path was well-worn and oft-traveled. When the foursome came out from under the gloom of the mountain canopy, off the path and onto a flat meadow near to the edge of one steep drop, they understood why.

Drizzt Do'Urden had seen the splendors of Mithril Hall, so had Catti-brie. With his magic, Harkle Harpell had visited many exotic places, such as the Hosttower of the Arcane in Luskan. Deudermont had sailed the Sword Coast from Waterdeep to exotic Calimport. But none of those places had ever taken the breath from any of the four like the sight before them now.

It was called the Spirit Soaring, a fitting name indeed for a gigantic temple—a cathedral—of soaring towers and flying buttresses, of great windows of colored glass and a gutter system finished at every corner with an exotic gargoyle. The lowest edges of the cathedral's main roof were still more than a hundred feet from the ground, and three of the towers climbed to more than twice that height.

The Baenre compound was larger, of course, and the Hosttower was more obviously a free-flowing creation of magic. But there was something more solemn about this place, more reverent and holy. The stone of the cathedral was gray and brown, unremarkable really, but it was the construction of that stone, the earthly, and even greater, strength of the place that gave them awe. It was as though the cathedral's roots were deep in the mountains and its soaring head touched the heavens themselves.

A beautiful melody, a voice rich and sweet, wafted out of the temple, reverberated off the stones. It took the four a moment to even realize that it was a voice, a human voice, for the Spirit Soaring seemed to have a melody all its own.

The grounds were no less spectacular. A grove of trees lined a cobblestone walk that led up to the temple's massive front doors. Outside that perfectly straight tree line was a manicured lawn, thick and rich, bordered by perfectly-shaped hedgerows and filled with various flower beds, all red and pink, purple and white. Several leafy bushes dotted the lawn as well, and these had been shaped to resemble various woodland animals—a deer and a bear, a huge rabbit and a group of squirrels.

Catti-brie blinked several times when she spotted the gardener, the most unusual dwarf she, who had been raised by dwarves, had ever seen. She poked Drizzt, pointing out the little fellow, and the others noticed, too. The gardener saw them, and began bobbing their way, smiling widely.

His beard was green—green!—split in half and pulled back over his large ears, then twisted with his long green hair into a single braid that dangled more than halfway down his back. He wore a thin sleeveless robe, pale green in color, that hung halfway to the knee, leaving bare his bowed legs, incredibly hairy and powerfully muscled. Bare too were the dwarf's large feet, except for the thin straps of his open-toed sandals.

He cut an intersecting course, coming onto the cobblestones thirty feet ahead of the foursome. There he skidded to a stop, stuck two fingers in his mouth, looked back over his shoulder and gave a shrill whistle.

"What?" came a call a moment later. A second dwarf, this one looking more like what the foursome would expect, rose up from the shade of the tree closest to the temple door. He had broad, square shoulders and a yellow beard. Dressed all in brown, he wore a huge axe strapped on his back and a helmet adorned with deer antlers.

"I told ye I'd help ye!" the yellowbeard roared. "But ye promised me sleep time!" Then this second dwarf noticed the foursome and he stopped his tirade immediately and bobbed down the path toward the group.

The green-bearded dwarf got there first. He said not a word, but gave a dramatic bow, then took up Catti-brie's hand and kissed it. "Hee hee hee," he squeaked with a blush, moving in turn from Catti-brie to Deudermont, to Drizzt, to . . .

Back to Drizzt, where the little one ducked low, peeking up under the full hood.

The drow obliged him, pulling back the hood and shaking out his thick white mane. First meetings were always difficult for Drizzt, especially so far from those places where he was known and accepted.

"Eek!" the little one squealed.

"A stinkin' drow!" roared the yellowbeard, running down the path, tearing the axe off of his back as he came.

Drizzt wasn't surprised, and the other three were more embarrassed than startled.

The greenbeard continued to hop up and down and point, benign enough, but the yellowbeard took a more direct and threatening course. He brought his axe up high over his head and bore down on Drizzt like a charging bull.

Drizzt waited until the last possible second, then, using the magical anklets and his honed reflexes, he simply side-stepped. The yellowbeard stumbled as he passed, running headlong into the tree behind the drow.

The greenbeard looked to the other dwarf, then to Drizzt, seeming for a moment as if he, too, meant to charge. Then he looked back to the other dwarf, noting the axe now stuck in the tree. He walked toward the yellowbeard, bracing himself and slapping the dwarf hard on the side of the head.

"A stinkin' drow!" the yellowbeard growled, taking one hand from his axe handle to fend off the continuing slaps.

Finally he managed to yank his axe free, but when he leaped about, he found three of the four, the drow included, standing impassively. The fourth, though, the auburn-haired woman, held a bow taut and ready.

"If we wanted ye dead, we'd've cut ye down afore ye got up from yer nap," she said.

"I mean no ill," Drizzt added. "I am a ranger," he said, mostly to the greenbeard, who seemed the more level-headed of the two. "A being of the forest, as are you."

"Me brother's a druid," the yellowbeard said, trying to appear firm and tough, but seeming rather embarrassed at the moment.

"Doo-dad!" the greenbeard agreed.

"Druid dwarf?" Catti-brie asked. "I've lived most o' me life with dwarves, and have never heared of a druid among the race."

Both dwarves cocked their heads curiously. Surely the young woman sounded dwarfish with her rough accent.

"What dwarves might that be?" the yellowbeard asked.

Catti-brie lowered Taulmaril. "I am Catti-brie," she said. "Adopted daughter of Bruenor Battlehammer, Eighth King of Mithril Hall."

The eyes of both dwarves popped open wide, and their mouths similarly dropped open. They looked hard at Catti-brie, then at each other, back to Catti-brie, and back to each other. They bumped their foreheads together, a firm, smacking sound, then looked back to Catti-brie.

"Hey," the yellowbeard howled, poking a stubby finger Drizzt's way. "I heared o' ye. Ye're Drizzt Dudden."

"Drizzt Do'Urden," the drow corrected, giving a bow.

"Yeah," the yellowbeard agreed. "I heared o' ye. Me name's Ivan, Ivan Bouldershoulder, and this is me brother, Pikel."

"Me brudder," the greenbeard agreed, draping an arm across Ivan's sturdy shoulders.

Ivan glanced back over his shoulder, to the deep cut he had put in the tree. "Sorry about me axe," he said. "I never seen a drow elf."

"Ye come to see the cathedr . . . the catheter . . . the cathe . . . the durned church?" Ivan asked.

"We came to see a man named Cadderly Bonaduce," Deudermont answered. "I am Captain Deudermont of the *Sea Sprite*, sailing out of Waterdeep."

"Ye sailed across land," Ivan said dryly.

Deudermont had his hand up to wave away that expected response before the dwarf ever began it.

"We must speak with Cadderly," Deudermont said. "Our business is most urgent."

Pikel slapped his hands together, put them aside his tilted head, closed his eyes and gave a snore.

"Cadderly's takin' his nap," Ivan explained. "The little ones wear him out. We'll go and see Lady Danica and get ye something to eat." He winked at Catti-brie. "Me and me brother're wanting to hear more about Mithril Hall," he said. "Word says an old one's running the place since Bruenor Battlehammer packed up and left."

Catti-brie tried to hide her surprise, even nodded as though she was not surprised by what Ivan had to say. She glanced at Drizzt, who had no response. Bruenor had left? Suddenly both of them wanted to sit and talk with the dwarves as well. The meeting with Cadderly could wait.

The inside of the Spirit Soaring was no less majestic and awe-inspiring than the outside. They entered the main area of the cathedral, the central chapel, and though there were at least a score of people within, so large was the place that the four strangers each felt alone. All of them found their eyes inevitably moving up, up to the soaring columns, past several ledges lined with decorated statues, past the glow coming in through the stained glass windows, to the intricately carved vaulting of the ceiling more than a hundred feet above them.

When he finally managed to move the stricken four through the main area, Ivan took them through a side door, into rooms more normally sized. The construction of the place, the sheer strength and detail of the place, continued to overwhelm them. No supporting arch or door was without decoration, and one door they went through was so covered in runes and sculptures that Drizzt believed he could stand and study it for hours and hours without seeing every detail, without deciphering every message.

Ivan knocked on a door, then paused for an invitation to enter. When it came, he swung the door open. "I give ye Lady Danica Bonaduce," the dwarf said importantly, motioning for the others to follow.

They started in, Deudermont in the lead, but the captain stopped short, was nearly tripped, as two young children, a boy and a girl, cut across his path. Seeing the stranger, both skidded to a halt. The boy, a sandy-haired lad with almond-shaped eyes, opened his mouth and pointed straight at the drow.

"Please excuse my children," a woman across the room said.

"No offense taken," Drizzt assured her. He bent to one knee, and motioned the pair over. They looked to each other for support, then moved cautiously to the drow, the boy daring to reach up and touch Drizzt's ebony skin. Then he looked at his own fingers, as if to see if some of the coloring had rubbed off.

"No black, Mum," he said, looking to the woman and holding up his hand. "No black."

"Hee hee," Pikel chuckled from the back.

"Get the brats outa here," Ivan whispered to his brother.

Pikel pushed through so that the children could see him, and their faces brightened immediately. Pikel stuck a thumb into each ear and waggled his fingers.

"Oo, oi!" the children roared in unison, and they chased "Uncle Pike" from the room.

"Ye should be watching what me brother's teaching them two," Ivan said to Danica.

She laughed and rose from her chair to greet the visitors. "Surely the twins are better off for having a friend such as Pikel," she said. "And such as Ivan," she graciously added, and the tough-as-iron dwarf couldn't hide a blush.

Drizzt understood that the woman was a warrior simply by the way she walked across the room, lightly, silently, in perfect balance through the complete motion of every step. She was slight of build, a few inches shorter than Cattibrie and no more than a hundred and ten pounds, but every muscle was honed and moved in harmony. Her eyes were even more exotic than those of her children, almond-shaped and rich brown, full of intensity, full of life. Her hair, strawberry blond and as thick as the drow's white mane, bounced gaily about her shoulders as though the abundance of energy that flowed within this woman could not be contained.

Drizzt looked from Danica to Catti-brie, saw a resemblance there in spirit, if not in body.

"I give ye Drizzt Dudden," Ivan began, pulling the deer-antlered helmet from his head. "Catti-brie, daughter of Bruenor of Mithril Hall, Captain Deudermont of the *Sea Sprite,* outa Waterdeep, and . . ." The yellow-bearded dwarf stopped and looked curiously at the skinny wizard. "What'd ye say yer name was?" he asked.

"Harpell Harkle . . . er, Harkle Harpell," Harkle stuttered, obviously enchanted by Danica. "Of Longsaddle."

Danica nodded. "Well met," she said to each of them in turn, ending with the drow.

"Drizzt Do'Urden," the ranger corrected.

Danica smiled.

"They came to speak to Cadderly," Ivan explained.

Danica nodded. "Go and wake him," she said, still holding Drizzt's hand. "He will not want to miss an audience with such distinguished visitors."

Ivan hopped away, rambling down the hallway.

"Ye've heared of us?" Catti-brie asked.

Danica looked at her and nodded. "Your reputation precedes you," she assured the young woman. "We have heard of Bruenor Battlehammer and the fight to reclaim Mithril Hall."

"And the war with the drow elves?" Drizzt asked.

Danica nodded. "In part," she replied. "I hope that before you leave you will find the time to tell us the story in full."

"What do ye know o' Bruenor's leavin'?" Catti-brie asked bluntly.

"Cadderly knows more of that than I," Danica replied. "I have heard that Bruenor abdicated his reclaimed throne to an ancestor."

"Gandalug Battlehammer," Drizzt explained.

"So it is said," Danica went on. "But where the king and the two hundred loyal to him went, that I do not know."

Drizzt and Catti-brie exchanged glances, both having a fair guess as to where Bruenor might have gone.

Ivan returned then, along with an old, but sprightly man dressed in a tan-white tunic and matching trousers. A light blue silken cape was pulled back from his shoulders, and a wide-brimmed hat, blue and banded in red topped his head. At the front center of the hat band sat a porcelain and gold pendant that depicted a candle burning above an eye, which all of the four recognized as the holy symbol of Deneir—the god of literature and art.

The man was of average height, around six feet, and was muscular, despite his advanced age. His hair, what was left of it, was mostly silver in hue, with a hint of brown. Something about his appearance seemed strangely out of place to the companions. Drizzt finally recognized it to be the man's eyes, striking gray orbs that seemed full of sparkle, the eyes of a younger man.

"I am Cadderly," he said warmly with a humble bow. "Welcome to the Spirit Soaring, the home of Deneir and of Oghma, and of all the goodly gods. You have met my wife, Danica?"

Catti-brie looked from the old Cadderly, to Danica, who could not have been much older than Catti-brie, certainly not yet out of her twenties.

"And yer twins," Ivan added with a smirk, eyeing Catti-brie as she studied Danica. It seemed to perceptive Drizzt and Deudermont that the dwarf was familiar with such confusion upon such an introduction, a fact that led them both to think that Cadderly's advanced age was no natural thing.

"Ah, yes, the twins," Cadderly said, shaking his head and unable to contain a smirk at the mere thought of his boisterous legacy.

The wise priest studied the expressions of the four, appreciating their gracious withholding of the obvious questions. "Twenty-nine," he remarked offhandedly. "I am twenty-nine years old."

"Thirty in two weeks," Ivan added. "Though ye're not looking a day over a hunnerd and six!"

"It was the task of building the cathedral," Danica

explained, and there was just a hint of sorrow and anger in her controlled tones. "Cadderly gave to the place his life force, a choice he made for the glory of his god."

Drizzt looked long and hard at the young woman, the dedicated warrior, and he understood that Danica, too, had been forced into a great sacrifice because of Cadderly's choice. He sensed an anger within her, but it was buried deep, overwhelmed by her love for this man and her admiration for his sacrifice.

Catti-brie didn't miss any of it. She, who had lost her love, surely empathized with Danica, and yet, she knew that this woman was undeserving of any sympathy. In those few sentences of explanation, in the presence of Cadderly and of Danica, and within the halls of this most reverent of structures, Catti-brie understood that to give sympathy to Danica would belittle the sacrifice, would diminish what Cadderly had accomplished in exchange for his years.

The two women looked into each other's eyes, locking gazes, Danica's exotic almond-shaped orbs and Catti-brie's large eyes, the richest shade of blue. Catti-brie wanted to say, "At least you have your lover's children," wanted to explain to Danica the emptiness of her own loss, with Wulfgar gone before . . .

Before so much, Catti-brie thought with a sigh.

Danica knew the story, and simply in sharing that long look with Catti-brie, she understood and appreciated what was in the woman's heart.

The eight—for Pikel soon returned, explaining that the children were sleeping in the gardens and being watched over by several priests—spent the next two hours exchanging tales. Drizzt and Cadderly seemed kindred spirits and indeed, had shared many adventures. Both had faced a red dragon and lived to tell the tale, both had overcome legacies of their past. They hit it off splendidly, as did Danica and Catti-brie, and though the dwarven brothers wanted to hear more of Mithril Hall, they found it hard in cracking into the conversation between the women, and the one between Drizzt and Cadderly. Gradually they gave up, and spent their time engaged with Harkle. He had been to

Mithril Hall and had participated in the drow war, and turned out to be quite the storyteller, highlighting his tales with minor illusions.

Deudermont felt strangely removed from it all. He found himself missing the sea and his ship, longing to sail again out of Waterdeep Harbor to chase pirates on the open waters.

It might have gone on for all of the afternoon, except that a priest knocked on the door, informing Danica that the children were awake. The woman started to leave with the dwarves, but Drizzt stopped her. He took out the panther figurine and called to Guenhwyvar.

That set Ivan back on his heels! Pikel squealed, too, but in glee, the dwarfish druid always willing to meet with such a magnificent animal, despite the fact that the animal could tear the features from his face.

"The twins will enjoy their time with Guenhwyvar," the drow explained.

The great cat ambled out of the room, Pikel in close pursuit, grabbing the panther's tale that Guenhwyvar might pull him along.

"Not as much as me brother," Ivan, still a bit shaken, remarked.

Danica was going to ask the obvious question of safety, but she held the thought in check, realizing that if the panther wasn't to be trusted, Drizzt would never have brought it in. She smiled and bowed graciously, then left with Ivan. Catti-brie would have gone, but Drizzt's posture, suddenly formal, told her that it was time to speak of business.

"You have not come here merely to exchange tales, fine though they may be," Cadderly said, and he sat up straight, folding his hands in front of him, ready to hear their most important story in full.

Deudermont told it, Drizzt and Catti-brie adding in points they thought necessary, and Harkle constantly highlighting the story with remarks that really had nothing to do with anything as far as the other four could tell.

Cadderly confirmed that he had read of Caerwich and the blind seer. "She speaks in riddles that are not always what they seem," he warned.

"So we have heard," Deudermont agreed. "But this is one riddle my friends cannot ignore."

"If the seer spoke truthfully, then a friend lost, my father Zaknafein, is in the clutches of an evil being," Drizzt explained. "A minion of Lloth, perhaps, or a matron mother of one of Menzoberranzan's ruling houses."

Harkle bit hard on his lip. He saw a mistake here, but had to consider the limitations of his spell. He had read the blind seer's poem, word by word, at least a score of times, committing it fully to memory. But that was privileged information, beyond the scope of his spell. The fog of fate facilitated what would be, but if Harkle used the information that the spell privately gave to him, then he might be altering fate. What that might mean, catastrophe or better conclusion, the wizard could only guess.

Cadderly nodded, not disagreeing with Drizzt's reasoning, but wondering where he might fit in all of this, wondering what role the visitors expected him to play.

"I expect it is a handmaiden," Drizzt went on. "An extraplanar being of the Abyss."

"You wish me to use my powers to confirm this," Cadderly reasoned. "Perhaps to bring forth the beast that you might bargain or battle for your father's soul."

"I understand the depth of my request," Drizzt said firmly. "A yochiol is a powerful being . . ."

"I learned long ago not to fear evil," Cadderly calmly assured him.

"We have gold," Deudermont offered, thinking the price would be high.

Drizzt knew better. In the short time he had been with Cadderly, the drow understood the man's heart and motivations. Cadderly would not take gold, would take no payment at all. He was not surprised when Cadderly answered simply, "One soul is worth saving."

# Chapter 14

## THE FLUSTERED WIZARD

here's Deudermont?" Catti-brie asked of Harkle when the wizard stumbled into a small side room where the young woman was sitting with Drizzt.

"Oh, out and about, out and about," the distracted Harpell replied. There were two chairs in the room, both set before a large window that looked out over the majestic Snowflakes. Drizzt and Catti-brie occupied these, half-facing each other and half-looking out to the beautiful view. The dark elf reclined, his feet up on the window's wide sill. Harkle considered the scene for just a moment, then seemed to collect his wits and moved right between the two. He motioned Drizzt to take his feet away, then hopped up to sit on the window sill.

"Do join us," Catti-brie said with obvious sarcasm—obvious to Drizzt at least, for Harkle smiled dumbly.

"You were discussing the poem, of course," the wizard reasoned. It was partially true. Drizzt and Catti-brie were talking as much about the news that Bruenor had left Mithril Hall as about the all-important poem.

"Of course you were," Harkle said. "That is why I have come."

"Have you deciphered any more of the verse?" Drizzt asked, not too hopeful. The drow liked Harkle, but had learned not to expect too much from the wizard. Above all else, Harkle and his kin were unpredictable sorts, oftentimes of great help, as in the fight for Mithril Hall, and at other times more a detriment than an advantage.

Harkle recognized the drow's ambivalent tone, and he found that he wanted to prove himself at that moment, wanted to tell the drow all of the information in his magical journal, to recite the poem word by word, exactly as the seer had told it. Harkle bit back the words, though, fearful of the limitations of his spell and the potential consequences.

"We're thinking it's Baenre," Catti-brie said. "Whoever's holding the Baenre throne, I mean. 'Given to Lloth and by Lloth given,' is what she said, and who better than the one sitting on Baenre's throne for the Spider Queen to give such a gift?"

Harkle nodded, letting Drizzt take up the thought, but believing that they were slipping off track.

"Catti-brie thinks that it is Baenre, but the seer spoke of the Abyss, and that makes me believe that Lloth has engaged a handmaiden," said Drizzt.

Harkle bit hard on his lip and nodded unconvincingly.

"Cadderly has an informant in the Abyss," Catti-brie added. "An imp, or something akin to that. He'll summon the beastie and try to find us a name."

"But I fear that my road . . ." Drizzt began.

"Our road," Catti-brie corrected, so firmly that Drizzt had to concede the point.

"I fear that our road will once again lead to Menzoberranzan," Drizzt said with a sigh. He didn't want to go back there, that much was obvious, but it was clear also that the ranger would charge headlong into the accursed city for the sake of a friend.

"Why there?" Harkle asked, his voice almost frantic. The wizard saw where the seer's poem had guided Drizzt, and knew that the second line, the one concerning Drizzt's father's ghost, had forced the ranger to think of Menzoberranzan as the source of it all. There were references in the poem to Menzoberranzan, but there was one word in particular that led Harkle to believe that the drow city was not their ultimate goal.

"We have already discussed that," Drizzt replied. "Menzoberranzan would seem to be the dark road the seer spoke of."

"You think it is a handmaiden?" Harkle asked Drizzt. The drow half-nodded, half-shrugged.

"And you agree?" Harkle questioned Catti-brie.

"Might be that it is," Catti-brie replied. "Or might be a matron mother. That'd be me own guess."

"Aren't handmaidens female?" Harkle's question seemed irrelevant.

"All of Lloth's closest minions are female," Catti-brie replied. "That's why the Spider Queen's one to be fearin'," she added with a wink, trying to break some of the tension.

"As are all of the matron mothers," Harkle reasoned.

Drizzt looked to Catti-brie; neither of them quite understanding what the unpredictable wizard might be getting at.

Harkle flapped his arms suddenly, looking as if he was about to burst. He hopped down from the window, nearly overturning Drizzt in his chair. "She said *he*!" the flustered wizard cried. "The blind hag said *he*! 'The traitor to Lloth is sought by *he* who hates him most!'" Harkle stopped and gave a great, exasperated sigh. Then there came a hissing sound and a line of gray smoke began wafting out of his pocket.

"Oh, by the gods," the wizard moaned.

Drizzt and Catti-brie both jumped to their feet, more because of the wizard's surprisingly acute reasoning than because of the present smoky spectacle.

"What foe, Drizzt?" Harkle pressed with all urgency, the wizard suddenly suspecting that his time was short.

"He," Catti-brie echoed over and over, trying to jog her memory. "Jarlaxle?"

"'Who is most unshriven,'" Harkle reminded her.

"Not the mercenary, then," said Drizzt, for he had come to the conclusion that Jarlaxle was not as evil as many. "Berg'inyon Baenre, perhaps. He has hated me since our days in the Academy."

"Think! Think! Think!" Harkle shouted as a great gout of smoke rose up from his pocket.

"What are you burning?" Catti-brie demanded, trying to pull the Harpell around so that she could better see. To her surprise and horror, her hand went right through the wizard's suddenly-less-than-corporeal form.

"Never mind that!" Harkle snapped at her. "Think, Drizzt Do'Urden. What foe, who is most unshriven, who festers in the swirl of Abyss and hates you above all? What beast must be freed, that only you can free?" Harkle's voice seem to trail away as his form began to fade.

"I have exceeded the limits of my spell," the wizard tried to explain to his horrified companions. "And so I am out of it, I fear, sent away . . ."

Harkle's voice came back strong, unexpectedly. "What beast, Drizzt? What foe?" And then he was gone, simply gone, leaving Drizzt and Catti-brie standing and staring blankly in the small room.

That last call, as Harkle faded from view, reminded Drizzt of another time when he had heard such a distant cry.

"Errtu," the drow whispered breathlessly. He shook his head even as he spoke the obvious answer, for, though Harkle's reasoning seemed sound, it didn't make sense to Drizzt, not in the context of the poem.

"Errtu," Catti-brie echoed. "Suren that one's hating ye above all, and Lloth'd likely know him, or know of him."

Drizzt shook his head. "It cannot be, for never did I meet the tanar'ri in Menzoberranzan, as the blind seer declared."

Catti-brie thought on that one for a moment. "She never said Menzoberranzan," the woman replied. "Not once."

"In the home that was . . ." Drizzt began to recite, but he nearly gagged on the words, on the sudden realization that his interpretation of their meaning might not be correct.

Catti-brie caught it, too. "Ye never called that place yer home," she said. "And ye often told me that yer first home was . . ."

"Icewind Dale," Drizzt said.

"And it was there that ye met Errtu, and made o' him an enemy," Catti-brie reasoned, and Harkle Harpell seemed a wise man indeed at that moment.

Drizzt winced, remembering well the power and wickedness of the evil balor. It pained the ranger to think of Zaknafein in Errtu's clutches.

* * * * *

Harkle Harpell lifted his head from his huge desk and stretched with a great yawn.

"Oh, yes," he said, recognizing the pile of parchments spread on the desk before him. "I was working on my spell."

Harkle sorted them out and studied them more closely.

"My new spell!" he cried in glee. "Oh, it is finally completed, the fog of fate! Oh, joy, oh happy day!" The wizard leaped up from his chair and twirled about the room, his voluminous robes flying wide. After so many months of exhausting research, his new spell was finally complete. The possibilities rolled through Harkle's mind. Perhaps the fog of fate would take him to Calimshan, on an adventure with a pasha, perhaps to Anauroch, the great desert, or perhaps even to the wastelands of Vaasa. Yes, Harkle would like to go to Vaasa and the rugged Galena Mountains.

"I will have to learn more of the Galenas and have them fully in mind when I cast the spell," he told himself. "Yes, yes, that's the trick." With a snap of his fingers, the wizard rushed to his desk, carefully sorted and arranged the many parchments of the long and complicated spell and placed them in a drawer. Then he rushed out, heading for the library of the Ivy Mansion, to gather information on Vaasa and neighboring Damara, the famed Bloodstone Lands. He could hardly keep his balance, so excited was he about what he believed to be the initial casting of his new spell, the culmination of months of labor.

For Harkle had no recollection of the true initial casting. All of the last few weeks had been erased from his mind as surely as the pages of the enchanted journal that accompanied the spell were now blank once more. As far as Harkle knew, Drizzt and Catti-brie were sailing off the coast of Waterdeep, in a pirate hunting ship whose name he did not know.

* * * * *

Drizzt stood beside Cadderly in a square room, gorgeously decorated, though not a single piece of furniture was in it. The walls were all of polished black stone, bare, except for twisted iron wall sconces, one set in the exact center of each wall. The torches in these were not burning, not in the conventional sense. They were made of black metal, not wood, each with a crystal ball set at its top. The light—it seemed that Cadderly could conjure whatever colored light he chose—emanated from the balls. One was glowing red now, another yellow, and two green, giving the room a strange texture of colors and depth, with some hues seeming to penetrate more deeply into the glassy surface of the polished walls than others.

All of that held Drizzt's attention for a while, an impressive spectacle indeed, but it was the floor that most amazed the dark elf, who had seen so many amazing sights in his seven decades of life. The perimeter of the floor was black and glassy, like the walls, but the bulk of the floor area was taken up by a mosaic, a double-lined circle. The area between the lines, about a foot wide, was filled with arcane runes. A sign was etched inside, its starlike tips touching the innermost circle. All of these designs had been cut into the floor, and were filled with crushed gemstones of various colors. There was an emerald rune beside a ruby star, both of which were between the twin diamond lines of the outer circles.

Drizzt had seen rooms like this in Menzoberranzan, though certainly not as fabulously made. He knew its function. Somehow it seemed out of place to him in this most goodly of structures, for the twin circles and the sign were used for summoning otherworldly creatures, and because those runes that decorated the edges were of power and protection, the creatures summoned were not likely of a goodly weal.

"Few are allowed to enter this place," Cadderly explained, his voice grave. "Just myself, Danica, and Brother Chaunticleer among the residents of the library. Any guests that require the services of this place must pass the highest of scrutiny."

Drizzt understood that he had just been highly complimented, but that did not dissuade the many questions that bobbed about in his thoughts.

"There are reasons for such callings," Cadderly went on, as if reading the drow's mind. "Sometimes the cause of good can be furthered only by dealing with the agents of evil."

"Is not the summoning of a tanar'ri, or even a minor fiend, in itself an act of evil?" Drizzt asked bluntly.

"No," Cadderly replied. "Not in here. This room is perfect in design and blessed by Deneir himself. A fiend called is a fiend trapped, no more a threat in here than if the beast had remained in the Abyss. As with all questions of good and evil, the intent of the calling is what determines its value. In this case, we have discovered that a soul undeserving of such torture has fallen into the hands of a fiend. We may retrieve that soul only by dealing with the fiend. What better place and better way?"

Drizzt could accept that, especially now, when the stakes were so high and so personal.

"It is Errtu," the drow announced with confidence. "A balor."

Cadderly nodded, not disagreeing. When Drizzt had informed him of his new suspicions given his talk with Harkle Harpell, Cadderly had called upon a minor fiend, a wicked imp, and had sent it on a mission seeking confirmation of the drow's suspicions. Now he meant to call back the imp and get his answers.

"Brother Chaunticleer communed with an agent of Deneir this day," Cadderly remarked.

"And the answer?" the ranger asked, though Drizzt was a bit surprised by the apparent route Chaunticleer had taken.

"No agent of Deneir could give such an answer," Cadderly replied at once, seeing that the drow's reasoning was off course. "No, no, Chaunticleer desired information about our missing wizard friend. Fear not, for Harkle Harpell, it seems, is back at the Ivy Mansion in Longsaddle. We have ways of contacting him, even of retrieving him, if you so desire."

"No!" Drizzt blurted, and he looked away, a bit embarrassed by his sudden outburst. "No," he repeated more quietly. "Harkle Harpell has certainly done enough already. I would not endanger him in this issue that does not truly concern him."

Cadderly nodded and smiled, understanding the truth of the drow's hesitance. "Shall I call now to Druzil, that we might get our answer?" he asked, though he didn't even wait for a response. With a word to each sconce, Cadderly turned all the lights in the room to a velvety purple hue. A second chant made the designs in the floor glow eerily.

Drizzt held his breath, never comfortable in the midst of such a ceremony. He hardly listened as Cadderly began a soft, rhythmic chant, rather he focused on the glowing runes, concentrated on his suspicions and on the possibilities the future might hold.

After several minutes there came a sharp hissing sound in the middle of the circles, and then an instant of blackness as the fabric of the planes tore asunder. A sharp crackle ended both the hissing and the tear, leaving a very angry looking bat-winged and dog-faced imp sitting on the floor, cursing and spitting.

"Well, greetings my dear Druzil," Cadderly said cheerily, which of course made the wicked imp, the unwilling servant, grumble all the more. Druzil hopped to his feet, his small horns hardly reaching the height of Drizzt's knee, and folded his leathery wings about him.

"I wanted you to meet my friend," Cadderly said casually. "I haven't yet decided whether or not I will have him cut you into little pieces with those fine blades of his."

The evil gaze from Druzil's black eyes locked onto Drizzt's lavender orbs. "Drizzt Do'Urden," the imp spat. "Traitor to the Spider Queen."

"Ah, good," Cadderly said, and his tone told the imp that he had unwittingly offered up a bit of information by admitting his recognition of the drow. "You know of him, thus you have spoken with some fiend who knows the truth."

"You desired a specific answer, and only one," Druzil rasped. "And promised a year of peace from you in return!"

"So I did," Cadderly admitted. "And have you my answer?"

"I pity you, foolish drow," Druzil said, staring again intently at Drizzt. "I pity you and laugh at you. Foolish drow. The Spider Queen cares little for you now, because she has given out your punishment as a reward to one who helped her in the Time of Troubles."

Drizzt pulled his gaze from Druzil to regard Cadderly, the old priest standing perfectly calm and collected.

"I pity any who so invokes the rage of a balor," Druzil went on, giving a wicked little laugh.

Cadderly saw that the imp's attitude was difficult for Drizzt, who was under such intense stress from this all. "The balor's name!" the priest demanded.

"Errtu!" Druzil barked. "Mark it well, Drizzt Do'Urden!"

Fires simmered behind Drizzt's lavender eyes, and Druzil could not bear their scrutiny.

The imp snapped his evil gaze over Cadderly instead. "A year of peace, you promised," he rasped.

"Years are measured in different ways," Cadderly growled back at him.

"What treachery—" Druzil started to say, but Cadderly slapped his hands together, uttering a single word, and two black lines, rifts in the fabric of the planes, appeared, one on either side of the imp, and came together as forcefully as Cadderly's hands came together. With a boom of thunder and a waft of smoke, Druzil was gone.

Cadderly immediately brightened the light in the room, and remained quiet for some time, regarding Drizzt, who stood with his head bowed, digesting the confirmation.

"You should utterly destroy that one," the drow said at length.

Cadderly smiled widely. "Not so easy a task," he admitted. "Druzil is a manifestation of evil, a type more than an actual being. I could tear apart his corporeal body, but that merely sends him back to the Abyss. Only there, in his smoking home, could I truly destroy Druzil, and I have little desire to visit the Abyss!" Cadderly shrugged, as if it really mattered very little. "Druzil is harmless enough," the priest explained, "because I know him, know of him, know where to find him, and know how to make his miserable life more miserable still if the need arises."

"And now we know that it is truly Errtu," Drizzt said.

"A balor," Cadderly replied. "A mighty foe."

"A foe in the Abyss," said Drizzt. "A place where I also have no desire to ever go."

"We still need answers," Cadderly reminded. "Answers that Druzil would not be able to provide."

"Who, then?"

"You know," Cadderly answered quietly.

Drizzt did know, but the thought of summoning in the fiend Errtu was not a pleasant one to Drizzt.

"The circle will hold the balor," Cadderly assured him. "You do not have to be here when I call to Errtu."

Drizzt waved that notion away before Cadderly ever finished the sentence. He would be there to face the one who hated him most, and who apparently held captive a friend.

Drizzt gave a deep sigh. "I believe that the prisoner the hag spoke of is Zaknafein, my father," he confided to the priest, for he found that he truly trusted Cadderly. "I am not yet certain of how I feel about that."

"Surely it torments you to think your father in such foul hands," Cadderly replied. "And surely it thrills you to think that you might meet with Zaknafein once more."

Drizzt nodded. "It is more than that," he said.

"Are you ambivalent?" Cadderly asked, and Drizzt, caught off his guard by the direct question, cocked his head and studied the old priest. "Did you close that part of your life, Drizzt Do'Urden? And now are you afraid because it might again be opened?"

Drizzt shook his head without hesitation, but it was an unconvincing movement. He paused a long while, then sighed deeply. "I am disappointed," the drow admitted. "In myself, for my selfishness. I want to see Zaknafein again, to stand beside him and learn from him and listen to his words." Drizzt looked up at Cadderly, his expression truly serene. "But I remember the last time I saw him," he said, and he told Cadderly then of that final meeting.

Zaknafein's corpse had been animated by Matron Malice, Drizzt's mother, and then imbued with the dead drow's spirit. Bound in servitude to evil Malice, working as her assassin, Zaknafein had then gone out into the Underdark in search of Drizzt. At the critical moment, the true Zaknafein had broken through the evil matron mother's will for a fleeting moment, had shone forth once again and spoken to his beloved son. In that moment of victory, Zaknafein's spirit had proclaimed its peace, and Zaknafein had destroyed his own animated corpse instead, freeing Drizzt and freeing himself from the grasp of evil Malice Do'Urden.

"When I heard the blind hag's words and spent the time to consider them, I was truly sorry," Drizzt finished. "I believed that Zaknafein was free of them now, free of Lloth and all the evil, and sitting in a place of just rewards for the truth that was always in his soul."

Cadderly put a hand on Drizzt's shoulder.

"To think that they had captured him once again . . ."

"But that may not be the case," Cadderly said. "And if it is true, then hope is not lost. Your father needs your help."

Drizzt set his jaw firmly and nodded. "And Catti-brie's help," he replied. "She will be here when we call to Errtu."

# Chapter 15

# DARKNESS INCARNATE

is smoking bulk nearly filled the circle. His great leathery wings could not extend to their fullest, else they would have crossed the boundary line where the fiend could not pass. Errtu clawed at the stone and issued a guttural growl, threw back his huge and ugly head and laughed maniacally. Then the balor suddenly calmed, and looked forward, his knowing eyes boring into the gaze of Drizzt Do'Urden.

Many years had passed since Drizzt had looked upon mighty Errtu, but the ranger surely recognized the fiend. His ugly face seemed a cross between a dog and an ape, and his eyes—especially those eyes—were black pits of evil, sometimes wide with outrage and red with flame, sometimes narrowed, slanted, intense slits promising hellish tortures. Yes, Drizzt remembered Errtu well, remembered their desperate fight on the side of Kelvin's Cairn those years before.

The ranger's scimitar, the one he had taken from the white dragon's lair, seemed to remember the fiend, too, for Drizzt felt it calling to him, urging him to draw it forth and strike at the balor again that it might feed upon Errtu's fiery heart. That blade had been forged to battle creatures of fire, and seemed particularly eager for the smoking flesh of a fiend.

Catti-brie had never seen such a beast, darkness incarnate, evil embodied, the most foul of the foul. She wanted to take up Taulmaril and shoot an arrow into the beast's ugly face, and yet she feared that to do so would loose wicked Errtu upon them, something the young woman most certainly did not desire.

Errtu continued to chuckle, then with terrifying speed, the great fiend lashed out toward Drizzt with its many-thonged whip. The weapon snapped forward, then stopped fast in midair, as though it had hit a wall, and indeed it had.

"You cannot send your weapons, your flesh, or your magic through the barrier, Errtu," Cadderly said calmly—the old priest seemed not shaken in the least by the true tanar'ri.

Errtu's eyes narrowed wickedly as the balor dropped his gaze over Cadderly, knowing that it was the priest who had dared to summon the balor. Again came that rumbling chuckle and flames erupted at Errtu's huge, clawed feet, burning white and hot, blazing so high that they nearly blocked the companions' view of the balor. The three friends squinted against the intense, stinging heat. At last, Catti-brie fell away with a shout of warning, and Drizzt heeded that call, went with her. Cadderly remained in place, though, standing impassively, confident that the rune-etched circles would stop the fires. Sweat beaded on his face, droplets falling from his nose.

"Desist!" Cadderly yelled above the crackle. Then he recited a string of words in a language that neither Drizzt nor Catti-brie had ever heard before, an arcane phrase that ended with the name of Errtu, spoken emphatically.

The balor roared as if in pain, and the fire walls fell away to nothingness.

"I will remember you, old man," the great balor promised. "When I walk again on the plane that is your world."

"Do pay me a visit," Cadderly replied evenly. "It would be my pleasure to banish you back to the filth where you truly belong."

Errtu said no more, but growled and focused once more upon the renegade drow, the most-hated Drizzt Do'Urden.

"I have him, drow," the fiend teased. "In the Abyss."

"Who?" Drizzt demanded, but the balor's response was yet another burst of maniacal laughter.

"Who do you have, Errtu?" Cadderly asked firmly.

"No questions must I answer," the balor reminded the priest. "I have him, that you know, and the one way you have of getting him back is to end my banishment. I will take him to this, your land, Drizzt Do'Urden, and if you want him, then you must come and get him!"

"I will speak with Zaknafein!" Drizzt yelled, his hand going to the hilt of his hungry scimitar. Errtu mocked him, laughed at him, thoroughly enjoying the spectacle of Drizzt's frustration. It was just the beginning of the drow's torment.

"Free me!" the fiend roared, silencing the questions. "Free me now! Each day is an eternity of torture for my prisoner, your beloved fa—" Errtu stopped abruptly, letting the teasing word hang in the air. The balor waggled a finger at Cadderly. "Have I been tricked?" Errtu said, feigning horror. "Almost did I answer a question, something that is not required of me."

Cadderly looked to Drizzt, understanding the ranger's dilemma. The priest knew that Drizzt would willingly leap into the circle and fight Errtu here and now for the sake of his lost father, of a friend, or of any goodly person, but to free the fiend seemed a desperate and dangerous act to the noble drow, a selfish act for the sake of his father that might jeopardize so many others.

"Free me!" roared the balor, his thunderous voice echoing about the chamber.

Drizzt relaxed suddenly. "That I cannot do, foul beast," he said quietly, shaking his head, seeming to gain confidence in his decision with every passing second.

"You fool!" Errtu roared. "I will flail the skin from his bones! I will eat his fingers! And I will keep him alive, I promise, alive and conscious through it all, telling him before each torture that you refused to help him, that you caused his doom!"

Drizzt looked away, relaxed no more, his breathing coming in hard, angry gasps. He knew the truth of Zaknafein, though, understood his father's heart, and knew that the weaponmaster would not wish Drizzt to free Errtu, whatever the cost.

Catti-brie took Drizzt's hand, as did Cadderly.

"I'll not tell you what to do, good drow," the old priest

offered, "but if the fiend imprisons a soul undeserving of such a fate, then it is our responsibility to save . . ."

"But at what price?" Drizzt said desperately. "At what cost to the world?"

Errtu was laughing again, wildly. Cadderly turned to quiet the fiend, but Errtu spoke first. "You know, priest," the fiend accused. "You know!"

"What does the ugly thing mean?" Catti-brie asked.

"Tell them," Errtu bade Cadderly, who seemed uncomfortable for the first time.

Cadderly looked at Drizzt and Catti-brie and shook his head.

"Then I shall tell them!" Errtu shouted, the balor's tremendous, throaty voice echoing again about the stone room, paining their ears.

"You shall be gone!" Cadderly promised, and he began a chant. Errtu jerked suddenly, violently, then seemed smaller, seemed as if he was falling back in on himself.

"I am free now!" the balor proclaimed.

"Wait," Drizzt bade Cadderly, and the priest obeyed.

"I shall go where I please, foolish Drizzt Do'Urden! By your will I have touched the ground of the Prime Material Plane, and thus my banishment is at its end. I can return to the call of any!"

Cadderly began his chant again, more urgently, and Errtu began to fade away.

"Come to me, Drizzt Do'Urden," the balor's now-distant voice beckoned. "If you would see him again. I'll not come for you."

Then the fiend was gone, leaving the three companions exhausted in the empty room. Most weary among them was Drizzt, who slumped back against the wall, and it seemed to the others as if the solid stone was the only thing keeping the weary ranger on his feet.

"Ye didn't know," Catti-brie reasoned, understanding the guilt that so weighed on her friend's shoulders. She looked to the old priest who hardly seemed bothered by the revelations.

"Is it true?" Drizzt asked Cadderly.

"I cannot be certain," the priest replied. "But I believe

that our summoning of Errtu to the Prime Material Plane might have indeed ended the balor's banishment."

"And ye knew it all along," Catti-brie said in accusing tones.

"I suspected," Cadderly admitted.

"Then why did you let me call to the beast?" Drizzt asked, completely surprised. He would never have figured that Cadderly would end the banishment of such an evil monster. When he looked at the old priest now, though, it seemed to Drizzt as if Cadderly wasn't bothered in the least.

"The fiend, as is always the case with such denizens, can get to the Prime Material Plane only with assistance from a priest or a wizard," Cadderly explained. "Any of that ilk who so desired such a beast could find many, many waiting for their call, even other balors. The freeing of Errtu, if indeed Errtu is free, is not so much a travesty."

Put in that context, it made sense to Drizzt and to Catti-brie. Those who desired to call a fiend to their service would find no shortage; the Abyss was full of powerful denizens, all eager to come forth and wreak havoc among the mortals.

"The thing I fear," Cadderly admitted, "is that this particular balor hates you above all, Drizzt. He may, despite his last words, seek you out if he ever gets back to our world."

"Or I will seek out Errtu," Drizzt replied evenly, unafraid, and that brought a smile to Cadderly's lips. It was just the response he had hoped to hear from the courageous drow. Here was a mighty warrior in the war for good, Cadderly knew. The priest held great faith that if such a battle were to come about, Drizzt and his friends would prevail, and the torment of Drizzt's father would come to an end.

\* \* \* \* \*

Waillan Micanty and Dunkin Tallmast arrived at the Spirit Soaring later that day, and found Captain Deudermont outside the structure, relaxing in the shade of a tree, feeding strange nuts to a white squirrel.

"Percival," Deudermont explained to the two men, holding his hand out to the squirrel. As soon as Percival snatched the treat, Deudermont pointed out Pikel Bouldershoulder, hard at work as always, tending his many gardens. "Pikel over there informs me that Percival is a personal friend of Cadderly's."

Waillan and Dunkin exchanged doubting looks, neither having a clue as to what Deudermont might be talking about.

"It is not important," the captain remarked, rising to his feet and brushing the twigs from his trousers. "What news on the *Sea Sprite*?"

"The repairs are well underway," replied Waillan. "Many of Carradoon's fishermen have joined in to help. They have even found a tree suitable to replace the mast."

"A friendly lot, these men of Carradoon," Dunkin put in.

Deudermont regarded Dunkin for a while, pleased at the subtle changes he had witnessed in the man. This was not the same surly and conniving emissary who had first come to the *Sea Sprite* in the name of Lord Tarnheel Embuirhan in search of Drizzt Do'Urden. The man was a fine sailor and a fine companion according to Waillan, and Deudermont planned to offer him a full-time position as a crewman aboard the *Sea Sprite* as soon as they figured out how to get the ship back in the Sea of Swords where she belonged.

"Robillard is in Carradoon," Waillan said unexpectedly, catching the captain off guard, though Deudermont never doubted that the wizard had survived the storm and would eventually find them. "Or he was. He might have gone back to Waterdeep by now. He says that he can get us back where we belong."

"But it will cost us," added Dunkin. "For the wizard will need help from his brotherhood, an exceptionally greedy lot, by Robillard's own admission."

Deudermont wasn't very concerned about that. The Lords of Waterdeep would likely reimburse any expenses. The captain did note Dunkin's use of the word "us," and that pleased him more than a little.

"Robillard said that it would take him some time to organize it all," Waillan finished. "But we're two weeks from repairing the *Sea Sprite* in any case, and with the help, it's easier fixing her here than in Waterdeep."

Deudermont only nodded. Pikel came bobbing over then, stealing the attention of Waillan and Dunkin. That was fine with Deudermont. The details of returning the *Sea Sprite* where she belonged would work themselves out, he did not doubt. Robillard was a competent and loyal wizard. But the captain saw a parting of the ways in his immediate future, for two friends (three, counting Guenhwyvar) wouldn't likely go back with the ship, or if they did, they wouldn't likely remain with her for long.

# Chapter 16
## THE BAIT

cewind Dale," Drizzt said, before the three had even left the room of summoning.

Cadderly looked surprised, but as soon as Catti-brie heard the words, she understood what Drizzt was talking about and agreed with his reasoning. "Ye're thinking that the fiend'll go after the crystal shard," she explained, more for Cadderly's sake than for any need of confirmation.

"If ever Errtu does get back to our world, then he will certainly go for the artifact," Drizzt replied.

Cadderly knew nothing about this crystal shard they referred to, but he realized that the pair believed they were on to something important. "You are sure of this?" he asked Drizzt.

The drow nodded. "When first I met Errtu, it was on a windswept mountain above the Spine of the World, in the place called Kelvin's Cairn in Icewind Dale," he explained. "The fiend had come to the call of the wizard who possessed Crenshinibon— the crystal shard—a most powerful artifact of evil."

"And where is this artifact?" Cadderly asked, suddenly seeming quite concerned. The priest had some experience in dealing with evil artifacts, had once put his own life and the lives of those he loved in jeopardy for the sake of destroying such an item.

"Buried," Catti-brie replied. "Buried under a mountain o' snow and rock by an avalanche down the side o' Kelvin's Cairn." She looked more at Drizzt than the priest as she spoke, her expression showing that she was beginning to doubt the drow's reasoning.

"The item is sentient," the ranger reminded her. "A malignant tool that will not accept such solitude. If Errtu gets back to our world, he will go to Icewind Dale in search of Crenshinibon, and if he is near to the thing, it will call out to him."

Cadderly agreed. "You must destroy this crystal shard," he said so determinedly that he caught them by surprise. "That is paramount."

Drizzt wasn't sure that he agreed with that priority, not with his father apparently held prisoner by the balor. But he did agree that the world would be a better place without the likes of Crenshinibon.

"How does one destroy so powerful an artifact?" the ranger dared to ask.

"I do not know. Each artifact has specific ways in which it may be undone," Cadderly replied. "A few years ago, when I was young, it was asked by my god to destroy the Ghearufu, a sentient and evil thing. I had to seek . . . to demand assistance from a great red dragon."

"A few years ago when I was young," Catti-brie repeated under her breath, so that neither of the others could hear.

"Thus I put it upon you now to find and destroy Crenshinibon, this artifact that you call the crystal shard."

"I'm not knowin' any dragons," Catti-brie remarked dryly.

Drizzt actually did know of another red, but he kept that quiet, having no desire to face the great wyrm called Hephaestus again and hoping that Cadderly would offer an alternative.

"When you have the item in your possession and Errtu is dealt with, then bring it back to me," Cadderly said. "Together, with the guidance of Deneir, we will discover how the crystal shard might be destroyed."

"Ye make it sound so easy," Catti-brie added, and again, her tone was ripe with sarcasm.

"Hardly," Cadderly said. "But I hold fast my faith. Would it please you more if I said 'if' instead of 'when'?"

"I'm gettin' yer point," Catti-brie replied.

Cadderly smiled broadly and draped an arm about the young woman's sturdy shoulders. Catti-brie didn't shy away from that embrace in the least, finding that she truly liked the priest. There was nothing about Cadderly that made her uncomfortable, except perhaps the casual way in which Cadderly dealt with such powers as Errtu and the crystal shard. Now that was confidence!

"We can't be gettin' the crystal shard out from under the pile," Catti-brie reasoned to Drizzt.

"Likely, it will find its own way out," Cadderly said. "Likely, it already has."

"Or Errtu will discover it," said Drizzt.

"So we're to go to Icewind Dale and wait?" Catti-brie huffed, suddenly realizing the depth of the task before them. "Ye're wanting to sit and serve as guardians? For how many centuries?"

Drizzt also wasn't pleased by the prospect, but the responsibility seemed clear to him, now that Errtu was apparently freed. The thought of seeing Zaknafein again would hold the drow even if it meant centuries of servitude.

"We will take it as the fates give it to us," Drizzt told Catti- brie. "We have a long road ahead of us, and yes, perhaps a long wait after that."

"There is a temple of Deneir in Luskan," Cadderly interjected. "That is near to this place called Icewind Dale, is it not?"

"The closest city south of the mountains," Drizzt replied.

"I can get you there," Cadderly said. "Together the three of us can walk the wind to Luskan."

Drizzt considered the prospects. It was nearly midsummer and many merchants would be on their way through Luskan, bound for Ten-Towns to trade for the valuable knucklehead trout scrimshaw. If Cadderly could get them to Luskan quickly, they would have little trouble in joining a caravan to Icewind Dale.

Only then did Drizzt realize yet another obstacle. "What of our friends?" he asked.

Catti-brie and Cadderly looked to each other. In the excitement, they had both nearly forgotten about Deudermont and the stranded *Sea Sprite.*

"I cannot take so many," Cadderly admitted. "And certainly, I cannot take a ship!"

Drizzt thought it over for a moment. "But we must go," he said to Catti-brie.

"I'm thinking that Deudermont's to like sailin' on a lake," Catti-brie retorted sarcastically. "Not many pirates about, and if he opened the *Sea Sprite*'s sails wide, then suren he'd find himself a mile into the stinkin' woods!"

Drizzt seemed to deflate under the weight of her honest words. "Let us go and find the captain," he replied. "Perhaps we will retrieve Harkle Harpell. He put the *Sea Sprite* in Impresk Lake, let him get her back where she belongs!"

Catti-brie mumbled something under her breath, her tone too low for Drizzt to decipher the actual words. He knew what she thought of Harkle though, and could imagine them readily enough.

The three found Deudermont, Waillan and Dunkin sitting with Ivan and Pikel along the walk outside of the Spirit Soaring's front doors. Deudermont told them the news of Robillard and the plan to get back where they belonged, which came as a great relief to both Drizzt and Catti-brie. The two looked to each other, and Deudermont knew them well enough to understand the gist of what was going on.

"You are leaving us," he reasoned. "You cannot wait the two or three weeks it will take Robillard to facilitate our return."

"Cadderly can get us to Luskan," Drizzt replied. "In less than two or three weeks, I hope to be in Ten-Towns."

The news put a pall on the previously lighthearted conversation. Even Pikel, who hardly knew what the others were talking about, issued a long and forlorn, "Ooooo."

Deudermont tried to find a way out of this, but he recognized the inevitable. His place was with the *Sea Sprite*, and given the high stakes, Drizzt and Catti-brie had no choice but to follow the words of the blind seer. Besides, Deudermont had not missed their expressions when Ivan had informed them that Bruenor had left Mithril Hall. Drizzt said he was going back to Ten-Towns, to Icewind Dale, and that was likely where Bruenor had gone.

"Perhaps if we get back to the Sword Coast before the weather turns toward winter, I'll sail the *Sea Sprite* around the bend and into the Sea of Moving Ice," Deudermont said, his way of bidding his friends farewell. "I would like to visit this Icewind Dale."

"My home," Drizzt said solemnly.

Catti-brie nodded to Drizzt and to Deudermont. She was never comfortable with goodbyes and she knew that was exactly what this was.

It was time to go home.

# Chapter 17
## THE FEEL OF POWER

tumpet Rakingclaw plodded through the snow halfway up the side of Kelvin's Cairn. The dwarf knew that her course was risky, for the melt in Icewind Dale was on in full and the mountain was not so high that its temperature remained below the point of freezing. The dwarf could feel the wetness seeping through her thick leather boots, and more than once she heard telltale rumblings of the complaining snow.

The stubborn dwarf plowed on, thrilled by the potential danger. This whole slope could go tumbling down; avalanches were not uncommon on Kelvin's Cairn, where the melt came fast. Stumpet felt like a true adventurer at that moment, braving ground she believed no one had trod in many years. She knew little of the region's history, for she had gone to Mithril Hall along with Dagna and the thousands from Citadel Adbar and had been too busy working in the mines to pay attention to the stories the members of Clan Battlehammer told of Icewind Dale.

Stumpet did not know the story of the most famous avalanche on this very mountain. She did not know that Drizzt and Akar Kessel had waged their last battle here before the ground had fallen out from under them, burying Kessel.

Stumpet stopped and reached into a pouch, producing a bit of lard. She uttered a minor enchantment and touched the lard to pursed lips, enacting a spell to help her ward off the chill. The season was fast turning to summer down below, but the wind up here was cold still and the dwarf was wet. Even as she finished, she heard another rumble and looked up to the mountain's peak, which was still two hundred feet away. For the first time she wondered if she could really get there.

Kelvin's Cairn was certainly not a large mountain. If it had been near Adbar, Stumpet's birthplace, or near Mithril Hall, it wouldn't even have been called a mountain at all. It was just a hillock, a thousand-foot-high clump of rock. But out here on the flat tundra, it seemed a mountain, and Stumpet Rakingclaw was a dwarf who considered the challenge of climbing to be the primary purpose of any mountain. She knew that she could have waited until late summer, when there would have been little snow remaining on Kelvin's Cairn and the ground would be more accessible, but the dwarf had never been known for her patience. Anyway, the mountain wouldn't be much of a challenge without the dangerous, shifting snow.

"Don't ye be falling on me," Stumpet said to the mountain. "And don't ye take me all the way back down!"

She spoke too loudly and, as if in answer, the mountain gave a tremendous groan. Suddenly Stumpet was sliding backward.

"Oh, damn ye!" she cursed, taking up her huge pick, looking for a hold. She tumbled over backward, but kept herself oriented enough to dodge a jutting stone and to set her pick firmly into its side. Her muscles strained as the snow washed past, but it was not too deep and the force of it not too strong.

A moment later all was quiet again, save the distant echoes, and Stumpet pulled herself out of the giant snowball that she and the supporting rock had become.

Then she noticed a curious shard of ice lying on the now bare ground. Coming free of the snow pile, the dwarf gave the strangely shaped item little thought. She moved up to a spot of bare ground and brushed herself off as thoroughly as possible before the snow could melt on her and further wet her already sopping clothing.

Her eyes kept roving back to the crystal. It didn't seem so extraordinary, just a hunk of ice. And yet, the dwarf got the distinct feeling deep in her gut that it was more than that.

For a few moments, Stumpet managed to fend off the unreasonable urges and concentrate on getting herself ready to continue her climb.

The piece of crystal kept calling to her, just below her conscious level, beckoning her to pick it up.

Before she realized what she was doing, she had the item in hand. Not ice, she realized immediately, for it was warm to the touch, warm and somehow comforting. She held it up to the light. It appeared to be a square-sided icicle, barely a foot long. Stumpet paused and removed her gloves.

"Crystal," she muttered in confirmation, for the warm item did not have the slick feel of ice. Stumpet closed her eyes, concentrating on her tactile sense, trying to feel the true temperature of the item.

"Me spell," the dwarf whispered, thinking she had figured out the mystery. She chanted again, dispelling the magic she had just enacted to fend off the cold.

Still the crystal shard felt warm. Stumpet rubbed her hands across its side and its warmth spread out even to her wet toes.

The dwarf scratched the stubble on her chin and looked around to see if anything else might have dislodged in the small avalanche. She was thinking clearly now, reasoning through this unexpected mystery. But all she saw was white and gray and brown, the unremarkable tapestry that was Kelvin's Cairn. That didn't deter her suspicions. Again she held the crystal shard aloft, watching the play of sunlight through its depths.

"A magical ward against the cold," she said aloud. "A merchant brought ye on a trip to the dale," she reasoned. "Might be that he was seeking some treasure up here, or just that he came up here to get a better look around, thinking that ye'd protect him. And from the cold, ye did," she reasoned confidently, "but not from the snowfall that buried him!"

There, she had it figured out. Stumpet felt herself lucky indeed to have found such a useful item in the empty wasteland that was Kelvin's Cairn. She looked to the south, where the tall peaks of the Spine of the World, perpetually covered in snow, loomed in a gray mist. Suddenly, the dwarven priestess was thinking of where this crystal shard might take her. What mountain would be beyond her if she carried such protection? She could climb them all in a single journey, and her name would be revered among the dwarves!

Already Crenshinibon, the crystal shard, the sentient and insidious artifact was at work, imparting subtle promises of Stumpet's deepest desires upon her. Crenshinibon recognized this wielder, not only a dwarf, but a dwarven priestess, and was not pleased. Dwarves were a stubborn and difficult lot, and resistant to magic. But still, the most evil of artifacts was glad to be out of the snow, glad that someone had returned to Kelvin's Cairn to bear Crenshinibon away.

The crystal shard was back among the realm of the living now, back where it might cause more havoc.

* * * * *

He crept along the tunnels, measuring his steps by the rhythmic pounding of dwarven hammers. The fit of the tight place was not comfortable, not for one used to the stars as his ceiling, and tall Kierstaad sometimes had to get down on his knees to pass through low archways.

Hearing footsteps, he paused at one corner and flattened himself as much as possible against the wall. He was unarmed, but he would not be welcomed here in the dwarven mines, not after Bruenor's unsavory encounter with Berkthgar. Kierstaad's father, Revjak, had been better in dealing with the dwarf, welcoming Bruenor's return, but even in that meeting, the strain had been obvious. Berkthgar and his followers were putting tremendous pressure on Revjak for a complete return to the ancient ways of mistrusting anyone who was not of the tribe. Revjak was wise enough to know that if he fought Berkthgar too boldly on this issue, he might lose control of the tribe altogether.

Kierstaad saw it, too, and his feelings were mixed. He remained loyal to his father, and believed that the dwarves were his friends, but Berkthgar's arguments were convincing. The ancient ways—the hunt across the tundra, the prayers to the spirits of those animals who were taken—seemed so refreshing to the young man who had spent the last few years of his life dealing with wretched merchants or battling dark elves.

The approaching dwarves turned away at the intersection, never noticing Kierstaad, and the barbarian breathed easier. He paused a moment to get his bearings, recalling which tunnels he had already passed through and where he believed the personal quarters of the leader would be. Many of the dwarves were out of the mines this day, having gone to Bryn Shander to collect the supplies Bruenor had purchased. Those remaining were in the deeper tunnels, eagerly opening up veins of precious minerals.

Kierstaad encountered no others as he made his way, often backtracking, sometimes going in circles. At last he came to a small corridor with two doors on either side and another at the very end. The first room seemed very undwarflike. Plush carpets and a bed stacked high with mattresses and higher still with warm comforters told the barbarian who it was that used this room.

"Regis," Kierstaad said with a soft chuckle, nodding as he spoke the name. The halfling was supposedly everything the barbarian people despised, lazy, fat, gluttonous, and worst of all, sneaky. Yet, Kierstaad's smile (and the smiles of many other barbarians) had widened every time Regis had come bobbing into Settlestone. Regis was the only halfling Kierstaad had ever met, but if "Rumblebelly," as many called him, was indicative of the race, Kierstaad thought that he would like to meet many more. Gently he closed the door, with one last smirk at the pile of mattresses—Regis often boasted that he could make himself comfortable any place, at any time.

Indeed.

Both rooms across the hall were unoccupied, each holding a single bed more suited to a human than a dwarf. This, too, Kierstaad understood, for it was no secret that Bruenor hoped that Drizzt and Catti-brie would someday return to his side.

The end of the hall was likely a sitting room, the barbarian reasoned. That left one door, the door to the chambers of the dwarven king. Kierstaad moved slowly, tentatively, fearing that a cunning trap had been set.

He cracked open the door, just an inch. No pits opened below his feet, no stones fell from the ceiling onto his head. Gaining confidence, the young barbarian pushed the door wide.

Bruenor's room, there could be no doubt. A scattering of parchments sat atop a wooden desk across the way, extra clothes were piled nearly as high as Kierstaad in one corner. The bed was not made, was a tumble of blankets and pillows.

Kierstaad hardly noticed any of it. The moment the door had opened, his eyes had fixed upon a single object set on the wall at the head of Bruenor's bed.

Aegis-fang. Wulfgar's warhammer.

Hardly breathing, Kierstaad crossed the small room to stand beside the mighty weapon. He saw the gorgeous runes etched into its gleaming mithril head—the twin mountains, the symbol of Dumathoin, dwarven god and keeper of secrets. Looking closer, Kierstaad made out portions of another rune buried under the twin mountain disguise. So perfect was the overlay that he could not determine what it might be. He knew the legend of Aegis-fang, though. Those hidden runes were the marks of Moradin, the Soul Forger, greatest of the dwarven gods on one side, and the axe of Clangeddin, the dwarven battle god, on the other.

Kierstaad stood for a long time, staring, thinking of the legend that was Wulfgar, thinking of Berkthgar and Revjak. Where would he fit in? If the conflict exploded between the former leader of Settlestone and the current leader of the Tribe of the Elk, what role might Kierstaad play?

A greater one, he knew, if he held Aegis-fang in his hands. Hardly considering the movement, Kierstaad reached out and clasped the warhammer, lifting it from its hooks.

How heavy it seemed! Kierstaad brought it in close, then, with great effort, lifted it above his head.

It banged against the low ceiling, and the young man

nearly fell sidelong as it bounced out too wide for him to properly control its momentum. When he at last regained his balance, Kierstaad laughed at his foolishness. How could he hope to wield mighty Aegis-fang? How could he hope to follow in the giant footsteps of mighty Wulfgar?

He brought the fabulous warhammer in close to his chest again, wrapping his arms about it reverently. He could feel its strength, its perfect balance, could almost feel the presence of the man who had wielded it so long and so well.

Young Kierstaad wanted to be like Wulfgar. He wanted to lead the tribe in his own vision. He didn't agree with Wulfgar's course any more than he now agreed with Berkthgar's, but there was a place in between, a compromise that would give the barbarians the freedom of the old ways and the alliances of the new. With Aegis-fang in hand, Kierstaad felt as if he could do that, could take control and lead his people on the best possible course.

The young barbarian shook his head and laughed again, mocking himself and his grand dreams. He was barely more than a boy, and Aegis-fang was not his to wield. That thought made the young man glance back over his shoulder, to the open door. If Bruenor returned and found him in here holding the warhammer, the taciturn dwarf would likely cut him in half.

It wasn't easy for Kierstaad to replace the hammer on its hooks, and it was harder still for him to leave the room. But he had no choice. Empty-handed, he quietly and cautiously snuck back out of the tunnels, back under the open sky, and ran all the way back to his tribe's encampment, some five miles across the tundra.

\* \* \* \* \*

The dwarf reached as high as she possibly could, her stubby fingers brushing aside the crusty snow and grasping desperately at the rock. The last ledge, the doorway to the top, the very top.

Stumpet groaned and strained, knowing it to be an impossible obstacle, knowing that she had overreached her bounds and was surely destined to fall thousands of feet to her death.

But then, somehow, she found the strength. Her fingers latched on firmly and she pulled with all her might. Little legs kicked and scraped at the rock, and suddenly she was over, onto the flat plateau at the top of the tallest mountain in all the world.

The resilient dwarf stood tall on that high place and surveyed the scene below her, the world conquered. She noted the crowds then, thousands and thousands of her bearded minions, filling all the valleys and all the trails. They were cheering, bowing before her.

Stumpet came awake drenched in sweat. It took her several moments to orient herself, to realize that she was in her own small room in the dwarven mines in Icewind Dale. She gave a slight smile as she recalled the vivid dream, the breathtaking last surge that got her over the top. But that smile was lost in confusion as she considered the subsequent scene, the cheering dwarves.

"Why'd I go and dream that?" Stumpet wondered aloud. She never climbed for glory, simply for the personal satisfaction that conquering a mountain gave to her. Stumpet didn't care what others thought of her climbing prowess, and she rarely even told anyone where she was going, where she had been, or whether or not the climb had been a success.

The dwarf wiped her forehead and slipped back to her hard mattress, the images of the dream still vividly clear in her mind. A dream or a nightmare? Was she lying to herself about the truth of why she climbed? Was there indeed a measure of personal satisfaction, a feeling of superiority, when she conquered a mountain? And if that was the case, then was that feeling a measure of superiority not only over the mountain, but over her fellow dwarves?

The questions nagged the normally-unshakable cleric, the usually humble priestess. Stumpet hoped the thoughts weren't true. She thought more of herself, her true self, than to be concerned with such pettiness. After a long while of tossing and turning, the dwarf finally fell back to sleep.

\* \* \* \* \*

No more dreams came to Stumpet that long night. Crenshinibon, resting in a locker at the foot of the dwarf's bed, sensed Stumpet's dismay and realized that it had to be careful in imparting such dreams. This dwarf was not an easy one to entice. The artifact had no idea of what treasures it could promise to weaken the will of Stumpet Rakingclaw.

Without those insidious promises, the crystal shard could grab no firm hold over the dwarf. But if Crenshinibon became more overt, more forceful, it could tip Stumpet off to the truth of its origins and its designs. And certainly the artifact did not want to arouse the suspicions of one who could call upon the powers of goodly gods, perhaps even learning the secrets of how to destroy Crenshinibon!

The crystal shard closed in its magic, kept its sentient thoughts deep within its squared sides. Its long wait was not quite over, it realized, not while it was in the hands of this one.

# Part 4

## ICEWIND DALE

remember well that occasion when I returned to Menzoberranzan, the city of my birth, the city of my childhood. I was floating on a raft across the lake of Donigarten when the city came into view, a sight I had feared and longed for at the same time. I did not ever want to return to Menzoberranzan, and yet, I had to wonder what going there would feel like. Was the place as bad as my memories told me?

I remember well that moment when we drifted past the cavern's curving wall, the sculpted stalagmites coming into view.

It was a disappointment.

I did not feel any anger, nor any awe. No warmth of nostalgia, true or false, washed over me. I did not dwell in the memories of my childhood, not even in the memories of my good times with Zaknafein.

All that I thought of in that critical moment was the fact that there were lights burning in the city, an unusual and perhaps significant event. All that I thought of was my critical mission, and how I must move fast to get the job done. My fears, for indeed they remained, were of a rational nature. Not the impulsive *and unreasonable fears wrought of childhood memories, but the very real trepidations that I was walking into the lair of a powerful enemy.*

*Later, when the situation allowed, I reflected on that moment, confused as to why it had been so disappointing, so insignificant. Why hadn't I been overwhelmed by the sight of the city that had been my home for the first three decades of my life?*

*Only when I turned around the northwestern corner of the Spine of the World mountain range, back into Icewind Dale, did I realize the truth. Menzoberranzan had been a place along my journey, but not a home, never a home. As the blind seer's riddle had inferred, Icewind Dale had been my home that was first. All that had come before, all that had led to that windswept and inhospitable place—from Menzoberranzan, to Blingdenstone, to the surface, even to the enchanted grove of my ranger mentor, Montolio DeBrouchee—had been but a road, a path to follow.*

*These truths came clear to me when I turned that corner, facing the dale for the first time in a decade, feeling the endless wind upon my face, the same wind that had always been there and that gave the place its name.*

*It is a complicated word: home. It carries varied definitions to nearly every person. To me, home is not just a place, but a feeling, a warm and comfortable sensation of control. Home is where I need make no excuses for my actions or the color of my skin, where I must be accepted because this is my place. It is both a personal and a shared domain, for it is the place a person most truly belongs, and yet it is so only because of those friends around him.*

*Unlike my first glimpse of Menzoberranzan, when I looked upon Icewind Dale I was filled with thoughts of what had been. There were thoughts of sitting on the side of Kelvin's Cairn, watching the stars and the fires of the roaming barbarian tribes, thoughts of battling tundra yeti beside Bruenor. I remembered the dwarf's sour expression when he licked his axe and first learned that the brains of a tundra yeti tasted terrible! I remembered my first meeting with Cattibrie, my companion still. She was but a girl then, a trusting and beautiful spirit, wild in nature yet always sensitive.*

*I remembered so very much, a veritable flood of images, and though my mission on that occasion was no less vital and pressing than the one that had taken me to Menzoberranzan, I thought nothing of it, didn't consider my course at all.*

*At that moment, it simply didn't matter. All that I cared about was that I had come home.*

—Drizzt Do'Urden

# Chapter 18
## WALKING THE WIND

rizzt and Catti-brie accompanied Deudermont, Waillan and Dunkin back to Carradoon to say their farewells to the crewmen they had worked beside for more than five years, friends all. Drizzt was impatient and didn't want to delay his return to Icewind Dale any longer than necessary, but this short trip was important. It was a fond farewell with promises that they would meet again.

The two friends—Drizzt called in Guenhwyvar later—dined with Deudermont and Robillard that night. Robillard, seeming more animated and friendly than usual, promised to use his magic to whisk them back to the Spirit Soaring, to get them on their way.

"What?" the wizard asked as the other three exchanged knowing glances and grins, all of them thinking exactly the same thing.

Robillard had changed in the last few weeks, especially since the wild battle on the beach of Caerwich. The fact was, Harkle had rubbed off on him.

"What?" Robillard demanded again, more forcefully.

Deudermont laughed and lifted his glass of wine in a toast. "To Harkle Harpell," the captain said, "and the good he has left in his wake!"

Robillard snorted, ready to remind them that the *Sea Sprite* was locked tight in a lake hundreds of miles from the Sword Coast. But as he considered the continuing smirks on his companions' faces, the wary wizard realized the truth of Deudermont's toast, realized that it was aimed at him.

Robillard's first instinct was to yell out a protest, perhaps even to rescind his offer to take Drizzt and Catti-brie back to the cathedral. But they were right, the wizard finally had to admit to himself, and so he lifted his glass. Though he kept quiet, Robillard was thinking that maybe he would go to the famed Ivy Mansion in Longsaddle and pay his eccentric friend a visit.

It was difficult for Drizzt, Catti-brie, and Deudermont to say goodbye. They shared hugs and promised that they would meet again, but they all knew the depth of the task facing Drizzt and Catti-brie. There was a very real possibility that neither of them would ever leave Icewind Dale alive.

They all knew this, but none of them mentioned that possibility, acting as though this was merely a short interruption to their friendship.

\* \* \* \* \*

Twenty minutes later, Drizzt and Catti-brie were back at the Spirit Soaring. Robillard said his farewells, and then disappeared in a flash of magical energy.

Ivan, Pikel and Danica greeted them. "Cadderly's gettin' ready," the stout, yellow-bearded dwarf remarked. "Takes the old man longer, ye know!"

"Hee hee hee," Pikel piped in.

Danica feigned a protest, but in truth—and Catti-brie saw it—she was glad that the dwarves continued to taunt Cadderly's advanced age. They did it only because they believed that the priest was growing stronger, even younger, and their taunts were filled with hope, not malice.

"Come," Danica bade Catti-brie. "We have not had enough time together." The woman cast a sour look at Ivan and Pikel, bobbing along on their heels. "Alone," she finished pointedly.

"Ooooo," moaned Pikel.

"Does he always do that?" Drizzt asked Ivan, who sighed and nodded.

"Ye think ye got long enough to tell me o' Mithril Hall?" Ivan asked. "I heared o' Menzoberranzan, but I'm not for believing what I heared."

"I will tell what I may," Drizzt replied. "And you will indeed have a difficult time in believing many of the splendors I describe."

"And what of Bruenor?" Ivan added.

"Booner!" put in the excited Pikel.

Ivan slapped his brother on the back of the head. "We'd go with ye, elf," the yellow-bearded dwarf explained, "but we've got chores to do here right now. Takin' care o' the twins and all that, and me brother with his gardens." As soon as he mentioned Pikel, Ivan turned fast to regard his brother, as if expecting another silly remark. Pikel did seem like he wanted to say something, but he began to whistle instead. When Ivan turned back to Drizzt, the drow had to shake his head and bite his lip. For, in looking over the yellow-bearded Ivan, Drizzt caught the face, thumbs in ears, fingers wagging, tongue stuck out to its limits, that Pikel offered.

Ivan spun back, but Pikel was standing calm again, whistling away. They went through three more such exchanges before Ivan finally gave up.

Drizzt had known these two for only two days, but he was thinking that they were grand fun, and he was imagining the good times the Bouldershoulders would inflict on Bruenor if ever they met!

\* \* \* \* \*

For Danica and Catti-brie, that last hour together was much more serious and controlled. They went to Danica and Cadderly's private quarters, a grouping of five rooms near the rear of the great structure. They found Cadderly in the bedroom, praying and preparing, so they quietly left him alone.

Their talk at first was general in nature, Catti-brie telling of her past, of how she had been orphaned when very young and then taken under the wing of Bruenor, to be raised among the dwarves of Clan Battlehammer. Danica spoke of her training in the teachings of Grandmaster Penpahg D'Ahn. She was a monk, a disciplined warrior, not so unlike Catti-brie.

Catti-brie wasn't used to dealing with women of her own age and of a similar mind. She liked it, though, liked Danica quite a bit, and could imagine a great friendship between the two if time and the situation would permit. In truth, the situation was also awkward for Danica, her life had been no easier and her contact with women of her own age no more common.

They spoke of the past and finally, of the present, of their hopes for the future.

"Do you love him?" Danica dared to ask, referring to the dark elf.

Catti-brie blushed, and really had no answer. Of course she loved Drizzt, but she didn't know if she loved him in the way that Danica was speaking of. Drizzt and Catti-brie had agreed to put off any such feelings, but now, with Wulfgar gone for so many years and Catti-brie approaching the age of thirty, the question was beginning to resurface.

"He is a handsome one," Danica remarked, giggling like a little girl.

Indeed, that's what Catti-brie felt like, reclining on the wide davenport in Danica's sitting room: a girl. It was like being a teenager again, thinking of love and of life, allowing herself to believe that her biggest problem was in trying to decide if Drizzt was handsome or not.

Of course, the weight of reality for both these women was fast to intrude, fast to steal the giggles. Catti-brie had loved and lost, and Danica, with two young children of her own, had to face the possibility that her husband, unnaturally aged by the creation of the Spirit Soaring, would soon be gone.

The conversation gradually shifted, then died away, and then Danica sat quiet, staring intently at Catti-brie.

"What is it?" Catti-brie wanted to know.

"I am with child," Danica said, and Catti-brie knew at once that she was the first person the monk had told, even before Cadderly.

Catti-brie waited a moment, waited to see the smile widen on Danica's face to make sure that, for the young monk, being pregnant was indeed a good thing, and then she grinned broadly and wrapped Danica in a tight hug.

"Do not say anything to Cadderly," Danica begged. "I've already planned how I will tell him."

Catti-brie sat back. "And yet ye told me first," she said, the gravity of that reality evident in her solemn tones.

"You are leaving," Danica answered matter-of-factly.

"But ye hardly know o' me," Catti-brie reminded her.

Danica shook her head, her strawberry blonde hair flying wide and her exotic almond-shaped eyes locking fast with Catti-brie's deep blue eyes. "I know you," Danica said softly.

It was true enough, and Catti-brie felt that she knew Danica as well. They were much alike, and both came to realize that they would miss each other a great deal.

They heard Cadderly stirring in the room next door; it was almost time to go.

"I will come back here someday," Catti-brie promised.

"And I will visit Icewind Dale," Danica responded.

Cadderly entered the room and told them that it was time for Catti-brie and Drizzt to leave. He smiled warmly, and was gracious enough to say nothing of the moisture that rimmed the eyes of the two young women.

\* \* \* \* \*

Cadderly, Drizzt and Catti-brie stood atop the highest tower of the Spirit Soaring, nearly three hundred feet above the ground, the wind whipping against their backs.

Cadderly chanted quietly for some time, and gradually, both friends began to feel lighter, somehow less substantial. Cadderly grabbed a hand of each and continued his chant, and the threesome faded away. Ghostlike, they walked off the tower top with the wind.

All the world sped past, blurry, in a fog, a dreamlike vision. Neither Drizzt nor Catti-brie knew how long they were flying, but dawn was breaking along the eastern horizon when they slowed and then stopped, becoming more substantial again.

They were in the city of Luskan, along the northernmost stretch of the Sword Coast, just south of the western lip of the Spine of the World mountains and barely two hundred miles, by horse or by foot, from Ten-Towns.

Cadderly didn't know the city, but the priest's aim was perfect and the three came out of their enchantment right in front of the temple of Deneir. Cadderly was well received by his fellow priests. He quickly secured rooms for his friends and while they were sleeping, went out with one of the Luskan priests to make the arrangements for Drizzt and Catti-brie to hook up with a caravan heading for Icewind Dale.

It was easier than Cadderly expected, and that made him glad, for he feared that Drizzt's heritage would outweigh any words he might offer. But Drizzt was known among many of the merchants in Luskan, as was Catti-brie, and their fighting prowess would be a welcome addition to any caravan traveling north to the dangerous land that was Icewind Dale.

The two were awake when Cadderly got back to the Deneirian temple, speaking with the other priests and gathering supplies for the long road ahead. Drizzt accepted one gift reverently, a pair of waterskins filled with blessed water from the temple's font. The drow didn't see any practical use for the water, but the significance that a human priest of a goodly god had given it to him, a drow elf, was not lost on him.

"Your fellows are a good lot," Drizzt remarked to Cadderly, when he, the old priest, and Catti-brie were at last alone. Cadderly had already explained the provisions that had been made, including the time and place, where Drizzt and Catti-brie were to meet with the caravan. The merchants were putting out this very day, giving the pair less than an hour to get out on the road. They knew that this was yet another parting.

"They do Deneir proud," Cadderly agreed.

Drizzt was busy with his pack then, and so Catti-brie quietly pulled Cadderly aside. Her thoughts were on Danica, her friend.

Cadderly smiled warmly, seeming to understand what this private conversation might be about.

"Ye've got many responsibilities," Catti-brie began.

"My god is not so demanding," Cadderly said coyly, for

215

he knew that Catti-brie was not speaking of his duties to Deneir.

"I'm meaning the twins," Catti-brie whispered. "And Danica."

Cadderly nodded. No argument there.

Catti-brie paused for a long while, seeming to struggle with the words. How might she put things so as not to insult the old priest?

"Ivan told me something about yer . . . condition," Catti-brie admitted.

"Oh?" Cadderly replied. He wasn't going to make this easy for the young woman.

"The dwarf says ye expected to die as soon as the Spirit Soaring was completed," Catti-brie explained. "Says ye looked like ye would, too."

"I felt like I would," Cadderly admitted. "And the visions I had of the cathedral made me believe that to be the truth."

"That was more than a year ago," Catti-brie remarked.

Cadderly nodded again.

"The dwarf says ye look like ye're getting younger," Catti-brie pressed. "And stronger."

Cadderly's smile was wide. He understood that Catti-brie was looking out for Danica's interests and her apparently deep friendship with his wife warmed his heart profoundly. "I cannot be certain of anything," he said to her, "but the dwarf's observations seem to be accurate. I am stronger now, much stronger and more energetic than when the cathedral was first completed." Cadderly reached up and pulled straight a few strands of hair, mostly gray, but with several sandy-colored strands mixed in. "Brown hairs," the old priest went on. "It was white, all white, when first the cathedral was completed."

"Ye're gettin' younger!" Catti-brie proclaimed with much enthusiasm.

Cadderly blew a long and deep sigh, and then, couldn't help but nod. "So it would seem," he admitted.

"I cannot be sure of anything," he said as if he was afraid of speaking his hopes out loud. "The only explanation that I can figure is that the visions shown to me—visions of my impending death—and the fatigue I felt at the completion of the Spirit Soaring were a test of my ultimate loyalty to the precepts and commandments of Deneir. I honestly expected to die as soon as the first service in the new cathedral was completed, and indeed, when it was done, a great weariness overcame me. I went to my room—I was practically carried by Danica and Ivan—and went to sleep, expecting to never again open my eyes upon this world. I accepted that." He paused and closed his eyes, recalling that fateful date.

"But now," Catti-brie prompted.

"Perhaps Deneir tested me, tested my loyalty," Cadderly said. "It might be that I passed that test, and so now my god has chosen to spare me."

"If he's a goodly god, then the choice is made," Catti-brie said firmly. "No good god'd take ye from Danica and the twins, and . . ." She paused and bit her lip, not wanting to give away Danica's secret.

"Deneir is a goodly god," Cadderly replied with equal determination. "But you speak of the concerns of mortals and we cannot understand Deneir's will or his ways. If Deneir takes me from Danica and my children, then that does not make him anything less than the goodly god that he truly is."

Catti-brie shook her head and didn't seem convinced.

"There are higher meanings and higher principles than we humans can understand," Cadderly said to her. "I hold faith that Deneir will do what is ultimately right by his needs and his designs, which outweigh my own."

"But ye hope it's true," Catti-brie said, her tone showing the words to be an accusation. "Ye hope ye get young again, as young as yer bride, that ye might live out yer life beside her and with yer kids!"

Cadderly laughed aloud. "True enough," he finally admitted, and Catti-brie was appeased.

So was Drizzt, listening in with those keen drow ears of his, only half his attention focused upon the task of packing his haversack.

Catti-brie and Cadderly shared a hug, and then the old priest, who seemed not so old, went to Drizzt and offered a sincere handshake. "Bring to me the artifact, this crystal

217

shard," Cadderly said. "Together we will discover a way to rid the world of its evil.

"And bring your father as well," Cadderly went on. "I feel that he would enjoy a stay at the Spirit Soaring."

Drizzt gripped Cadderly's hand all the tighter, thankful for the priest's confidence that he would succeed. "The artifact will give me . . . give us," he corrected, looking to Cattibrie, "the excuse we need to make the journey back to Carradoon."

"A journey I must make now," Cadderly said, and so he left the pair.

They said nothing when they were alone, just went about finishing their preparations for the road.

The road home.

# Chapter 19

# AND ALL THE WORLD
# IS THEIRS

evjak knew that it would come to this, had guessed it as soon as he had realized that Berkthgar did not mean to split off from the Tribe of the Elk to recreate one of the other tribes.

So now Revjak stood facing the brutish barbarian within a ring of all their people. Everyone in the tribe knew what was to come, but it had to be done properly, by the rules of ancient traditions.

Berkthgar waited for the gathering to quiet. He could be patient because he knew that the whispers were leaning in his favor, that the arguments for his ascension were gaining momentum. Finally, after what seemed to Revjak to be many minutes, the crowd went silent.

Berkthgar lifted his arms high to the sky, his hands reaching wide. Behind him, strapped diagonally across his back, loomed Bankenfuere, his huge flamberge. "I claim the Right of Challenge," the huge barbarian declared.

A chorus of cheers rose up, not a strong as Berkthgar would have liked, but showing that he had quite a bit of support.

"By what birthright do you make such a claim?" Revjak responded properly.

"Not by blood," Berkthgar promptly answered, "but by deed!" Again came the cheers from the younger man's supporters.

Revjak shook his head. "There is no reason, if blood does not demand a challenge," he protested, and his supporters, though not as vocal as Berkthgar's, gave their own burst of cheering. "I have led in peace and in strength," Revjak finished firmly, a claim that was all too true.

"As have I!" Berkthgar was quick to interrupt. "In Settlestone, so far from our home. I have brought our people through war and peace, and have led the march all the way back to Icewind Dale, our home!"

"Where Revjak is King of the Tribe of the Elk," the older man put in without hesitation.

"By what birthright?" Berkthgar demanded.

Revjak had a problem here, and he knew it.

"What birthright does Revjak, son of Jorn the Red, who was not a king, claim?" Berkthgar asked slyly.

Revjak had no answer.

"The position was given to you," Berkthgar went on, telling a tale that was nothing new to his people, but from a slightly different perspective than they normally heard. "It was handed to you, through no challenge and no right, by Wulfgar, son of Beornegar."

Kierstaad watched it all from the sidelines. At that moment, the young man came to understand the real reason why Berkthgar had launched a campaign to discredit Wulfgar. If the legend of Wulfgar still loomed larger than life to the barbarians, then his father's claim as king would be strong indeed. But with Wulfgar somewhat discredited . . .

"Who rightly claimed the kingship from Heafstaag, who was by birthright, rightly king," Revjak reasoned. "How many here," he asked the general gathering, "remember the battle wherein Wulfgar, son of Beornegar, became our king?"

Many heads bobbed, mostly of the older folk who had remained in Icewind Dale through all the years.

"I, too, remember the battle." Berkthgar growled defiantly. "And I do not doubt Wulfgar's claim, nor all the good he did for my people. But you have no claim of blood, no more than my own, and I would lead, Revjak. I demand the Right of Challenge!"

The cheers were louder than ever.

Revjak looked to his son and smiled. He could not avoid Berkthgar's claim, no more than he could possibly defeat the huge man in combat. He turned back to Berkthgar.

"Granted," he said, and the cheers were deafening then, from both Berkthgar's supporters and Revjak's.

"In five hours, before the sun runs low along the horizon," Berkthgar began.

"Now," Revjak said unexpectedly.

Berkthgar eyed the man, trying to discern what trick he might be pulling. Normally a Right of Challenge would be answered later in the day on which it was made, after both combatants had the time to prepare themselves mentally and physically for the combat.

Berkthgar narrowed his blue eyes and all the crowd hushed in anticipation. A smile widened on the huge man's face. He didn't fear Revjak, not now, not ever. Slowly, the huge man's hand went up over his shoulder, grasping the hilt of Bankenfuere, drawing the massive blade up from its scabbard. That sheath had been cut along its top edge so that Berkthgar could draw the weapon quickly. He did so, hoisting the heavy blade high into the sky.

Revjak took up his own weapon, but, to his observant and worried son, he did not seem ready for combat.

Berkthgar approached cautiously, feeling the balance of Bankenfuere with every step.

Then Revjak held up his hand and Berkthgar stopped, waiting.

"Who among us hopes for Revjak to win?" he asked, and a loud cheer of many voices went up.

Thinking the question to be no more than a ruse to lower his confidence, Berkthgar issued a low growl. "And who would see Berkthgar, Berkthgar the *Bold*, as King of the Tribe of the Elk?"

The cheer was louder still, obviously so.

Revjak moved right up to his opponent, unthreateningly, one hand up and his axe's head low to the ground. "The challenge is answered," he said, and he dropped his weapon to the ground.

All eyes widened in disbelief, Kierstaad's perhaps widest of all. This was dishonor! This was cowardice among the barbarians!

"I cannot defeat you, Berkthgar," Revjak explained, speaking loudly so that all would hear. "Nor can you defeat me."

Berkthgar scowled mightily. "I could cut you in half!" he declared, taking up his sword in both hands so powerfully that Revjak half expected him to do so right then and there.

"And our people would suffer the consequences of your actions," Revjak said quietly. "Whoever might win the challenge would be faced with two tribes, not one, split apart by anger and wanting revenge." He looked to the general gathering again, speaking to all his people. "We are not strong enough yet to support that," he said. "Whether we are to strengthen the friendship with Ten-Towns and the dwarves who have returned, or whether we are to return to our ways of old, we must do so together, as one!"

Berkthgar's scowl did not relent. Now he understood. Revjak could not defeat him in combat—they both knew that—so the wily older man had usurped the very power of the challenge. Berkthgar truly wanted to cut him in half, but how could he take any actions against the man?

"As one," Revjak repeated, and he held out his hand, bidding his opponent to clasp his wrist.

Berkthgar was wild with rage. He hooked his foot under Revjak's dropped axe and sent it spinning across the circle. "Yours is the way of the coward!" he roared. "You have proven that this day!" Up went Berkthgar's huge arms, up and out wide as if in victory.

"I have no claim of blood!" Revjak yelled, commanding attention. "Nor do you! The people must decide who will rule and who will step aside."

"The challenge is of combat!" Berkthgar retorted.

"Not this time!" Revjak shot back. "Not when all the tribe must suffer your foolish pride." Berkthgar moved again as if to strike, but Revjak ignored him and turned to the gathering. "Decide!" he commanded.

"Revjak!" yelled one man, but his voice was buried by a band of young warriors who cried out for Berkthgar. They, in turn, were outdone by a large group calling for Revjak. And so it went, back and forth, mounting cries. Several fights broke out, weapons were drawn.

Through it all, Berkthgar glowered at Revjak, and when the older man matched that intense stare, Berkthgar merely shook his head in disbelief. How could Revjak have done such dishonor to their people?

But Revjak held faith in his choice. He was not afraid to die, never that, but he truly believed that a fight between himself and Berkthgar would split the tribe and bring hardship to both groups. This was the better way, as long as things didn't get out of hand.

And they seemed to be heading in just that direction. Both sides continued to yell out, but now each cry was accompanied by a lifting of sword and axe, open threats.

Revjak watched the crowd carefully, measuring the support for him and for Berkthgar. Soon enough he understood and admitted the truth.

"Stop!" he commanded at the top of his voice, and gradually, the shouting match did diminish.

"With all your strength, who calls out for Berkthgar?" Revjak asked.

A great roar ensued.

"And who for Revjak?"

"Revjak who would not fight!" Berkthgar quickly added, and the cheers for the son of Jorn were not as loud, or as enthusiastic.

"Then it is settled," Revjak said, more to Berkthgar than to the crowd. "And Berkthgar is King of the Tribe of the Elk."

Berkthgar could hardly believe what had just transpired. He wanted to strike down the wily older man. This was to be his day of glory, a victory of mortal combat, as had been the way since the dawn of the tribes. But how could he do that? How could he slay an unarmed man, one who had just proclaimed him as the leader of all his people?

"Be wise, Berkthgar," Revjak said quietly, moving close, for the buzz of the astonished gathering was loud indeed. "Together we will discover the true way for our people, what is best for our future."

Berkthgar shoved him aside. "I will decide," he corrected loudly. "I need no advice from a coward!"

He walked out of the circle then, his closest supporters falling in line behind him.

Stung by the rejection of his offer, but not really surprised, Revjak took comfort in the fact that he had tried his best to do what was right for his people. That counted little, though, when the man looked upon his son, who had just completed the rights of passage into manhood.

Kierstaad's expression was one of disbelief, even of shame.

Revjak lifted his head high and walked over to the young man. "Understand," he commanded. "This is the only way."

Kierstaad walked away. Logic might have shown him the truth of his father's bravery this day, but logic played a very minor role in the young man's consciousness. Kierstaad felt ashamed, truly ashamed, and he wanted nothing more than to run away, out onto the open tundra, to live or to die.

It hardly seemed to matter.

\* \* \* \* \*

Stumpet sat on the very highest peak of Kelvin's Cairn, which seemed an easy climb to her. Her waking thoughts, like most of her dreams, were now squarely focused on the south, on the towering peaks of the Spine of the World. Fleeting images of glory and of victory raced through the dwarf's mind. She pictured herself standing atop the tallest mountain, surveying all the world.

The impracticality of the image, the sheer irrationality of it, did not make its way into Stumpet Rakingclaw's conscious thoughts. The constant barrage of images, the stream of delusion, began to erode the normally-pragmatic dwarf's rational sensibilities. For Stumpet, logic was fast losing to desires, desires that were not truly her own.

"I'm on me way, towering peaks," the dwarf said suddenly, addressing those distant mountains. "And not a one o' ye's big enough to keep me down!"

There, she had said it aloud, had proclaimed her course. She immediately began gathering together her things, then swung herself over the edge of the peak and began her scramble to the mountain's base.

In her haversack, Crenshinibon verily purred with elation. The powerful artifact still had no designs on making Stumpet Rakingclaw its wielder. The sentient crystal shard knew the stubbornness of this one, despite the delusions it had gradually enacted over the dwarf. Even worse, Crenshinibon understood Stumpet's place in her society, as a priestess of Moradin, the Soul Forger. Thus far, the artifact had managed to generally sidetrack any of Stumpet's attempts at communing with her god, but sooner or later, the dwarf would seek that higher level, and would likely learn the truth of the "warming stick" that she kept in her pack.

So Crenshinibon would use her to get away from the dwarves, to escape to the wilds of the Spine of the World, where it might find a troll or a giant, or perhaps even a dragon to serve as its wielder.

Yes, a dragon, Crenshinibon hoped. The artifact would like to work in collusion with a dragon!

Oblivious to such wishes, even to the fact that her "warming stick" could wish at all, poor Stumpet cared only about conquering the mountain range. And even she wasn't sure of why she cared.

\* \* \* \* \*

On the very first night of his rule, Berkthgar began to reveal the precepts that the barbarians of Icewind Dale would follow, a way of life such as they had lived until only a decade hence, before Wulfgar had defeated Heafstaag.

All contact with the folk of Ten-Towns was ordered to stop, and, on pain of death, no barbarian was to speak with Bruenor Battlehammer or any of the bearded folk.

"And if one of the bearded folk is found in need on the open tundra," Berkthgar said, and it seemed to Kierstaad that the man was looking directly at him as he spoke, "leave him to die!"

Later that night, Kierstaad sat alone under the wide canopy of stars, a tortured soul. Now he understood what his father had tried to do that afternoon. Revjak could not defeat Berkthgar, everyone knew that, and so the older man had tried to work out a compromise, one that would benefit all the barbarians. In his mind, Kierstaad realized that Revjak's abdication when the majority favored Berkthgar was a wise, even courageous thing to do, but in his heart and in his gut, the young man still felt the shame of his father's unwillingness to fight.

Better if Revjak had taken up his axe and died at Berkthgar's hands, Kierstaad believed, or at least a part of him believed. That was the way of their people, the ancient and sacred way. What might Tempus, the god of the barbarians, the god of battle, think of Revjak this day? What place in the afterworld might a man such as Revjak, who refused honest and rightful combat, find?

Kierstaad put his head in his hands. Not only was his father dishonored, but so were he and his family.

Perhaps he should proclaim allegiance to Berkthgar and reject his father. Berkthgar, who had been with Kierstaad all the years in Settlestone, who had been beside Kierstaad when the young man had made his first hunting kill on the open tundra, would welcome such support. He would see it, no doubt, as a solidification of his position as leader.

No. He could not abandon his father, however angry he might be. He would take up his weapon against Berkthgar if need be, and kill the man or die in order to restore his family's honor. He would not desert his father.

That option also seemed ridiculous to the young man, and he sat alone, overwhelmed, under the vastness of Icewind Dale's canopy, a tortured soul.

# Chapter 20
## EARNING THEIR PAY

oth Drizzt and Catti-brie had become quite proficient at riding horses on their trip from Mithril Hall to Waterdeep. But that had been six years before, and the only thing the companions had ridden since then were waves. By the time the caravan got around the western edge of the Spine of the World, five days out from Luskan, the two had settled back into the rhythm, though both had painful sores on their legs and buttocks.

They were at the lead, far ahead of the caravan when they reached the dale.

Reached the dale!

Drizzt was about to call for Catti-brie to slow up, but she, as awestruck as the drow, was pulling tight her reigns before he ever began the command.

They were home, truly home, within a hundred miles of the place where they had first met and where their lives and their most important friendships had been shaped and forged. All the memories washed over them at that moment as they looked across the windswept tundra, heard that forlorn moan, the incessant call of the winds blowing off the glaciers to the north and east. The icewind that gave the dale its name.

Catti-brie wanted to say something to Drizzt, something profound and meaningful, and he fostered the same desires. Neither could find the words. They were too overwhelmed by simply seeing the spectacle of Icewind Dale again.

"Come along," Drizzt said finally. The drow looked back over his shoulder, to see the six wagons of the caravan gaining ground, then looked ahead, to the beautiful and wonderful emptiness that was Icewind Dale. Kelvin's Cairn was not in sight, was still too far away, but it would not be long.

Suddenly the drow desperately wanted to see that mountain again! How many hours and days had he spent on the side of that rocky place?

How many times had he sat upon the barren stones of Kelvin's Cairn, looking at the stars and at the twinkling campfires of the distant barbarian encampments?

He started to tell Catti-brie to begin moving, but again, the woman seemed to share his thoughts, for she set her mount off and running before he could get his own horse moving.

Something else struck Drizzt Do'Urden then, another memory of Icewind Dale, a warning from his ranger sensibilities that this was not a safe place. Turning the final corner around the Spine of the World had put them truly in the wilderness again, where fierce tundra yeti and tribes of wild goblins roamed. He didn't want to steal the moment from Catti-brie, not yet, but he hoped that she was sharing his thoughts once again.

Unwary people did not survive long in the unforgiving land called Icewind Dale.

They met up with no trouble that day or the next, and were on the road early before the dawn, making great progress. The mud from the spring thaw had dried and the ground was solid and flat beneath them, the wagon wheels turning easily.

The sun came up in their faces, stinging their eyes, particularly Drizzt's lavender orbs, designed by heredity for the lightless Underdark. Even after more than two decades on the surface, after six years of sailing the bright waters of the Sea of Swords, Drizzt's sensitive eyes had not fully adjusted to the surface light. He didn't mind the sting, though, reveled in it, greeting the bright dawn with a smile, using the light as a reminder of how far he had come.

Later that morning, when the sun climbed high in the clear southeastern sky and the horizon before them became distinct and perfectly clear, they caught what Drizzt claimed to be their first true sight of the area that had been their home, a single flash that Drizzt decided had to be a reflection of the sun off the crystalline snow topping Kelvin's Cairn.

Catti-brie was not so sure of that. Kelvin's Cairn was not so high, and they were still two days of hard riding away. She didn't express any doubts, though, hoping that the drow was right. She wanted to be home!

As did Drizzt, and their pace quickened, became so great that they left the wagons even farther behind. Finally, reason and a terse call from the driver of the lead wagon reminding them of their duty, slowed them down. The pair exchanged knowing smiles.

"Soon," Drizzt promised.

The pace was still swift, for a short while. Then, Drizzt began to slow his horse, glancing all around, sniffing the air.

That was all the warning Catti-brie needed. She brought her horse to a trot and scanned the ground.

Everything seemed unremarkable to Drizzt. The ground was flat, brown and gray, and unbroken. He could see nothing unusual, and could hear nothing save the clip-clop of hooves on the hard ground and the moan of the wind. He could smell nothing other than the wet scent that Icewind Dale's summer wind always carried. But that did not allow the drow to sit easier on his mount. No signs, but that was the way with monsters in the dale.

"What do ye know?" Catti-brie whispered finally.

Drizzt continued to look about. There was about a hundred yards between them and the wagons, and the distance was fast closing. Still, Drizzt's eyes told him nothing, nor did his keen ears, nor even his sense of smell. But that sixth warrior sense knew better, knew that he and Catti-brie had missed something, had passed something by.

Drizzt took the onyx figurine from his pouch and softly called to Guenhwyvar. As the mist grew and the panther took shape, the drow motioned for Catti-brie to ready her bow, which she was already doing, and then to circle back toward the wagons, flanking right while he flanked out to the left.

The young woman nodded. The hairs on the back of her neck were tingling, her warrior instincts yelling at her to be ready. She had an arrow on Taulmaril, holding the weapons easily in one hand while her other guided the horse.

Guenhwyvar came onto the tundra with her ears flat, knowing from both the secretive tone of Drizzt's call and her own incredible senses that enemies were about. The cat looked right to Catti-brie, then left to Drizzt, then padded silently up the middle, ready to spring to the aid of either.

Noticing the movement of his point guards, and then the presence of the panther, the lead driver slowed his wagon, then called for a general halt. Drizzt held high a scimitar, showing his agreement with the stop.

Now far to the right, Catti-brie was the first to spot an enemy. It was deep into the soil, just the top of its shaggy brown head visible, poking from a hole. A tundra yeti, the fiercest hunter of Icewind Dale. Shaggy brown in the summer, snow white in the winter, tundra yetis were known to be masters of camouflage. Catti-brie nodded at that assessment, almost in appreciation of their skills. She and Drizzt, no novices, had walked their mounts right past the beasts, oblivious to the danger. This was Icewind Dale, the young woman promptly reminded herself. Merciless and unforgiving of the smallest error.

But the error this time was the yeti's, Catti-brie decided grimly, lifting her bow. Off streaked an arrow, hitting the unsuspecting beast right in the back of the head. It lurched forward, rebounded back violently, then slumped dead in its hole.

A split second later, the very ground seemed to explode as half a dozen yetis leaped up from similar trenches. They were powerful, shaggy beasts, looking like a cross between a human and a bear—and indeed, the lore of Icewind Dale's barbarian tribes claimed that they were exactly that!

Back behind Drizzt and Catti-brie, right in the middle of the flanking pair, Guenhwyvar hit one beast in full stride. She knocked it back into its hole, the panther's momentum carrying her in right behind it.

The yeti grabbed on with all its might, thinking to squeeze the life from the cat, but Guenhwyvar's powerful rear legs raked at the beast and held it at bay.

Meanwhile, Drizzt went into a full gallop, racing right beside one spinning yeti and double slashing at it with his scimitars as he held fast to his mount with his strong legs.

The bloodied beast fell away, roaring and howling in protest, and Drizzt, bearing down on a second yeti, paid it no more heed. This second yeti was ready for him, and even worse, it was ready for his horse. Yetis had been known to stop a horse at full charge, breaking the animal's neck in the process.

Drizzt couldn't risk that. He angled his charge to the left of the yeti, then lifted his left leg over the saddle and dropped from his speeding mount into a run, his enchanted anklets allowing him to get his feet under him in but a few speedy strides.

He went by the surprised yeti in a wild, slashing blur, scoring several wicked hits before he was too far away to strike. Drizzt kept running, knowing that the yeti, far from finished, had turned in pursuit. When he had put enough ground between himself and the beast, he turned back, angling for another swift pass.

Then Catti-brie, too, went into a full gallop, using her legs to hold herself steady and she leaned low in the saddle, taking a bead on the next closest beast.

She fired, and missed, but had another arrow up and ready in an instant and fired again, taking the yeti in the hip.

The beast flailed at the arrow and spun in a circle, taking another arrow, and then another in the chest as it came around to face the closing woman. Still it was standing, stubbornly, as Catti-brie came upon it. Ready to improvise, the woman hooked Taulmaril over the horn of her saddle and in one flashing motion, drew out Khazid'hea, her fabulous sword.

Catti-brie rambled past, swiping hard in a downward arc, the fine edge of Khazid'hea caving in the dying beast's skull, finishing the grim task. Down went the beast, its brain spilling from its skull onto the brown plain.

Catti-brie went right by the dying thing, replaced her sword and fired off her fifth shot with Taulmaril, this one popping into the shoulder of the next beast in line, dropping its arm lifeless to its side. Looking past the wounded yeti, Catti-brie saw the last of the yetis, which were closest to the lead wagons. In the distance she also noted the other caravan guards, a dozen sturdy fighters, riding hard to catch up to the battle.

"This fight's our own," the woman said quietly, determinedly, and as she closed on the wounded yeti, she hooked Taulmaril over the horn of her saddle and once more drew out Khazid'hea.

Still down in the tight hole, Guenhwyvar found her mighty claws gave her the advantage. The yeti tried to bite, but the panther was quicker, her neck more flexible. Guenhwyvar angled under the yeti's chin, her jaws snapping onto the shaggy neck.

Her claws kept up their raking motions, kept the yeti's considerable weapons at bay, while the deadly jaws clamped tight and suffocated the beast.

The panther came out of the hole as soon as the yeti had stopped its fighting. Guenhwyvar looked left and right, to Drizzt and Catti-brie. She issued a roar and raced right, where the situation seemed far more dangerous.

Drizzt was charging at the yeti he had wounded, but pulled up short, forcing the yeti, which had been ready to meet the charge, to overcompensate. It leaned too far forward. The drow's scimitars cut fast and hard, ripping into the yeti's hands, severing several of the beast's fingers.

The yeti howled and pulled in its arms. Drizzt, so impossibly quick, chased them back, snapping Twinkle into the yeti's upper arm, and scoring a hit down low, at the beast's waist, with his other blade. Then Drizzt went deftly out to the side, out of range before the beast could counter.

The yeti was not a stupid thing, not where combat was concerned, and it understood that it was overmatched. It turned to flee, long and loping strides that could outrun almost any man, or any elf.

But Drizzt wore the enchanted anklets, and he paced the beast easily. He was behind it and then beside it, scoring hit after hit, turning the dirty, shaggy coat bright red with spilling blood. The ranger knew the truth of tundra yetis, knew that they were not simple animal hunters. They were vicious monsters that murdered for sport as well as for food.

So he continued to pace it, would not let it flee, easily dodging the feeble attempts the beast made to strike at him, and scoring his own brutal hits repeatedly. Finally, the yeti pulled up and turned in a final, desperate rush.

Drizzt, too, charged, scimitars extended, one taking the yeti in the throat, the other in the belly.

Agile Drizzt came out the other side, right under the stumbling yeti's reaching arm. The drow skidded to a stop and banged his blades hard against the yeti's back, but the beast was already on the way down, already defeated. It fell headlong into the dirt.

Now it became a race between Catti-brie and the one remaining uninjured enemy to get to the yeti she had wounded in the arm.

Catti-brie won that race, and slashed hard as the yeti reached for her with its one working arm. Khazid'hea, fine-edged Khazid'hea, took that arm off cleanly, severing it at the shoulder.

The yeti went into a crazed dance, spinning all about and then toppling to the ground, its lifeblood gushing forth.

Catti-brie rushed away from it, not wanting to get caught up in that frenzied thrashing, and knowing that the fight was not yet won. She turned just in time to meet the charge of the last yeti, extending her sword and bracing herself.

The beast came straight in, arms out wide and extended. Khazid'hea went right through its chest, but still its strong arms grasped Catti-brie's shoulders and its momentum barreled her over backward.

As she flew and fell, Catti-brie realized the danger of a five hundred pound yeti coming down atop her. Then, suddenly, she was still falling, but the yeti was gone, simply gone, its momentum reversed by the flying Guenhwyvar.

Catti-brie hit the ground hard, managed to roll to absorb some of the force, and then came back to her feet.

The fight was over, though, with Guenhwyvar's strong jaws clamped tight on the throat of the already dead yeti.

Catti-brie looked up from the cat, into the stare of blank amazement splayed across the faces of the other caravan guards.

Six dead tundra yetis in a matter of minutes.

Catti-brie couldn't restrain a smile, nor could Drizzt as he came up to join her, as the men turned their horses away, shaking their heads in disbelief.

According to Cadderly, Drizzt's reputation as a fighter had gotten them onto the caravan in the first place, and now, the pair realized, that reputation would spread wide among the merchants of Luskan. Would spread wide, as would the clear acceptance of this most unusual drow elf.

\* \* \* \* \*

Soon after, the friends were back on their mounts and back in the lead.

"Three for me," Catti-brie remarked offhandedly.

Drizzt's lavender orbs narrowed as he considered her. He understood the game, had played it often with Wulfgar and even more so with Bruenor, during the days of their exploits.

"Two and a half," Drizzt corrected, remembering the panther's role in killing the last of the beasts.

Catti-brie did the math quickly in her head and then decided that there was no harm in giving the drow the argument, though she believed that the last yeti was dead before Guenhwyvar ever got to it. "Two and a half," she replied, "but only two for yerself!"

Drizzt couldn't suppress a chuckle.

"And only one and a half for the cat!" Catti-brie added with a superior snap of her fingers.

Guenhwyvar, loping along beside the horses, issued a growl, and both Catti-brie and Drizzt burst out in laughter, figuring that the too-intelligent panther had understood every word.

The caravan continued into Icewind Dale without further incident, arriving ahead of schedule in Bryn Shander, the primary marketplace in the dale and the largest of the ten towns that gave this region of the dale its name. Bryn Shander was a walled city, built upon low hills and circular in design. It was located near to the exact center of the triangle created by the three lakes of Maer Dualdon, Lac Dinneshere, and Redwaters. Bryn Shander was the only town of the ten without a fishing fleet, the staple of Ten-Towns' economy, and yet it was the most thriving of the cities, the home of the craftsmen and the merchants, the hub of politics in all the region.

Drizzt's welcome there was not friendly, even after he was formally introduced to the gate guards, and one of them admitted that he remembered the drow ranger from when he was a boy. Catti-brie was well received, though, quite well, particularly because her father had returned to the dale and all in the city were anxious for the precious metals to begin their flow from the dwarven mines.

Because his time of work for the caravan merchants was ended, Drizzt would not have even entered Bryn Shander. He meant to turn instead straight north for the dwarven valley. Before they could settle up with the caravan leaders inside the city gates, though, the companions were informed that Cassius, the Spokesman of Bryn Shander had requested an audience with Catti-brie.

Though she was dirty from the long ride and wanted nothing more than to fall into a comfortable bed, Catti-brie could not refuse, but she insisted that Drizzt accompany her.

\* \* \* \* \*

"It went well," the young woman remarked, later that day, when she and Drizzt left the spokesman's mansion.

Drizzt didn't disagree. Indeed it had gone better than Drizzt had expected, for Cassius remembered Drizzt Do'Urden well, and had greeted the drow with an unexpected smile. And now Drizzt was walking openly down the streets of Bryn Shander, suffering many curious looks, but no open hostility. Many, particularly the children, pointed and whispered, and Drizzt's keen ears caught words such as "ranger" and "warrior" more than once, always spoken with respect.

It was good to be home, so good that Drizzt almost forgot the desperate search that had brought him here. For a short while at least, the drow didn't have to think of Errtu and the crystal shard.

Before they reached the gate, another of Bryn Shander's residents came running up to them, hollering their names.

"Regis!" Catti-brie shouted, turning to see the three-and-a-half-foot halfling. His curly brown hair was bobbing, as was his ample belly as he huffed along.

"You were leaving without even a visit!" the halfling cried, finally catching up to the pair. He was immediately scooped up in a tight hug by a speechless Catti-brie. "No 'well met' for your old friend?" Regis asked, falling back to his feet.

"We thought you would be with Bruenor," Drizzt explained honestly, and Regis was not offended, for the explanation was simple and truly believable. Surely if Drizzt and Catti-brie had known that the halfling was in Bryn Shander, they would have gone straight to see him.

"I split my time between the mines and the city," Regis explained. "Somebody has to serve as ambassador between the merchants and that surly father of yours!"

Catti-brie gave him another hug.

"We have dined with Cassius," Drizzt explained. "It seems that not much has changed in Ten-Towns."

"Except for many of the people. You know the way of the dale. Most don't stay long, or don't live long."

"Cassius still rules in Bryn Shander," Drizzt remarked.

"And Jensin Brent speaks still for Caer-Dineval," Regis reported happily. That was good news for the companions, for Jensin Brent was among the heroes of the battle for Icewind Dale against Akar Kessel and the crystal shard. He was among the most reasonable politicians either of them had ever known.

"The good with the bad," Regis went on, "for Kemp remains in Targos."

"Tough old orc-kin," Catti-brie replied quietly.

"Tougher than ever," Regis said. "Berkthgar has returned as well."

Drizzt and Catti-brie nodded. Both had heard rumors to that effect.

"He's running with Revjak and the Tribe of the Elk," the halfling explained. "We hear little from them."

His tone told the pair that there was more to that tale.

"Bruenor paid Revjak a visit," Regis admitted. "It did not go well."

Drizzt knew Revjak, understood the wise man's soul. He knew Berkthgar, too, and it didn't take the drow long to surmise the source of the apparent problems.

"Berkthgar's never truly forgiven Bruenor," Regis said.

"Not the hammer again," said an exasperated Catti-brie.

Regis could offer no explanations, but Drizzt resolved then and there to pay the barbarians a visit of his own. Berkthgar was a noble and powerful warrior, but he could be a stubborn one, and the drow suspected that his old friend Revjak might be needing some support.

But that was business for another day. Drizzt and Catti-brie spent the night with Regis in his Bryn Shander residence, and then the three were out bright and early the next day, setting a swift pace due north for the dwarven mines.

They arrived before midday, and as they came down into the valley, an anxious Catti-brie, who had grown up in this very place, took the lead from Regis. The young woman needed no guide in this familiar setting. She went straight to the common entrance to the dwarven complex and went in without hesitation, stooping to get under the low frame so easily that it seemed as if she had never been away from the place.

She verily ran along the dimly lit corridors, pausing briefly with every dwarf she encountered—bearded folk whose faces inevitably beamed when they recognized that Catti-brie and Drizzt had returned. Conversations were polite, but very short, a well-wish from the dwarf, an inquiry by Catti-brie or Drizzt about where they might find Bruenor.

At last they came to the room where Bruenor was reportedly at work. They heard the hammer banging within; the dwarf was forging, a rare event over the last decade, since the creation of Aegis-fang.

Catti-brie cracked open the door. Bruenor had his back to her but she knew that it was him by the sturdy set of his shoulders, the wild red hair, and the helmet with one horn broken away. With the sound of his hammer and the roaring fire just to the side of him, he did not hear them enter.

The three walked right up to the oblivious dwarf and Catti-brie tapped him on the shoulder. He half-turned, hardly glancing her way.

"Get ye gone!" the dwarf grumbled. "Can't ye see I'm fixin' . . ."

Bruenor's words fell away in a profound swallow. He continued to stare straight ahead for a long moment as if he was afraid to look, afraid that the quick glimpse had deceived him.

Then the red-bearded dwarf did turn, and he nearly swooned at the sight of his daughter returned, and of his best friend, come home to him after six long years. He dropped his hammer right on top of his own foot, but he didn't seem to notice as he shuffled over a step and wrapped both Catti-brie and Drizzt in a hug so tight that they thought the powerful dwarf would surely snap their spines.

Gradually, Bruenor let Drizzt slip out of that hug, and he wrapped Catti-brie all the tighter, mumbling, "me girl," over and over again.

Drizzt took the opportunity to bring in Guenhwyvar from her astral home, and as soon as the dwarf finally sorted himself out from Catti-brie, the panther buried him, knocking him prone and standing triumphantly above him.

"Get the durned cat off o' me!" Bruenor roared, to which Guenhwyvar casually licked him full in the face.

"Oh, ye stupid cat," the dwarf complained, but there was no anger in Bruenor's voice. How could he possibly be angry with his two, no three, friends returned?

And how could that anger, if there had been any, have held up against the howls of laughter from Drizzt, Catti-brie, and Regis. A defeated Bruenor looked up to the cat, and it seemed to him as if Guenhwyvar was smiling.

The five companions spent the remainder of that day, long into the night, trading tales. Bruenor and Regis had little to say, other than to quickly retell their decision to leave Mithril Hall in Gandalug's hands and return to Icewind Dale.

Bruenor couldn't fully explain that choice—his choice, for Regis merely had followed along—but Drizzt could. When Bruenor's grief over the loss of Wulfgar and his elation about the victory over the dark elves had finally dissipated, Bruenor had gotten restless, as had Catti-brie and Drizzt. The red-bearded dwarf was old, past two hundred, but not too old by the standards of the dwarven folk. He was not yet ready to settle down and live happily ever after. With Gandalug back in Mithril Hall, Bruenor, for once, could forget about responsibilities and consider his own feelings.

For their part, Drizzt and Catti-brie had much more to talk about, recounting tales of their pirate-chasing along the Sword Coast with Captain Deudermont. Bruenor, too, had sailed with the captain, though Regis did not know the man.

And the two had so many tales to tell! One battle after another—thrilling chases, music playing, and Catti-brie always straining to decipher the enemy's insignia from her high perch. When they got to the events of the last few weeks, though, Drizzt ended the recounting abruptly.

"And so it went," the drow said. "But even such times can become a hollow enjoyment. We both knew that it was time to come home, to find you two."

"How'd ye know where to find us?" he asked.

Drizzt stuttered over his answer for just a moment. "Why, that was how we knew it was time to come home," he lied. "We heard in Luskan that some dwarves had come through the city, returning to Icewind Dale. The rumors said that Bruenor Battlehammer was among them."

Bruenor nodded, though he knew that his friend was not telling him the truth, or at least, not all of it. Bruenor's party had purposely avoided Luskan, and though the people there certainly knew of the march, the dwarves had not "come through the city," as Drizzt had just claimed. The red-bearded dwarf said nothing, though, for he held faith that Drizzt would tell him the complete truth in good time.

He suspected that his friends had some monumental secret, and the dwarf figured that he knew what it was. How ironic, Bruenor privately considered, for a dwarf to have a drow elf for a son-in-law!

The group went quiet for a while, Drizzt and Catti-brie's tales having been told in full, at least, as in full as they were apparently going to be told at this sitting. Regis went out into the hall and returned in a moment with news that the sun was high in the eastern sky.

"Good food and warm beds!" Bruenor proclaimed, and so off they went, Drizzt dismissing Guenhwyvar and promising to recall the cat as soon as she was rested.

After the short sleep, they were back together—except for Regis, who considered anything less than ten hours too short— talking and smiling. Drizzt and Catti-brie revealed nothing new about the last few weeks of their adventure, though, and Bruenor didn't press the point, holding faith in his dear friend and his daughter.

For that brief moment, at least, all the world seemed bright and carefree.

# Chapter 21

## WHENEVER

rizzt reclined in the shade on the smooth and slanted side of a boulder, crossing his hands behind his head and closing his eyes, enjoying the unusually warm day—for it did not often get so warm in Icewind Dale, even in late summer.

Though he was far from the entrance to the dwarven mines, Drizzt did not fear his lapse of readiness, for Guenhwyvar reclined nearby, always alert. The drow was just about asleep when the panther issued a low growl, her ears going flat.

Drizzt sat up, but then Guenhwyvar calmed, even rolled over lazily and he knew that whoever was approaching was no threat. A moment later, Catti-brie walked around a bend in the trail to join her friends. Drizzt was pleased to see her—Drizzt was always pleased to see her—but then he noted the troubled look upon her fair features.

She walked right up and sat down on the boulder beside the dark elf. "I'm thinking that we have to tell them," she said immediately, ending any suspense.

Drizzt understood exactly what she was talking about. When they had recounted their adventures to Bruenor, it had been Drizzt, and Drizzt alone, who had fabricated the ending tales, Catti-brie going conspicuously silent. She was uncomfortable in lying to her father. So was Drizzt, but the drow wasn't certain of what he might say to Bruenor to explain the events that had brought them to the dale. He did not want to inject any unnecessary tension and as far as he knew, it could be years, even decades, before Errtu found his way to them.

"Eventually," Drizzt replied to Catti-brie.

241

"Why're ye wanting to wait?" the woman asked.

Drizzt paused—good question. "We need more information," he explained at length. "We do not know whether Errtu means to come to the dale, and have no idea of when that might be. Fiends measure time differently than do we; a year is not so long to one of Errtu's race, nor is a century. I see no need to alarm Bruenor and Regis at this time."

Catti-brie thought on that for a long while. "How're ye thinking to get more information?" she asked.

"Stumpet Rakingclaw," Drizzt replied.

"Ye hardly know her."

"But I will get to know her. I know enough of her, of her exploits in Keeper's Dale and in Menzoberranzan against the invading dark elves, to trust in her power and her sense."

Catti-brie nodded—from everything she had heard of Stumpet Rakingclaw, the cleric was an excellent choice. Something else bothered Catti-brie, though, something that the drow had hinted at. She sighed deeply, and that told Drizzt what was on her mind.

"We have no way of knowing how long it will be," the drow ranger admitted.

"Then are we to become guardians for a year?" Catti-brie asked, rather sharply. "Or a hundred years?" She saw the drow's pained look and regretted the words as soon as she had spoken them. Surely it would be difficult for Catti-brie, lying in wait as the months rolled by for a fiend that might not even show up. But how much worse it must be for Drizzt! For Drizzt was not just waiting for Errtu, but for his father, his tortured father, and every day that passed meant another day that Zaknafein was in Errtu's evil clutches.

The woman bowed her head. "I'm sorry," she said. "I should've been thinkin' of yer father."

Drizzt put a hand on her shoulder. "Fear not," he replied, "I think of him constantly."

Catti-brie lifted her deep blue eyes to look deeply into the drow's lavender orbs. "We'll get him back," she promised grimly, "and pay Errtu for all the pain he's given yer father."

"I know," Drizzt said with a nod. "But there is no need to raise the alarm just yet. Bruenor and Regis have enough to concern them with winter fast approaching."

Catti-brie agreed and sat back on the warm stone. They would wait as long as they had to, and then let Errtu beware!

And so the friends fell into the routine of everyday life in Icewind Dale, working with the dwarves over the next couple of weeks. Drizzt secured a cave to serve as an outer camp for his many forays onto the open tundra, and Catti-brie spent quite a bit of time there as well, beside her friend, silently comforting him.

They spoke little of Errtu and the crystal shard, and Drizzt hadn't yet approached Stumpet, but the drow thought of the fiend, and more particularly, of the fiend's prisoner, almost constantly.

Simmering.

\* \* \* \* \*

"You must come quicker when I call to you!" the wizard growled, pacing anxiously about the room. He hardly seemed imposing to the twelve-foot glabrezu. The fiend had four arms, two ending with mighty hands and two with pincers that could snap a man in half.

"My fellows, they do not tolerate delays," the wizard went on. The glabrezu, Bizmatec, curled up his canine lips in a sly smile. This wizard, Dosemen of Sundabar, was all in disarray, battling hard to win a foolish contest against his fellow guild members. Perhaps he had erred in preparing the circle . . .

"Do I ask much of you?" Dosemen wailed. "Of course I do not! Just a few answers to minor questions, and I have given much in return."

"I do not complain," Bizmatec replied. While the fiend spoke, he scrutinized the circle of power, the only thing holding back the glabrezu's wrath. If Dosemen had not properly prepared the circle, Bizmatec meant to devour him.

"But neither do you give to me the answers!" Dosemen

howled. "Now, I will ask once more, and you will have three hours, just three hours, to return with my answers."

Bizmatec heard the words distinctly, and considered their implications in a new and respectful light, for by that time, the fiend had come to know that the circle was complete and perfect. There could be no escape.

Dosemen began rattling off his seven questions, seven unimportant and obscure questions, worthless except that finding their answers was the contest the wizard's guild had begun. Dosemen's voice showed his urgency; he knew that at least three of his fellows had garnered several of the answers already.

Bizmatec was not listening, though, was trying to recall something he had heard in the Abyss, a proposition put forth by a tanar'ri much greater than he. The glabrezu looked at the perfect circle again and scowled doubtfully, and yet, Errtu had said that the power of the summoner or the perfection of the magical binding circle was not an issue.

"Wait!" Bizmatec roared, and Dosemen, despite his confidence and his anger, fell back and fell silent.

"The answers you require will take many hours to discover," the fiend explained.

"I do not have many hours!" Dosemen retorted, gaining back a bit of his composure with his rising ire.

"Then I have for you an answer," the glabrezu replied with a sly and wicked grin.

"You just said . . ."

"I have no answers to your questions," Bizmatec quickly explained. "But I know of one who does, a balor."

Dosemen paled at the mention of the great beast. He was no minor wizard, practiced at summoning and confident of his magic circle. But a balor! Never had Dosemen tried to bring in such a beast. Balors, and by all accounts there were only a score or so, were the highest level of tanar'ri, the greatest of the terrors of the Abyss.

"You fear the balor?" Bizmatec teased.

Dosemen pulled himself up straight, remembering that he had to show confidence in the face of a fiend. Weakness of attitude bred weakness of binding, that was the sorcerer's creed. "I fear nothing!" the wizard declared.

"Then get your answers from the balor!" Bizmatec roared. "Errtu, by name."

Dosemen fell back another step at the sheer power of the glabrezu's roar. Then the wizard calmed considerably and stood staring. The glabrezu had just given him the name of a balor, openly and without a price. A tanar'ri's name was among its most precious commodities, for with that name, a wizard such as Dosemen could strengthen the binding of his call.

"How much do you desire defeating your rivals?" Bizmatec teased, snickering with each word. "Surely Errtu will show you the truth of your questions."

Dosemen thought on it for just a moment, then turned sharply upon Bizmatec. He was still leery about the prospects of bringing in a balor, but the carrot, his first victory in one of the guild's bi-annual contests, was too juicy to ignore. "Be gone!" he commanded. "I'll waste no more energy upon the likes of you."

The glabrezu liked hearing that promise. He knew that Dosemen was speaking only of wasting his energy upon Bizmatec for the time being. The wizard had become quite a thorn to the glabrezu. But if the whispers filtering around the smoky layers of the Abyss concerning mighty Errtu were true, then Dosemen would soon enough be surprised and terrified by the ironic truth of his own words.

\* \* \* \* \*

Back in the Abyss, the interplanar gate fast closing behind him, Bizmatec rushed to an area of gigantic mushrooms, the lair of mighty Errtu. The balor at first moved to destroy the fiend, thinking the glabrezu an invader, but when Bizmatec spouted his news, Errtu fell back on his mushroom throne, grinning from horn to horn.

"You gave the fool my name?" Errtu asked.

Bizmatec hesitated, but there seemed no anger in Errtu's voice, only eager anticipation. "By the instructions I heard . . ." the glabrezu began tentatively, but Errtu's cackling laughter stopped him.

"That is good," the balor said. Bizmatec relaxed considerably.

"But Dosemen is no minor wizard," Bizmatec warned. "His circle is perfect."

Errtu chuckled again as if that hardly mattered. Bizmatec was about to reiterate that point, figuring that the balor simply believed that he would find a flaw where the glabrezu had not, but Errtu moved first, holding forth a small black coffer.

"No circle is perfect," the balor remarked cryptically and with all confidence. "Now, come quickly. I have another task for you, a service of guarding my most valuable prisoner." Errtu slid from his throne and started away, but stopped, seeing that the glabrezu was hesitating.

"The rewards will be great, my general," Errtu promised. "Many days running free on the Prime Material Plane; many souls to devour."

No tanar'ri could resist that.

Dosemen's call came a short while later, and though it was weak, the wizard having already expended much of his magical energy in summoning Bizmatec, Errtu scooped up his precious coffer and was quick to respond. He followed the interplanar gate to Dosemen's room in Sundabar, and found himself, as Bizmatec had warned, standing in the middle of a perfectly ingrained circle of power.

"Close fast the gate!" the balor cried, his thunderous, grating voice reverberating off the stone walls of the room. "The baatezu might follow me through! Oh, fool! You have separated me from my minions, and now the beasts of doom will follow me through the gate! What will you do, foolish mortal, when the pit fiends enter your domain?"

As any wise wizard would, Dosemen was already frantically at work in closing the gate. Pit fiends! More than one? No circle, no wizard, could hold a balor and a pair or more of pit fiends. Dosemen chanted and worked his arms in concentric circles, throwing various material components into the air.

Errtu continued to feign rage and terror, watching the wizard and then looking back as if he was viewing the very gate he had come through. Errtu needed that gate closed, for any working magic would soon be dispelled, and if the gate was still empowered at the time, the balor would likely be sent back to the Abyss.

Finally, it was done, and Dosemen stood calm—as calm as a wizard could while looking into the half-ape, half-dog face of a balor!

"I have summoned you for a simple—" Dosemen began.

"Silence!" roared mighty Errtu. "You have summoned me because you were instructed to summon me!"

Dosemen eyed the beast curiously, then looked to his circle, his perfect circle. He had to hold faith, had to consider the balor's words as a bluff.

"Silence!" Dosemen yelled back, and because his circle was indeed perfect, and because he had summoned the tanar'ri correctly, using its true name, Errtu had to comply.

So the balor was silent as he produced the black coffer, holding it up for Dosemen to see.

"What is that?" the wizard demanded.

"Your doom," Errtu answered, and he was not lying. Grinning wickedly, the balor opened the coffer, revealing a shining black sapphire the size of a large man's fist, a remnant of the Time of Troubles. Contained within that sapphire was an energy of antimagic, for it was a piece of dead magic zone, one of the most important remnants of the days when the avatars of the gods walked the Realms. When the shielding coffer was opened, Dosemen's mental binding over Errtu was gone, and the wizard's circle, though its tracings remained perfect, was no longer a prison for the summoned fiend, no longer a deterrence, nor were any of the protection spells that the wizard had placed upon his person.

Errtu, too, had no magic that he could hurl in the face of that dead magic stone, but the powerful tanar'ri, a thousand pounds of muscle and catastrophe, hardly needed any.

\* \* \* \* \*

Dosemen's fellow wizards entered his private room later that night, fearful for their guild-brother. They found a shoe, just one, and a splotch of dried blood.

Errtu, having replaced the sapphire in the coffer, which could shield even against such wicked antimagic, was far, far away by then, flying fast to the north and the west—to Icewind Dale, where Crenshinibon, an artifact that the balor had coveted through centuries, waited.

# Chapter 22
## LIKE OLD TIMES

he ranger ran with the wind in his ears, that constant humming. It had shifted more from the north now, off the glaciers and the great bergs of the Sea of Moving Ice, as the season drifted away from summer, through the short fall and into the long and dark winter.

Drizzt knew this change on the tundra as well as any. He had lived in Icewind Dale for just a decade, but in that time he had come to know well the land and its ways. He could tell by the texture of the ground exactly what time of year it was to within a ten-day. Now the ground was hardening once more, though there remained a bit of sliding under his moving feet, a subtle hint of mud below the dry surface, the last remnant of the short summer.

The ranger kept his cloak tight about his neck, warding off the chilly breeze. Though he was bundled, and though he could not hear much above the incessant moan of the wind, the drow was alert, always alert. Creatures venturing out onto the open plain of Icewind Dale who were not careful did not survive for long. Drizzt noted tracks of tundra yeti in several places. He also found one group of footprints close together, moving side by side, the way a goblin band might travel. He could read those prints, where they had come from and where they were going, and he had not come out from Kelvin's Cairn for any fight. He took special note of them now simply to avoid the creatures who had made them.

Soon Drizzt found the tracks he desired, two sets of prints from soft boots, man-sized, traveling slowly, as a hunter would stalk. He noted that the deepest depression by far was near the ball of the foot. Barbarians walked in a toe-heel manner, not the heel-toe stride used by most of the peoples of the Realms. There could be no doubt now for the ranger. He had ventured near to the barbarian encampment the night before, meaning to go in and speak with Revjak and Berkthgar. Listening secretly from the darkness, how-ever, the drow had discovered that Berkthgar intended to go out on a hunt the next day, alone with Revjak's son.

That news unsettled Drizzt at first—did Berkthgar mean to indirectly strike a blow at Revjak and kill the boy?

Drizzt had quickly dismissed that silly notion; he knew Berkthgar. For all their differences, the man was honorable and no murderer. More likely, Drizzt reasoned, Berkthgar was trying to win over the trust of Revjak's son, strength-ening his base of power within the tribe.

Drizzt had stayed out of the encampment all the night, in the darkness, undetected. He had moved safely away before the dawn and had subsequently circled far to the north.

Now he had found the tracks, two men, side by side. They were an hour ahead of him, but moving as hunters, and so Drizzt was confident that he would find them in but a few minutes.

The ranger slowed his pace a moment later when he found that the tracks split, the smaller set going off to the west, the larger continuing straight north. Drizzt followed the larger, figuring them to be Berkthgar's, and a few min-utes later, he spotted the giant barbarian, kneeling on the tundra, shielding his eyes and peering hard to the north and west.

Drizzt slowed and moved cautiously. He discovered that he was nervous at the sight of the imposing man. Drizzt and Berkthgar had argued many times in the past, usually when Drizzt was serving Bruenor as liaison to Settlestone, where Berkthgar ruled. This time was differ-ent, Drizzt realized. Berkthgar was back home now, need-ing nothing from Bruenor, and that might make the man more dangerous.

Drizzt had to find out. That was why he had come out from Kelvin's Cairn in the first place. He moved silently, step by step, until he was within a few yards of the still-kneeling, apparently oblivious barbarian.

"My greetings, Berkthgar," the ranger said. His sudden voice did not appear to startle the barbarian, and Drizzt believed that Berkthgar, so at home on the tundra, had sensed his approach.

Berkthgar rose slowly and turned to face the drow.

Drizzt looked to the west, to a speck on the distant tundra. "Your hunting partner?" he asked.

"Revjak's son, Kierstaad by name," Berkthgar replied. "A fine boy."

"And what of Revjak?" Drizzt asked.

Berkthgar paused a moment, jaw firm. "It was whispered that you had returned to the dale," he said.

"Is that a good thing in the eyes of Berkthgar?"

"No," came the simple reply. "The tundra is wide, drow. Wide enough so that we will not have to meet again." Berkthgar began to turn away, as if that was all that had to be said, but Drizzt wasn't ready to let things go just yet.

"Why would you desire that?" Drizzt asked innocently, trying to push Berkthgar into playing his hand openly. Drizzt wanted to know just how far the barbarians were moving away from the dwarves and the folk of Ten-Towns. Were they to become invisible partners sharing the tundra, or, as they once had been, sworn enemies?

"Revjak calls me friend," Drizzt went on. "When I left the dale those years ago, I named Revjak among those I would truly miss."

"Revjak is an old man," Berkthgar said evenly.

"Revjak speaks for the tribe."

"No!" Berkthgar's response came fast and sharp. Then he quickly calmed and his smile told Drizzt that the denial was true. "No more does Revjak speak for the tribe," Berkthgar went on.

"Berkthgar, then?" Drizzt asked.

The huge barbarian nodded, smiling still. "I have returned to lead my people," he said. "Away from the errors of Wulfgar and Revjak, back to the ways we once knew, when we were free, when we answered to no one but our own and our god."

Drizzt thought on that for a moment. The proud young man was truly deluding himself, the drow realized, for those old times that Berkthgar spoke of so reverently were not as carefree and wonderful as the huge man apparently believed. Those years were marked by war, usually between tribes competing for food that was often scarce. Barbarians starved to death and froze to death, and often wound up as meals for tundra yeti, or for the great white bears that also followed the reindeer herd along the coast of the Sea of Moving Ice.

That was the danger of nostalgia, Drizzt realized. One often remembered the good of the past while forgetting the troubles.

"Then Berkthgar speaks for the tribes," Drizzt agreed. "Will he lead them to despair? To war?"

"War is not always despair," the barbarian said coolly. "And do you forget so soon that following the course of Wulfgar led us to war with your own people?"

Drizzt had no response to that statement. It hadn't happened exactly like that, of course. The drow war was far more an accident of chance than of anything Wulfgar had done. But still, the words were true enough, at least from Berkthgar's stilted perspective.

"And before that, Wulfgar's course led the tribes to war in helping to reclaim the throne for your ungrateful friend," Berkthgar pressed.

Drizzt glared hard at Berkthgar. Again the man's words were true, if stilted, and the drow realized that there was no practical response he could offer to sway Berkthgar.

They both noticed then that the speck on the tundra was larger now as Kierstaad approached.

"We have found the clean air of the tundra again," Berkthgar proclaimed before the lad arrived. "We have returned to the old ways, the better ways, and those do not allow for friendship with drow elves."

"Berkthgar forgets much," Drizzt replied.

"Berkthgar remembers much," the giant barbarian answered, and walked away.

"You would do well to consider the good that Wulfgar did for your people," Drizzt called after him. "Perhaps

Settlestone was not the place for the tribe, but Icewind Dale is an unforgiving land, a land where allies are the most valuable assets for any man."

Berkthgar didn't slow. He came up to Kierstaad and walked right past the young man. Kierstaad turned and watched him for a short time, the young man quickly deciphering what had just happened. Then Kierstaad turned back to Drizzt and, recognizing the drow, sprinted over to stand before him.

"Well met, Kierstaad," Drizzt said. "The years have done you well."

Kierstaad straightened a bit at that remark, thrilled to have Drizzt Do'Urden say anything complimentary to him. Kierstaad was just a boy of twelve when Drizzt left Mithril Hall, and so he did not know the drow very well. He knew of Drizzt, though, the legendary warrior. Once Drizzt and Catti-brie had come to Hengorot, the mead hall in Settlestone, and Drizzt had leaped upon the table, giving a speech that called for a strengthened alliance between the dwarves and the barbarians. By all the old ways that Berkthgar so often spoke of, no drow elf should have been allowed in Hengorot, and certainly none would have been shown any respect. But the mead hall showed respect to Drizzt Do'Urden that day, a testament to the drow's battle prowess.

Kierstaad could not forget, too, the stories his father had told him of Drizzt. In one particularly vicious battle with the folk of Ten-Towns, the barbarian warriors invading Ten-Towns were badly beaten, in no small part because of Drizzt Do'Urden. After that fight, the ranks of the barbarians were greatly diminished. With winter coming on, it seemed that many hardships would befall those who had survived the war, particularly the very young and the very old, for there simply were not enough hunters left alive to provide for all.

But the fresh carcasses of reindeer had been found along the trail as the nomadic barbarians had moved west with the herd, killed cleanly and left for the tribe. The work of Drizzt Do'Urden, Revjak and many of the elders agreed, the drow who had defended Ten-Towns against the barbarians. Revjak had never forgotten the significance of that act of kindness, nor had many of the older barbarians.

"Well met, to you," Kierstaad replied. "It is good that you have returned."

"Not everyone agrees with that view," Drizzt remarked.

Kierstaad snorted and shrugged noncommittally. "I am sure that Bruenor is glad to see the likes of Drizzt Do'Urden again," he said.

"And of Catti-brie," Drizzt added. "For she returned at my side."

Again the young man nodded and Drizzt could tell that he wanted to say something more profound than the polite conversation. He kept looking back over his shoulder, though, to the departing form of Berkthgar, his leader. His loyalties were obviously split.

Finally, Kierstaad sighed and turned to face the drow directly, the internal battle decided. "Many remember the truth of Drizzt Do'Urden," he said.

"And of Bruenor Battlehammer?"

Kierstaad nodded. "Berkthgar leads the tribe, by right of deed, but not all agree with his every word."

"Then let us hope that Berkthgar soon remembers that truth," Drizzt replied.

Kierstaad glanced back one more time, to see that Berkthgar had stopped and had turned to regard him. The young barbarian understood then what was expected of him, and he gave a quick nod to Drizzt, not even offering a parting word, and ran off to join the giant man.

Drizzt spent a long time considering the implications of that sight, the young man blindly running to Berkthgar's will, though he did not share many of his leader's views. Then Drizzt considered his own course. He had meant to go back to the encampment for a word with Revjak, but that seemed a useless, even dangerous proposition now.

Now that Berkthgar spoke for the tribe.

\* \* \* \* \*

While Drizzt was running north of Kelvin's Cairn, another traveler was traversing the tundra to the south of the mountain. Stumpet Rakingclaw rambled on, her back

bent for the weight of her huge pack, her eyes focused on
that singular goal: the towering peaks of the Spine of the
World.

Crenshinibon, hanging through a loop on the dwarf's
belt, was silent and pleased. The artifact had invaded
Stumpet's dreams every night. Its communications with
the dwarf had been more subtle than was usual for the
domineering artifact, for Crenshinibon held a healthy
respect for this one, both dwarf and priestess of a goodly
god. Gradually, over the weeks, Crenshinibon had worn
away Stumpet's resistance, had slowly convinced the dwarf
that this was not a foolishly dangerous trek, but rather a
challenge to be met and conquered.

And so Stumpet had come out the previous day, striding
determinedly to the south, weapon in hand and ready to
meet any monsters, ready to climb any mountain.

She wasn't yet near the mountains, about halfway from
Redwaters, the southernmost of the three lakes. Crenshinibon
planned to remain silent. The artifact was a work of the ages
and a few days meant nothing to it. When they got to the
mountains, the wilderness, the artifact would find a more
suitable wielder.

But then, unexpectedly, the crystal shard sensed a presence, powerful and familiar.

A tanar'ri.

Stumpet stopped her run a moment later, her face
screwed up with curiosity as she considered the item on
her belt. She felt the vibrations from it, as though it was a
living thing. As she studied the item, she recognized those
vibrations as a call.

"What then?" the dwarf asked, lifting the crystal shard
from the loop. "What're ye about?"

Stumpet was still eyeing the shard when a ball of blackness swept out of the blue haze of the distant horizon,
hearing the call now and speeding fast on leathery wings.
Finally, the dwarf shrugged her shoulders. Not understanding, she replaced the shard, then looked up.

Too late.

Errtu came in hard and fast, overwhelming the dwarf
before she could even lift her weapon. In mere seconds, the

fiend held Crenshinibon in his clutches, a union both desired.

Stumpet, on the ground and dazed, her weapon knocked far from her hands, propped herself on her elbows and looked upon the tanar'ri. She started to call to her god, but Errtu would have none of that. He kicked her hard, launching her a dozen feet away and moved in for the torturous kill.

Crenshinibon stopped him. The artifact did not disdain brute force, nor did it hold any sympathy for the dwarf. But a simple reminder to Errtu that enemies such as Stumpet could be used to his advantage gave the fiend pause. Errtu knew nothing about Bruenor Battlehammer and the quest for Mithril Hall, knew nothing about the clan's departure from the dale, let alone their return. But the fiend did know of Drizzt's previous allegiance to the dwarves of Icewind Dale. If Drizzt Do'Urden was in the dale, or if he ever came back, he would likely once again befriend the dwarves that worked the mines south of the mountain called Kelvin's Cairn. This female, obviously, was of that clan.

Errtu towered over her, menacing her, preventing her from holding any concentration that she would need to cast a spell, or even to retrieve her weapon. The fiend held out one hand, on his second finger was a ring adorned with a blackish-purple gemstone. Errtu's black eyes blazed into orange flames as he began to chant in the guttural language of the Abyss.

The gemstone flared a purplish light that washed over Stumpet.

Suddenly Stumpet's perspective changed. She was no longer looking up at the fiend, but was rather looking down, on her own body! She heard Errtu's cackling laughter, sensed the approval of the crystal shard, and then watched helplessly as her form rose up from the ground and moved about, collecting the dropped items.

Zombielike, moving stiff-legged, the soulless dwarven body turned about and walked off to the north.

Stumpet's soul remained, trapped within the purplish gem, hearing the cackles, sensing the sentient waves that the evil artifact sent out to Errtu.

\* \* \* \* \*

That same night, Drizzt and Catti-brie sat atop Bruenor's climb with the red-bearded dwarf and Regis, basking in the starlight. Both the dwarf and the halfling recognized the uneasiness of their companions, sensed that Drizzt and Catti-brie were keeping a secret.

Many times, the drow and the woman exchanged concerned looks.

"Well," Bruenor said at length, unable to bear the cryptic glances.

Catti-brie chuckled, the tension relieved by her father's acute observations. She and Drizzt had indeed taken Bruenor and Regis up here this night to discuss more than the beauty of the moon and stars. After long discussion, the drow had finally agreed with Catti-brie's reasoning that it would not be fair to keep their friends in the dark of their true reasons for returning to Icewind Dale.

And so Drizzt told the tale of his last few weeks aboard the *Sea Sprite,* of the attack on Deudermont in Waterdeep and the run to Caerwich, of the journey to Carradoon caused by Harkle's spell and the windwalk with Cadderly that had brought them to Luskan. He left nothing out, not even the remnants he could remember of the blind hag's poem and the intimations that his father was a prisoner of Errtu, the great tanar'ri.

Catti-brie interjected her thoughts often, mostly reassuring her father that a big part of the reason that they decided it was time to come home was because this was home, was because Bruenor was here, and Regis was here.

Silence fell over the four after Drizzt finished. All gazes fell over Bruenor, waiting for his response as though it was a judgment of them all.

"Ye durned elf!" he bellowed at last. "Ye're always bringing trouble! Know that ye make life interesting!"

After a short, strained laugh, Drizzt, Catti-brie and Bruenor turned to hear what Regis had to say on the matter.

"I do have to widen my circle of friends," the halfling remarked, but like Bruenor's outrage, Regis's despair was a feigned thing.

Guenhwyvar roared in the night.

They were together again, the five friends, more than ready to face whatever odds, more than ready for battle.

They didn't know the depth of Errtu's terror, and didn't know that the fiend already had Crenshinibon in his evil clutches.

# Chapter 23
## CRYSHAL-TIRITH

 whisper of sound, a ball of flying blackness against the dark night sky, the fiend rushed north, past the three lakes, past Kelvin's Cairn, across the open tundra and over the encampment of Berkthgar's people. Errtu meant to go to the farthest reaches of the tundra to set up his fortresses, but when he got to that point, to the edge of the Sea of Moving Ice, the fiend discovered a better and more forlorn landscape. Errtu, a creature of the fiery Abyss, was no friend of snow and ice, but the texture of the great icebergs clogging the waters—a mountain range built among defensible, freezing moats—showed him potential he could not resist.

Out swooped the tanar'ri, across the first and widest expanse of open water, setting on the side of the visible cone of the closest tall iceberg. He peered out through the darkness, first using his normal vision, then letting his eyes slip into the spectrum of heat. Predictably, a cold blackness reflected back at him from both the normal and the infrared spectrums, cold and dead.

The fiend started to move on again, but felt the will of Crenshinibon, asking him to look more closely.

Errtu expecting to find nothing, didn't understand the point to such scrutiny, but he continued his scan. He was surprised indeed when he did see a patch of warmer air rising from a hollow on the side of an iceberg perhaps a hundred yards away. That was too far for Errtu to make out any distinct forms so the great tanar'ri gave a short flap of his leathery wings and halved the gap.

Closer still the balor crept, until Errtu could discern

that the heat was coming from a group of warm-blooded forms, huddled in a tight circle. A more knowledgeable traveler of Icewind Dale would have thought them to be seals, or some other marine animal, but Errtu was not familiar with the creatures of the north and so he approached cautiously.

They were humanoid, man-sized, with long arms and large heads. Errtu thought that they were dressed in furs, until he got close enough to recognize that they were not dressed at all, but had their own coat of thick, shaggy fur covered with a filmy, oily sheen.

*The beginnings of your army,* came an intrusion into the balor's thoughts, as eager Crenshinibon renewed its quest for ever more power.

Errtu paused and considered that thought for some time. The fiend wasn't planning to raise an army, not here in this forlorn wilderness. He would remain in Icewind Dale for a short time only, long enough to discover if Drizzt Do'Urden was about, and long enough to destroy the drow ranger if he was. When that business was finished, Errtu planned to be long gone from the emptiness of the dale and into more hospitable, more thickly inhabited regions.

Crenshinibon's suggestions did not relent, and after awhile, the tanar'ri came to see a potential value of enslaving some of the area's creatures. Perhaps it would be wise to fortify his position with some expendable soldiers.

The balor chuckled wickedly and muttered a few words, a spell that would allow him to converse with the creatures in their own guttural and grunting language—if that's what their snorts and snarls could be called. Errtu called upon his magical abilities once again and disappeared, reappearing on the slope right behind and above the shaggy creatures' impromptu encampment. Now the balor had a better look at the beasts, about two-score of them, he figured. Their shaggy fur was white, their heads large, though virtually without any discernable forehead. They were strongly built and jostled each other roughly, each apparently trying to get closest to the center of the huddle, what Errtu figured to be the warmest spot.

*They are yours!* Crenshinibon declared.

Errtu agreed. He felt the power of the crystal shard, a dominating force indeed. The balor leaped up to his full twelve foot height atop the ridge and bellowed to the shaggy humanoids in their own tongue, Errtu declaring himself their god.

The camp disintegrated into pandemonium, creatures running all about, slamming into each other, falling over each other. Down swooped Errtu into their midst, and when they moved out from the towering fiend, encircling him cautiously, the balor brought up a ring of low, simmering fire, a personal perimeter.

Errtu held high his lightning bolt sword, commanding the creatures to kneel before him.

Instead, the shaggy beasts shoved one of their own, the largest of the group, forward.

Errtu understood the challenge. The large, shaggy creature bellowed a single threat, but the word was caught in its throat as the tanar'ri's other weapon, that wicked many-thonged whip, snapped out and wrapped about the beast's ankles. A half-hearted tug from the mighty fiend jerked the creature onto its back and Errtu casually pulled it in so that it lay, screaming in agony, in the fiend's ring of fire.

Errtu didn't kill the creature. He gave a rolling snap on his whip a moment later and the thing flew out of the flames and rolled about on the ice, whimpering.

"Errtu!" the tanar'ri proclaimed, his thunderous voice driving back the cowed creatures. Cowed, but not kneeling, Errtu realized, and so he took a different tactic. Errtu understood the basic, instinctual way of these tribal beasts. Scrutinizing them and their trinkets in the light of the fire, the balor realized that they were likely less civilized than the goblins he was more used to dealing with.

*Cower them and reward them,* Crenshinibon imparted, a strategy that Errtu already had well under way. The cowering was done. With a roar the fiend leaped away, soaring over the top of the berg and into the blackness of the night. Errtu heard the continuing grunts and whispers as he departed, and he smiled again, thinking himself clever, imagining the faces of the stupid brutes when he gave them their reward.

Errtu didn't have to fly far to figure out what that reward might entail. He saw the fin of a creature, a huge creature, poking from the black surface of the water.

It was a killer whale, though to Errtu, it was merely a big fish, merely some meat he might provide. Down swooped the fiend, diving fast onto the back of the behemoth. In one hand Errtu held his lightning sword, in the other, the crystal shard. Hard struck the sword, a mighty blow, but harder still came the assault from Crenshinibon, its power loosed for the first time in many years, a line of blazing white fire that tore through whale flesh as easily as a beacon cut through the night sky.

Just a few minutes later, Errtu returned to the encampment of the shaggy humanoids, dragging the dead whale behind him. He flopped the creature into the midst of the stunned humanoids, and once again proclaimed himself as their god.

The brutes fell over the slain whale, chopping wildly with crude axes, tearing flesh and guzzling blood, a grisly ceremony.

Just the way Errtu liked it.

Within the span of a few hours, Errtu and his new minions located a suitable ice floe to serve as their stronghold. Then Errtu used the powers of Crenshinibon once more, and the creatures, already falling into worship for the fiend, leaped about in circles, crying Errtu's name, falling to their faces and groveling.

For, Crenshinibon's greatest power was to enact an exact replica of itself, huge in proportion, a crystalline tower—Cryshal-Tirith. At Errtu's invitation, the creatures searched all about the base of the tower, but they saw no entrance—only extraplanar creatures could find the door to Cryshal-Tirith.

Errtu did just that, and entered. The fiend wasted no time in calling back to the Abyss, in opening a gate that Bizmatec could come through with the balor's helpless and tormented prisoner in tow.

"Welcome to my new kingdom," Errtu told the tortured soul. "You should like this place." With that, Errtu snapped his whip repeatedly, beating the prisoner unconscious.

Bizmatec howled with glee, knowing that the fun had just begun.

They settled into their new stronghold over the next few days, Errtu bringing in other minor fiends, a horde of wretched manes, and even conversing with another powerful true tanar'ri, a six-armed marilith, coaxing her to join in the play.

But Errtu's focus did not wander too far from his primary purpose; he did not let the intoxication of such absolute power distract him from the truth of his minor conquest. Upon one wall of the tower's second level, there was set a mirror, a device for scrying, and Errtu perused it often, scouring the dale with his magical vision. Great indeed was Errtu's pleasure when he found that Drizzt Do'Urden was indeed in Icewind Dale.

The prisoner, always at Errtu's side, saw the specter of the drow elf, the human woman, a red-bearded dwarf and a plump halfling as well, and his expression changed. His eyes brightened for the first time in many years.

"You will be valuable to me indeed," Errtu remarked, deflating any hope, reminding the prisoner that he was but a tool for the fiend, a piece of barter. "With you in hand, I will bring the drow to me, and destroy Drizzt Do'Urden before your very eyes before I destroy you as well. That is your fate and your doom." The fiend howled with ecstasy and whipped his prisoner again and again, driving him to the floor.

"And you will prove of value," the balor said to the large, purple stone set on his ring, the prison of poor Stumpet Rakingclaw's consciousness. "Your body, at least."

Trapped Stumpet heard the distant words, but the spirit of the priestess was caught in a gray void, an empty place where not even her god could hear her pleas.

\* \* \* \* \*

Drizzt, Bruenor and the others looked on in helpless amazement as Stumpet walked back into the dwarven mines that night, her expression blank, devoid of any emotion at all. She moved to the main audience hall on the uppermost level, and just stood in place.

263

"Her soul's gone," was Catti-brie's guess, and the others, in examining the dwarf, in trying to wake her from her stupor, even going so far as to slap her hard across the face, couldn't rightly disagree.

Drizzt spent a long while in front of the zombielike dwarf, questioning her, trying to wake her. Bruenor dismissed most of the others, allowing only his closest friends—and ironically, not one of these was a dwarf—to remain.

On impulse, the drow begged Regis to give him the precious ruby pendant, and Regis readily complied, slipping the enchanted item from around his neck and tossing it to the drow. Drizzt spent a moment marveling at the large ruby, its incessant swirl of little lights that could draw an unsuspecting onlooker far into its hypnotic depths. Drizzt then put the item right in front of the zombie dwarf's face and began talking to her softly, easily.

If she heard him at all, if she even saw the ruby pendant, she did not show it.

Drizzt looked back to his friends, as if to say something, as if to admit defeat, but then his expression brightened in recognition, just a flicker, before it went grave once more. "Has Stumpet been out on her own?" Drizzt asked Bruenor.

"Try to keep that one in one place," the dwarf replied. "She's always out—look at her pack. Seems to me that she was off again, heading for what's needin' climbing."

A quick look at Stumpet's huge pack confirmed the red-bearded dwarf's words. The haversack was stuffed with food and with pitons and rope, and other gear for scaling mountains.

"Has she climbed Kelvin's Cairn?" Drizzt asked suddenly, things finally falling into place.

Catti-brie gave a low groan, seeing where the drow was taking this.

"Had her eyes set on the place from the minute we walked into Ten-Towns," Bruenor proclaimed. "I think she got it, said she did anyway, not so long ago."

Drizzt looked to Catti-brie and the young woman nodded her agreement.

"What are you thinking?" Regis wanted to know.

"The crystal shard," Catti-brie replied.

They searched Stumpet carefully then, and subsequently went to her private quarters, tearing the place apart. Bruenor called for another of his priests, one who could detect magical auras, but the enhanced scan was similarly unsuccessful.

Not long after, they left Stumpet with the priest, who was trying an assortment of spells to awaken or at least comfort the zombielike dwarf. Bruenor expanded the search for the crystal shard to include every dwarf in the mines, two hundred industrious fellows.

Then all they could do was wait, and hope.

Bruenor was awakened late that night by the priest, the dwarf frantic that Stumpet had just walked away from him, was walking right out of the mines.

"Did ye stop her?" Bruenor was quick to ask, shaking off his grogginess.

"Got five dwarves holding her," the priest answered. "But she just keeps on walkin', trying to push past 'em!"

Bruenor roused his three friends and together they rushed for the exit to the mines, where Stumpet was still plodding, bouncing off the fleshy barricade, but stubbornly walking right back into it.

"Can't wear her out, can't kill her," one of the blocking dwarfs lamented when he saw his king.

"Just hold her then!" Bruenor growled back.

Drizzt wasn't so sure of that course. He began to sense something here, and figured that it was more than coincidence. Somehow, the drow had the feeling that whatever had happened to Stumpet might be related to his return to Icewind Dale.

He looked to Catti-brie, seeing by her return gaze that she was sharing his feelings.

"Let us pack for the road," Drizzt whispered to Bruenor. "Perhaps Stumpet has something she wishes to show us."

Before the sun had begun to peek over the mountains in the east, Stumpet Rakingclaw walked out of the dwarven valley, heading north across the tundra, with Drizzt, Catti-brie, Bruenor, and Regis in tow.

Just as Errtu, watching from the scrying room of Cryshal-Tirith, had planned.

The fiend waved a clawed hand and the image in the mirror grew gray and indistinct, then washed away altogether. Errtu then went up into the tower's highest level, the small room in which the crystal shard hung, suspended in midair.

Errtu felt the curiosity of the item, for the fiend had developed quite an empathetic and telepathic bond with Crenshinibon. It sensed his delight, the fiend knew, and it wanted to know the source.

Errtu snickered at it and flooded the item with a barrage of incongruous images, defeating its mental intrusions.

Suddenly the fiend was hit with a shocking intrusion, a focused line of Crenshinibon's will that nearly tore the story of Stumpet from his lips. It took every ounce of mental energy the mighty balor could manage to resist that call, and even with that, Errtu found that he had not the strength to leave the room, and knew that he could not resist for long.

"You dare . . ." the fiend gasped, but the crystal shard's attack was undiminished.

Errtu continued a blocking barrage of meaningless thoughts, knowing his doom if Crenshinibon read his mind at that time. He gingerly reached around his hip, taking a small sack that he kept hooked and hanging from the lowest claw of his leathery wings.

In one fierce movement, Errtu brought the sack around and tore it apart, grabbing up the coffer and pulling it open, the black sapphire tumbling into his hand.

Crenshinibon's attack heightened; the fiend's great legs buckled.

But Errtu had gotten close enough. "I am the master!" Errtu proclaimed, lifting the antimagic gemstone near to Crenshinibon.

The ensuing explosion hurled Errtu back against the wall, shook the tower and the iceberg to their very roots.

When the dust cleared, the antimagic gemstone was gone, simply gone, with barely a speck of useless powder to show that it had ever been there.

*Never again do such a foolish thing!* came a telepathic command from Crenshinibon, the artifact following up that order with promises of ultimate torture.

Errtu pulled himself up from the floor, simmering and delighted all at once. The bared power of Crenshinibon was great indeed for it to have so utterly destroyed the supremely unenchanted sapphire. And yet, that subsequent command Crenshinibon had hurled the balor's way was not so strong. Errtu knew that he had hurt the crystal shard, temporarily, most likely, but still something he had never wanted to do. It couldn't be avoided, the fiend decided. He had to be in command here, not in the blind service of a magical item!

*Tell me!* the stubborn shard's intrusions came again, but, as with the outrage over the fiend's game with the antimagic gemstone, the telepathic message carried little strength.

Errtu laughed openly at the suspended shard. "I am the master here, not you," the great balor declared, pulling himself up to his full height. His horns brushed the very top of the crystallizing tower. Errtu hurled the empty, shielding coffer at the crystal, missing the mark. "I will tell when it pleases me, and will tell only as much as pleases me!"

The crystal shard, most of its energy sapped by the close encounter with the devilish sapphire, could not compel the fiend to do otherwise.

Errtu left the room laughing, knowing that he was again in control. He would have to pay close heed to Crenshinibon, would have to gain the ultimate respect of the item in the days ahead. Crenshinibon would likely regain its sapped strength, and Errtu had no more antimagic gems to throw at the artifact.

Errtu would be in command, or they would work together. The proud balor could accept nothing less.

# Part 5

MORTAL ENEMIES

erkthgar was right.

He was right in returning his people to Icewind Dale, and even more so in returning to the ancient ways of their heritage. Life may have been easier in Settlestone for the barbarians, their material wealth greater by far. In Settlestone, they had more food and better shelter, and the security of allies all around them. But out here on the open tundra, running with the reindeer herd, was their god. Out here on the tundra, in the soil that held the bones of their ancestors, was their spirit. In Settlestone, the barbarians had been far richer in material terms. Out here they were immortal, and thus, richer by far.

So Berkthgar was right in returning to Icewind Dale, and to the old ways. And yet, Wulfgar had been right in uniting the tribes, and in forging alliances with the folk of Ten-Towns, especially with the dwarves. And Wulfgar, in inadvertently leading his people from the dale, was right in trying to better the lot of the barbarians, though perhaps they had gone too far from the old ways, the ways of the barbarian spirit.

### R. A. Salvatore

*Barbarian leaders come to power in open challenge, "by blood or by deed," and that, too, is how they lead. By blood, by the wisdom of the ages, by the kinship evoked in following the course of best intent. Or by deed, by strength and by sheer physical prowess. Both Wulfgar and Berkthgar claimed leadership by deed— Wulfgar by slaying Dracos Icingdeath, and Berkthgar by assuming the leadership of Settlestone after Wulfgar's death. There the resemblance ends, though, for Wulfgar had subsequently led by blood, while Berkthgar continues to lead by deed. Wulfgar always sought what was best for his people, trusting in them to follow his wise course, or trusting in them to disapprove and deny that course, showing him the folly of his way.*

*Berkthgar is possessed of no such trust, in his people or in himself. He leads by deed only, by strength and by intimidation. He was right in returning to the dale, and his people would have recognized that truth and approved of his course, yet never did he give them the chance.*

*Thus Berkthgar errs; he has no guidance for the folly of his way. A return to the old does not have to be complete, does not have to abandon that which was better with the new. As is often the case, the truth sits somewhere in the middle. Revjak knows this, as do many others, particularly the older members of the tribe. These dissenters can do nothing, though, when Berkthgar rules by deed, when his strength has no confidence and thus, no trust.*

*Many others of the tribe, the young and strong men mostly, are impressed by powerful Berkthgar and his decisive ways; their blood is high, their spirits soar.*

*Off the cliff, I fear.*

*The better way, within the context of the old, is to hold fast the alliances forged by Wulfgar. That is the way of blood, of wisdom.*

*Berkthgar leads by deed, not by blood. He will take his people to the ancient ways and ancient enemies.*

*His is a road of sorrow.*

—Drizzt Do'Urden

# Chapter 24
## STUMPET'S WALK

rizzt, Catti-brie, Bruenor and Regis paced Stumpet as she continued her trancelike trek across the tundra, heading to the north and east. Her line was straight, perfectly straight, as if she knew exactly where she was going, and she walked tirelessly for many hours.

"If she's meaning to walk all the day, we'll not pace her," Bruenor remarked, looking mostly at Regis, who was huffing and puffing, trying to catch his breath and trying to keep up.

"Ye could bring in the cat to pace her," Catti-brie offered to the ranger. "Then Guen could come back and show us the way."

Drizzt thought on that for just a moment, then shook his head. Guenhwyvar might be needed for more important reasons than trailing the dwarf, he decided, and he did not want to waste the panther's precious time on the Prime Material Plane. The drow considered tackling Stumpet and binding her, and he was explaining to Bruenor that they should do just that, when suddenly the dwarven priestess simply sat down on the ground.

The four companions surrounded her, fearing for her safety, fearing that they had come to the place Errtu desired. Catti-brie had Taulmaril in hand and ready, scanning the noonday skies for sight of the fiend.

But all was quiet, the skies perfectly blue and perfectly empty, save a few puffy clouds drifting fast on stiff winds.

\* \* \* \* \*

Kierstaad heard his father talking with some of the older men about the march of Bruenor and Drizzt. More pointedly the young man heard his father's concerns that the friends were walking into some trouble once more. That same morning, his father left the barbarian encampment along with a group of his closest friends. They were going hunting, so they said, but Kierstaad, wise beyond his years, knew better.

Revjak was following Bruenor.

At first, the young barbarian was sorely wounded that his father had not confided in him, had not asked him to go along. But when he considered Berkthgar, the huge man living always on the verge of outrage, Kierstaad came to realize that he didn't need that anymore. If Revjak had lost the glory of the Jorn family, then Kierstaad, Kierstaad the man, meant to reclaim it. Berkthgar's hold on the tribe was tightening and only an act of heroic proportions would garner Kierstaad the needed accolades for a right of challenge. He thought he knew how to do that, for he knew how his dead hero had done it. Now Wulfgar's own companions were out in the wild and in need of help, he believed.

It was time for Kierstaad to make a stand.

He arrived at the dwarven mines at midday, quietly slipping into the small tunnels. Again, the chambers were mostly empty, the dwarves, as always, busy with their mining and crafting. Their industry apparently even outweighed any concerns they might hold for the safety of their leader. At first this struck Kierstaad as odd, but then he came to realize that the dwarves' apparent ambivalence was merely a show of respect for Bruenor, who needed no watching after, and who had been, after all, often out on the road with his nondwarven friends.

Much more familiar with the place now, Kierstaad had little trouble in getting back to Bruenor's room. When he had Aegis-fang in his hands once more, the warhammer feeling so solid and comforting, his course was clear to him.

It was midafternoon when the young barbarian managed to get back out onto the open tundra, Aegis-fang in hand. By all accounts, Bruenor and his companions had half a day's lead on him, and Revjak had been on the march for nearly eight hours. But they were likely walking, Kierstaad knew, and he was young. He would run.

\* \* \* \* \*

The reprieve lasted the remainder of the afternoon, until Stumpet just as suddenly and unexpectedly climbed back to her feet and plodded off across the barren tundra, walking purposefully, though her eyes showed only a blank, unthinking gaze.

"Considerate fiend, givin' us a rest," Bruenor remarked sarcastically.

None of the others appreciated the humor—if Errtu had arranged the impromptu rest, then the balor likely knew exactly where they were.

That thought hung on them with every step, until something else caught Drizzt's attention soon after. He was flanking the group, running swiftly, moving from one side to the other in wide arcs. After some time, he paused and motioned for Bruenor to slide out to join him.

"We are being followed," the drow remarked.

Bruenor nodded. No novice to the tundra, the dwarf had sensed the unmistakable signs: a flitter of movement far to the side, the rush of tundra fowl startled by passage, but too far off to have been disturbed by the companions.

"Barbarians?" the dwarf asked, seeming concerned. Despite the recent troubles between the peoples, Bruenor hoped that it was Berkthgar and his tribesmen. At least then, the dwarf would know what problems he was getting!

"Whoever stalks us knows the tundra—few fowl have been roused, and not a deer has skittered away. Goblinoids could not be so careful and tundra yeti do not pursue, they ambush."

"Men, then," replied the dwarf. "And the only men knowing the tundra well enough'd be the barbarians."

Drizzt didn't disagree.

They parted then, Bruenor going back to Catti-brie and Regis to inform them of their suspicions, and Drizzt swinging in another wide, trotting arc. There really wasn't much they could do about the pursuit. The ground was simply too open and flat for any evasive actions. If it was the barbarians, then it was likely that Berkthgar's people were watching more for curiosity than for any threat. Confronting the barbarians might just put problems where there were none.

So the friends walked on, throughout the rest of the day, and long into the night, until Stumpet finally stopped again, unceremoniously dropping to the cold and hard ground. The companions immediately went to work in setting up a formal camp this time. They figured that their rest would last for several hours and understood that the summer was fast on the wane, the chills of winter beginning to sneak into Icewind Dale, particularly during the ever-lengthening night. Catti-brie draped a heavy blanket around Stumpet, though the entranced dwarf didn't seem to notice.

The quiet calm lasted a long hour.

"Drizzt?" Catti-brie whispered, but she realized as soon as she had spoken that the drow was not really asleep, was sitting motionless and with his eyes closed, but was very much alert and very much aware that a small avian form had silently glided above the camp. Perhaps it had been an owl; there were huge owls in Icewind Dale, though they were rarely seen.

Perhaps, but neither of them could afford to think that way.

The slight, barely perceptible flutter came again, to the north, and a shape darker than the night sky glided silently overhead.

Drizzt came up in a rush, scimitars sliding free of his belt. The creature reacted at once, giving a quick flap of its wings to lift it out of Drizzt's deadly reach.

But not out of Taulmaril's range.

A silver-streaking arrow cut the night and slammed into the creature, whatever it was, before it cleared the encampment. Multi-colored sparks lit up the area and Drizzt caught his first true vision of the invader, an imp, as it tumbled from the air, shaken, but not really hurt. It landed hard, rolled to a sitting position, then quickly hopped up, flapping batlike wings to get itself into the air once more before the deadly drow could close in.

Regis had a lantern lit and opened wide by then, and Bruenor and Drizzt flanked the creature, Catti-brie standing back, her bow at the ready.

"My master said you would do that," the imp rasped to Catti-brie. "Errtu protects me!"

"I still put ye out o' the air," the woman replied.

"Why are you here, Druzil?" Drizzt asked, for he surely recognized the imp, the same imp Cadderly had used at the Spirit Soaring to gather information.

"Ye're knowin' this thing?" Bruenor asked the drow.

Drizzt nodded, but didn't reply, too intent on Druzil to banter.

"It did not please Errtu to learn that I was the one who told Cadderly," Druzil snarled in explanation. "Errtu uses me now."

"Poor Druzil," Drizzt said with much sarcasm. "Yours is a difficult lot."

"Spare me your false pity," the imp rasped. "I do so love working for Errtu. When my master is done with you here, we will go to Cadderly next. Perhaps Errtu will even make the Spirit Soaring our fortress!" Druzil snickered with every word, obviously savoring the thought.

Drizzt could barely contain a snicker as well. He had been to the Spirit Soaring and understood its strength and its purity. No matter how powerful Errtu might be, no matter how numerous and strong his minions, the fiend would not defeat Cadderly, not there, in that house of Deneir, in that house of goodness.

"Ye admit then that Errtu's behind the march, and behind the troubles of the dwarf?" Catti-brie asked, indicating Stumpet.

Druzil ignored the women. "Fool!" the imp snapped at Drizzt. "Do you think my master even cares about the fodder in this forlorn place? No, Errtu stays only to meet with you, Drizzt Do'Urden, that you might pay for the troubles you have caused!"

Drizzt moved instinctively, a fast stride toward the imp. Catti-brie lifted her bow, and Bruenor, his axe.

But Drizzt calmed quickly, expecting more information,

and he held his dangerous friends in check with an up-raised hand.

"I offer a deal from Errtu," Druzil said, speaking to Drizzt only. "Your soul for the soul of the tormented one, and for the soul of the female dwarf."

The way the imp described Zaknafein as "the tormented one," surely stung Drizzt to his heart. For a moment, the temptation of the offered deal nearly overwhelmed him. He stood with his head down suddenly, his scimitar tips dipping toward the ground. He would be willing to sacrifice himself to save Zaknafein, surely, or to save Stumpet, for that matter. How could he ever do less?

But then it occurred to Drizzt that neither of them, Zaknafein nor Stumpet, would want him to, that neither of them would subsequently be able to live with such knowledge.

The drow exploded into action, too fast for Druzil to react. Twinkle sliced deeply into the imp's wing, and the other scimitar, the one forged to fight creatures of fire, scratched at the spinning imp's chest, drawing upon Druzil's life force even though it had not sunk in deeply.

Druzil managed to twirl away, and was about to say something in a last desperate act of defiance, but all of the imp's magical shield had been burned away by Catti-brie's first shot. Her second one, perfectly aimed, blew the imp right out of the sky.

Drizzt was to the spot in an instant, his scimitar moving immediately to cave in Druzil's head. The imp shuddered once, and then melted away into a black and acrid smoke.

"I do not deal with denizens of the lower planes," the drow ranger explained to a fast-closing Bruenor, who had not been quick enough to get into the fight.

Still, Bruenor dropped his heavy axe on the dead imp's head for good measure, before the corporeal form faded away altogether. "Good choice," the dwarf agreed.

Soon after, Regis was snoring contentedly, and Catti-brie was fast asleep. Drizzt did not sleep, preferring to keep a watchful eye over his friends, though even the wary drow expected no more trouble from Errtu that night. He paced a perimeter about the camp, scanning the horizons and more often than not, looking up to the bright stars, letting his heart fly with the freedom that was Icewind Dale. At that moment, under that spectacle of sheer beauty, Drizzt understood why he had truly returned, and why Berkthgar and the others from Settlestone had come running home.

"Ye're not to find many monsters peeking at us from behind the durned stars," came a gruff whisper from behind. Drizzt turned as Bruenor approached. The dwarf was already dressed in his battlegear, his one-horned helmet tilted to the side and his many-notched axe comfortably resting across his shoulder, in anticipation of the coming march.

"Balors can fly," Drizzt reminded him, though they both knew that Drizzt was not looking up at the sky in anticipation of any enemy.

Bruenor nodded and moved beside his friend. There ensued a long period of quiet, each of them alone in the wind, alone among the stars. Drizzt sensed Bruenor's somber mood and knew that the dwarf had come out of the camp for a reason, likely to tell him something.

"I had to come back," Bruenor said at length.

Drizzt looked to him and nodded, but Bruenor was still staring up at the sky.

"Gandalug's got Mithril Hall," Bruenor remarked, and it sounded to Drizzt as though the red-bearded dwarf was making excuses. "Rightfully his."

"And you have Icewind Dale," Drizzt added.

Bruenor turned to him then, as if he meant to protest, to further explain himself. One look into Drizzt's lavender orbs told the dwarf that he didn't have to. Drizzt understood him and understood his actions. He had to come back. That was all that he needed to say.

The pair spent the rest of the night standing in the chill wind, watching the stars, until dawn's first glow stole the majestic view, or rather, replaced it with yet another. Stumpet was up soon after, walking zombielike again. The pair roused Catti-brie and Regis. The friends went off in pursuit, together.

# Chapter 25
## TO THE BERGS

ver a ridge, they saw the icebergs and shifting floes floating about in the dark waters of the Sea of Moving Ice. Logic told them that they should be nearing their goal, but all of them feared that Stumpet would keep moving, would pick her way across those treacherous expanses, from floe to floe, up and down the conical bergs. Crenshinibon was known to produce towers; another of the artifact's names was Cryshal-Tirith, which literally translated from elvish meant "crystal tower." A ridge blocked their view of the actual shoreline, but surely any tower before the sea would have been visible to them by this time.

Stumpet, seeming oblivious to it all, continued her march to the sea. She came over the ridge first, the friends rushing to keep close behind, when a barrage of icy snowballs assailed them all.

Drizzt went into a flurry, cut left and right, ducking and slapping away at the hurled missiles with his scimitars. Regis and Catti-brie fell flat to the ground, but the two dwarves, particularly poor Stumpet, who just continued her walking, got pummeled. Bloody welts rose on the priestess's face and she staggered more than once.

Catti-brie, recovered from the shock, put her feet under her and rushed ahead, tackling Stumpet and falling over her protectively.

The barrage stopped as abruptly as it had begun.

Drizzt had the onyx figurine on the ground in front of him, quietly calling in his panther ally. He saw the enemy then, they all did, though none of them knew what to make of the creatures. They came as ghosts, slipping from the white ice onto the still-brown shore so smoothly that they seemed part of the land. They were humanoid, bipedal, large and strong and covered in shaggy white hair.

"I'd be mean too, if I was that ugly," Bruenor remarked, moving close to Drizzt so they could calculate their next move.

"You are," Regis said from his prone position.

Neither the drow nor the dwarf had the time or compunction to respond to the halfling. More and more enemies came off the icy sea—flanking left and right—two score, three, and still they came.

"I'm thinking we might want to turn about," Bruenor remarked.

Drizzt hated that thought, but it seemed their only choice. He and his friends could dole out considerable damage, had battled many mighty enemies, but no less than a hundred of these creatures faced them now. They were obviously not stupid beasts, moving in an organized and cunning fashion.

Guenhwyvar was there then, beside her master, ready to spring.

"Perhaps we can scare them off," Drizzt whispered to Bruenor, and with a word, he sent the cat springing away, a powerful rush straight ahead.

A hail of iceballs slapped against the panther's black sides, and even those creatures directly in Guenhwyvar's line did not retreat, did not waver at all. Two of them were buried where they stood, but a host of others closed in, whacking at the cat with heavy clubs. Soon it was Guenhwyvar who was in full retreat.

Catti-brie, meanwhile, had climbed up from Stumpet—who immediately rose and resumed her march until Regis likewise tackled her—and strung Taulmaril. She quickly surveyed the scene and sent fly an arrow, putting the bolt right between the wide-spread legs of the largest creature to the left of her. Again, the merciful Catti-brie wanted only to scare the things away, and was surprised by the savage response. The creature didn't flinch, as though it didn't care whether it lived or died, and it responded, as did a score of creatures near to it, by hurling iceballs at the woman.

Catti-brie dove and rolled, but got hit several times. One strike on the temple nearly knocked her senseless. She came up in a short run, getting to the side of Drizzt, Bruenor, and the returned panther.

"I'm thinking that our road just turned the other way," she remarked, rubbing the bruise on her forehead.

"A true warrior knows when to turn away," Drizzt agreed, but his eyes continued to scan the icebergs on the dark sea, looking for some hint of Cryshal-Tirith, some hint that Errtu was nearby.

"Would someone please tell that to the damned dwarf!" called a flustered Regis, holding fast to one of Stumpet's sturdy legs. The entranced priestess merely walked along with him, dragging him across the tundra.

All about them, the creatures continued to flank, passing those nasty iceballs down the line for another barrage—one that the companions suspected would be accompanied by a wild charge.

They had to leave, but had not the time to drag Stumpet along with them. If she would not turn with them, surely she would be killed.

\* \* \* \* \*

"You sent them out!" Errtu roared accusingly at the crystal shard as it hovered in midair in the highest room of the Cryshal-Tirith. From the scrying mirror, the mighty balor watched his minions, the taers, as they blocked the passage of Drizzt Do'Urden, something Errtu most certainly did not desire.

"Admit it!" the fiend bellowed.

*You take dangerous chances concerning the rogue drow,* came the telepathic reply. *I cannot allow that.*

"The taers are mine to command!" Errtu screamed. The fiend knew that he merely had to think of his responses and the sentient crystal shard would "hear" them, but Errtu needed to hear the sound of his own roar at that grim time, had to vent his outrage verbally.

"No matter," the fiend decided a moment later. "Drizzt Do'Urden is no small foe. He and his companions will chase off the taers. You have not stopped him!"

*They are unthinking tools,* came Crenshinibon's casual and confident reply. *They obey my command, and will fight to the death. Drizzt Do'Urden is stopped.*

Errtu didn't doubt the declaration. Crenshinibon, though it had certainly been weakened by its joust with the antimagic sapphire, was strong enough to dominate the stupid taers. And those creatures, more than a hundred in number, were too strong and too numerous for Drizzt and his friends to defeat. They might escape—the fleet-footed drow at least—but Stumpet was doomed, as was Bruenor Battlehammer and the chubby halfling.

Errtu considered swooping out of his tower then, or of using his magical abilities to get to that beach, to face off with the drow then and there.

Crenshinibon read his thoughts easily and the image in the scrying mirror disappeared as did Errtu's magical teleportation options, for the balor wasn't even sure of where that particular beach might be. He could take wing, of course, and he had a general idea of where Stumpet would make the Sea of Moving Ice, but he realized that by the time he arrived, Drizzt Do'Urden would likely be dead.

The fiend turned angrily on the crystal shard, and Crenshinibon met his rage with a stream of soothing thoughts, of promises of greater power and glory.

The sentient artifact didn't comprehend the level of Errtu's hatred, didn't understand that the fiend's most important reason for coming to the Prime Material Plane was to exact revenge on Drizzt Do'Urden.

Errtu, impotent and confused, stalked from the room.

\* \* \* \* \*

"We cannot leave Stumpet," Catti-brie said, and of course, Drizzt and Bruenor agreed.

"Hit at them hard," the drow instructed. "Shoot your arrows to kill."

Even as he spoke the words, the iceball volley slapped in. Poor Stumpet got hit repeatedly; Regis took one in the head and let go of the dwarf. She continued her slow walk until three missiles hit her simultaneously, dropping her to the ground.

Catti-brie killed two taers in rapid succession, then rushed after Drizzt, Bruenor and Guenhwyvar as they charged to form a defensive ring about Stumpet and Regis. The taers were out of iceballs then, and on they came, fearlessly, brandishing clubs and howling like the north wind.

"There's only a hunnerd o' the durned things!" Bruenor blustered, hoisting his axe.

"And four of us!" yelled Catti-brie.

"Five," Regis corrected, stubbornly pulling himself to his feet.

Guenhwyvar roared. Catti-brie fired, killing yet another.

*Take me in hand!* came a desperate plea from Khazid'hea.

The woman sent off another arrow, and then the creatures were too close. She dropped her precious bow and drew out the eager Khazid'hea.

Drizzt cut in front of her, double-slashing a taer across the throat, falling into a spin to his knees and thrusting ahead with Twinkle, driving the curving blade deep into a creature's belly. His other scimitar slashed horizontally behind him, tripping up the next beast as it bore down on Catti-brie.

Her downward chop sent the sharp-edged Khazid'hea right through the thing's skull and halfway down its neck. But Catti-brie had to tear her sword free immediately, and Drizzt had to get back to his feet and go into yet another scrambling maneuver, for the throng swarmed about them, closing off any escape.

They knew they were doomed . . . until they heard the unified cry of "Tempus!"

Revjak and his twenty-five warriors came hard into the taer ranks, their huge weapons cutting a swath through the lines of surprised shaggy beasts.

Regis yelled out to their reinforcements, but was silenced by a taer club that slammed him on the shoulder, knocking the breath from him and sending him flying to the ground. Three of the creatures towered over him, ready to smash him down.

A flying Guenhwyvar slammed into them sidelong, the

panther spinning about with all four paws raking wildly. A fourth taer slipped by the embattled three, seeking the prone halfling and the unconscious dwarven female lying beside him.

It met a growling Bruenor, or more particularly, Bruenor's chopping axe.

Dazed, Regis was glad to see the boots of Bruenor as the sturdy dwarf straddled him.

Now Drizzt and Catti-brie worked side by side, the two friends who had been together, fighting together, for so many years.

Catti-brie caught the club of one taer in her free hand and sent Khazid'hea in a short arc, severing the creature's other arm just below the shoulder. To her surprise and horror, though, the taer continued to press forward, and another creature came in right beside it, on Catti-brie's left. Struggling to keep her grip firm on the first creature's club, and with her sword all the way on the other side, the woman had no practical defense against the newcomer.

She screamed in defiance and slashed again with her sword, angling higher this time, cutting halfway through the neck of the creature she held. As she moved, Catti-brie closed her eyes, not wanting to see the incoming club.

Drizzt's scimitar came across and under Khazid'hea's high cut, the drow lurching violently to get his blade all the way past Catti-brie to intercept the club. The parry was perfect, as a surprised Catti-brie realized when she opened her eyes.

The woman didn't hesitate. Drizzt had to go back to the two taers he was battling, but his desperate parry had given Catti-brie the moment she needed. She twisted wildly to face this second taer, cutting her blade the rest of the way through the dead and falling creature's neck, and then using its momentum as it pulled free to thrust it straight ahead, right into this newest foe's chest.

The taer fell back, but two others took its place.

As the ground around Bruenor filled with piled bodies and severed limbs, the dwarf accepted hit after hit from the taer's clubs, belting the beasts with his mighty axe in exchange.

"Six!" he yelled as his axe dove into the sloped forehead of yet another creature, but his call was shortened as yet another beast slammed him in the back.

That one hurt, truly hurt, but Bruenor knew that he had to ignore the pain. Gasping as he turned, he launched his axe in a two-handed semicircle, chopping it deep into the side of the taer as if the creature were a tree.

The taer flew sidelong as the axe barreled in, then stood twisted over the blade, dying fast.

Bruenor heard the roar behind him and was glad to know that Guenhwyvar had untangled herself once more and was protecting his back.

Then he heard another cry, a call to the barbarian god, as Revjak and his warriors joined up with the companions. Now the ring about Regis and Stumpet was secured; now the defense was sturdy enough for Guenhwyvar to go out into the taer ranks, a muscled black ball of devastation. Drizzt and Catti-brie cut through the first line and then charged into the second.

In a matter of mere minutes, every taer was dead or downed with injuries too grievous for it to continue the battle, even though Crenshinibon's commands went on, unabated in their relentless brainwashing assault.

Stumpet had recovered enough by then to get back to her feet and to stubbornly resume her march.

Drizzt, down on one knee, trying to catch his breath, called to Revjak, and the barbarian immediately ordered two of his strongest men to surround the dwarf and lift her off the ground. Stumpet offered no resistance, just held steady, staring blankly ahead, her feet pumping futilely in the empty air.

The smile Drizzt and Revjak exchanged was cut short, though, by a familiar voice.

"Treason!" roared Berkthgar as he and his warriors, more than twice the number Revjak had brought out, surrounded the group.

"This keeps gettin' better and better," Catti-brie said dryly.

"The laws, Revjak!" Berkthgar blustered. "You knew them and you disobeyed!"

"To leave Bruenor and his fellows to die?" Revjak asked incredulously, showing no fear, though it seemed to the companions that battle might soon be joined once more. "Never would I follow such a command," Revjak went on confidently. The warriors with him, many of them nursing wounds from the taer fight, were unified in their agreement.

"Some of our people do not forget the friendship shown to us by Bruenor and Catti-brie, by Drizzt Do'Urden and all the others," the older man finished.

"Some of us do not forget the war with Bruenor's folk and the folk of Ten-Towns," Berkthgar retorted, and his warriors bristled.

"I've heared enough," Catti-brie whispered, and before Drizzt could stop her, she stalked across the open ground to stand right before the huge and imposing barbarian.

"Suren, ye've diminished," Catti-brie said defiantly.

Calls behind the barbarian leader hinted that he should slap the impertinent woman aside. Good sense held Berkthgar in check. For, not only was Catti-brie a formidable opponent, as he had learned personally back in Settlestone when she had defeated him in private combat, but she was backed by Drizzt and by Bruenor, neither of whom the barbarian wanted to face. If he put a hand on Catti-brie, Berkthgar understood that the only thing that would keep the drow ranger off of him would be Bruenor, beating Drizzt to the attack.

"All the respect I once had for ye," Catti-brie went on, and Berkthgar was surprised by the sudden change in her tone and the direction of her words. "Ye were the rightful leader after Wulfgar," she said sincerely. "By deed and by wisdom. Without yer guidance, the tribe would have been lost so far away in Settlestone."

"Where we did not belong!" Berkthgar was quick to respond.

"Agreed," said Catti-brie, again catching the man off guard, cutting inside the direction of his ire. "Ye did right in returning to the dale and to yer god, but not to the ancient enemies. Think on the truth o' me father, Berkthgar, and on the truth o' Drizzt."

"Both killers of my kin."

"Only when yer kin came to kill," Catti-brie said, not backing down an inch. "What cowards would they be if they did not defend their home and kin! Do ye begrudge them for fightin' better than yer own?"

Berkthgar's breath came in short, angry puffs. Drizzt saw it and was quick to join Catti-brie. He had heard the quiet conversation, every word, and he knew where to take it up from there.

"I know what you did," the drow said. Berkthgar stiffened, thinking the words to be an accusation.

"To gain control of the united tribe you had to discredit he who came before you. But I warn you, for the good of all in the dale, do not get caught up in your own half-truths. The name of Berkthgar is spoken of reverently in Mithril Hall, in Silverymoon, in Longsaddle and Nesme, even in Ten-Towns and the dwarven mines. Your exploits in Keeper's Dale will not be forgotten, though you seem to choose to forget the alliance and the good that Bruenor's folk have done. Look to Revjak now—we owe him our lives—and decide, Berkthgar, what course is best for you and your people."

Berkthgar was quiet then, and both Catti-brie and Drizzt knew that to be a good thing. He was not a stupid man, though often he let his emotions cloud his judgment. He did look at Revjak, and at the resolute warriors standing behind the older man, a bit battered, certainly outnumbered, and yet showing no fear. The most important point to the huge barbarian was that neither Drizzt nor Catti-brie was denying his claim of leadership. They were willing to work with him, so it seemed, and Catti-brie had even publicly compared him favorably to Wulfgar!

"And let the hammer stay with Bruenor, where it rightfully belongs," Catti-brie dared to press, as if she was reading Berkthgar's every thought. "Yer own sword is the weapon of yer tribe now; its legend'll be no less than Aegis-fang's if Berkthgar chooses wisely."

That was bait that Berkthgar could not ignore. He visibly relaxed, so did the men following his every word, and Drizzt recognized that they had just passed an important test.

"You were wise in following Bruenor and his companions," Berkthgar said loudly to Revjak, as much an apology as anybody had ever heard the proud barbarian offer.

"And you were wrong in denying our friendship with Bruenor," Revjak replied. Drizzt and Catti-brie both tensed, wondering if Revjak had pushed a bit too hard, too fast.

But Berkthgar took no offense. He didn't respond to the charge. The barbarian didn't show that he agreed, but neither did he become defensive.

"Return with us now," he bade Revjak.

Revjak looked to Drizzt, then to Bruenor, knowing that they still needed his help. It was two of his men, after all, who were still holding Stumpet up in the air.

Berkthgar looked first to Revjak, then followed his gaze to Bruenor, and then looked past the dwarf and to the coast looming not so far away. "You are going out onto the Sea of Moving Ice?"

A frustrated Bruenor gave Stumpet a sidelong glance. "So it'd seem," the dwarf admitted.

"We cannot accompany you," Berkthgar said flatly. "And this is no choice of mine, but an edict of our ancestors. No tribesman may venture out onto the floating land."

Revjak had to nod his agreement. It was indeed an ancient edict, one put in for practicality because there was little to be gained and much to lose in venturing out onto the dangerous ice floes, the land of the white bear and the great whales.

"We would not ask for you to go," Drizzt quickly put in, and his companions seemed surprised by that. They were going off to fight a balor and all of his devious minions, and an army of powerful barbarians might come in handy! But Drizzt knew that Berkthgar would not go against that ancient rule, and he did not want Revjak to split any further from the leader, did not want to jeopardize the healing that had begun here. Also, none of Revjak's warriors had been killed against the taers, but that would not likely hold true if they followed Drizzt all the way to Errtu. Drizzt Do'Urden had enough blood on his hands already. For the drow ranger, this was a private battle. He would have preferred it to be him against Errtu, one against one, but he knew that Errtu would not be alone, and he could not deny his closest friends the chance to stand beside him as he would stand beside them.

"But ye admit that yer folk owe this much, at least, to Bruenor?" Catti-brie had to ask.

Again Berkthgar didn't openly answer, but his silence, his lack of protest, was all the confirmation that the woman needed to hear.

The companions bandaged up their bruises as well as possible, bid their farewells, and thanked the barbarians. Revjak's men put Stumpet down then, and she resumed her march. The companions plodded off after her.

The Tribe of the Elk turned south in a unified march, Berkthgar and Revjak walking side by side.

\* \* \* \* \*

Sometime later, Kierstaad came upon the scene of a hundred taer bodies bloating in the afternoon sun. It didn't take the wily young barbarian long to figure out what had happened. Obviously the barbarians with his father had joined in the fight beside Bruenor's group, and so many different prints were to be found that Kierstaad understood that another group—certainly one led by Berkthgar—had also come upon the scene.

Kierstaad looked to the south, wondering if his father had been escorted back to the encampment as a prisoner. He almost turned then and ran off in pursuit, but the other tracks—the ones of two dwarves, a drow, a woman, a halfling and a hunting cat—compelled him to the north.

Aegis-fang in hand, the young barbarian picked his way down to the cold coast and then out onto the broken trail of ice floes. He was breaking the ancient edicts of his people, he knew, but he dismissed that. In his mind and in his heart, he was following the footsteps of Wulfgar.

# Chapter 26
## NOT BY SURPRISE

he glabrezu was adamant, not backing down from his story despite the mounting threats of a nervous and desperate Errtu.

"Drizzt Do'Urden and his friends have passed the taers," Bizmatec insisted once more, "leaving them dead and torn on the plain."

"You have seen this?" Errtu asked for the fifth time, the great balor clenching and unclenching his fist repeatedly.

"I have seen this," Bizmatec replied without hesitation, though the glabrezu did lean back warily from the balor. "The taers did not stop them, hardly slowed them. They are mighty indeed, these enemies you have chosen."

"And the dwarf?" Errtu asked, his frustration turning fast to eagerness. As he spoke, the balor tapped his bejeweled ring to show that he was referring to the imprisoned female dwarf.

"Leads them still," Bizmatec answered with a wicked smile, the glabrezu thrilled to see the eagerness, the sheer wickedness bringing the light back to Errtu's glowing eyes.

The balor left with a great flourish, a victorious spin and flap of leathery wings that got it to the landing of the crystalline tower's open first level. Up Errtu climbed, maddened by hunger, by desire to show Crenshinibon its failure.

"Errtu has put us in line with worthy enemies," Bizmatec remarked again, watching the balor's departure.

The other tanar'ri in the tower's lowest level, a six-armed woman with the lower torso of a snake, smirked, seeming truly unimpressed. There were no worthy enemies to be found among the mortals of the Prime Material Plane.

High above his minions, Errtu clambered into the small room at the tower's highest level. The fiend went to the narrow window first, peering out in the hopes that he might catch a glimpse of the approaching quarry. Errtu wanted to make a dramatic statement to Crenshinibon, but the fiend's excitement betrayed his thoughts to the sentient, telepathic artifact.

*Your path remains one of danger,* the crystal shard warned.

Errtu spun away from the window and issued a hearty, croaking laugh.

*You must not fail,* the artifact's telepathic message went on. *If you and yours are defeated, then defeated am I, placed in the hands of those who know my nature and . . .*

Errtu's continued laughter rebuked any more telepathic intrusions.

"I have met the likes of Drizzt Do'Urden before," the great balor said with a feral snarl. "He will know true sorrow and true pain before I release him into death! He will see the deaths of his beloved, of those who were foolish enough to accompany him and of he who I hold as prisoner." The great fiend turned back angrily toward the window. "What an enemy have you made, foolish drow rogue! Come to me now that I might exact my revenge and give to you the punishment you deserve!"

With that, Errtu kicked the small coffer still lying on the floor where the fiend had dropped it after the volatile reaction between the crystal shard and the antimagic sapphire. Errtu started to leave, but reconsidered for just a moment. He would be facing Drizzt and all of his companions soon, including the imprisoned priestess. If Stumpet came face to face with the fiend's entrapping gemstone, her spirit might find its way aback to her body.

Errtu pulled off his ring and showed it to Crenshinibon. "The dwarven priestess," the fiend explained. "This holds her spirit. Dominate her and lend what aid you may!"

Errtu dropped the ring to the floor and stormed from the chamber, back down to his minions to prepare for the arrival of Drizzt Do'Urden.

Crenshinibon felt keenly the tanar'ri's rage and the

sheer wickedness that was mighty Errtu. Drizzt and his friends had gotten past the taers, so it seemed, but what were they compared to the likes of Errtu?

And Errtu, the crystal shard knew, had powerful allies lying in wait.

Crenshinibon was satisfied, was quite secure. And to the evil artifact, the thought of using Stumpet against the companions was certainly a pleasant one.

\* \* \* \* \*

Stumpet continued her march across the treacherous and broken ice, leaping small gaps, sometimes splashing her feet into the icy water, but pulling them out with apparently no regard for the freezing wetness.

Drizzt understood the dangers of the water. He wanted to tackle Stumpet once more and pull off her boots, wrapping her feet in warm and dry blankets. The drow let it go. He figured that if frozen toes were the worst of their troubles, they would certainly be better off than he had hoped. Right now, the best thing he could do for Stumpet, for all of them, was to get to Errtu and get this grim business over with.

The drow kept one hand in his pocket as he marched, fingers feeling the intricate detailing of the onyx figurine. He had sent Guenhwyvar home shortly after the taer fight, giving the cat what little rest she might find before the next battle. Now, in looking around, the drow wondered about the wisdom of that decision, for he knew that he was out of place in this unfamiliar terrain.

The landscape seemed surreal, nothing but jagged white mounds, some as high as forty feet, and long sheets of flat whiteness, often cracked by zigzagging dark lines.

They were more than two hours off the beach, far out into the ice-clogged sea, when the weather turned. Dark and ominous clouds rose up, the wind bit harder, colder. Still they plodded on, crawling up the side of one conical iceberg, then sliding down the other side. They came into an area of more dark water and less ice, and there they caught their first sight of their goal, far away to the north and west. The crystalline tower gleamed above the berg cones, shining even in the dull gray daylight. There could be no doubt, for the tower was no natural structure, and though it appeared as if it was made of ice, it seemed unnatural and out of place among the hard and stark whiteness of the bergs.

Bruenor considered the sight and their present course, then shook his head. "Too much water," he explained, pointing to the west. "Should be going straight out that way."

By all appearances, it seemed as if the dwarf was right. They were traveling generally north, but the ice floes seemed more tightly packed to the west.

Their course was not for them to decide though, and Stumpet continued on her oblivious way to the north, where it seemed as if she would soon be stopped by a wide gap of open water.

Appearances could be deceiving in the surreal and unfamiliar landscape. A long finger of ice bridged that watery gap, turning them more directly toward the crystal tower. When they crossed over, they came into another region of clogged icebergs, and looming before them, barely a quarter of a mile away, was Cryshal-Tirith.

Drizzt brought in Guenhwyvar once more. Bruenor knocked Stumpet down and sat on her, while Catti-brie scrambled up the tallest nearby peak to get a better feeling for the area.

The tower was on a large iceberg, set right in back of the thirty foot high conical tip of the natural structure. Catti-brie guessed she and her companions would cross onto the berg from the southwest, on a narrow strip of ice about a dozen feet wide. One other iceberg directly west of the tower, was close enough, perhaps, to make a leap onto the main area, but other than that, the fiend's fortress was surrounded by ocean.

Catti-brie marked one other point: a cave entrance on the southern face of the conical peak that was almost directly across from the tower on the other side of the berg. It was at least a man's height up from the wider flat area on the southern side of the berg, the area they would cross, the area that seemed as if it would soon become a killing ground. With a resigned sigh, the woman slid back down and reported it all to her friends.

"Errtu's minions will meet us soon after we cross the last stretch," Drizzt reasoned, and Catti-brie nodded with every word. "We will have to fight them all the way to the cave entrance, and even more so within."

"Let's get on with it, then," Bruenor grumbled. "Me durned feet're getting cold!"

Catti-brie looked to Drizzt, as though she wanted to hear some options. Few seemed apparent, though. Even if that leap was possible for Catti-brie, Drizzt, and Guenhwyvar, Bruenor, in his heavy armor, could not hope to make it, nor could Regis. And if they went that way, Stumpet—who could only walk—would be alone.

"I'll not be much good in a fight," Regis said quietly.

"That never stopped ye before!" Bruenor howled, misunderstanding. "Ye meanin' to sit here—"

Drizzt stopped the dwarf with an upraised hand, guessing that the remarkably resourceful halfling had something important and valuable in mind.

"If Guenhwyvar could get me across that gap, I might make it quietly to the tower," the halfling explained.

The faces of his companions brightened as they began to consider the possibilities.

"I have been in Cryshal-Tirith before," Regis went on. "I know how to get through the tower, and how to defeat the crystal shard if I make it." He looked to Drizzt as he said this and nodded. Regis had been with Drizzt on the plain north of Bryn Shander, when the drow had beaten Akar Kessel's tower.

"A desperate chance," Drizzt remarked.

"Yeah," Bruenor agreed dryly. "Not like walking into the middle of a tanar'ri horde."

That brought a chuckle—a strained one indeed—from the group.

"Let Stumpet up," Drizzt bade Bruenor. "She will take us in to whatever Errtu has planned. And you," he added, looking to the halfling, "may Gwaeron Windstrom, servant of Mielikki and patron of rangers, be with you on your journey. Guenhwyvar will get you across. Understand, my friend, that if you fail and Crenshinibon is not defeated, Errtu will be all the stronger!"

Regis nodded grimly, took a firm hold of the scruff on the back of Guenhwyvar's neck, and split apart from the group, thinking that his one chance would be to get to the iceberg quickly and secretly. He and the cat were soon out of sight, moving up and down across the rough terrain. Guenhwyvar did most of the work, her claws cutting deep into the ice, grabbing holds where she could find them. Regis merely kept his hold on her and tried to keep his legs moving quickly enough so that he would not be too much of a burden.

They nearly met with disaster coming down the slippery backside of one steep cone. Guenhwyvar dug in, but Regis stumbled and went down. His momentum as he slipped past the cat cost Guenhwyvar her tenuous hold. Down they careened, heading for the black water. Regis stifled a cry, but closed his eyes and expected to splash into his freezing doom.

Guenhwyvar caught a new hold barely inches from the deadly cold sea.

Shaken and bruised, the pair pulled themselves up and started off once more. Regis bolstered his resolve, burying his fears by reminding himself repeatedly of the importance of his mission.

\* \* \* \* \*

The companions understood how very vulnerable they were as they crossed the last expanse of open ice to get to the huge iceberg that held Cryshal-Tirith. They sensed that they were being watched, sensed that something terrible was about to happen.

Drizzt tried to hurry Stumpet along. Bruenor and Cattibrie ran up ahead.

Errtu's minions were waiting, crouched within the cave entrance and behind the icy bluffs. Indeed the fiend was watching the group, as was Crenshinibon.

The artifact thought the balor a fool, risking so much for so little real gain. It used the gemstone ring to connect with Stumpet, to see through the imprisoned dwarf's eyes, to know exactly where the enemies were.

Suddenly, the very tip of Cryshal-Tirith glowed a fierce red, stealing the grayness of the approaching storm in a pinkish haze.

Catti-brie yelled to Drizzt; Bruenor grabbed the woman and tugged her forward and to the ground.

Drizzt barreled into Stumpet, but merely bounced off. He skittered past—he had to move—then skidded, trying desperately to slow, as a line of blazing fire shot out from the tower's tip and sliced through the ice walk in front of the drow.

Thick steam engulfed the area and the stunned ranger. Drizzt could not fully stop and so he yelled out and charged ahead, leaping and rolling with all his strength.

Only good luck saved him. The line of fire halted abruptly from the tower, and then began again, this time over the standing dwarven priestess, cutting another line behind her. The force of the blow sent flecks of ice flying, thickened the steam. The now-severed floe, two hundred square feet of drifting ice, floated to the southeast, turning slowly as it drifted.

Stumpet had nowhere to go, so she merely stood perfectly still, her gaze impassive.

On the main iceberg, the three friends were up and running once more.

"Left!" Catti-brie called as a creature clambered over the ridge that was the side of the central cone. The woman nearly gagged on her word at the sight of the horrid thing, one of the least of the Abyss's creatures that were called manes. It was the dead spirit of a wretch from the Prime Material Plane. Pale white skin, bloated and overloaded with oozing liquids, hung in loose flaps along the thing's torso, and many-legged parasites clung to its hide. It was only three feet tall, Regis's size, but it sported long and obviously sharp claws and nasty teeth.

Catti-brie blew it away with a single silver-streaking arrow, but a group of its friends, showing no regard whatsoever for their safety, scrambled over the ridge right behind it.

"Left!" the woman cried again, but Drizzt and Bruenor could not afford to heed those words.

For many more manes had come ambling out of the cave entrance, barely thirty feet away, and two flying fiends, giant bugs that seemed a horrid cross between a human and a giant fly, came out above the horde.

Bruenor met the closest fiends with a vicious chop of his axe. The single stroke did the trick, but the destroyed fiend, rather than lie down dead, exploded into a puff of noxious, acidic fumes that burned at the dwarf's skin and lungs.

"Durned slime-orcs," the red-bearded dwarf grumbled, and he was not deterred, blasting away a second fiend, and then a third in rapid succession, filling the air about him with fumes.

Drizzt was hitting at manes and moving so quickly that the ensuing cloud of evil vapors did not even touch him. He had a line of them down, but then had to fall flat to avoid the low pass of one of the flying tanar'ri, chasme they were called.

By the time the drow regained his footing, a gang of manes had closed around him, reaching eagerly with their long and nasty claws.

Catti-brie nearly wretched again at the mere sight of the flying fiends. She had downed half a dozen manes already, but now she had to turn her attention to the horrible bugs.

She whirled and fired at the closest, nearly point-blank, and sighed with sincere relief as her arrow threw the fiend backward and to the ground.

Its companion, though was gone, simply disappeared in a display of fiendish magic.

It stood quietly behind Catti-brie.

* * * * *

Regis and Guenhwyvar saw the commotion, saw the lines of blazing white fire and heard the ensuing battle. They picked up their pace as much as possible, but the terrain was not favorable, not at all.

Again the halfling was merely holding on, letting Guenhwyvar tow him in full flight. Regis bumped and bounced, but didn't complain. Whatever his pains, he was certain that his friends were feeling worse.

\* \* \* \* \*

"Behind ye!" Bruenor yelled, bursting free of the horde of manes. One of the wretched creatures clung fast to the dwarf, its claws deep into the back of his neck, but he hardly cared.

All that mattered was Catti-brie, and she was in dire trouble. The dwarf couldn't get to the fiend behind her, but the one she had hit was back up, walking this time, and was directly between Bruenor and his beloved daughter.

Not a good place to be.

Catti-brie spun on her heels as the chasme struck. She accepted the vicious hit on her shoulder and rolled with it, doing two complete somersaults across the ice before putting her feet back underneath her.

Bruenor's twirling axe hit the other chasme full force in the back, blasting it to the ground for the second time. Still the stubborn thing tried to rise, but the running dwarf summarily buried it, diving upon it and grabbing up his weapon. He tore the axe free and pounded away repeatedly, driving the chasme into the ice, splattering the white surface with green and yellow gore.

Still the other fiend hung on the back of the furious dwarf, scratching and biting. It was starting to do some real damage, but that ended as abruptly as the cut of a drow's scimitar.

The remaining chasme was airborne once more, and Catti-brie had her bow in line. She scored a brutal hit and the fiend had seen enough. It flew right past her and over the ridge, toward the back side of the glacier.

As she turned to follow its flight, Catti-brie had to lower her bow to a different target, one of the score of manes who, by this time, had come scrambling over the ridge.

The chasme under Bruenor seemed to deflate—there really was no other way to describe how the fiend's body flattened, like a waterskin emptying its contents.

Drizzt pulled the dwarf up and roughly turned him

about. The immediate threat to Catti-brie had been halted, but they had lost ground and the horde of oozing manes had regrouped.

No matter for the two seasoned friends. A quick glance told them that Catti-brie had the group to the side under control and so they charged, side by side, tearing into the closest ranks of least tanar'ri.

Drizzt, with his deadly, slashing scimitars and his quick feet, made the most progress, slicing through reaching arms and dodging manes with abandon, laying six of them low in a matter of seconds. The drow hardly registered that his opponent had changed a moment later, until his wild swing was met, not by one, but by three separate ringing parries.

The horde thinned in this area, the lesser fiends giving a respectful distance to the six-armed monstrosity that now faced off against Drizzt Do'Urden.

Catti-brie saw the fight and recognized the drow's predicament. She rushed to her right, toward the shoreline, trying to get an angle for a shot, paying no heed to unblinking Stumpet on the drifting floe, now some forty feet out from the iceberg. Her wounded shoulder continued to pump out blood—nasty indeed was the strike of a chasme—but she couldn't stop and bandage it.

Down the woman skidded to one knee. The angle was difficult, especially with the active drow between her and the six-armed tanar'ri. But Catti-brie knew that Drizzt would want her to try, that he needed her to try. Up came Taulmaril, Catti-brie's fingers finding their hold on the string behind the arrow's fletchings.

"The drow cannot fight his own battles?" came a question behind the woman, a deep, throaty voice. "We must talk about that." It was the glabrezu, Bizmatec.

Catti-brie threw herself forward and ducked her shoulder, moving her arm out to full extension to protect the bow, and more particularly, to protect the integrity of the readied arrow. Agile Catti-brie fired off her shot before she even completed the spin, grimacing as her shoulder spouted a red stream. This newest opponent's expression went from amazement to agony as the silver-streaking arrow skipped off the inside of the glabrezu's huge thigh.

Catti-brie winced then, for the arrow continued out from the shore, skipping across the water and onto the drifting chunk of ice barely a few feet from oblivious Stumpet. The woman realized that she shouldn't have wasted the time to follow the arrow, though, for the twelve-foot glabrezu, all muscle and horrible pincers, roared in outrage and closed the gap to Catti-brie with one long stride.

In came a monstrous claw that could easily snap the woman in half, setting into place about Catti-brie's slender, vulnerable waist.

In one fluid motion, Catti-brie punched her hand between the bow and its string, reaching across her body and tearing Khazid'hea from its sheath. Catti-brie cried out and tried futilely to fall away, snapping off a weak backhand with the weapon, hoping to wedge the blade into the fiend's pincers and turn aside his attack.

Khazid'hea, so very sharp, hit the inside edge of the pincer and kept on going, slicing right through.

*I feared I was forgotten!* the sentient sword relayed to Catti-brie.

"Never that," the woman replied grimly.

Bizmatec howled again and brought his great arm snapping across, the remaining side of the pincers knocking Catti-brie flat to the ground. In stalked the glabrezu, lifting a huge foot to squash the woman.

Khazid'hea, coming up fast and sure, made the fiend reconsider the wisdom of that maneuver, and took one of the toes from Bizmatec's huge foot in the process.

Again the glabrezu howled in rage. Bizmatec hopped back and Catti-brie climbed to her feet, readying herself for the next assault.

The ensuing attack was not what the woman expected. Bizmatec loved to toy with mortals, particularly humans, to torment them and finally, to tear them apart slowly, limb by limb. This one was too formidable for such tactics, the wounded tanar'ri decided, and so Bizmatec called upon magical powers.

Catti-brie felt her back foot slip out from under her, and when she tried to recover, she realized that she was no longer standing on the ice, was floating in the air.

"No, ye cheatin' dog-faced smoke-sucker!" Catti-brie protested, to no avail.

Bizmatec waved his huge hand and Catti-brie drifted by, ten feet in the air now, and moving out over the open water. The woman growled defiantly. Understanding what the fiend had in mind, she took up Khazid'hea in one hand, holding it more like a spear than a sword, and hurled it to the side, to the ice floe holding Stumpet. The sword hit the ice near to the dwarf, and sunk in to the hilt.

Catti-brie wasn't watching, was scrambling to regain her balance and to ready her bow. She did so, but Bizmatec merely laughed at her and released his magical energy.

Catti-brie splashed into the icy water, lost her breath immediately, and could feel her toes quickly going numb.

"Stumpet!" Catti-brie yelled to the dwarf, and Khazid'hea called out to the priestess as well, a mental plea for Stumpet to pull the sword from the ice. Stumpet stood impassively, perfectly oblivious to the threatening scene.

Bruenor knew what had happened to Catti-brie. The dwarf had seen her rise into the air, had heard the splash and her subsequent cries for Stumpet. Every paternal instinct within Bruenor told him to run from the fight and leap into the water after his dear daughter, and yet he knew that to be a foolhardy course. It would not only get him killed (for he cared little for personal safety where Catti-brie was concerned) but would doom his daughter as well. The only thing Bruenor could do for Catti-brie was win the fight quickly, and so the dwarf went at the manes with abandon, chopping enemies nearly in half with his mighty axe and screaming all the while. His progress was amazing and all the area near him was cloudy with puffs of yellowish gas.

Bruenor's fortune reversed in the flare of a sudden burst of fire. The dwarf fell back and yelped, stunned for a moment, his face red from the flash. He shook his head fiercely and came back to his senses as Bizmatec entered the fray, the huge fiend clubbing Bruenor on the head with what remained of his right claw, his left pincers going for the fast kill at the dwarf's throat.

Drizzt heard it all, the fate of both Catti-brie and Bruenor. The drow did not allow the intimations of guilt to creep into his senses. Long ago, Drizzt Do'Urden had learned that he was not responsible for all of the sorrow in the world, and that his friends would follow the course of their own choosing. What Drizzt felt was outrage, pure and simple, and adrenaline coursed through his veins, carrying him to greater heights of battle.

But how could someone parry six attacks?

Twinkle went left, left, left, then back to the right, each swing picking off a rushing blade. Drizzt's other blade, verily pulsing with hunger, came in a vertical swipe, tip pointing to the ground, blocking two of the marilith's swords at once. Twinkle flew back the other way, angling up to block, and then turning down to intercept. Then the drow hopped as high as he could, purely on instinct, as the marilith half-spun, her green and scaly tail whipping past in an attempt to take the drow's feet out from under him.

Advantage gained, Drizzt hit the ground running, straight ahead, his scimitars flying out in front in a wild offensive flurry. But though he was inside the angles of the fiend's six swords, his attack was defeated as the marilith simply disappeared—pop!—and reappeared right behind him.

Drizzt knew enough about fiends to react to the move. As soon as his target vanished, he dove into a headlong roll, twisting as he came back to his feet. His hungry scimitar shot out to the side as he rose, cutting down a fiend that had ventured too near, but Drizzt hardly followed the attack, his quick feet already turning on the ice to reverse his direction, to get him back at the marilith.

Again came the ringing of parry and counter, sounding almost as a single, long wail, as eight blades wove a blurring dance of death.

It seemed almost a miracle, a virtual impossibility, but Drizzt scored the first hit, Twinkle taking the marilith in one of her numerous shoulders, rendering that arm useless.

And then there were five swords charging hard at the drow's face and he had to fall away.

\* \* \* \* \*

Regis and Guenhwyvar made it at last to the narrowest point in the channel between the icebergs, and it seemed a desperate leap to the frightened halfling. Even worse, a new problem presented itself, for the area across from them was not an empty, secret run to the crystal tower, but was filling fast with wretched manes.

Regis would have turned back then, preferring to try and find his friends, or, if they were already gone, to turn tail and run, all the way back to the tundra, all the way back to the dwarven mines. Images of coming back with an army of dwarves (of coming back *behind* an army of dwarves!) flitted through the halfling's mind, but it soon proved to be a moot notion.

Regis was holding fast to Guenhwyvar, and he soon realized that the dedicated panther had no intention of even slowing. The halfling grabbed all the tighter. He yelped in fear as the great cat jumped, soaring out over the black water, across the gap to skid hard on the ice, scattering the nearest group of manes. Guenhwyvar could have made short work of those horrid creatures, but the panther knew her mission and went at it with single-minded abandon. With Regis holding on desperately and howling in terror, Guenhwyvar ran on, cutting left and right, dodging manes and leaving them far behind. In a matter of seconds, the pair went over a ridge and came down into an empty little vale, right at the base of Cryshal-Tirith. The manes, apparently too stupid to follow prey that had gone out of sight, did not come in fast pursuit.

"I have to be insane," Regis whispered, looking again at the crystal tower that had served as a prison to him when Akar Kessel had invaded Icewind Dale. And Kessel, though a wizard, was but a man. This time a fiend, a great and powerful balor, controlled the crystal shard!

Regis could not see any door to the four-sided tower, as he knew he would not. An added defense of the tower was that Cryshal-Tirith's entrance was not visible to creatures of the plane of existence on which the tower stood, with the single exception of the crystal shard's wielder. Regis could not see the door, but Guenhwyvar, a creature of the Astral Plane, surely could.

Regis hesitated, managed to hold Guenhwyvar back for a moment. "There are guards," the halfling explained. He remembered the giant and powerful trolls that had been in the last Cryshal-Tirith, and imagined what monsters Errtu might have put in place.

Even as he spoke, the pair heard a buzzing sound and looked up. Regis nearly fainted dead away as a chasme swooped over the ridge and bore down on them.

\* \* \* \* \*

Not bothered at all at being bonked on the head, Bruenor got his axe up to intercept the nipping pincer. The dwarf bolted ahead, or at least, he tried. When that attack didn't work, he wisely reversed his course and went into a quick tactical retreat.

"Bigger beastie, bigger target," Bruenor snarled, straightening the one-horned helmet on his head. He whipped his axe to the side, knocking back a pair of manes, then roared and charged straight in at Bizmatec, showing no fear whatsoever.

The four-armed glabrezu met the charge with a pounding half-claw and a pair of punching fists. Bruenor scored a hit, but got slugged twice in return. Dazed, the dwarf could only look on helplessly as the fiend's good pincer came rushing in again.

A silver streak passed right by the dwarf, the arrow hitting the fiend in his massive chest and driving Bizmatec back a staggering step.

There was Catti-brie, in the water still, thrashing about, bobbing high so that she could bring Taulmaril, which she had turned sidelong, free of the water long enough to get off a shot. Firing the bow at all was amazing, but for her to actually hit the mark . . .

Bruenor couldn't understand how she came high again, impossibly high, until the dwarf realized that Catti-brie had her foot on a submerged piece of ice. Up she went, letting fly another deadly arrow.

Bizmatec howled and staggered back another step.

Catti-brie howled, too, in glee, but hers was not a sincere cry. She was glad that she was exacting some revenge on the fiend, and glad that she was aiding her father, but she could not deny that her legs were already numb, that her shoulder continued to bleed, and that her time for this fight was not long. All around her, the black and cold water waited impatiently, a prowling animal waiting to gobble up the doomed woman.

Her third shot missed the mark, but it came close enough so that Bizmatec had to duck suddenly. The fiend twisted and bent low, then his eyes widened considerably when he realized that he had just put his forehead in perfect alignment with Bruenor's rushing axe.

The explosion dropped Bizmatec to his knees. The fiend felt the fierce yank as Bruenor tore his axe free. Then came another explosion and a silver streak to the side that blasted away the manes that were trying to come to the glabrezu's aid. Where was Errtu now? Then came a third hit, and the world was swirling, darkening, as the spirit of Bizmatec careened along the corridor that would take him back to the Abyss for a hundred years of banishment.

Bruenor came out from the black smoke, all that remained of the glabrezu, with renewed abandon, hacking at the fast-thinning ranks of manes, working his way to Drizzt. He couldn't actually see the drow, but he could hear the ring of steel, the impossibly fast repetition of blade striking blade.

He did manage to get a glimpse of Catti-brie, and his heart soared with hope, for his daughter had somehow splashed her way over to the same ice floe that bore Stumpet.

"Come on, dwarf," Bruenor muttered intensely. "Find yer god and save me girl!"

Stumpet didn't move as Catti-brie continued to flounder. The woman was too engaged, as was her father, to notice another large form making its way toward the battle, moving swiftly and gracefully across the ice.

\* \* \* \* \*

From a short distance back within the cave opening, Errtu watched it all with pure enjoyment. The fiend felt no loss as Bizmatec was pounded away into nothingness, cared little for the chasme, and nothing at all for the manes. Even the marilith, in such desperate combat with Drizzt, merely concerned the balor because Errtu feared that she might kill the drow. As for the generals and his soldiers, they were replaceable, easily replaceable. There was no shortage of willing fiends waiting eagerly in the Abyss.

So let the companions win out here on the open berg, Errtu figured. Already the woman was out of the fight, and the dwarf was battered. And Drizzt Do'Urden, though he was fighting so very well, was surely tiring. By the time Drizzt got into the cave, he would likely be alone, and no single mortal, not even a drow elf, could stand up to the mighty balor.

The fiend smiled wickedly and watched the continuing fight. If the marilith gained too much of an advantage, Errtu would have to intervene.

* * * * *

Crenshinibon also viewed the battle with great interest. The crystal shard, intent on the main fight, was oblivious to the enemies who had come to Cryshal-Tirith's doorstep. Unlike Errtu, the artifact wanted the fight done with, wanted Drizzt and his friends simply destroyed before they ever got near the cave. Crenshinibon would have liked to send out another line of fire—the drow was a more stationary target now, locked in combat as he was—but the first such attack had severely weakened the shard. The encounter with the antimagic sapphire had taken a toll. Crenshinibon could only hope the damage would eventually heal.

For now, though . . .

The wicked artifact found a way. It reached out telepathically to the ring Errtu had left on the floor, to the trapped dwarf held within that gem prison.

On the ice floe, Stumpet finally moved, and Catti-brie, not understanding, smiled hopefully when she noticed the priestess's approach.

307

* * * * *

In the never-ending wars of the Abyss, the fiends known as mariliths have a reputation as generals, as the finest tacticians. But Drizzt soon realized that the creature with seven appendages was not so coordinated in her movements. The marilith's routines did not vary, simply because of the confusion any wielder would find in trying to coordinate the movements of six separate blades.

And so the drow was doing better, though his arms tingled with numbness from the sheer number of parries he had been through.

Left, left, then right went Twinkle, complimenting the up and down movements of the other scimitar, and Drizzt was quick to jump when the marilith's tail, predictably, came slashing around.

The fiend disappeared once more, and Drizzt decided to spin about. The marilith expected him to do that, he realized, and so he came straight ahead instead, and scored a vicious hit as the creature reappeared, exactly where she had just been.

"Oh, my son," the marilith said unexpectedly, falling back.

That gave Drizzt pause, but he was still in a ready crouch, still able to double-slash into gas the two manes that ventured near.

"Oh, my son," the fiend said again, in a voice that was so familiar to the beleaguered drow. "Can you not see through the disguise?" his enemy went on.

Drizzt sucked in a deep breath, trying not to look at the deep and bleeding slash he had put across the marilith's left breast, wondering suddenly if he had struck foolishly.

"It is Zaknafein," the creature went on. "A trick of Errtu, forcing me to fight against you . . . as Matron Malice did with Zin-carla!"

The words stunned Drizzt profoundly, locked his feet into place. His knees nearly buckled as the creature gradually shifted shape, went from a six-armed monstrosity to a handsome drow male, a male that Drizzt Do'Urden knew so very well.

Zaknafein!

"Errtu wants you to destroy me," the creature said. The marilith did well to hide a snicker. She had scoured Drizzt's thoughts to come up with this ploy, and had followed their ensuing course, letting Drizzt lead, every step. As soon as she had proclaimed this to be a trick of the balor, Drizzt had thought of Matron Malice, whoever that was, and of Zin-carla, whatever that was. The marilith was more than prepared to play along.

And it was working! Drizzt's scimitars sagged. "Fight him, my father!" Drizzt yelled. "Find your freedom, as you did from Malice!"

"He is strong," the marilith replied. "He . . ." The creature smiled, her two remaining weapons dipping low. "My son!" came the soothing, familiar voice.

Drizzt nearly swooned. "We must aid the dwarf," he started to say, willing to believe that this was indeed Zaknafein, and that his father could find his way out of Errtu's mental clutches.

Drizzt was willing to believe that, but his scimitar, forged to destroy such creatures of fire, most certainly was not. The scimitar could not "see" the marilith's illusion, could not hear the soothing voice.

Drizzt actually took a step to the side, toward Bruenor, when he recognized the continued throbbing, the unrelenting hunger, of that blade. He took another step, just to get his feet properly positioned, and then hurled himself at the illusion of his father, his rage doubling.

He was met by the five remaining blades as the marilith quickly resumed her more natural form, and the battle began anew.

Drizzt called upon his innate magic and limned the fiend with purplish faerie fire, but the marilith laughed and countered the magical energy, dousing the fire with a thought.

Drizzt heard the familiar shuffling behind him and immediately brought up a globe of impenetrable darkness, right over himself and the creature.

The marilith taunted him. "You think I cannot see?" the fiend roared gleefully. "I have lived longer in darkness than you, Drizzt Do'Urden!"

Her unabated attacks seemed to confirm her words. Sword rang out against scimitar, against scimitar, against scimitar against . . . axe.

The creature didn't understand for a split second, a fatal hesitation. Suddenly she realized that Drizzt was no longer in front of her, but the drow's dwarven ally! And if Bruenor was in front . . .

The marilith reached into her innate magic once more, thinking to teleport away to safety.

Drizzt's strike came first, though, his hungry scimitar driving through the marilith's backbone.

His darkness globe went away then, and Bruenor, in front of the fiend, howled insanely as the tip of Drizzt's scimitar blasted out of the marilith's chest.

Drizzt held on, even managed a twist or two, as the scimitar fed, energy coursing along its blade and hilt.

The marilith spat curse after curse. She tried to attack Bruenor, but could not lift her arms as that wicked, cursed blade gulped at her life force, draining it away. The marilith was less substantial suddenly, her flesh melting away to smoky nothingness.

She promised Drizzt Do'Urden a thousand tortured deaths, promised that she would one day return to exact horrific revenge.

Drizzt had heard it all before.

"There's more and worse inside," Drizzt said to Bruenor when the business was finished.

Bruenor gave a quick look over his shoulder and saw Stumpet closing on his struggling daughter—what the dwarf thought to be a good thing. There was nothing more that Bruenor could do for her. "Let's go then!" he bellowed in reply.

Only a few manes remained—more were coming over the ridge from the back side of the iceberg—and the friends charged on, side by side. They blew away any of the meager resistance, went into the cave hard and fast, where the last group of manes waited, and were summarily destroyed.

The only light the companions had with them came from Drizzt's blades. Twinkle glowed its usual blue, while the other blade flared brightly, a different hue of blue. This scimitar glowed only in extreme cold, and it was glowing more fiercely after its most recent feast.

The cave seemed larger from the inside. The floor inside the entrance sloped down steeply to add to its depth, though the whole of the place was thick with icy stalagmites and stalactites, most reaching from floor to ceiling, which was now more than thirty feet above the pair.

When the fight was ended, Drizzt pointed across the way, to a steep incline, a path up the opposite wall, which ended on a landing that seemed to turn around a blocking sheet of thick ice.

They started across the jagged floor, but stopped when they heard the maniacal laughter. Errtu appeared, and cold became hot as the mighty balor loosed his devastating fire.

\* \* \* \* \*

It was a simple case of underestimation. The chasme knew about the material world, had been here before, and understood what to expect from the creatures that lived here.

But Guenhwyvar was not of the material world, and was above what a normal cat could do.

The chasme rushed over the pair, thinking itself high enough to be safe. Great indeed was the fiend's surprise when the mighty cat leaped straight up, crossing thirty feet in a mere instant, great claws hooking fast onto the buglike torso.

Down they went in a heap, Guenhwyvar raking wildly with her back legs, holding fast with her front and biting with all the considerable strength of her powerful jaws.

Regis looked to the rolling pair, quickly surmising that he could do little to help. He called repeatedly for Guenhwyvar, then looked about, seeing that some of the manes were fast returning, this time continuing over the ridge to close in.

"Hurry, Guenhwyvar!" the halfling cried, and the panther did just that, redoubling her devastating kicks.

311

Then it was Guenhwyvar alone on the ground, pulling herself from the fast-dissipating black smoke. The cat came right to Regis, and started for the door, but Regis, an idea popping into his head, tugged hard to stop her momentum.

"There's a window on the top floor!" the halfling explained, for he had no desire to fight his way through the tower's guardians, which might, he realized, include Errtu. He knew this was a desperate chance, for the window on Cryshal-Tirith's top floor was as often a portal to another place as a normal entrance or exit for the tower.

Guenhwyvar scanned the indicated area quickly, then changed direction. Regis went right onto the panther's back, fearing that he would slow the cat's desperate run if his legs could not keep up.

Up the side of the conical mound went Guenhwyvar. Claws digging in, legs churning with all her strength, she came to a relatively flat area, gained a burst of speed, and leaped out for the tower, for the small window.

The pair hit the side of Crenshinibon hard, Regis somehow scrambling over the panther to get his body through the narrow portal. He landed hard and rolled backward, finally putting his back to the wall. He started to call out for Guenhwyvar to come in.

But he heard the cat's roar, and then heard Guenhwyvar spring away from the tower's side, the panther going fast to the aid of her master.

That left Regis alone in the small room to face the crystal shard.

"Great," the terrified halfling said dryly.

# Chapter 27
## SHOWDOWN

rizzt and Bruenor quickly came to understand the absolutely unfavorable conditions in which they had met Errtu. The fiend's fires raged, turning the ice cave into a sloshing quagmire. Huge blocks fell from the ceiling, forcing the friends to dodge and twist, the cold water weighing them down.

Even worse, whenever the great balor moved away from the pair, taking away his fiendish heat, the water began to refreeze about Drizzt and Bruenor, slowing them.

Throughout the ordeal, they heard the taunting laughter of the mighty Errtu.

"What torment awaits you, Drizzt Do'Urden!" the fiend bellowed.

Drizzt heard the sudden splash behind him, felt the suddenly intense heat, and knew that the fiend had used his magic, had teleported to arrive right behind the drow. Drizzt started to turn, was quick enough to dodge, but the fiend merely stuck his lightning sword into the water behind the drow, and the energy released from the blade jolted Drizzt's every muscle.

Drizzt spun, gritted his teeth to prevent himself from biting off his own tongue. Around came Twinkle, a perfect parry, catching Errtu's second attack in mid-swing.

The fiend laughed all the louder as his devilish blade released another jolt, a burst of electrical energy that rushed through Drizzt's scimitar and into the drow, coursing down his body and popping his knees so painfully that he lost his balance and nearly lost consciousness.

He heard Bruenor's roar, and the sloshing as the dwarf

pounded his way toward him. The dwarf couldn't get there in time, Drizzt realized. Errtu's sudden assault had beaten him.

But suddenly, the fiend was gone, simply gone. It took Drizzt only a moment to understand; Errtu was playing with them! The fiend had waited all these years to exact revenge on Drizzt, and now the wicked balor was truly enjoying himself.

Bruenor skidded by as Drizzt regained his footing. The pair heard the sound of Errtu's taunting laughter once more, from across the way.

"Beware, for the fiend can appear wherever he chooses," Drizzt warned, and even as he spoke the words, he heard the crack of a whip and the cry of the dwarf. Drizzt spun about as Bruenor was tugged from his feet.

"Ye don't say?" the dwarf asked, scrambling furiously to get himself in line for a strike as Errtu jerked him backward, away from Drizzt.

Bruenor realized the depth of his troubles then, for in looking back, he saw a wall of fire looming before him, sizzling and sputtering as it turned the ice to steam. Behind it stood Errtu reeling him in with the whip, grinning wickedly.

Drizzt felt the strength drain from his body; he knew how Errtu meant to torment him now. Bruenor was doomed.

\* \* \* \* \*

Regis didn't know it, but his presence alone in that small room at the top of Cryshal-Tirith saved Catti-brie. Stumpet was near to her, at the edge of the ice. To Catti-brie's horror, the dwarf did not try to help her get her numbed form over the edge of the floe, but rather began pushing and kicking at her, trying to dislodge her and drop her back into the water.

Catti-brie fought back as fiercely as she could, but without firm footing and with her legs completely numb, she was losing the struggle.

But then Regis went into the tower, and the crystal shard had to release Stumpet from its domineering hold and concentrate on this newest threat.

Stumpet stopped fighting, went perfectly still. As soon as she realized the truth of the immobile dwarf, Catti-brie grabbed a hold on Stumpet's sturdy leg, using the dwarf's bulk to pull herself clear of the water.

After a considerable struggle, the woman managed to get shakily to her feet. Drizzt and Bruenor were gone by then, into the cave, but there remained manes to shoot, including a group that had leaped into the water and were thrashing about, gradually closing the gap to Catti-brie and Stumpet, the last remaining visible enemies.

Up came Taulmaril.

* * * * *

Bruenor struggled with all his might. He grabbed on to the remaining stump of one destroyed stalagmite, but the icy thing was too slick for him to get a firm hold. It wouldn't have helped anyway, not with Errtu—so huge and strong—pulling against him. The dwarf howled in pain as his feet went into the fiendish fire.

Drizzt scrambled so fast that his feet slipped out from under him. He kept moving, though, churning his knees, banging them hard. The drow hardly cared for his pain. Bruenor needed him, that was all that mattered. He rushed with all speed, found a proper foothold amidst the quagmire, and shoved off, diving straight out, his arm extended and holding straight the ice-forged scimitar, sliding its curving blade right beside his friend.

In that area, Errtu's fires were extinguished, put out by the magic of the scimitar.

Both friends tried to rise, and both were blasted back to the wet ground as the balor plunged his lightning sword into the watery ice, taunting them all the while.

"Yes, a reprieve!" the fiend bellowed. "Well done, Drizzt Do'Urden, foolish drow. You have extended my pleasure, and for that—"

The fiend's sentence ended with a grunt as Guenhwyvar soared in, slamming Errtu hard, knocking him off-balance on the slick floor.

Drizzt was up and charging. Bruenor worked fast to untangle himself from the binding thongs of the fiend's whip. And Guenhwyvar raked wildly, biting and clawing.

Errtu knew the cat, had faced Guenhwyvar on that same occasion when Drizzt had banished him, and the balor felt the fool for not anticipating that the animal would soon arrive.

No matter, though, Errtu reasoned, and with a huge shrug of powerful muscles, the fiend launched the cat away.

In came Drizzt, his hungry scimitar thrusting for the fiend's belly.

Errtu's lightning sword swiped down in a parry, and that, too, was an attack, as the energy coursed from weapon to weapon, and subsequently into Drizzt, hurling him backward.

Bruenor was in fast and the dwarf's axe chopped hard into Errtu's leg. The fiend roared and swatted the dwarf, and Bruenor flew backwards. Out came the fiend's leathery wings, up he rose, above the reach of the mighty friends. Guenhwyvar leaped again, but Errtu caught her in mid-flight, locked her with a telekinesis spell, as the glabrezu had done with Catti-brie.

Still, for Drizzt and Bruenor, shaking off their earlier wounds, Guenhwyvar was helping, was keeping the fiend's considerable magical energies engaged.

"Let my father go!" Drizzt cried out.

Errtu laughed at him, and the reprieve was at its end. Errtu's spell hurled the panther aside, and the fiend came on in all his wrath.

\* \* \* \* \*

It was a small room, perhaps a dozen feet in diameter and with a domed ceiling reaching up to the tower's pinnacle. In the middle of the room, hanging in the empty air, loomed Crenshinibon, the crystal shard, the heart of the tower, pulsing with a pinkish-red color as though it were a living thing.

Regis glanced around quickly. He spotted the coffer lying on the floor—he knew it from somewhere, though he couldn't immediately place it—and the gem-studded ring, but what significance they held, the halfling could not be sure.

And he didn't have the time to figure it out. Regis had talked extensively with Drizzt after the fall of Kessel, and he knew well the technique the drow had used to defeat the tower on that occasion, simply by covering the pulsing shard with blocking flour. So it was with the halfling now as he pulled the small pack from his back and strode confidently in.

"Time to sleep," Regis taunted. He was almost right, but not in the manner he meant, for he was almost knocked unconscious. The halfling and Drizzt had erred. In the tower on the plain outside of Bryn Shander those years ago, Drizzt had covered not Crenshinibon, but one of the shard's countless images. On this occasion, it was the real crystal shard, the sentient and powerful artifact, serving as the tower's heart. Such a meager attack was defeated by a pulse of energy that disintegrated the flour as it descended, burned the sack in the halfling's hands, and hurled Regis hard against the far wall.

The dazed halfling groaned all the louder when the trap door in the room's floor flew open. The stench of trolls wafted in, followed closely by a huge and wide hand with sharpened claws and rubbery, putrid green skin.

\* \* \* \* \*

Catti-brie could hardly feel her extremities, her teeth chattered uncontrollably and she knew that her bowstring was cutting deeply into her fingers, though she felt no pain there. She had to continue, for the sake of her father and of Drizzt.

Using solid Stumpet as a support, the young woman steadied herself and let fly an arrow, taking down the fiend closest to the cave entrance. Again and again, Catti-brie let fly, her enchanted quiver providing her with endless ammunition. She decimated most of the manes remaining on the ice beach, and blew away those coming over the ridge. She nearly shot Guenhwyvar, too, before she recognized the speeding cat. Her heart was lifted with some hope as the mighty panther rushed into the cave.

Soon all that remained of the manes were the few in the water, swimming fast for Catti-brie. Catti-brie worked frantically—most of her shots hit the mark—but one did get up on the ice floe, and came rushing in.

Catti-brie looked to her sword, buried to the hilt in the ice, and knew that she could not get to it in time. Instead, she used her bow like a club, whacking the fiend hard across the face.

The wretched thing skidded in, off-balance, and even as the two connected, Catti-brie snapped her forehead right into the ugly fiend's nose. Up came the tip of her bow, driving hard under the thing's saggy chin, poking through the oozing skin. The creature exploded into noxious gas, but it had done its work. The momentum of its rush, combined with the sudden gaseous cloud, sent Catti-brie moving backward, past the dwarf and into the water.

Up she came, gasping for breath, flailing with arms that she could not feel. Her legs were useless to her now. She managed somehow to grab on to the very edge of the ice floe, locking her fingers into a small crevice, for she knew that her strength was already going away. She cried out for Stumpet, but even those muscles of her mouth would not respond to her mind's command.

Catti-brie had survived the fiends, it seemed, only to be destroyed by the natural elements of Icewind Dale, the place she had called home for most of her life. That irony was not lost on her as all the world grew cold.

\* \* \* \* \*

Regis's back skimmed the curving ceiling as the nine-foot troll, the larger of the two that had entered the room, lifted him high into the air to look into its ghastly face. "Now youses goes into me belly!" the horrid thing proclaimed, opening wide its considerable maw.

The mere fact that the troll could speak gave Regis an idea, a desperate glimmer of hope.

"Wait!" he bade the creature, reaching under his tunic. "I have treasure to offer." Out came the halfling's prized pendant, the magnificent, hypnotic ruby dancing on the end of the chain just inches from the startled, and suddenly intrigued, troll's eyes.

"This is only the beginning," Regis stammered, fighting hard to improvise for the consequences of failure were all too evident. "I have a mound of these—look at how wonderfully it spins, drawing your eyes . . ."

"Ere now, be ye to eats the thing or not?" the second troll demanded, shoving the first one hard. But that troll was caught fast by the charm, and was already thinking that it didn't want to share the booty with its companion.

Thus, the horrid thing was more than open to Regis's ensuing suggestion as the halfling casually glanced at the second troll and said, "Kill him."

Regis dropped hard to the floor, and was nearly squashed as the two trolls fell into a wild wrestling match. The halfling had to move fast, but what was he to do? His rolling evasion took him to the gem-studded ring, which he promptly pocketed, and to the open and empty coffer, which he suddenly recognized.

It was the same coffer the glabrezu had been carrying when Regis and his companions had come upon evil Matron Baenre in the tunnels under Mithril Hall, the same coffer that had held the stone—the black sapphire that had stolen away all the magic.

Regis scooped up the thing and dashed past the rolling trolls, bearing down fast on the crystal shard. A flood of mental images assaulted him then, nearly buckling his legs. The sentient artifact, sensing the danger, entered the halfling's mind, dominating poor Regis. Regis wanted to move forward, he really did, but his feet would not obey.

And then he wasn't sure that he wanted to move forward at all. Suddenly Regis had to wonder why he had wanted to destroy the crystal tower, the beautiful and marvelous structure. And why would he desire the destruction of Crenshinibon, the creator, when he might use the artifact to his own benefit?

What did Drizzt know anyway?

Though he was a confused and nearly lost soul at that

point, the halfling thought to lift his own ruby pendant up before his eyes.

Immediately Regis found himself swirling into the item's depths, following the red flickers deeper and deeper. Most people got lost in that charm, but it was there, deep within the hypnosis of his gemstone, that Regis found himself.

He dropped the pendant chain and leaped forward, snapping the shielding coffer over Crenshinibon just as it released another pulse of deadly energy.

The coffer swallowed the item and its attack, and Regis plucked the shard out of the air.

Immediately the tower, the gigantic image of the crystal shard, began to shudder, the initial rumbles of its death throes.

"Oh, not again," the halfling muttered, for he had been through this before, and had escaped only with aid of Guenhwyvar, while Drizzt had escaped by . . .

Regis turned to the window, leaped up to its sill. He glanced back at the trolls, hugging instead of wrestling as their tower home shivered beneath them. In unison, they turned to regard the smiling halfling.

"Another day perhaps," Regis said to them, and then, without looking down, he leaped out. Twenty feet down, he hit the side of the iceberg cone, bouncing and sliding wildly to come to a sudden, jolting stop in the icy snow. The crystal tower crumbled around him, huge blocks narrowly missing the stunned and bruised halfling.

\* \* \* \* \*

The earthquake on the iceberg brought a temporary halt to the fighting within the cave, a temporary reprieve for those being badly beaten by the powerful tanar'ri. But poor Bruenor, standing by the cave wall, fell down as a wide crack opened at his feet. Though the break wasn't very deep, barely to Bruenor's waist, when the shaking ended, the dwarf found himself wedged in tightly.

The loss of Crenshinibon did nothing to diminish Errtu's powers, and the obvious fall of the tower only heightened the balor's rage.

Guenhwyvar came flying back in at him, but the fiend skewered the cat in mid-flight with his mighty sword, holding Guenhwyvar aloft with one powerful hand.

Drizzt, on his knees in the slush, could only watch in horror as Errtu calmly stalked in, as the panther twitched and tried futilely to free herself, growling with agony.

It was over, Drizzt knew. All of it had come to a sudden, crashing end. He could not win out. He wished that Guenhwyvar could get off of that sword—if she did, Drizzt would send her over to Bruenor and then dismiss her. Hopefully she would take the dwarf with her to the relative safety of her astral home.

But that couldn't happen. Guenhwyvar twitched again and slumped, and then dissipated into gray smoke, her corporeal form defeated and sent away from the Prime Material Plane.

Drizzt pulled out the figurine. He knew that he could not recall the cat, not for some days. He heard the hiss as the fiend's fires neared him and were extinguished by his trusty blade, and he looked from the figurine to grinning Errtu, towering over him, barely five feet away.

"Are you ready to die, Drizzt Do'Urden?" the fiend asked. "Your father can see us, you know, and how pained he is that you will die slowly before me!"

Drizzt didn't doubt the words, and his rage came up in full. But it wouldn't help him, not this time. He was cold, weary, filled with sorrow, and defeated. He knew that.

\* \* \* \* \*

Errtu's words were half true. The prisoner, behind a partially opaque wall of ice at the side of the cave's upper landing, could indeed see the scene, highlighted by the blue glow of Drizzt's scimitars and the orange flames near Errtu.

He clawed at the wall futilely. He cried as he had not cried in so many years.

\* \* \* \* \*

"And what a fine pet your cat will make for me," Errtu teased.

"Never," the drow growled, and purely on impulse, Drizzt threw the figurine with all his might, back through the cave entrance. He didn't hear the splash, but he was confident that he had heaved it far enough to reach the sea.

"Well done, me friend," a grim Bruenor said from the side.

Errtu's grin became a grimace of outrage. Up came the deadly sword, hanging right over Drizzt's vulnerable head. The drow lifted Twinkle to block.

And then a hammer twirled in end over end to slam hard into the balor, accompanied by the hearty call of "Tempus!"

Without fear, Kierstaad rushed into the cave, skidding right through the breach in Errtu's flames caused by Drizzt's scimitar, skidding right into the face of the tanar'ri, and howling for Aegis-fang all the way. Kierstaad knew the hammer's legend, knew that it would return to his hands.

But it didn't. It was gone from the ground near the fiend, but for some reason that Kierstaad did not understand, it had not materialized in his waiting hands.

"It should have come back!" he cried in protest, to Bruenor mostly, and then Kierstaad was flying, slapped away by the fiend. He smacked hard into an ice mound, rolled off the thing and fell heavily, groaning, to the slushy floor.

"It should have come back," he said once more, before his consciousness drifted away.

\* \* \* \* \*

Aegis-fang couldn't go back to Kierstaad, for it had returned to its rightful owner, to Wulfgar, son of Beornegar, watching the scene from behind an ice wall. Wulfgar had been Errtu's prisoner for six long years.

The feel of the weapon transformed Wulfgar, gave him back a measure of himself along with the familiarity of this warhammer, forged for him by the dwarf who loved him.

He remembered so much at that moment, so much that he had, by necessity, forced himself to forget in the years of hopelessness.

Truly the strong barbarian was overwhelmed, but not so much so that he didn't think of the immediate need. He roared out to Tempus, his god—how good it felt to hear that name coming from his lips again!—and began taking down the wall with mighty chops of his powerful hammer.

\* \* \* \*

Regis felt a call in his mind. At first he thought it to be the crystal shard, and then, when he convinced himself that the artifact was safely and completely locked away in the coffer, he guessed it to be the ruby pendant.

When that proved false, Regis finally discerned the source: the gemstone ring in his pocket. Regis took it out and stared hard at it. He feared that it was yet another manifestation of Crenshinibon and lifted his arm back to hurl it into the sea.

But then Regis recognized the little voice in his head.

"Stumpet?" he asked, curiously, peering hard into the stone. He moved as he spoke, coming to kneel right beside one of the broken tower blocks. Out came his little mace.

\* \* \* \* \*

The thunder of the barbarian's hits shook the whole of the cave, so much so that a suddenly nervous Errtu could not help but look back. And when the balor did, Drizzt Do'Urden struck hard.

Twinkle gashed against the fiend's calf, while Drizzt launched his other blade higher, aiming for Errtu's groin. The scimitar's pointy tip dug in, and how Errtu howled! Again came that welcomed throbbing along Drizzt's arm as the scimitar fed on the fiend's life force.

But the turn in the battle was temporary. Errtu quickly slapped Drizzt away, then disappeared, coming back into view high among the icy fingers that hung down from the ceiling.

"Up, Bruenor," Drizzt called. "We have been given a reprieve, for Zaknafein will soon be among us."

The drow looked to the red-bearded dwarf as he spoke, and Bruenor had nearly wriggled his way out of the hole.

Up Drizzt scrambled, up and ready, but something about the look that came over Bruenor's face as the dwarf gazed to the side, weakened Drizzt's knees. He followed the dwarf's stare across the chamber, to the ice wall, where he expected to see Zaknafein.

He saw Wulfgar instead, with unkempt, wild hair and beard, but Wulfgar no doubt, hoisting Aegis-fang high and roaring with pure hatred.

"Me boy," was all the dwarf could whisper, and Bruenor slumped back into the hole.

Errtu went at Wulfgar hard, swooping in, his whip cracking and his sword blazing.

A hurled Aegis-fang nearly knocked the fiend from the air. Still the balor swept by, entangling Wulfgar's ankles with his whip and tugging the man from the ledge to send him bouncing among the ice mounds of the slushy floor.

"Wulfgar," Drizzt called out, and he winced as the man tumbled. It would take more than a fall to stop the tormented Wulfgar, now that he was among his friends, now that he held his mighty hammer. Up he sprang, roaring like some animal, and Aegis-fang, beautiful and solid Aegis-fang, was back in his hand.

Errtu went into a frenzy, determined to squash this minor uprising, to destroy all of Drizzt's friends, and then the drow himself. Balls of darkness appeared in the air, obscuring Wulfgar's vision as he tried to line up another throw. The fiend cracked his whip and zipped all about the cave, sometimes in swift flight, other times calling upon magic to teleport himself from place to place.

The chaos was complete, and every time Drizzt tried to get to Bruenor, Wulfgar, or even to fallen Kierstaad, there was Errtu, smacking him away. Always the drow parried the lightning sword, but each hit jolted him and hurt him. And every time, before Drizzt could begin to counter, Errtu was gone, simply gone, to wreak havoc in another part of the cave with another of the drow's friends.

* * * * *

She wasn't cold anymore, was far beyond that simple sensation. Catti-brie was walking in darkness, fleeing the realm of mortals.

A strong hand grabbed her by the shoulder, the physical shoulder, bringing her senses back in tune with her corporeal body, and then she felt herself being lifted from the water.

And then . . . the woman felt warmth, magical warmth, seeping through her body, returning life where there was barely any.

Catti-brie's eyes fluttered open to see Stumpet Rakingclaw working furiously over her, calling upon the dwarven gods to breathe life back into this woman who had been as a daughter to Clan Battlehammer.

* * * * *

Lightning simmered every time Errtu used that mighty sword. The rumbling of thunder and the fiend's victorious roars were matched by the beating of great leathery wings, the roars of Wulfgar to his battle god, and the cries of "Me boy!" from a wild-eyed, and still trapped Bruenor. Drizzt shouted, trying to bring some semblance of order to his companions, some common strategy that might corner and at last defeat wicked Errtu.

The fiend would have none of that. Errtu swooped and disappeared, struck fast and hard and was simply gone. Sometimes the balor hung up high amidst the stalactites, using his fires to loosen and drop the natural spikes at the companions scrambling below. Other times, Errtu had to come down to keep them apart, and even with the balor's tremendous efforts, Drizzt wove his way stubbornly toward Bruenor.

Wherever the fiend chose to appear, he could not remain in place and visible for very long. Even though the quagmire continued to slow any moves the drow might try, and even though the dwarf remained stuck in the stubborn crevice, the tormented prisoner, and his mighty hammer were always quick to the call. On several occasions Errtu vanished just an instant before Aegis-fang slammed into the wall, marking the spot where the fiend had been.

And so Errtu retained the upper hand, but in that craziness, the fiend could score no decisive hits.

It was time to win.

Bruenor was almost out of the crack, stuck by a single leg, when the mighty balor appeared, right behind him.

Drizzt, yelled out a warning, and purely on instinct, the dwarf whipped about, throwing himself as far into the fiend as possible, grabbing the balor's leg, wrenching his own knee in the process. Errtu's sword came swishing down, but Bruenor was in too close for it to cleave him. Still the dwarf was battered hard, and the energy jolt nearly popped his knees out of joint, especially the twisted one.

Bruenor grabbed on all the harder, knowing he could not hurt the balor, but hoping he could keep the fiend in place long enough for his friends to strike. His hair singed and his eyes stung as the fiend's fires came up, but they were gone in an instant and Bruenor knew that Drizzt was nearby.

Errtu's whip cracked, slowing the drow's approach. Drizzt went in a complete spin to dodge, skidding down to one knee, and he stumbled as he tried to get back to his feet.

The whip cracked again, but it could do little to slow the progress of twirling Aegis-fang. The hammer caught the balor on the side, slamming Errtu back against the ice wall, and the fiend's respect for the man that had been his prisoner soared. Errtu had been hit by Aegis-fang once already, when Kierstaad had entered the fray, and so he understood the power of the weapon. But that first throw could not prepare Errtu for the power that was Wulfgar. Kierstaad's throw had stung him; Wulfgar's had truly hurt.

In came Drizzt, but the balor lashed out hard with his foot, tearing Bruenor from the crevice and launching the dwarf a dozen feet across the cave floor. The fiend used his magic to disappear immediately, and Drizzt went sliding into empty wall.

"Fools!" the balor bellowed from the cave's exit. "I will retrieve the crystal shard and meet with you again before you leave this sea. Know that you are doomed!"

Drizzt scrambled, Wulfgar tried to line up a parting shot, and even Bruenor worked hard to stagger back to his feet, but none of them would get to Errtu in time.

The fiend turned away from them and started to fly off, but his surprise was complete, his momentum fully halted, by a silver-streaking arrow that hit him right in the face.

Errtu howled and Wulfgar threw, the hammer smashing hard into the fiend, crushing bones.

Catti-brie let fly again, putting one right into his chest. The balor howled again and stumbled backward into the cave.

Bruenor hobbled toward him, catching his axe as Drizzt tossed it to him. He reversed his grip to add to the momentum of the throw and buried the many-notched blade deep into the fiend's backside.

Errtu howled and Catti-brie hit him again, right beside her last shot.

Drizzt was there, Twinkle striking hard. He plunged his other blade plunging deep into the fiend's side, right under Errtu's arm as the fiend tried to lift his own sword to fend off the drow. Then Wulfgar was there, pounding away beside his father. Catti-brie kept the exit blocked by a steady line of streaking arrows.

And Drizzt held on, leaving his gulping blade deep in the fiend's flesh, while Twinkle worked furiously, cutting wound after wound.

With a last burst of energy, Errtu turned about, throwing off Bruenor and Wulfgar, but not Drizzt. The mighty balor looked right into the drow's lavender eyes. Errtu was defeated—even then, the fiend could feel his corporeal form beginning to melt away—but this time, the balor meant to take Drizzt Do'Urden back to the abyss.

Up came the balor's sword and his free hand came across, accepting the sting as it connected with Twinkle, moving the blocking weapon aside.

Drizzt had no defense. He let go of his embedded scimitar and tried to fall away. Too late.

The lightning flared along the blade's edge as it slashed toward the drow's head.

A strong hand shot out before the horrified drow's eyes and caught the fiend by the wrist, somehow stopping the cut, somehow holding mighty Errtu at bay, the lightning weapon barely inches from the target. Errtu glanced across to see Wulfgar, mighty Wulfgar, teeth clenched and muscles standing out like steel cords. All the years of frustration were in that iron grip, all the horrors the young barbarian had known were transformed then into sheer hatred for the fiend.

There was no way that Wulfgar, or any man, could hold back Errtu, but Wulfgar denied that logic, that truth, with the stronger truth that he would not let Errtu hurt him anymore, would not let the fiend take Drizzt from his side.

Errtu shook his half-canine, half-ape head in disbelief. It could not be!

And yet it was. Wulfgar held him, and soon, the balor was gone, in a waft of smoke and a wail of protest.

The three friends fell together in a tearful hug, too overwhelmed to speak, to even stand, for many, many moments.

# Chapter 28

## THE SON
## OF BEORNEGAR

atti-brie saw Regis stumbling his way over the ridge to the left of the cone. She saw Drizzt and Bruenor, leaning heavily on each other for support as they exited the cave. And she saw Kierstaad, being carried over the shoulder of . . .

Stumpet, with her spells of healing, had done much to bolster the woman, and so the dwarf was surprised when Catti-brie gave a stifled yelp and fell down her knees. The dwarven priestess looked to her with concern, then followed her blank stare across the way, recognizing the source immediately.

"Hey," Stumpet said, scratching her stubbly face, "is that. . ."

"Wulfgar," Catti-brie breathed.

Regis joined the four at the edge of the iceberg, and was similarly knocked off his feet when he saw who it was that they had rescued from the clutches of evil Errtu. The halfling squeaked repeatedly and launched himself into the barbarian's arms, and Wulfgar, on the slick ice and with Kierstaad on his shoulder, pitched over backward, nearly cracking his head.

The huge man didn't mind, though. Errtu and his wicked minions were gone and now was the time for celebration!

Almost.

Drizzt searched frantically along the stretch of the

iceberg in front of the cave entrance, cursing himself repeatedly for losing faith in himself and his friends. He questioned Regis, then called out to Catti-brie and Stumpet, but none of them had seen it.

The figurine that allowed the drow to call to Guenhwyvar was gone, swallowed up in the dark sea.

With Drizzt in such a fit, Bruenor surveyed the situation and quickly took command, setting the friends to work. The first order of business was to get Catti-brie and Stumpet back to them—and fast, for Drizzt, Bruenor, and Wulfgar were wet and fast freezing, and Kierstaad needed immediate attention from the cleric.

On the ice floe, Stumpet pulled a grappling hook and heavy line from her pack, and, with the practiced throw of a seasoned climber, put the hook on the iceberg barely ten feet from her companions. Bruenor secured it quickly, then went beside Wulfgar, who was already pulling hard to bring the floating ice to shore, and pulling all the harder as he looked upon Catti-brie, his love, the woman who was to be his wife all those years ago.

Drizzt was of little help. He knelt over the edge of the iceberg, put his scimitars into the water to try and illuminate it. "I need some protection so I can go down there!" the drow called to Stumpet, who was pulling on her end of the rope and trying to offer some words of comfort to the pained ranger.

Regis, standing beside Drizzt, shook his head knowingly. The halfling had put out a line of his own, weighted at the end. He had fifty feet of cord into the water and still had not felt bottom. Even if Stumpet could enact a spell to keep Drizzt warm and to allow him to breathe underwater, he could not go that deep for very long, and could not hope to find the black figurine in the dark water.

Catti-brie and Bruenor exchanged a quick hug at the shoreline—Stumpet went right to work on Kierstaad—and then the woman and Wulfgar squared off uncomfortably.

Truly the barbarian looked ragged, his blond hair flying wildly, his beard down to his chest, and a hollow look in his eyes. He was still huge, still so well-muscled, but a slackness had come into his limbs, more a loss of spirit than of

girth, Catti-brie knew. But it was Wulfgar, and whatever
scars Errtu had put on him seemed irrelevant to the
woman at that moment.

Wulfgar's heart pounded in his still-massive chest.
Catti-brie did not look so different at all. A bit thicker perhaps, but that sparkle remained in her deep blue eyes, that
love of life and adventure, that spirit that could not be
tamed.

"I thought ye . . ." Catti-brie began, but she stopped and
took a deep, steadying breath. "I never once forgot ye."

Wulfgar grabbed her up in his arms, pulling her tight to
him. He tried to talk to her, to explain that only thoughts
of her had kept him alive during his ordeal. But he couldn't
find the words, not a one, and so he just held her as tight
as he could and they both let the tears come.

It was a heartwarming sight for Bruenor, for Regis, for
Stumpet, and for Drizzt, though the drow could not take
the moment to consider and enjoy it. Guenhwyvar was
gone from him, a loss as great as the loss of his father, as
the loss of Wulfgar. Guenhwyvar had been his companion
for so many years, often his only companion, his one true
friend.

He could not say goodbye to her.

It was Kierstaad, coming out of his stupor with the help
of some dwarven healing magic, who broke the spell. The
barbarian understood the trouble they were still in, especially with the sky growing thick with moisture and with
the short day fast on the wane. It was colder out here than
on the tundra, much colder, and they had little materials to
set and maintain a fire.

Kierstaad knew a different way to shelter them. Still
on the ground, propped on his elbows, he took up the call
from Bruenor and began directing the movements. Using
Khazid'hea, Catti-brie cut out blocks of ice, and the others piled them as instructed, soon building a domelike
structure—an ice hut.

Not a moment too soon, for the dwarven priestess was
out of spells and the cold was creeping back into the companions. Soon after, the sky opened up, unleashing a driving sleet, and then later, a fierce snowstorm.

But inside the shelter, the companions were safe and warm.

Except for Drizzt. Without Guenhwyvar, the drow felt as if he would never be warm again.

\* \* \* \* \*

The next dawn was dim and gray, the air even colder than the previous, freezing night. Even worse, the friends found that they were trapped, stranded, for the night winds had shifted the ice that gave this sea its appropriate name and their berg was too far from any others for them to get across.

Kierstaad, feeling much better, climbed to the top of the conical tip and took up his horn, blowing wildly.

But the only answer came in the form of echoes, bouncing back across the flatness of the dark sea from the numerous other ice mountains.

Drizzt spent the morning in prayer, to Mielikki and to Gwaeron Windstrom, seeking guidance from them, asking them to return to him his panther, his precious friend. He wanted Guenhwyvar to lift out of the sea, back into his arms, and prayed for just that, but Drizzt knew that it didn't work that way.

Then he had an idea. He didn't know if it was god-inspired or one of his own, and he didn't care. He went to Regis first, Regis who had carved so very many wonderful objects with the bone of knucklehead trout, Regis who had created the very unicorn that hung around Drizzt's neck.

The halfling cut an appropriate-sized block of ice and went to work, while Drizzt went to the back side of the iceberg, as far from the others as possible, and began to call.

Two hours later, the drow returned, a young seal flopping along behind him, a newfound friend. As a ranger, Drizzt knew animals, knew how to communicate with them in rudimentary terms, and knew which movements would frighten them, and which would give them confidence. He was pleased upon his return to see that Catti-brie and Bruenor, using a bow and a hastily-strung, makeshift net, had caught some fish, and the drow was quick to proffer one and toss it to the seal.

"Hey!" Bruenor howled in protest, and then the dwarf's face brightened. "Yeah," he said, rubbing his hands briskly together as he thought he understood the drow's intent, "fatten the thing up."

Drizzt's ensuing scowl, as serious as the drow had ever been, ended that train of thought.

The drow went to Regis next, and was amazed and thrilled by the halfling's work. Where there once had been an unremarkable block of ice there was now a near likeness, in size and shape, of the onyx figurine.

"If I had more time," Regis started to say, but Drizzt stopped him with a wave of his hand. This would suffice.

And so they began training the seal. Drizzt tossed the ice statue into the water, yelled, "Guen!" and Regis rushed to the edge of the iceberg and scooped out the figurine in the same net Bruenor had put together for fishing. When Regis turned net and statue over to Drizzt, the drow rewarded him with one of the fish. They repeated it over and over, and finally, Drizzt put the net in the seal's mouth, tossed the figurine into the water and yelled, "Guen!"

Sure enough, the clever creature snorted and plunged in, quickly retrieving the halfling's sculpture. Drizzt glanced around at his friends, daring a smile of hope as he tossed a fish to the eager seal.

They went at it for more than twenty minutes, with each successive throw going farther out into the black water. Every time, the seal retrieved it perfectly, and every time, was rewarded by excitement and, more importantly, by a fish.

Then they needed a break, for the seal was tired and was no longer hungry.

The next few hours were terminally long for poor Drizzt. He sat in the ice hut, warming with his friends, while the others talked, mostly to Wulfgar, trying to bring the barbarian back to the world of the living.

It was painfully obvious to them all, especially to Wulfgar, that he had a long, long road yet to travel.

During that time, Kierstaad would occasionally go out

onto the iceberg and blare his horn. The young barbarian was growing quite concerned, for if they were drifting away at all, it was farther out from the shore, and there seemed no way to navigate back to their homes. They could catch their fish, the dwarven priestess and the ice hut could do much to keep them warm, but out on the Sea of Moving Ice was no way to spend Icewind Dale's winter! Eventually, Kierstaad knew, a blizzard would catch up to them, burying them in their hut while they slept, or a hungry white bear would come calling.

Drizzt was back to his work with the seal that afternoon, ending by having Regis distract the seal, while the drow splashed the water and called out, pretending to toss in the statue.

In leaped the seal, excitedly, but that lasted only a few moments, and finally, the frustrated creature clambered back onto the iceberg, barking in protest.

Drizzt did not reward it.

The drow kept the seal inside the ice hut that night and most of the next morning. He needed the creature to be hungry, very hungry, for he knew that they were running out of time. He could only hope that the iceberg hadn't drifted too far from the statue.

After a couple of throws, the drow used the same distractions and sent the seal in on a futile hunt. A few minutes passed, and when it seemed as if the seal was growing frustrated, Drizzt secretly slipped the figurine into the water.

The happy seal spotted it and brought it out, and was rewarded.

"It doesn't sink," Regis remarked, guessing the problem. "We have to get the seal used to diving for it." Following the logic, they weighed down the statue with Stumpet's grappling hook, which was easily bent by Wulfgar. Drizzt was careful on the next couple of throws, making sure that the seal could follow the statue's descent. The cunning animal performed perfectly, gliding under the dark water, out of sight, and returning with the figurine in the net every time.

They tried the ruse again, distracting the seal, while Drizzt slapped the water, and all of them held their breath when the seal went far under.

It surfaced many, many yards from the iceberg, barked to Drizzt and then disappeared again. This happened many times.

And then the seal came up right near the iceberg, leaping with joy up beside the drow, its mission complete.

With Guenhwyvar's figurine in the net.

The friends took up a huge cheer, and Kierstaad blew furiously on his horn. This time, the young barbarian's call was answered by more than echoes. Kierstaad looked to the others hopefully, then blew again.

Drifting through the misty sea came a single boat, Berkthgar standing tall atop its prow while a host of both dwarves and barbarians pulled with all their strength.

Kierstaad responded once more, and then handed his horn over to Wulfgar, who blew the strongest and clearest note ever heard in Icewind Dale.

From out on the dark water, Berkthgar looked upon him, and so did Revjak. It was a moment of confusion and then elation, even for proud Berkthgar.

\* \* \* \* \*

On the night of their return to the dwarven mines, Drizzt retired with mixed emotions. He was so glad, impossibly thrilled, to have Wulfgar back at his side, and to have come away from an encounter with such powerful enemies with all of his friends, Guenhwyvar included, virtually unharmed.

But the drow could not help thinking about his father. For months he had pursued this course in the belief that it would lead to Zaknafein. He had built the fantasy of being with his father and mentor once more, and though he did not for a moment begrudge the fact that Errtu's prisoner was Wulfgar and not Zaknafein, he could not easily let go of those fantasies.

He went to sleep troubled, and in that sleep, the drow dreamed.

He was awakened in his room by a ghostly presence. He went for his scimitars, but then stopped abruptly and fell back on his bed, recognizing the spirit of Zaknafein.

335

"My son," the ghost said to him, and Zaknafein was smiling warmly, a proud father, a contented spirit. "All is well with me, better than you can imagine."

Drizzt couldn't find the words to reply, but his expression asked every question in his heart anyway.

"An old priest called me," Zaknafein explained. "He said that you needed to know. Fare well, my son. Keep close to your friends and to your memories, and know in your heart that we will meet again."

With that, the ghost was gone.

Drizzt remembered it all vividly the next morning, and he was indeed comforted. Logic told him that it had been a dream—until he realized that the ghost had been speaking to him in the drow tongue, and until he realized that the old priest Zaknafein had referred to could only be Cadderly. .

Drizzt had already decided that he would be going back to the Spirit Soaring after the winter, bearing the crystal shard— securely tucked into the shielding coffer—as he had promised.

As the days went by and the memory of his ghostly encounter did not fade, the drow ranger found true peace, for he came to understand and to believe that it had been no dream.

\* \* \* \* \*

"They offered me the tribe," Wulfgar said to Drizzt. It was a crisp wintry morning outside the dwarven mines, more than two months after their return from the Sea of Moving Ice.

Drizzt considered the not-unexpected news and the healthier condition of his returned friend. Then he shook his head—Wulfgar had not yet recovered, and should not take on the burden of such responsibility.

"I refused," Wulfgar admitted.

"Not yet," Drizzt said comfortingly.

Wulfgar looked to the blue sky, the same color as his eyes, which were shining again after six years of darkness. "Not ever," he corrected. "That is not my place."

Drizzt wasn't sure that he agreed. He wondered how much of Wulfgar's refusal was fostered by the overwhelming adjustment the barbarian was trying to make. Even the simplest things in this life seemed unfamiliar to poor Wulfgar. He was awkward with everyone, especially Catti-brie, though Bruenor and Drizzt had little doubt that the spark was rekindling between the two.

"I will guide Berkthgar, though," Wulfgar went on. "And will accept no hostility between his people, my people, and the folk of Icewind Dale. We each have enough real enemies without creating more!"

Drizzt didn't argue that point.

"Do you love her?" Wulfgar asked suddenly, and the drow was off his guard.

"Of course I do," Drizzt responded truthfully. "As I love you, and Bruenor, and Regis."

"I would not interfere—" Wulfgar started to say, but he was stopped by Drizzt's chuckle.

"The choice is neither mine nor yours," the drow explained, "but Catti-brie's. Remember what you had, my friend, and remember what you, in your foolishness, nearly lost."

Wulfgar looked long and hard at his dear friend, determined to heed that wise advice. Catti-brie's life was Catti-brie's to decide and whatever, or whomever, she chose, Wulfgar would always be among friends.

The winter would be long and cold, thick with snow and mercifully uneventful. Things would not be the same between the friends, could never be after all they had experienced, but they would be together again, in heart and in soul. Let no man, and no fiend, ever try to separate them again!

\* \* \* \* \*

It was one of those perfect spring nights in Icewind Dale, not too cold, but with enough of a breeze to keep the skin tingling. The stars were bright and thick. Drizzt couldn't tell where the night sky ended and the dark tundra began. And it didn't matter to him, Bruenor or Regis.

Guenhwyvar was similarly content, prowling about on the lower rocks of Bruenor's Climb.

"They're friends again," Bruenor explained, speaking of Catti-brie and Wulfgar. "He's needin' her now, and she's helping to get him back."

"You do not forget six years of torment at the hands of a fiend like Errtu in short order," Regis agreed.

Drizzt smiled widely, thinking that his friends had found their place together once more. That notion, of course, led the drow to wonder about his own place.

"I believe that I can catch up with Deudermont in Luskan," he said suddenly, unexpectedly. "If not there, then certainly in Waterdeep."

"Ye durned elf, what're ye runnin' from this time?" the dwarf pressed.

Drizzt turned to regard him and laughed aloud. "I am not running from anything, good dwarf," the drow replied. "But I must, on my word and for the good of all, deliver the crystal shard to Cadderly at the Spirit Soaring, in faraway Carradoon."

"Me girl said that place was south o' Sundabar," Bruenor protested, thinking he had caught the drow in a lie. "Ye ain't for sailin' there!"

"Far south of Sundabar," Drizzt agreed, "but closer to Baldur's Gate than to Waterdeep. The *Sea Sprite* runs swiftly; Deudermont can get me much nearer to Cadderly."

Bruenor's bluster was defeated by the simple logic. "Durned elf," the dwarf muttered. "I'm not much for goin' back on a durned boat! But if we must . . ."

Drizzt looked hard at the dwarf. "You are coming?"

"You think we would stay?" Regis replied, and when Drizzt turned his startled gaze on the halfling, Regis promptly reminded him that it was he, and not Drizzt, who had captured Crenshinibon.

"Of course they're goin'," came a familiar voice from the darkness some distance below. "As are we!"

A moment later, Catti-brie and Wulfgar walked up the steep path to join their friends.

Drizzt looked to them all, one by one, then turned away to regard the stars.

"All my life, I have been searching for a home," the drow said quietly. "All my life, I have been wanting more than that which was offered to me, more than Menzoberranzan, more than friends who stood beside me out of personal gain. I always thought home to be a place, and indeed it is, but not in any physical sense. It is a place in here," Drizzt said, putting a hand to his heart and turning back to look upon his companions. "It is a feeling given by true friends.

"I know this now, and know that I am home."

"But ye're off to Carradoon," Catti-brie said softly.

"And so're we!" Bruenor bellowed.

Drizzt smiled at them, laughed aloud. "If circumstances will not allow me to remain at home," the ranger said firmly, "then I will simply take my home with me!"

From somewhere not so far away, Guenhwyvar roared. They would be out on the road, all six, before the next dawn.

FORGOTTEN REALMS®
RETURN OF THE ARCHWIZARDS
BOOK I

# *The Summoning*

Troy Denning

March, 2001

# I

Like every burial cairn Galaeron Nightmeadow had ever entered, this one stank of the sweat and breath of those who had opened it, of musty human armpits and cumin-heavy belches and braids slicked with bear grease. What he did not smell was blood, which meant these crypt breakers were more skillful than most. Usually, two or three met their ends just digging the fill gravel out of the entrance passage.

As Galaeron led his patrol deeper into the cairn, his dark sight began to function, illuminating the passage walls in shades of cool blue. Inscribed into the flat wall stones were ancient elven glyphs recounting, had there been time to read them, the lives and deeds of the ones buried within. Like most entrance tunnels, this one was low and narrow, with just enough height to stand upright and barely enough room for an elf's slender shoulders. How the burly humans had found room in the cramped space to clear the corridor of its fill gravel he could not imagine, but they had deftly avoided all the customary traps, spanning the death pits with rough-hewn planks and bracing ceiling deadfalls with stout posts of oak.

Galaeron followed the tunnel straight back to the burial chamber. He was greatly surprised to find the room both quiet and dark, given that a pair of his elves were outside guarding twenty shaggy horses and three red-faced sentries. Nor could there be any doubt the humans had actually reached the crypt. The bronze shield that had once served as its door had been melted almost into nothingness, a crude but effective entry that hinted at plenty of powerful magic, especially since they would have first needed to annul the crypt's magic seals.

Galaeron slipped cautiously into the chamber. Seven dead elves lay undisturbed on their ancient biers, their flesh and hair perfectly preserved by the crypt's now-shattered magic, their bejeweled weapons and gold-trimmed armor still lying untouched beneath a thick layer of dust. By their amber skin and ornate bronze armor, Galaeron knew these to be Aryvandaaran nobles, high lords of the aggressive Vyshaan clan who had touched off the First Crown War and plunged the entire elven civilization into three thousand years of carnage. Though he wished them no peace in their sleep, he had sworn as a Tomb Guard to protect all elven burials and would do what he could to bring their crypt breakers to justice.

In the far corner of the tomb, Galaeron found a knotted rope leading down into a freshly opened hole. The shaft had apparently been excavated by the same magic that had destroyed the bronze door, for there was no dirt or rubble heaped around the collar. Trying to imagine what the humans might be seeking that had more value to them than the priceless armor and enchanted weapons of the Vyshaan lords, he led the patrol down the rope.

Thirty feet down, the shaft opened into a labyrinth of low, square-cut dwarven tunnels. By the look of the workings, it had been old when Evereska was young. Dust clung to the walls two fingers thick and lay on the floor a foot deep. The humans' path twisted and twined its way through the powdery stuff more or less eastward, looking for all the world like a trail through snow.

Galaeron sent two scouts ahead, then, recalling the care his quarry had displayed in defeating the crypt traps, ordered a three-elf rear guard to follow a hundred feet behind. Stooping over almost double to avoid hitting their heads on the low dwarven ceiling, the patrol moved into the blackness. Galaeron left his sword in its scabbard and moved to his customary position three places back from the leader. Though all Tomb Guards could fight with both spell and steel, he usually served as the patrol's primary magic-user. Not only was his magic quicker and more versatile than that of most elves, he had learned in the few battles he had actually fought against crypt breakers that humans usually targeted spell-flingers first, and he preferred to shoulder that burden himself.

The human trail ran more or less eastward for a
thousand yards, circling past a dozen ancient cave-
ins before narrow seams of sand began to appear in
some ceiling cracks, suggesting to Galaeron's experienced eye that they had crossed under Anauroch
itself. Not long after, the distant clatter of falling rock
began to echo through the tunnels, and Cotovaari
returned to report.

*We must be careful with these spiders. They look to
have venom.* A svelte wood elf with a cupid's bow
smile and brown eyes the size of a doe's, her slender
hands streaked through the darkness in finger talk.
*And their pet has fangs of its own.*

*Pet?* Galaeron's fingers weaved a red-tinged bas-
ket of fading heat lines in the air before him. *What
kind of pet?*

Cotovaari smiled coyly. *Better you should see for
yourself.*

She spun away and started up the passage, leaving Galaeron knowing little more than he had before
her report. He shook his head in resignation and followed. If the patrol wanted a wood elf for a scout,
Cotovaari had to be allowed her fun.

Aragath, the second scout—and thankfully a
moon elf—lay near the inside wall of a gentle curve,
his head silhouetted against a flickering blue glow
that filled the tunnel ahead. The clatter of falling
rock was louder here, and punctuated by the quiet
grunts and gruff talk of men at work. Galaeron lay
down on his belly and crawled up beside Aragath.
After stooping over so long, stretching out on the
floor was a relief for his aching back—even if it did
mean breathing through his fingers so the dust did

not make him sneeze.

Galaeron peered around the corner and almost cried out in shock. Less than ten paces away hovered a leathery orb of gray-green flesh, nearly three feet in diameter and shaped more or less like a head. A huge bulbous eye bulged out from the center of its face, and beneath that gaped a enormous mouth filled with triangles of sharp teeth. Atop its pate writhed ten thick tentacles, each ending in a single bloodshot eye. Nine of these tentacles had been folded over a small length of wood and bound in place so that the eyes could look no place but the top of the gruesome head. The tenth tentacle was slowly sweeping back and forth, spraying a brilliant blue beam across a four-foot width of stone wall. Wherever the light touched, six inches of stone deteriorated into yellow smoke.

Galaeron swallowed, hardly able to believe what he was seeing. The creature was an eye tyrant, one of the rarest and most feared killers of the Underdark. Galaeron had never fought one himself, but he had seen a trophy specimen in the Evereskan Academy of Magic. According to the histories, the monster had taken possession of King Sileron's crypt in the Greycloak Hills, then gorged itself on two patrols of Tomb Guards before the great Kiinyon Colbathin finally killed it.

So stunned was Galaeron to see one of the horrid creature that he barely noticed its companions until a section of roof collapsed and several men crawled into the hollow to clear the rubble. All were heavy-boned and huge, with thighs as large as an elf's waist and dark braids swinging about their shoulders.

Their high boots and battle-worn scale mail were trimmed in black sable, while the belts that girded their thick waists appeared to be made from the scales of a white dragon.

As the men worked, the eye tyrant's blue gaze drifted downward, cutting a swath of smoking emptiness only inches above their backs. They dropped to their bellies and grunted something in a harsh, rasping language, then a small fist appeared on the other side of the monster and clasped one of its bound eyestalks. Though the hand was hairless and smooth, it was also strong, pulling so hard Galaeron thought the tentacle would pop off.

*"Shatevar!"* A female face appeared in the narrow gap between the ceiling and the eye tyrant's head. Her features were heavy and rough by elf standards, yet striking and surprisingly beautiful, with hair the color of coal, deep emerald eyes, and broad lips as red as a cardinal. Her second hand came into view and pressed a dagger blade to the trapped eyestalk, then she said in Common, "Try that again and I'll make a cyclops out of you."

"Then keep your oafs out of my way," hissed the eye tyrant, its voice deep and gurgling. "I'm too tired to watch them."

"Tired or dead, your choice."

As the two argued, Galaeron tried to take count of the humans, but quickly gave up. Behind the eye tyrant stood two men holding what appeared to be glassy black swords. The weapons might have been obsidian, save that they were perfectly molded, with shadow-smooth blades and none of the conchoidal flaking marks that normally distinguished obsidian blades. There were four more men along the near wall, squatting on their haunches with their scabbards resting across their knees. Judging by the shimmering pommels of their leather-wrapped hilts, these weapons were also made of black glass. It was impossible to see how many more men might be lurking on the other side of the eye tyrant, for the brilliance of its disintegration beam washed out Galaeron's dark sight and prevented him from seeing anything beyond the woman. Still, there had only been twenty horses outside, so he did not think his patrol too badly outnumbered.

Galaeron backed away from the corner, then stood and issued his orders in finger talk. He did not relish trying to capture someone who made slaves of eye tyrants, but there really was no choice in the matter. Word of such a strange encounter was bound to circulate through Evereska, and any leeway given such a small company of humans would reflect badly on the entire patrol. The matter would not trouble Galaeron overmuch, as it was his reputation as a malcontent that had landed him a monotonous posting along the Desert Border in the first place, but there were those among his elves who still hoped to make a name for themselves in the Tomb Guards.

Once his warriors had readied themselves, Galaeron used a spell to turn himself and four more Tomb Guards invisible, even to their own dark sight. Trusting the rest of the patrol to follow, he led the way around the corner, the magic of his boots smothering all sound as he skulked along the wall opposite the crouching humans. As he advanced, he saw that the passage was intersected by two more behind the eye tyrant's guards, creating in effect a broad, if all too low, chamber.

Unfortunately, even magic spells and elven boots could not keep dust from billowing up as someone walked through it. Galaeron was two paces from the eye tyrant when one of the humans on the opposite wall pointed at the gray cloud around Galaeron's feet and said something in his harsh language. The warrior started to rise off his haunches, already reaching for his sword.

The heavy pulse of bow strings throbbed through the passage. Four white arrows streaked out of the empty air and struck their targets in the unarmored calves, the points sinking only to the depth of a fingertip. The astonished humans leaped up, banging their skullcaps on the low ceiling as they turned to face their attackers, then their eyelids rolled down and they collapsed facedown into the dust.

Rendered visible by their attacks, Cotovaari and the other three elves who had fired rushed forward, exchanging their bows for their swords and pausing to turn the heads of the sleeping warriors sideways so they would not smother in the thick dust. . . .

## Sembia
# The Halls of Stormweather
### A new FORGOTTEN REALMS series

In the mean streets of Selgaunt everything has a price, and even the wealthiest families will do anything to survive. The cast of characters: the capable but embattled patriarch of the Uskevren family, a young woman who is more than just a maid, the son who carries a horrifying curse, a wife with past as long as it is dark, a servant with more secrets than his master could ever guess, and much more.

Seven talented authors introduce the FORGOTTEN REALMS to a new generation of fans. Featuring novellas by Ed Greenwood, Clayton Emery, Richard Lee Byers, Voronica Whitney-Robinson, Dave Gross, Lisa Smedman, and Paul Kemp.

Available July 2000

## Sembia
# Shadow's Witness
### Paul Kemp

Erevis Cale must battle ghosts from his own dark past if he is to save the family he dearly loves. The first full-length novel in this exciting new series—your gateway to the FORGOTTEN REALMS !

Available November 2000